THE SORCERER'S TRAP

Lorimer glared balefully at his quarry. Nothing of the sorcerer's face showed except his eyes. "Throw down those ridiculous weapons," he ordered. "If you *were* able to kill me, I would restore myself with another body, and my power would only be the greater."

The horse paced forward without flinching. Lorimer raised his staff and began muttering the words of a spell.

Ivarr abandoned his bold stance and scuttled around a large rock. Before him lay a jumble where no horse would ever risk its legs. He plunged into it, leaping over boulders and sliding down the face of others. Exulting at his escape, he tumbled over a small ledge and dropped into a clearing among the stones.

He fell directly at the feet of Lorimer, who stood patiently waiting.

Also by Elizabeth H. Boyer

THE SWORD AND THE SATCHEL

and published by Corgi Books

THE ELVES
AND
THE OTTERSKIN

ELIZABETH H. BOYER

CORGI BOOKS

THE ELVES AND THE OTTERSKIN

A CORGI BOOK 0 552 12759 0

First publication in Great Britain

This edition published by arrangement with Ballantine Books, a division of Random House Inc.

PRINTING HISTORY

Corgi edition published 1986

Copyright © 1981 by Elizabeth H. Boyer

This book is set in 10 on 11pt Times

Corgi Books are published by Transworld Publishers Ltd.,
61-63 Uxbridge Road, Ealing, London W5 5SA,
in Australia by Transworld Publishers (Aust.) Pty. Ltd.,
26 Harley Crescent, Condell Park, NSW 2200, and in New
Zealand by Transworld Publishers (N.Z.) Ltd., Cnr. Moselle
and Waipareira Avenues, Henderson, Auckland.

Made and printed in Great Britain by
Cox & Wyman Ltd., Reading, Berks.

This work is dedicated to and inspired by
the vast and lonely desert places of the
Canyonlands of Southern Utah, and the
desert man of Death Hollow.

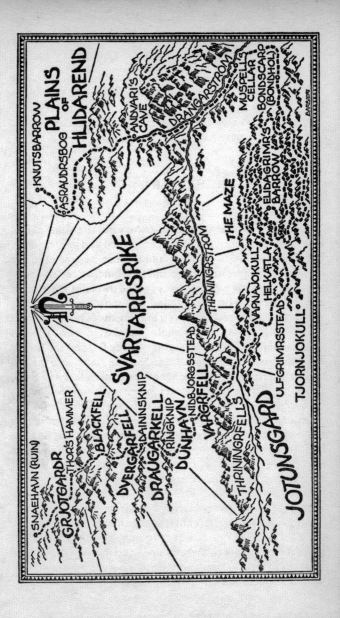

CHAPTER ONE

Second sons of poor fishermen always got the short shrift, Ivarr reflected darkly as the old cart rattled and jerked along. The horse pulling it was much older than he was, and the cart itself was certainly from the first landing on Skarpsey long ago. Ivarr glanced sideways at the owner of these relics and summed her up as the oldest and most sinister-looking woman he had ever seen—even barring the fact that she was the famous witch of Hvitafell. She darted him a sharp glance, as if reading his thoughts, and he flapped the frayed reins in a useless attempt to startle some speed into the old nag. It merely swivelled one ear around and rolled its left eye in long-suffering disdain. Its other eye was missing— probably required in some unsavoury spell of old Birna's.

Indentured to a witch! Ivarr heaved a sigh for himself and hunched his shoulders resentfully. That was typical luck for his father, Hoskuld of Fishless. Luck had abandoned Hoskuld long ago as a hopeless cause, leaving him to drift from misfortune to misfortune like a ship with no rudder in a rocky fjord. His wife and seven children and various sponging relatives were his helpless cargo.

The whole mucky bargain had begun harmlessly enough. Hoskuld and Thorgerdr were arguing, as usual, about the lack of food, firewood, and clothing, and the overabundance of family to feed, warm, and shelter. Thorgerdr argued, that is, and Hoskuld leaned upon the mantel, contemplating his

7

own inner thoughts. The five youngest children rolled around on the floor like good-natured bear cubs, ignoring their parents and the damage their flailing limbs did to the meager furnishings of the house. Ivarr and his older brother Sveinn exchanged worried glances. If the next winter was anything like the last one, none of the family would survive.

Hoskuld finally bestirred himself to respond to a particularly withering insult from his good wife. "I've got it all thought out," he said. "I shall go a-viking next spring as soon as the ice melts, and then we'll never have to worry about getting gold or food again."

"You, a-viking? Hah!" said Thorgerdr. "And in the meantime all we have to do is quit eating. If I have to ask my brothers again for food this year—"

"We have our chieftain," said Hoskuld hastily. "Old Breiskaldi won't let us starve, exactly, if we work for what we get. And we do have two strong sons who can herd his sheep, feed his horses, or whatever."

Thorgerdr's angry reply camouflaged Ivarr's groan of dismay. Sveinn nudged him warningly—their mother was in what they called her berserker state, in which she was known for her irrational acts of pure rage. But Ivarr whispered angrily at his brother, "I'm not working for that old tyrant again this winter. He'll work us to death and you know it." He sank his chin into his hands and glared at his exhausted old boots which were leaking toes all around. "What I wouldn't give to get away from Fishless. I'd do anything. I wish I were old enough to go a-viking."

"You'd have to ask Mother first."

The knock at the door was unheard for a few minutes as the squabbling continued, and the five fat little younglings knocked the table over and broke a crock of cream. The crash seemed to bring everyone to his senses. Thorgerdr snapped, "And that was my last crock!"

"Ah well," said Hoskuld soothingly. "The cow is nearly dry anyway, so we won't be missing it for long."

Thorgerdr flung up her hands. "Such a man!" she shrieked, and was getting into full cry on her "Such a man" tirade

8

when the door opened and the old woman stepped inside.

"Good day," she said, her eyes travelling around the house and finally settling on Sveinn and Ivarr. "The gods bless your house and all within—looks as if they've been a bit neglectful of you lately. This place has a singularly luckless atmosphere, I might say." The cream, which was creeping toward her toes, filled the house with a sour smell.

Thorgerdr began to cluck and fluster, settling the visitor in a chair, fetching her a cool drink, and offering her a place to stay the night. Fishless was a good day's journey from the next settlements up or down the coast. Visitors and travellers were always made welcome, even if the family went hungry the next day and Ivarr and Sveinn had to sleep in the cow shed.

When all the social amenities were taken care of, and the proper questions asked and answered about inconsequential things such as weather and common acquaintances, the old woman took a slender clay pipe from a black pouch at her waist and began to smoke it. The five younger brothers and sisters stood around her in an admiring and mostly naked semicircle, mouths agape and eyes goggling.

Thorgerdr knew the fame of the old woman of Hvitafell as a healer, and she was dying to know why such a personage would purposely want to visit her, but she concealed her curiosity. Hoskuld leaned against the mantel shelf, already forgetting they had company.

"Now you know who I am, and I've heard something of you," she began. "They call me Birna the witch of Hvitafell behind my back, just as they call your husband Hoskuld the Luckless behind his. I've come here looking—" She eyed Ivarr and Sveinn piercingly. "—for a young man to hire for some work. I'm getting too old to tend to my livestock and do the trading and harvesting. I live in a little shieling alone in the big fell near Hvitaness. I have one horse, three cows, and a flock of sheep and goats, and twenty geese. It's rather a lot for one old woman, in addition to my duties as a healing physician for man and beast. So I came here to take one of these great hungry boys off your hands, and I shall furnish his keep in exchange for work. In addition to that, I shall pay

9

you each month with a share of milk or cheese or wool, and four marks in silver at the offset. Of course he'll be expected to work hard to earn his keep, though." Her eyes were quick and sharp, noting the glance that passed between Ivarr and Sveinn.

Thorgerdr's eyes were alight in an instant, but she said, "Well, I'm sure you know that sons are a scarce commodity—" She had five of the creatures, all hungry. "—and one hates to barter them away. And I couldn't spare you my eldest, so it would have to be Ivarr." She managed to sound apologetic and portentous at the same time.

"Well, what's wrong with him?" Birna's eyes flashed over him from head to toe. "He looks suitable. A little lean for his size, perhaps, but he'll get all he wants to eat at my house. I just hope he's not a daydreamer." She darted a snappy glance at Hoskuld, who merely shifted his weight to his other angular leg and gazed out the window.

Thorgerdr's eyes followed the old woman's hands to a heavy little pouch that clinked as it was put upon the table. Her eyes never left it as she said reluctantly, "I suppose we can ask Ivarr if he wants to work for you. But I hate to think of a son of mine being a servant. Perhaps—"

"I'll go, I'll go." Ivarr could scarcely stand still. "I'll be glad to go, Mother. You were just saying yourself how we wouldn't have enough food for the winter, and what a nuisance we were, and —"

"I shall have to think about it," said Thorgerdr, with a chilling glare at Ivarr. He knew she would finally agree, but not until she had extorted more money from the old woman.

"You're not exactly selling him," said Birna. This widened the eyes of the five younglings; they would forever after tell every soul they encountered how their mother had sold their second older brother to a witch.

Five marks and a more specific amount of wool and cheese sealed the deal. "What exactly shall his duties be?" asked Thorgerdr, after they had struck palms and poured cups of ale.

Birna shrugged and sipped her ale. "The usual work

10

around a farm—tending the animals, milking, shearing, hay-mowing, that sort of thing. And it would also be helpful if he had a working knowledge of magic, but that would be too much to expect, I fear.''

Thorgerdr froze, and Hoskuld stood up straight, his wandering attention at last brought home. ''Magic?'' he asked, rather vaguely. ''I fear the lad's education is sadly lacking in that aspect, in particular. In fact, you're not likely to find a good witch or wizard in all of the East Quarter, or the West or South either. Now the North—'' He plucked absently at his nether lip, already beginning to slide away into another reverie. ''No, it was the style not long ago to burn such folks, to discourage them.''

Birna made a snorting sound. ''If that's so, they skipped me then. No respectable witch or wizard would permit her or himself to be burned by a tribe of ignorant fishy-smelling, sheep-eating Sciplings. Ignorant people like that are the ones responsible for driving the Alfar back into the unseen realm, much to the detriment of us who live here. This boy Ivarr has been told about the Alfar at least, I assume?''

''Elves, you mean?'' Thorgerdr hated being at a disadvantage. Her face was red and her expression defensive. ''Whatever is the use? None have been reported around here in more than a hundred years, you know—''

''And folks have begun to disbelieve in that short a time. Hah!'' Birna sighed and shook her head, as if having second thoughts about taking a heathen into her household. ''Well, no matter. I'll set him straight soon enough.'' The sharp glance she darted Ivarr gave him his first clue it might not be an entirely jolly process, either.

Birna stayed the night and was ready to depart early the next morning—earlier than Hoskuld was usually awake, let alone out of bed. Ivarr put his small parcel of belongings into the cart, shivering with early-morning cold and apprehension. His parents had argued most of the night about hiring their son out to a witch, but the final consensus seemed to be that they still had four other sons, so they could afford to gamble with Ivarr, especially in the light of the five

11

marks and the monthly stipend.

Birna perched on the seat of the rickety cart as if it were a throne. "I hope you can drive a horse," she greeted him.

"I expect I can manage," he said, eyeing the horse and wondering if she expected him to bring the dead back to life. The horse stood in the shafts fast asleep, its lips hanging and ears flopping.

Behind such a horse it took them two days to get to Hvitaness and up the mountain to Birna's shieling. The house was a tight little turf hut sunk into a green hillside, surrounded by neat animal pens and turf barns. Everything was spotlessly tidy, without a sag or a squeak—a marked contrast to Hoskuld's disgraceful attempts at farming.

"As you shall see, your main task will be helping me with my practice." Birna showed him rows of herbs hanging from her ceiling to dry, various small skins tacked to the wall, and a large assortment of boxes and bottles, all carefully labelled. "I shall require you to gather for me certain plants and substances in their season and deliver them or fetch them as you are told. My knees and back are getting weak, and even my own spells and herbs won't cure what's practically worn out. You shall go where I can't, and people may come here at times to be healed. But most importantly, you will be required to listen to all I say and learn all I teach you. I won't be here forever and I want someone to be able to take my place when I'm dead. If you are good enough, that is, and aren't as stupid as most Sciplings. That's why I've spent the last two days telling you about Light Alfar and Dark Alfar, dwarves, giants, trolls, and whatnot. If you are to be my assistant and someday replace me, you'll have to listen especially quick, my boy, or you'll find yourself food for the trolls."

Ivarr's head still reeled with all the information she had put into it with the perfect confidence that he would absorb it. The problem was, he could scarcely understand it—two realms existing side by side, and the Sciplings having no idea the Alfar realm existed.

"Will I have to go into that invisible realm you men-

12

tioned?'' he asked, feeling a long, long way from Fishless.

"Certainly. There's not much call for real magic in this realm, except for healings and fighting sendings; once in a while we'll get to deal with a ghost walking and making a nuisance of itself; and someone always wants a charm to make the weather pleasant, or rain, or somesuch. But in the other realm is where you'll find real magic. You're not afraid, are you?'' She pointed to a stool for him to sit on and began pouring tea and cutting slabs of cold smoked mutton. She also had rhubarb soup, one of Ivarr's favourites. "It's nothing to dread. All you require is the drops in your eyes and the proper spell in the proper place. I can see you'll need time to get used to the ideas of magic and power and the two worlds. I shall allow you two years, during which time I'll make certain you become acquainted with all these strange ideas the Sciplings try to disclaim. Later, I shall introduce you to some Alfar. Lesson two shall be trolls, then wizards, and so on, until we get to necromancers.'' Her voice changed and she put the pot down with a thump. "I hope you'll be happy here, young fellow, and find it an interesting life. I know it has its dangers and rewards.''

"I think I'll like it,'' said Ivarr, thinking of the dangers and wondering what the rewards might be.

"Good, good.'' The old woman could actually smile—a wintery smile, but her eyes warmed.

She was a hard taskmaster, after the absentminded maunderings of Hoskuld and the distracted fury of Thorgerdr. She made him learn the names of the herbs she harvested, and what they were good for; before long she was sending him out to the fells to gather them alone. He learned to make salves, potions, poultices, and simple charms. At night she drilled him with the legends and lore and history of the Alfar, and how the greed for gold had caused the Dark Alfar to split off from the kings of light and become the master miners of the earth, forsaking the world above ground for their gold and powers of darkness. She told him about dwarves and their three degrees of power—white, brown, and the powerful black dwarves. He learned the names of their domains

13

and leaders and wizards; they became as familiar as the names of the chieftains and lords of the Four Quarters.

In this way a year passed, and Ivarr began to enjoy his role as the witch's assistant. The farmsteads around Hvitaness and north and south along the coast called upon her for her healing arts, and were grudgingly beginning to accept Ivarr's skills also. They often succeeded when all other attempts had proved fruitless. When Birna was feeling out of sorts, she sent Ivarr to apply the poultice or administer the herb or charm—at least to the four-legged patients. Birna herself treated the human patients, who feared and respected her abilities. Ivarr itched to get his hands on some of the secret cures and spells she used, but she steadfastly told him he was not yet ready, although Ivarr himself was bursting with confidence.

By the end of the second year, Ivarr was fuming with impatience. He pestered Birna to give him something difficult to do, begged for new charms to try, and was always wanting to know exactly when he could go to the Alfar realm and actually meet Alfar and wizards. He was getting bored with holding her satchel and handing her things while she was getting all the credit for curing the patients.

Steadfastly Birna would answer, "Later, later, after your lessons are finished. You are not yet ready. There's plenty of time, and you're still very young. Be assured, you shall have your purpose. Wait, learn, and grow strong."

"But what purpose?" Ivarr demanded one day. "You won't let me try my own skills anyplace where it really matters. How will I ever learn if all I get to do is hold your satchel and hand you this or that, or pour horrible-smelling swill down a sick calf's throat? And you get to do exciting things like fixing corpses so they won't walk and stopping sendings. What exactly is this purpose you keep talking about?"

Birna sighed impatiently. "You'll find out soon enough. It's only been two years, and you're not ready yet."

"But there is something special you want me to do? How am I to learn it if you won't even tell me what it is? What's

14

the sense in waiting? You're not getting any younger, you know, and the longer you wait, the more time is wasted if I'm supposed to do something special with these things you're teaching me. Or the things you only hint at, Birna."

"Impudent boy! How would you like it if I changed you into a goat—a most obnoxious young billy goat is exactly what you remind me of," she retorted, nodding at him furiously.

Ivarr quickly made a few signs behind his back for protection. He wasn't sure even yet what to make of her notorious powers. He had seen her do many things, and there were other things he had almost seen, or suspected, which she wouldn't permit him to ask questions about. Was she merely an herbalist, with a few good luck or fertility charms thrown in, or was she something quite different? She never answered him directly when he asked if she were Alfar, and usually turned snappish on him.

This time, however, he decided to goad her a little. "And that's another thing," he said, sidling around closer to the door for a fast escape if one became necessary. "You once mentioned fylgja forms, and I've long suspected you occasionally turned yourself into a sly old grey fox which I see spying on me almost every day. If you can do it, why can't you teach me how to do it for myself? Or is that something only the Alfar can do?"

"You impertinent young rogue!" She whirled around from her wool-carding, but he was out the door like a racehorse, whisking around the corner of the house out of sight but not out of hearing. "Do you hear me, you great oaf?" shrilled Birna. "I know you're just around that corner, so listen up. I can see you're starting to think this whole business is nothing but a lark. I shall have to change that, yes indeed. You're losing your respect. Yes, I believe it's time to teach you a little fear."

Ivarr peered around the corner uneasily, somewhat taken aback by the tone of her voice. She was carding wool again, ignoring him, but the expression around her mouth was peculiar. Sometimes she said things to frighten him into

15

obedience, but this time he had the feeling she meant what she said. He decided it would be a good idea to disappear for the day and perhaps she would forget her threats.

Ivarr had spent all his free time for the past two years exploring the ravines and slopes of the fells above Hvitaness. By this time he knew them well and knew those ancient hills held many curious old secrets. He prowled around barrow mounds so old no one knew who was buried there, and forgotten ship-rings, and other stone circles and solitary stones which had been planted by living hands. Birna was also snappish about the stones and told him to stay away from them, saying only that they were ancient guideposts put up by long-forgotten people for unknown destinations.

When Ivarr returned that evening to milk the cows and do the work, he attempted to behave himself and not ask so many questions. Birna seemed to have forgotten about her threat, much to Ivarr's relief.

In the days to come, Birna gradually let Ivarr do more than assist. After half the year had passed, he was beginning to be more satisfied, but he was still aware of mysteries she kept dangling just out of his reach.

One evening in early winter they were returning home in the dark, although it was hardly into the late afternoon of the day. It was foggy also, so Ivarr was not too surprised when Birna turned from the usual path.

"Haven't you made a mistake, Birna?" he asked.

"No indeed. The last mistake I made was years ago and it nearly cost me my life. I do not make mistakes any longer, as they can be very time-consuming and expensive. Now follow me closely. If I should lose you now I can't imagine what trouble it would cause."

Ivarr was suddenly reminded of her old threat to teach him fear. It was such an unwelcome thought on a night like this that he curtailed his questions and hurried after her. She strode along, showing no indication that her knees or back were getting old, as she had claimed. Now that he thought about it, she never showed the least sign of disability.

Finally she halted and reached out her hand to touch an

upright stone. Ivarr's skin prickled when he realized they were standing inside one of the old stone circles. He found himself holding a fold of Birna's cloak and he didn't care to let go of it, either.

"Birna?" he whispered.

She was standing stock-still, concentrating. Her eyes flew open and she pushed him behind a stone, "Quiet now and watch. Something is going to happen. You stay here." She left him there, retreating to the top of the hill.

Ivarr crouched unhappily behind the big stone, not liking to get too near it, nor too far away, either. His hair bristled, as if lightning were about to strike nearby.

Then a light flickered in the shadows beside one of the stones. A small fire sputtered into life and Ivarr stared at it like a bird staring into a snake's eyes. Suddenly he became aware of a dark shape taking form behind the fire, a tall shadowy outline of a man with his hood drawn close around his face so nothing showed. In one hand he held a curiously carved staff with the head of an adder and two tiny red eyes. When the stranger seemed solid enough, he turned to peer around into the shadows, and Ivarr's heart thumped nervously. He seemed to look straight at Ivarr's hiding place. Then he strode to the centre of the circle where a low mound stood, and the fire glinted on the emblems and devices he wore around his neck and fastened to his belt. Ivarr could now see his beard and part of his face. He shuddered, not liking what it reminded him of. The summer before, the peat cutters had found a corpse in the bog, perfectly preserved by unknown chemicals. This stranger's face reminded Ivarr of the corpse's face—skin that looked like dried leather stretched thinly over the bones of the skull and hollow eye sockets sunken into shadows.

The stranger opened a small bag similar to Birna's. What followed was a series of spells calculated to raise a corpse from his grave. This Ivarr knew from illicit snooping into Birna's books of spells.

The necromancer took a parchment from his satchel and a stick carved with runes. He began to roll the stick back and forth across the mound, meanwhile reading from the paper in a droning chant the words which Ivarr knew were written in the necromancer's own blood. Other formulas were added to the chant, and the earth on the mound began to heave and stir.

Unearthly moaning sounds and muttering voices carried to Ivarr's pale, cold ears, but he was too paralyzed to run. The necromancer continued his spells, undaunted by either the sounds or the grisly sight of a head beginning to emerge from the earth.

"Lorimer, Lorimer," moaned a hoarse voice. "Let me sleep in peace."

Lorimer chanted his spells faster and rolled the runewand more briskly. The ghost rose further out of the grave, a boney, misshapen creature with a huge knobbly skull and remnants of a hairy hide still clinging to the bones. When lumps of soil threatened to tumble off the grave, Lorimer quickly caught them before they escaped; once the grave was closed again, any clods of earth that fell off could not be replaced.

"What are you troubling me for this time?" wailed the ghost. "Can't you let a body lie quiet?"

"Not when I think it might be useful." Lorimer stopped his spells with the ghost still buried up to his middle·in the earth, where it struggled ineffectually for a few moments to escape. Lorimer then extended a cup to the ghost, which it snatched from his hands eagerly and drained in three large gulps, letting dark thick trickles escape down its chin.

"The blood always makes you glad enough to talk," said Lorimer.

"Get on with it, then," growled the ghost, rather more lively now. "Two questions and no more."

Lorimer leaned forward. "How can I turn Svartarr, king of the black dwarves, against his old friend and ally Elbegast of the Light Alfar?"

The ghost sighed. "Elbegast—Alfar. What a bane they are, even to an old dead troll like me. But I have seen the future, and I have a plan for you which will destroy Elbegast

18

and his Snowfell, if you are clever enough. I have also seen five men of the Alfar in Svartarrsrike.''

"Yes, I know which ones. They are spies for Elbegast, but easy game for the rebels who follow me.''

"No, fool. Listen to me,'' the rasping voice continued. "Let Svartarr do that when the time comes. You must arrange a trap for these five spies, a web of outlawry, murder, and revenge. I see much blood and gold spilled. And I see that Svartarr has a young son, a boy who likes to go about in the disguise of an otter. The death of a prince would excite every loyal black dwarf, would it not? Particularly if it were a secret murder?''

"Ah yes, I begin to see. These five Alfar spies shall soon become murderers and outlaws. Svartarr will demand weregild for the prince, but I have ways of seeing to it that it shall never be paid. Then Svartarr will take vengeance upon Elbegast.''

"No. I have a better idea. See to it Svartarr gets the otter pelt. Tell him to put a spell on it so it will get larger and larger for every bit of gold placed upon it. This way, Svartarr will get all the gold, and since the pelt can never be completely covered to pay the prince's weregild, Svartarr will have to attack Elbegast.'' The ghost made a grab for Lorimer just as the necromancer turned and stalked away.

"You've been most helpful, Grus. If you'd been this co-operative when you were alive, I wouldn't have killed you. And now for my last question. Listen carefully, Grus. How can I overthrow Svartarr and seize Svartarrsrike for my own kingdom?''

"Greedy, greedy, aren't you? Well, let me think a moment. Svartarr—yes, it may be possible. Let's see— blast, I keep getting one of those wretched Scipling savages into my thoughts.'' His voice began to splutter and gasp. "Lorimer, you're in danger of your life. I see a terrible sword coming out of a barrow mound, a dwarfish sword with your death written upon it. A hero, a Scipling, will wield it, and you will perish on the soil you covet.''

Lorimer tossed his head and uttered a mirthless chuckle.

"I refuse to contemplate a death at the hands of a mere Scipling. I have died five deaths and returned stronger each time. No Sciplings, Grus. But because of your kind warning, I shall take care to kill any Scipling hero I find wandering in the Alfar realm." He unsheathed his sword, a long slender blade that gleamed with a faint blueness in the moonlight. "And now because you've been so helpful, I'm going to take you with me on my travels, Grus."

The ghost waved its arms and made a fearful grimacing cackle. "You know very well what I'd do to you the instant I got my legs free of this grave. I'm older than you are, Lorimer, and far stronger."

Lorimer raised his sword. "I'm aware of that, old friend. But you'll be hard put to do anything to me with no arms or legs, I fear." With one whistling blow he swept off the corpse's head, and it rolled across the circle almost to Ivarr's feet. Lorimer strode after it, and snatched it up by the hair. "You shall tell me more about this Scipling hero, Grus, and I fear you really have no choice, unless you want me to leave you where the rats can find you or any number of other unpleasant things."

The head rolled its gleaming green eyes and it sputtered and snarled. "You can't do this, it's not—it's not decent. What about my poor body? You won't just leave it like that, will you?"

Lorimer laughed harshly and put the head into a leather pouch hanging from his belt. He turned his attention back to the grave, much to Ivarr's relief, after standing close enough to him to reach out and touch him.

Lorimer began his spells and chanting, alternately cursing Grus, whose body was fiercely resisting reinterment.

Grus chuckled unpleasantly. "It doesn't want to go, Lorimer. Perhaps we'd ought to take it along.'

"You wretched little brute, it will go back into the ground, or I'll—"

"Hsst! Lorimer, Birna's coming! Get us out of here, fast!"

Lorimer whirled around to stare into the darkness in the

direction of the hill, his cloak swirling and surging in an unfelt wind. Quickly he nodded the fire out. Then he gripped his staff and raised it aloft. With a burst of luminous smoke, the necromancer disappeared.

CHAPTER TWO

Ivarr huddled behind the stone, not daring to look around it at the grave and the headless ghost. He could not remove the picture of the ghost from his mind as its hands ran over the ground searching for the head.

When he finally did peek around the stone, certain he would see the apparition still searching around for its head, he was completely amazed to see nothing of the kind. Nothing was there but a slight mound in the grass which showed no sign of ever being disturbed. Nor was there a charred circle where a fire had burned.

Ivarr raced for the top of the hill, but Birna hadn't waited for him. He ran homeward, never minding the bushes that clawed at him like scraggy little hands or the streamlets and pools he splashed through. He didn't know how he arrived there, but he came stumbling in just as Birna was taking the kettle off the coals to pour two cups of strong tea.

"A necromancer!" he gasped. "In the stone circle! And he called a ghost out of that grave and cut its head off!"

Birna nodded and fastened the door shut with a jerk of her head. Her hooded eyes glowed in their nets of wrinkled skin. "Remember your lessons now and give me the points that enabled you to recognize a personage of power, whether of ice and darkness or fire and light."

Ivarr circled the room distractedly, finally seizing upon an old staff. "This is no time for lessons. We've got to defend

ourselves. They know who you are and they must be somewhere nearby—"

"Nonsense. There are no necromancers between here
and the northmost tip of Skarpsey. You're dawdling, Ivarr.
Tell me how one recognizes a personage of power."

"Birna! You can't just sit there swallowing tea and
nagging me about some inconsequential lessons at a time
like this! We're in danger! Get up and start working some
spells, or grab a club. I wish I had a sword or at least a bow
and arrows—" He flew around the tiny house from one
window to the other, checking the bar on the door half a
dozen times.

"Ivarr, will you stop this insane behaviour and listen to
me?" Birna rose up with flashing eyes and a commanding
shout. Ivarr slunk into his chair at once. "If anyone was
threatening us, I would be the first to know, don't you
suppose? You forget how insignificant two years of training
is to the many years I have practiced. The lesson you have
seen was well-nigh wasted upon you, yet you've been
clamouring at me for a year to test you. Well, this was your
test, and I must say you've done rather poorly."

Ivarr shrivelled miserably. "But I did see something," he
said. "Did you know Lorimer was going to appear right
there at that particular time?"

Birna sighed and picked up her wool and began carding.
After a moment of briskly scraping the fibres back and forth
she replied, "You still don't know what you saw."

Ivarr stared at her, trying to decide if she was testing his
memory or his powers of conviction. "I saw a necromancer,
Lorimer, who was raising a ghost from a grave," he said
stubbornly. "I'm certain of it—aren't I?"

"No," said Birna. "What you saw is what we call a ghoul.
It wasn't the real Lorimer or the real Grus. It was the image
of them after the real event. I've told you frequently that
everything done leaves its impression, and most particularly
deeds that are crimes or murders or other evil things. Using
certain spells, a gifted magical personage can recall any
important action that took place in a certain spot. If Lorimer

23

had really been there, do you think you could have stood not ten paces away and him not see you? We could go back and do it all over again, if you'd like, but I want you to be certain you'll recognize Lorimer if you ever see him again.''

Ivarr leaned his chin into his hands. ''I'll know him a mile away. There's no need to go through that again. Only an image, you say? And the real necromancer is far away from here doing something quite different?''

Birna glared at him, not at all pleased, and he suddenly felt tired and discouraged. She said sharply, ''Now I know you're not as stupid as you're pretending to be. You've forgotten the most important part of the whole lesson, Ivarr.''

''I'm not pretending. I am stupid,'' he growled, trying to think and straighten out his fear-befuddled wits. ''Oh yes, I remember now. The five Alfar spies and Svartarr. He wants Svartarrsrike for his own, so he's going to—''

''Yes, I've known about it for quite some time, Ivarr. Longer than I've known you.''

''Has anyone warned Svartarr? What does Elbegast plan to do?''

''They don't know about it. Time in the Alfar realm is quite a different commodity than here. Now that's enough talk about the ghoul for tonight. You won't speak of this to a solitary living soul. And now that you've seen Lorimer, I feel I must give you a warning. I believe it is no longer safe for you to wander around after dark alone in the fells. Now don't interrupt me, let me finish. You can still be out late after visits to sick folks or animals as long as I am there to protect you.''

Ivarr gaped at the little shrewlike Birna and tried not to laugh. She was not nearly so tall as his shoulder and, although she was amazingly tough and strong, she weighed no more than a child.

She glowered at him fiercely, as if reading his thoughts. ''It's a feeling I have,'' she snapped, ''and don't you dare disobey. The time will come when you'd be glad for my protection. Now away with you to your bed, hasten, hasten!''

Ivarr hoped she would forget about her feeling. He enjoyed coming and going alone and working his own cures on the livestock of Hvitaness. But if Birna was there, she would get all the credit and praise.

When word arrived one afternoon that an important farmer's horse was sick, Ivarr attempted to dissuade Birna from going. "Bjargisstead is a long way to walk. I can speed over there and back alone much quicker if you don't care to trouble yourself. I know that old horse just needs a nettle infusion to get him on his feet."

"Hah. You're saying I'm too old and decrepit, is that it?"

"That's putting it bluntly, Birna, but I can walk faster than you."

"Bah. If I wanted to, I could fly over there before you'd even got your elbows off the table. You hoped I'd forgotten about what I said about walking alone after dark, didn't you?"

"Well, of course. I'm almost a man grown and not afraid of the dark. It hurts my pride something terrible to have to be protected by a little old stick of a woman." He tried to look aggrieved, but all he could do was scowl. "Wouldn't it be more appropriate for me to be watching over you? I've had the feeling since I got here that you could just as easily get along without me— or maybe it would be easier if I wasn't here getting in your way and asking a lot of questions."

Birna smiled her rare smile and gave him a quick pat on the arm. "What a lot of blither. You'll have your opportunity, lad. Now let's get over to Bjargi and his sick horse."

The horse was an old and esteemed member of the family, nearly twenty years old and nearly blind, but much beloved. He had to be examined and treated with all due consideration of his status in the family, and by the time this was done, with all of Bjargi's family hanging around to make sure it was done right and a thousand questions asked and answered, it was long after dark. To Ivarr's disgust, Birna refused an offer of supper and set off into the fells, lighting a small lantern to hang on the end of her staff. Her long cloak covered her from head to toe—to protect her from the night

25

vapours, she said, but is also had the effect of rendering her as black as the shadows. She walked along surprisingly quick and quiet, and her eyes and ears seemed to observe more than Ivarr's did in broad daylight. As they walked, no time was wasted; Birna was teaching him a catalogue of the dwarf king several hundred years before the first viking cast his envious eyes upon Skarpsey's pleasant shore.

Suddenly she halted, gripping Ivarr's arm warningly, and her "Hsst!" silenced any protests. Ivarr strained his ears and rolled his eyes around until they ached. Birna's hand tightened on his arm, silently turning his attention to the left. His spine was bathed in icy perspiration and he felt the same prickly feeling of horror he had experienced on the night of the ghoul. All he saw was a darker shadow flitting across their path, with a faint halo of luminescence about it.

After it had gone, Birna started him down the path again at the same no-nonsense pace. "A black dwarf, or I don't know a dwarf from a hay hook," she grumbled.

"Here, in this realm?" whispered Ivarr with a squeak.

"Spying, no doubt, for Lorimer. We shall have to be more cautious, if that's what things are coming to. I simply can't let you out of my sight for a moment." She prodded him anxiously with the staff, as if to make sure he was really still there, and not an illusion.

"But what—I don't understand—"

"Hush now. This is no place to discuss anything. Ears everywhere."

It was four days before Ivarr could persuade Birna to answer his questions. He had to help her slaughter the sheep for winter, smoking part of the meat, drying some and salting some away in barrels.

"Winter is getting very close," she said sitting down at last and taking out her odd little pipe. "The first snow will arrive any day now, and there's something I must show you before it comes. I expect it will answer all your questions at last."

Ivarr looked at her uncertainly. "After feeling that cold wave of power pass by us that night we went to Bjargisstead, I'm not sure I'm so curious anymore."

"That was only a minor black dwarf, hurrying home to supper, no doubt," said Birna. "We have a much more serious situation on our hands now." She gazed around the storage room where they had been salting meat. It was a cozy, crowded room, full to bursting with stored food and goods for trading and fragrant with the delicious smell of smoked mutton, which was to be eaten on Midwinter's Day. Ivarr had always liked the storage room but now the image of the necromancer sprang into his mind, and Ivarr felt the first feather-light touch of fear.

Birna was gazing out the open door to the steep green fell beyond. "Hvitafell has its safe places," she said, "as well as its dangerous ones. They say the great smiths of the dwarves used to keep their forges here inside the mountain. The first Sciplings to settle here used to leave a horse to be shod and a piece of gold on a stone, and the next morning the horse would have a set of new shoes and the gold would be gone. That's how close the two realms used to be. It has been a long, long time since a Scipling crossed over from this realm into that."

"You mean I'm to go over, at last?" Ivarr swallowed dryly. His old excitement was somehow contaminated with a dose of healthy fear.

Birna inclined her head in a single nod. "Last night while you were asleep I had a visitor from the other side."

Ivarr leaped up. "Why didn't you waken me? You know I've been dying to see a real Alfar!" He paced around the tiny room, anguished. "What about my lessons? And I was up in the loft just above; why didn't you—"

Birna held up her hand for silence. "We talked of nothing but you, if you really must know. I thought it better if you didn't hear until the next step is taken. I have done my part in preparing you. It's time for you to go on, Ivarr, whether I think you are ready or not."

"Go on? Where? Can't I stay here any longer? You want me to go back to Fishless?"

Birna shook her head, casting her eyes upward. "We shall go back to the kitchen and I shall explain."

Making tea and putting together a meal seemed to help Birna organize her thoughts. She tore apart a fresh loaf of bread, spread butter on it, and watched Ivarr devour it. He wondered at her silence and likewise kept silent until he had eaten the bread and drunk a cup of Birna's very special ale from a small cask she kept hidden until special occasions took place.

"And now," prompted Ivarr gently. "The messenger?"

Birna roused herself from her scowling reverie. "Ah yes, the messenger. He came to tell me that Ottar, the son of Svartarr, has been killed and the murder assigned to the five Alfar spies. In cases such as this, the Alfar laws are similar to our own. The nearest kin of the victim has the right to self-judgement over the murderers. Svartarr captured them the day after the killing had been reported."

"And killed them?" asked Ivarr.

"Weregild." Birna shook her head. "Svartarr released the five spies, but as long as they are in Svartarrsrike they are outlaws, which means no one can give them any help or food or shelter without risking outlawry also. The Alfar have until the autumn equinox to cover the otterskin with gold. If they can't, then Svartarr will exact a blood price on a great many Alfar."

"The pelt of an otter isn't very large," said Ivarr, but Birna glowered at him. "Did I forget something?"

"The pelt," she snapped, "is not merely the skin of a dead animal. It will take barrowloads of gold to cover it. When gold is placed upon it it grows larger. Perhaps the pelt, like Svartar's grief, has no limits. He is like a creature possessed."

Ivarr nodded. "Yes, well, it's going to be a frightful mess, I fear. But what has all that to do with you or me, actually? We're a world away from it, and we've built up a cozy little business here. I thought I was being trained to take your place one day a long time hence. This talk of moving me on is very upsetting. I like it here, Birna."

"Yes, you are getting a trifle too comfortable here," Birna said. "But I've done my best in the time allotted and I believe you won't be totally shocked by what you find on the other side." Then she muttered almost to herself, "May the gods preserve us both if I've made a mistake."

And that was positively the last Ivarr could get out of her. Early the next morning she led him up into the heights of Hvitafell. Saving her breath for climbing, she strode ahead in silence, pausing only to catch her wind and fan her face. Ivarr fetched her an icy drink from a freshet battering its rocky way downward to the sea. After a brief rest, she left the path and struck across the meadow. Close to its centre, she stopped and poked at something on the ground. "There," she said, tapping firmly on a smooth white stone, "What do you see?"

"A white stone, smoothly rounded, about the size of a round tub," Ivarr peered at it intently, "Some moss on it, too. Is something under it, besides the everlasting rocky soil of Skarpsey?"

Birna made no answer. She extended her staff at arm's length, up the smooth green side of the fell. "And what do you see up there?"

Ivarr knew better than to say, "Nothing," even when it was the truth. Birna was likely to whack him for such an answer. "I see a hillside and plenty more rocks. Bushes, a hare—"

Birna made her disapproving sound. "What about the rocks?"

"Black. Volcanic." Ivarr shrugged. Then he understood. "This rock is white and smooth, probably from a riverbed. It had to be put there by human hands—or somebody. Heavy, too. I wonder how they carried it?" He began to look around. Birna pointed again. He raised his eyes to the skyline. "A notch cut in the hill, Birna. By hands."

"Now you're seeing," she said with a nod.

Ivarr turned and looked downhill. One of the solitary standing stones stood there, tilting slightly to the east, as if nodding to the rising sun. The two white stones and the notch were arranged in a straight line leading toward the inland, where nobody ventured.

29

"It's called a ley line, or line of power," said Birna. "They are everywhere, passing through holy hills and circles and barrows and springs. In ancient dark times this was the only safe way to travel, in either realm. Of course we haven't used whatever strange old powers that lurked in the ley lines and circles, not in centuries. But should you need to find a safe place sometimes, these lines will never guide you wrong. Remember that, and remember that high places are usually safe places. When you need to find a ley line, you simply dowse for it with a pendulum. You remember our experiments with dowsing for hidden objects, metal, and so forth. On the places where two lines cross is safety—" She stopped a moment, suddenly breathless. "You must remember—about high places—safe places. Low places—" Gasping, she glared around at the empty autumn landscape. "—Or dark places—are evil. The white stones—" She clutched at her throat, wheezing. Her lips were a strange blue colour.

"Birna! What is it?" Ivarr steadied her as she swayed.

"Power—evil," she gasped, starting to stagger toward the upright stone, about fifty yards down the hillside. "They're trying to get you. Run—dance in a circle—concentrate. Three or nine— times—" Her voice failed and she floundered to her knees despite Ivarr's attempts to hold her up. She clutched her chest, grimacing with pain.

"Birna, what'll I do?" She groped for her satchel, wheezing. He grabbed it and dumped out its contents on the ground. She fumbled among the vials and pouches and at last seized a small blue vial. Ivarr was terrified at the blue tint her face was turning, and it sounded as if each tearing, ragged gasp would be the last. Her fingers and his struggled to pull the stopper from the blue vial.

Glancing up for an instant, he thought he saw a man in a black cloak standing beside the notch in the skyline, arms upraised, fists shaking in a gesture peculiar only to magic. It was only an instantaneous glimpse; Birna suddenly tore the stopper from the vial and, in two lightning flicks of her hand, she dashed some of the contents in each of his eyes. It stung, and he exclaimed, "Birna, how can I help you if I can't see? What on earth! I'm falling!"

The impression of falling passed and he rubbed his eyes with the back of his hand until he could finally see through a film of tears. He was still kneeling on the ground beside Birna, but her tortured breathing was silenced. His own breathing and heartbeat seemed to stop, too, as he looked down at her. The blue colour was fading, leaving a pallor foreign to her natural ruddy colour. Her eyes were open, staring into the sky, and the faint smile on her lips gave her an expression of surprised gladness. Ivarr felt her wrists and throat and found no heartbeat. She was dead.

Hollowly, he sat and stared, too stunned to move. In a moment the sun touched her pale features, and suddenly her form began to fade and melt away before his eyes. Reaching out with some idea of halting the unnatural process that was robbing him of her, he found himself holding only her empty cloak. Birna's body and her essence were both gone.

He stood up shakily, gathering the heavy black cloak into his arms. Something fell into the dirt at his feet—a slender, silvery knife with a gold-embossed handle, small and deadly for a feminine hand. He put it in his belt and his senses began returning. Blinking his still-burning eyes, he looked around in gathering consternation. A cold wind was jerking at his clothes, and the pleasant green meadow of Hvitafell had simply vanished. Instead, he was standing in a rocky, rubbly ruin atop a slight hill, looking down into a valley ravaged by wind and glacier. The wind streamed over the standing stones at his back and howled away down the desolate valley between two rugged back fells.

Ivarr cowered backward against the stones. Nothing was familiar in the least. He could hear the thunder of a high sea far to the west where the sun was sinking, and the sea-mist rose up sullenly. He could discern no sign of habitation—no scattered sheep grazing, no wisp of smoke from a lonely shieling.

In a small voice he called, "Birna?" But the wind snatched the sound away and hurled it among the jumbled stones.

CHAPTER THREE

Slowly Ivarr edged himself away from the rocks, recovering from his astonishment. He walked around the hilltop, studying the landscape, wondering where Birna would have wanted him to go. The stones themselves were no help, leaning sadly in three directions, and the other six were lying down, gathering overcoats of lumpy moss. He ran his hand over the rough surface of the largest stone, and his fingers suddenly jumped into a carving of some sort. It was lettering in the strange spiky script that he had seen thousands of times in Birna's house. Runic—the writing of sorcery and magic. Looking closer in the failing light, he discerned the symbol of Thor, the hammer-wielding god who appealed most to the numerous black dwarf smiths. Ivarr's own ancestors had paid homage to Thor, so he felt almost encouraged by this sign, whose meaning he shared with the unknown black dwarves. He stared in the direction the symbol pointed. Eastward, he saw a green plain dotted with small round hills which looked like barrow mounds. Grimly he tightened the laces on his boots, hoping he would get to the barrows before nightfall. An open barrow was shelter, however unappealing.

Resolutely he strode toward the east, clambering over the smoothly pitted black boulders of a rusty lava flow and skirting the inevitable chasms and crevices where deep still water waited for the unwary. Before long, he recognized the creeping feeling that indicated he was being watched. As casually as possible, he sat down in a protected place where he could watch in all directions. He saw nothing, no one, for a long time, and then a weasel stood up and stared at him boldly, even venturing a few steps closer before vanishing suddenly like a puff of smoke. Land-vaettir, thought Ivarr grimly. Someone had created the little creatures to watch and spy over this particular bit of territory. Often, Birna had told him, the land-vaettir were aggressively hostile, when the avowed owner of the area did not wish to be disturbed.

By the time he reached the barrow mounds, the day was speedily darkening. He peered around in dismay for a reasonable place to hide for the night and decided with a shiver that a barrow field was certainly not a reasonable sleeping place. He looked into one open mound where he could have hid, but some small warning whisper made him change his mind. In the open, at least, he could perhaps run away from whatever came after him, so he curled up in the comfort of a cluster of sharp-kneed rocks to wait for morning. Sleep was out of the question. Birna's knife was a small comfort to him. He crouched there, thinking of her and knowing she had sent him here for some specific purpose at the cost of her own life. The image of a man in a black cloak with upraised fists was burned into his memory, like a burning coal imbedded in hard wood.

To add further to his uneasiness, the night was alive with stealthy noises. The wind muttering under its breath began to sound like approaching voices. The dead might be stirring. He gripped the knife and huddled his cloak more tightly around himself, hoping he looked like a rock. It was enough to fool a small white owl, who landed silently on a rock nearby and began a series of gruff, muffled hoots. More doleful company Ivarr could not imagine. He tossed a pebble at the creature, but it only glared at him and clashed its sharp little hooked beak.

Then he heard a sound in the great emptiness of the valley. After a moment he became certain it was the sound of a horse carefully picking its way over a rugged lava flow, slipping from time to time with its iron shoes, or causing a rock to fall. It snorted repeatedly, dissatisfied with the choice of terrain.

Ivarr was glad for Birna's old black cloak. It smothered him perfectly into the darkness, all but a small gap for him to watch through. Whoever the rider was, he would have to step right on Ivarr before he would see him. Ivarr spent a few moments considering the old stories he had heard about the legendary Night-Rider, a ghostly horseman who prowled the lonely fells looking for a victim to carry back with him to the cold kingdom of the dead. In spite of himself, he began to feel the same choking horror he had felt when he saw Lorimer's ghoul.

Suddenly the owl flew up in the horse's face, flapping noisily and striking with its sharp talons. The horse reared back with a frightened squeal, and the rider drew a short sword with a swift yank, but the owl had vanished. The horse backed away stubbornly from the place of its fright, refusing to consider approaching it again. The rider sat glaring, a great shadowy figure in the faint light of the moon and stars. Ivarr noticed how the horse's keen ears kept flicking in his direction, and his fear tightened a notch.

"Gizur!" bellowed the rider suddenly, causing both Ivarr and the horse to jump. The voice was harsh, a bellow of rage. "I know you're here hiding, you upstart. It is I, Lorimer, the greatest sorcerer who ever was, and I command you to show yourself."

A burst of derisive hoots was his answer. Lorimer spurred his horse around in that direction, swinging his sword in a glowing blue arc. "I know your fylgja, Gizur. Come out and meet me, wizard to wizard." Lorimer halted to listen as the owl replied mockingly. He whirled his horse around to plunge in another direction. "Gizur, you're not deceiving me. I know you're bringing a Scipling over from the other side, hoping he can help those wretched Alfar. But you know he can't. Gizur! Do you hear me?"

The owl hooted twice, and chuckled. Lorimer swung his sword until it hummed. "What do you want? A duel of power? Then show yourself. Come, you can even strike the

34

first blow." He sheathed the sword and waited. The owl hooted, further away. "Who does he think he is? Impudent upstart! He's not even on the Guild register yet."

The muffled voice of Grus chuckled. "I think that owl is more interested in catching a rat for its supper than in talking to one."

"Silence. That's him, I know it's him. Gizur! If that's your answer, then I shall have to talk to your Scipling. He's hiding near here, like a rabbit under a bush. Are you going to give him up so easily, Gizur?"

The owl made no reply. Ivarr crouched, ready to spring away. Suddenly Lorimer thrust out his staff with a blazing light at the end of it, almost right into Ivarr's face. He could feel a blast of cold and he staggered back, almost blinded.

"There he is, Grus. What do you think? Am I in peril from this creature?"

"I don't like him," said Grus from his perch in Lorimer's hand. He had a face like a wizened cat and his eyes glowed balefully.

Lorimer chuckled without mirth, not taking his eyes off Ivarr. His face looked like a leather mask, dried into a malevolent sneer, and was rendered even more awful by the lurid light of the staff.

"You've nothing to fear, Scipling, if you do as I say. Come out here so we can see you. It's not every day we see such an oddity in our realm. Who sent you through? What are you going to do here?"

"I'm not sure I care to answer any questions," Ivaar said, fingering the edge of Birna's knife. It felt woefully short and dull.

Grus cackled, and Lorimer snapped, "Quiet, troll, or I'll find a bog for you. Come here Scipling. You're just a young fellow, aren't you? Are you the one Birna has been training? You don't even have a weapon, do you?"

"There's nothing I can possibly tell you," Ivarr said, edging away.

Grus made a frightful grimace. "Nothing! You can tell us everything Birna wouldn't want us to know, if she were alive, you silly fool. You can't expect to live until dawn anyway, so you may as well be a benefit to us before you die.''

Ivarr halted his cautious sidling. "How did you know Birna was dead?"

"That's not important," Lorimer said. "Why did she send you and not the hero? Is he coming later on? Answer me quickly; I'm getting short of patience."

"Not nearly as short as I," cackled Grus, winking wickedly. "I'm a head shorter than anyone I know."

"Answer!" Lorimer commanded.

Levelly Ivarr replied, "I don't have anything to say to you about anything whatsoever, unless you care to tell me who killed Birna."

"What do you know about Ottar?" The question took Ivarr by surprise. He gasped, feeling like an eavesdropper caught in the act, and couldn't find words to answer immediately.

"He knows! He knows!" crowed Grus. "Look at his silly Scipling face. Sciplings! They can't ever keep a secret."

Lorimer thrust the staff almost into Ivarr's face. "What do you know about the death of Ottar? Speak up, or I'll blast you instantly. Tell me all you know and how you know it.'

Ivarr had retreated as far as he could against the stones at his back. He could only stare at the necromancer's face beyond the flare of the staff. "At the stone circle, where you called Grus and cut his head off," he stammered. "Birna told me it was only a ghoul—"

"He knows," said Grus. "You'd better kill him, Lorimer."

"Shut up," Lorimer snarled. "Curse Birna for her meddling. I wonder who else she told, if she told this boy. If I had known how she talked, I wouldn't have let her die so pleasantly. I thought she was sending through a threat to my plan, but I suppose she was stopped before she sent the hero. All is not wasted then, and we have the good fortune to be rid of Birna at last. A young Scipling without a sword or a name will vanish soon enough."

Ivarr could scarcely believe what his ears were hearing. "You killed her, and you're bragging about it? It was you I saw on the fell?"

Lorimer leered through the flame. "So you saw me, eh? Yes, I killed her before she could get her guard up. She could have saved herself, but I suppose she thought I'd get you—as if you could possibly worry me in the least. Was she sending you to help those wretched outlaws who murdered Ottar, Svartarr's son?"

"Not that I know of," Ivarr said with cold fury. "But since I'm here, I'm going to take my vengeance on you if it takes me all my life. You're a murderer—no, worse. A secret murderer."

Lorimer's reply was an arrogant grunt. "Well, that shan't take long at all, if you're calling me to the holmgang right now. Is that it, Scipling? A fight to the death of one of us?" He slung his cloak aside to draw his sword and leaped down from his horse.

"Be careful, Lorimer," said Grus. "This could be the death of you."

Ivarr whipped Birna's knife from his belt, holding it extended before him like a sword. To his amazement, it gleamed with a hot white light, illuminating a tracery of thin black runes.

"An Alfar knife," Grus chuckled. "Why, Lorimer, I believe you're afraid."

Lorimer shoved the troll's head into one of his pockets and pushed his horse away with his free hand. The staff, which he had stood in a crack in the rock, blazed with a redder, lurid light. The muffled voice of Grus called out, "Halloa, Scipling, and goodbye. Perhaps he'll keep your head as well as mine. As they say among these necromancers, two heads are better than one, if they're preserved right." He laughed until Lorimer gave him a sharp whack with his hand.

"Well, Scipling, if you don't care to talk, then we can fight. I feel quite lucky today—Birna dead and you soon to follow her. But I am curious still. If you're not the hero she sent to help the outlaws, who are you and why are you

37

here?'' Lorimer's sword described glowing designs against the darkness.

"I can't tell you that," Ivarr said doggedly, wishing he himself knew the answer. "And I wouldn't if I could."

Lorimer raised his sword aloft to attack, but at that instant a pale mass plummeted from the darkness, striking him in the face and spinning away with a mirthful hooting. Ivarr glimpsed black extended talons and a sharp hooked beak. Lorimer barely had time to duck as the owl hurtled past his head again.

"Gizur! May the draugar eat your soul!" Lorimer snarled. Three dark scores across his forehead sluggishly oozed black blood. He whirled around and peered into the darkness, ignoring Ivarr.

The owl chuckled again and this time it sounded almost human. Then a very human voice spoke from the gloom. "Lorimer, how pleasant to see you again. I'd wondered how long it would be since that last duel before we came together again. What's this unfortunate creature you've been tormenting here?"

"Only a squeaking rat from the Scipling realm. Some hero Birna sent you. He looks as if he'd be more at home in a farmyard." Lorimer's teeth showed in a feral smile. "Run along, Gizur, before I am forced to lose my temper with you."

"And leave Birna's Scipling in your clutches? Not likely." Gizur was suddenly illuminated by a whoof of flame as he lit the end of his staff, so that light stood around him like a halo. He was a sturdy-looking fellow with a handsome red beard. He wore reindeer boots with the trousers stuffed into the elaborate tops, and his shirt and cloak showed a lot of fine handiwork. His hat, a three-cornered affair with lopping flaps, showed his native region and ancestry.

Lorimer gripped his staff and peered at his opponent. "Now we see each other clearly for the first time. No more hiding and spying, as you've been doing. I see you're from the east. I've never heard of a good wizard from east of

38

Snaehavn yet. Are you quite sure you're the standard Guild issue?''

"Certain enough that I'm willing to fight you for that young Scipling there. About to kill him, were you? Rather a lot of trouble if you're so sure he's totally useless to us.''

Lorimer answered with a snort and retreated to capture his horse.

"Don't let him escape!'' Ivarr exclaimed. "He killed Birna!''

"Birna dead?'' Gizur asked. "Lorimer, you must reckon for that.''

Lorimer laughed, an evil sound. "Much good that will do you or her. I killed her, as I've often wished to kill her. Let her avengers beware!'' He leaped astride his horse, while it plunged in nervous circles, and raised his staff aloft with a curse. Instantly the air exploded in a fiery concussion. Shattered fragments of ice hailed down like a shower of needles.

"Foxed you again,'' Gizur said, not relaxing his defensive stance.

"Not for long!''Lorimer vanished in a gust of icy wind, accompanied by the derisive screeching of Grus.

"So you're Birna's apprentice.'' Gizur and Ivarr silently sized each other up. Ivarr still held his knife ready.

"Since we both know who I am, you tell me who you are,'' Ivarr said.

"Gizur, fire wizard, friend to those with good intentions and foe to those without. Now it's my turn for a question. Are you truly the one Birna planned to send? You're different from what we expected.''

"I've got two arms and two legs, the same as you. What do you mean, different? Birna sent me as she was dying. I'm not sure why, but now I know what I must do—avenge her murder on Lorimer.''

"Of course you must, but you'll need help only a qualified fire wizard can give you. I shall be glad to assist you in any way I can. In fact, your vengeance will fit in nicely with our plans.''

39

"Indeed. Does everyone here have a plan?" Ivarr asked warily.

Gizur nodded his head. "Anybody who wants to live very long does. Just as everyone must have allies, since war is what we're talking about. Birna and I were allies, and she intended to send you to me, although your arrival was not as planned. I nearly missed you. But we can't remain here much longer or Lorimer's rebel dwarves are likely to come looking for us. I hope you trust me enough to accompany me to a safe place."

"A high place?" asked Ivarr. "Or a low place?"

Gizur nodded approvingly. "Birna taught you a few things, I see. We're going to a high place so you needn't keep scowling at me. And you can put that knife back into your belt; it's rather dangerous. When we get to where we're going, I shall explain to you the mess Birna has put you into." As he talked, he slapped his pockets and punched at a small black satchel. At last he pounced upon a piece of cord, tied a small stone in one end, and began to dowse. The pendulum wagged back and forth lazily as he turned and suddenly began to gyrate in tight purposeful circles. The circular path it described began to glow eerily. The wizard peered sidewise at Ivarr. "Oh, not impressed, eh? I imagine Birna was much better at it, or else magic bores you."

Ivarr managed a small rueful smile. "Magic is anything but boring. After today, I wonder if I'll ever be surprised at anything. Today has been—" He didn't finish, thinking of Birna lying among the cold stones. At least he had her cloak and knife to keep his memory fresh.

Gizur clapped a warm hand on his shoulder. "What you need is some food and rest. You've come a long way to get here, even if you don't realize it. Follow me and don't lag or stray to one side or the other. We'll be at a safe hill in about an hour."

They walked briskly, and Ivarr had to struggle to keep up. Rocks tripped him, and he never got enough of glancing behind him for possible danger.

Dawn was beginning to show very slightly when they

reached their objective. It was an old ruin, standing like jagged teeth in an old jawbone against the blue-black sky. Gizur advanced from stone to stone, peering with care around each corner. Ivarr had never seen such a sinister, gloomy place. Ruined walls leaned over him, seemingly held together with nothing but clumps of moss. Heaps of grass-grown rubble indicated where walls had stood. Gizur led him down silent grassy hallways with no roofs, up hillsides where crumbling stairs were nearly covered with dirt, and finally they arrived in a great roofless hall. Ivarr had never seen anything like the tall arched windows that still let light into the gloom. The houses and halls of the Sciplings were sensible, cozy longhouses built of turf, not stone and mortar.

"Built by the Alfar," Gizur said. "Centuries before Sciplings settled Skarpsey. There have always been wars, though, so we'll never have a shortage of ruins and barrow mounds."

Gizur kicked together a few pieces of wood near a fallen slab in the centre of the cavernous hall, With a nod, he lit the fire, watching it blaze into life and cast a warm glow on the ancient walls.

"Now we shall wait a bit. Curl up and go to sleep if you can. The friends I'm expecting are going to be a bit late—as usual," he added.

Ivarr curled up, enjoying the warmth, but certain he wouldn't sleep. He stared into the flickering curtain of orange flame, slowly drifting into deep and delicious sleep.

The next thing he knew, he heard voices. There were sounds of men tramping around and shouting.

"Gizur, you old salamander, where are you?" yelled someone, very near.

Ivarr leaped up in alarm, before someone stepped on him. His knife was in his hand. He found himself confronting a short, white bearded fellow in a maroon cloak. The man gasped and stumbled backward, fumbling for his sword and raising an unearthly bellow for help.

41

CHAPTER FOUR

Four other intruders froze in their tracks, hands stopped in midair. One even halted in the middle of a gusty sneeze. It looked as if their hearts had stopped beating. Then they exploded. Two fled at top speed, shedding their packs as they went; one drew a sword and held it in both hands uncertainly; and the last one rushed at Ivarr like a charging berserker, stopping just behind his companion in the maroon cloak and dancing around, waving a hand axe in a frightful display of bravery.

Ivarr brandished his knife at them experimentally and was astonished to see them both leap backward in fright. Then the one in maroon fixed his large, frightened eyes on the knife, as an elderly hare caught in a trap might eye the approach of his assassin. He drew his sword but trembled so hard that he had difficulty in getting it clear of its sheath.

The axe wielder suddenly stopped his prancing and threatening, to stare. "Why, that's one of our knives!" he declared angrily. "How dare you attack and menace us with one of our own weapons? You'd better give it back or it will certainly go the worse for you."

The old fellow lost his frightened hare aspect and rested the tip of his sword on the ground. "Now isn't that peculiar? How can you be an enemy of ours if you have a knife made in Snowfell? For a moment we thought you were perhaps a dark Alfar, in that black cloak. Who are you and what are you doing here, of all places?"

"I don't tell my name to everyone who wants to know it," Ivarr said stiffly. "I came here with a wizard to meet someone—although it looks as if he's not here at the moment. I'm sure he hasn't gone far." He looked around warily for Gizur and saw the other three strangers creeping forward by cautious degrees. Two were quite old, white-bearded, jolly looking sorts who would look more at home with drinking horns in their hands than swords. One wore an eyepatch, and the other was rather fat.

"What—who is he, Skapti?" the plump one called in a voice that quavered slightly. His butter-yellow breeches were astonishing in such a grim old place. "A dark Alfar? A draug?"

"He's probably a wizard of some sort, so stay back," declared the axe waver, flourishing the axe in one hand and a knife in the other. He was much younger than the others, as lean and wiry as a weasel hiding behind a hedge of black whiskers. His intense black eyes fastened upon Ivarr with glittering defiance. "Come on, you old cowards, we can handle one of them among the five of us. Skapti, throw a spell on him. Finnvard, Egills, you get ready to—"

"Shut up, Flosi!" snapped Skapti, the leader in maroon. "I shall decide what's to be done, if you don't mind. What if this is the fellow Birna was sending to help us out of this mess?" He tugged on one tufted red ear. A lifetime of such tugging had stretched it somewhat longer than the other.

"And if I am?" inquired Ivarr, still holding the knife at ready.

Finnvard of the yellow breeches exclaimed, "Oh, we're saved, we're saved! I never thought anything would turn out right for us after Flosi killed that wretched otter."

"I didn't say—" Ivarr began, realizing these were the outlaws.

"He's not much to look at," Egills declared, looking at Ivarr from head to foot with his one good eye, then lifting his patch so his blind eye could also register its opinion. He replaced the patch with a disapproving snap. "I never thought we had a fool's chance, even with the help of that

43

red- bearded wizard. Now I'm sure of it.''

Ivarr backed away. ''I never once consented to help a bunch of outlaws escape justice,'' he snapped. ''Let alone murderers of a young child. Whatever fate Svartarr deals you probably isn't cruel enough. You don't even act as if you're ashamed.''

The remaining outlaw, a tall thin fellow who hadn't said a word, suddenly appeared at his side. ''Gently, gently, fellows, we're not understanding one another. Put away all your weapons so we can talk in a peaceable manner. It's no good this way.''

Ivarr looked into his calm grey eyes and pleasant countenance and consideringly lowered his knife. ''Then you'd better talk quickly, and I'll decide for myself if it's safe to put my knife away in the company of outlaws or not.''

''Fair enough. I am Eilifir, usually called the Silent. We are men of the Alfar—or elves, as you Sciplings persist in calling us. We are spies for Elbegast, our king, and I have reason to believe that men and Alfar will find it to their advantage to be on the same side in this conflict. And it is true we have killed Ottar, but not as you think. It was not so much a murder as an accident. He was in the guise of his namesake, the otter, and Flosi had the misfortune to kill him.''

''My hands were about to freeze off,'' Flosi said.

Old Egills growled. ''You'd better close your mouth, you dolt. We wouldn't be in this fix if not for you. What a predicament. Outlawed by Svartarr, hunted like rats by Lorimer, and no doubt strung up by the heels by Elbegast once he hears what we've done. And now here we sit hobnobbing with this young rapscallion who no doubt is waiting for the moment to bash in our skulls and steal whatever we've got, and all because that wizard has abandoned us!'' He ended in a roar that quivered the ends of his drooping mustaches.

Finnvard's round pink face went pale as he listened. ''Then we're still doomed?'' he asked, clasping his hands. ''I never had problems like this when I was the chief pastry

44

cook in Snowfell." With a trembling hand, he carefully blotted his brow and lowered himself to a mossy rock before his shaking knees betrayed him.

"I can't imagine how such a coward ever got to be a spy," Flosi said in disgust. "They should have left him in the kitchen with his crumpets and trifles. He even looks out of place here." He glared at Ivarr as if it were his fault.

Egills glared at Flosi, bristling with enmity. "You shut your beak and keep it shut, you young pup. One of Finnvard is worth ten of your sort. You were thrown out of six different schools for general misbehaviour. Finnvard, at least, is honestly and genuinely incompetent, but you Flosi, are a waste of everyone's time."

"You're no great prize yourself," Flosi retorted. "You've been in the spies from the very beginning, and if that's not a testimony to your lack of ability—"

"Flosi, hush!" Skapti said, darting uneasy glances at Ivarr, who was listening with both ears.

"The only reason we're spies is because we're all misfits, incompetents, or cooks!" shouted Flosi, waving his axe wildly. "Elbegast has dumped us here with the hope he'll never see us again!"

Finnvard began to moan and blubber, and Egills and Flosi began a shouting match that certainly looked as if it ought to end in bloodshed. Skapti looked imploringly at Eilifir, and Ivarr looked for a way to escape. A low window ledge seemed to beckon, so he leaped into it and almost knocked Gizur off his feet as the wizard was coming in from the other side.

"Breakfast," Gizur said, holding up a stick with a dozen dead birds slung over it. "I see Skapti and the others are here. I daresay they were rather glad to see you."

"I want to go back," said Ivarr, "Get yourself another hero. All those fellows do is fight and quarrel with each other, and nobody pays any attention to the leader, and that fellow in the yellow pants is about as useless an individual as I've ever seen. I'd rather jump in the lake with a millstone around my neck than try to help—"

Skapti had pattered after Ivarr, wringing his hands and waving at Gizur to get his attention. Now he interrupted. "Gizur, you can't let him leave, or we'll never get that were-gild, and Elbegast won't like paying it himself, not one bit. You've got to do something, Gizur."

"How do I get back to my own realm?" Ivarr demanded, ignoring him.

"Not before breakfast, I should hope," Gizur said amiably, looping his staff through Ivarr's arm somehow and towing him around a crumbling corner. "Now what's this nonsense about going back? Birna could have easily saved herself, but she chose to send you to us instead."

"They want a hero. I'm no hero," Ivarr growled stubbornly.

"Well, you may not think so at the moment, but I assure you, we need you most desperately and you are the only one who will do. Who else has such a motive for killing Lorimer? Our success depends upon outwitting and killing Lorimer, and your estimation of yourself and the opinion of your fellow Sciplings depend upon avenging the murder of Birna."

"Of course, but I never bargained for those—those outlaws." Ivarr glared back at the Alfar, who were quarreling and scowling.

Gizur raised his gingery eyebrows. "Then how do you propose to do it, may I ask? You haven't a crumb of supplies about you, nor even a weapon nor an eider to sleep in. How will you defend yourself from packs of hungry trolls, or hostile land-spirits, or malicious wizards such as Lorimer? This realm is well-noted for its restless and very evil draugar who creep from their graves in search of warm, living blood to drink. I assure you, you won't last long here by yourself."

After a moment of thought, Ivarr sighed and nodded his head. "I can see you're right. But what is it you expect me to do for you?"

"I'll discuss it later—" began the wizard, but at that moment Skapti and Flosi came around the corner, arguing loudly.

46

"Hello, Gizur's back!" Flosi exclaimed. "Well, have you got this mess straightened out? Why on earth did Birna send us this fellow? He's only a young sprat and has no power besides. I can't believe Birna would send us a hero with no power. Have you told him about the dragon yet?"

"Shut up, Flosi!" Skapti commanded fiercely, reading Gizur's smouldering expression and Ivarr's astonished one correctly. "You're a far worse bargain yourself, I can tell you. The whole lot of us are a bad lot for any hero to acquire, but—"

"Acquire!" Ivarr looked from the truculent faces of Flosi and Egills to the buttery Finnvard, who seemed to be melting with perpetual fright. "Dragon! Nobody said anything about a dragon to me."

"Silence!" Gizur struck his staff on the rock so it spat sparks.

"That's a good way to burn somebody," Flosi said indignantly, pointing to Gizur's smoking staff.

"Now we shall explain to Ivarr who and what we are." Gizur said. "He no doubt thinks we're much worse than we really are."

"Basically it's true," Skapti sighed. "We are the bottomest of Elbegast's worst spies. None of us has even mastered his powers, so we were sent to the borders of Svartarrsrike, where nothing has happened in centuries— until we got there, that is. We were mucking around in the bogs, nearly frozen to death and up to our eyes in mud. None of us endure the cold very well, Flosi least of all. So in spite of Elbegast's specific orders, Flosi killed an otter."

"To make mittens," Flosi added. "My hands were ready to drop off, like two icebergs."

"But the otter, we found out later, was Ottar, the dwarf king's son, in his fylgja disguise as an otter," continued Skapti. "As I said, Flosi killed him, and by the end of that day Svartarr's dwarves were swarming around us like angry hornets. I thought for certain we were dead Alfar."

"I didn't even get to keep the pelt," Flosi said indignantly, with a challenging glance at Gizur.

"The pelt," Skapti said severely, looking at Flosi, "was taken to Svartarr, and we were taken to Svartarr, and you can't imagine the row. In the end he decided to be merciful and forgive us if we would cover the pelt with gold—"

"The advice of our friend Lorimer, by the way," said Gizur.

"Oh yes, Lorimer," said Skapti. "It was he who raised the hue and cry, evidently, and I suspect he has something to do with the fact that the otterskin grows larger and larger with each piece of gold you put on it. We turned out our pockets and succeeded in making the pelt the size of a calf. The next thing that happened was us promising somehow that we would cover the pelt with gold by autumn. You, of course, understand how reluctant we are to take our troubles to Elbegast, so we hired a wizard from the Fire Wizards' Guild to help us, and he has a plan for getting the weregild, but he's going to be the one who tells you about it." He sighed and shook his head, looking terribly anxious as he tugged at his favorite ear.

Gizur rose from his position beside the roasting birds. "If that's all any of you has to say, now we can get down to the important business. Let's eat. Skapti, break out that horrid stale oatmeal hardtack. Someone fetch some water for tea. And it would be a very good idea if someone were up on that wall, watching for Lorimer's rebels."

"Why is Lorimer stalking you?" Ivarr asked. "He engineered the killing of Ottar and the agreement on the weregild, so why does he want to kill you?"

"Because of you," Gizur replied agreeably. "With the aid of a hero trained by Birna, we might have a chance of actually getting enough gold to cover that pelt."

"That's what comes of complicating yourself with wizards and heroes," Flosi muttered darkly.

The roasted birds did not take long to eat; the hardtack was a different matter. Sitting around chewing on it and washing down the scratchy crumbs with hot tea was almost pleasant. Even the Alfar became more jolly, playing tricks on each other and singing bits of songs. Eilifir made himself

48

conspicuous by his refusal to indulge in the passionate bantering and quarreling of the others. His beard was a rich gold colour, unstreaked with white. In spite of his habitual silence, when he did consent to speak he seemed kindly enough to Ivarr.

"What I'd like to hear more about is this dragon," Ivarr said.

Eilifir sat up and crossed his legs. "First let me explain. The fate of the Ljosalfar rests upon our shoulders. What we will do will decide whether or not a great many Alfar will be killed by vengeance-seeking dwarves. And you know how these things start—one killing or burning leads to another, and before long every clan is involved in a blood feud and there's not enough gold in all of Skarpsey to pay the weregilds demanded."

"Get on with it," Flosi said, eavesdropping on their conversation unabashedly. "Tell him about the dragon."

Ivarr eyed Flosi with icy dislike, and Flosi glared back at him. He guessed that he and Flosi approximated the same age, however the ages of Alfar were figured; and he also knew a prodigious antipathy between them would flourish for as long as they were together.

Gizur elbowed Flosi aside and sat down beside Ivarr, bestowing a withering scowl upon Flosi. "I shall explain the dragon. Which is not to be confused with a lingorm; technically they are quite different." He then launched into a minute comparison of lingorms and dragons which Ivarr could scarcely listen to.

"Excuse me for interrupting," he said at last, "but I would rather hear what the dragon has to do with the killing of Ottar, if you don't mind."

"The gold which we are going to get," Eilifir said in his calm, refined voice, "is in a river cave in the possession of an old white dwarf called Andvari. Doubtless you have heard the legends and tales about Fafnir and Andvari?" He raised one eyebrow questioningly, and Ivarr shook his head. Eilifir looked pained, and shut his eyes.

Gizur explained, "Andvari acquires his gold a bit at a

time as it washes down the river. He crouches in a cave behind the highest waterfall on the Drangarstrom and darts out to retrieve any gold he sees. He has a salmon form; otherwise the river would batter him to pieces. Sometime in the past dark history, a dragon took up residence in his cave with him, since dragons have a great fancy for gold. When these outlaws summoned wizardly aid and I agreed to help them, I recommended that they rob Andvari as the quickest way to get such a staggering amount of gold.''

''We'll be stealing barrow gold?'' Ivarr asked.

''Andvari is an outlaw himself. It's a crime to keep anything removed from a barrow,'' Skapti said.

''It belongs more rightfully to us than Andvari,'' Flosi declared. ''He's only a white dwarf.''

''A white dwarf with a dragon,'' Egills added gloomily. ''It's your privilege to attempt to kill Fafnir.''

''Oh, indeed, just that simple?'' Ivarr retorted. ''And how am I supposed to do that? Somehow Birna neglected to tell me much about killing dragons. We were rather busy with bog-spavins and evil eye charms and missed the dragons, somehow.''

''Tell him about Glimr,'' Eilifir said, lighting his pipe by casually pressing his finger in the bowl.

''What or who is Glimr?'' Ivarr demanded.

Gizur began to smile, and his fox-coloured eyes shone with the secret he was keeping. ''A sword,'' he whispered, as if the rocks had ears. ''A sword anyone would yearn to possess. Glimr is its name, and it was made of the finest metal the black dwarf smiths could find. In the proper hands it will defend its master with the strength of ten good men, and it is so woven with spells and enchantments that it will not break even on the hardest stones or skulls.''

Flosi leaned over Gizur's shoulder and said, ''But the trouble is, it's in a barrow mound, and a haunted barrow at that. Thousands of bloodthirsty fire jotuns are guarding it, great giants who wield firebolts as a pitchy log spits sparks. And what's more, its true master is old Elidagrimr, one of the fiercest and most honourably dead of our ancient heroes, and you can bet he won't allow anyone even to touch his sword, or he'll come rattling and clattering after you, all rags and loose teeth and bones. And draugar never rest until they've revenged themselves upon the one who has wronged them. Stealing their weapons has to be the most grievous affront of all. It takes a tremendously brave fellow, or an absolute fool, to go robbing barrows, and that's what Gizur expects you to do. Now I expect you're more than ready to go back to shearing sheep and gutting fish."

"If I do, I wouldn't regret it much," Ivarr retorted, "although you certainly would before long."

Egills snapped, "Flosi, if you would keep your mouth shut for five minutes, we might persuade Ivarr we're not all as moronic as you. Can't you stop buzzing around like the vicious little horsefly you are? We wouldn't even be here if it weren't for you."

The outlaws glowered at each other as if they were ready to draw their knives and fly at each other's throats.

"Well, what's the big to-do about robbing a barrow?" demanded Ivarr. "I've known plenty of men who have done it and lived to brag about it, and they were anything but Alfar or wizards. If we much-despised Sciplings can get away with it, then certainly you fellows ought to."

"Hah," grunted Egills, morosely biting the end of his beard. "The sum total of our knowledge of magic and luck would fit on the end of a pin. You have to get the sword yourself and use it on old Fafnir, or he can sit on that gold forever. After Svartarr squashes us like miserable insects, I expect Fafnir can do as he pleases. He always has, anyway." He began punching Finnvard, who was collapsing limply, moaning in despair.

Gizur drew a deep breath, exhaled it slowly, and combed his fingers through his beard as if he felt more like pulling it out by the handful. "If you'd all care to listen and stop moaning, I shall tell you how we shall go about finding Elidagrimr's barrow. Skarpsey is full of old barrows and bones, and it won't be easy to locate one particular barrow with a specific skeleton inside. Now as it happens, I know who

51

might be able to help us—a very old smith named Dainn, who used to make swords for the Alfar kings, before the dwarves turned hostile. Before Svartarr, in other words.''

Skapti scowled at the map Gizur was removing from his satchel. "But black dwarves are beastly hard to find below ground. And if he's that old, how do you know he hasn't gone into the mound by now?"

"We'll hope he hasn't," said Gizur. "That would be very inconvenient for us. As you can see from the map, we'll be making a considerable journey to find him." He controlled the map with a rock on each corner and pointed to a range of mountains. "His forge lies here on the eastern slopes of the Dvergarfell. If he is still alive and still friendly to the Alfar, if we can convince him to reveal his secret, and if we can safely lay our hands upon the sword of Elidagrimr, it will be a relatively simple matter to rob Andvari of his gold. If we can keep Lorimer off our backs long enough, that is."

The Alfar stared at him, and Flosi exclaimed, "Now that's a fair-sized lot of ifs, isn't it? I thought we hired you to make our problem easier to solve, not to tack on a dozen others to complicate the original issue. At first all we had was Svartarr to worry about."

Gizur gripped his staff, and its silver cat's head knob began to snort little jets of smoke. "If you have a better idea, Flosi, you may go after it alone, or if you think you can do a better job of wizarding than I can, then pay me my wages and I'll depart herewith." He stood up and raised his staff as if he were about to incant himself away at that instant.

"I didn't say that," grumbled Flosi, a trifle anxiously, and Finnvard looked as if he were ready to faint away, crushing dry old Egills beneath him, a rather insubstantial prop for his considerable bulk.

Skapti elbowed Flosi savagely and declared, "Flosi's nothing but a buzzing nuisance, Gizur, so you've got to ignore anything he says. In spite of all appearances, I am the leader of this group, and I will be the one who decides, right?" The Alfar gaped back at him, paralyzed by indecision.

"Well then," Gizur snorted, "let's get packing."

CHAPTER FIVE

A cold wind whipped through the ruins of the old fortress as they left it. Gizur parcelled out for Ivarr a large lump of supplies wrapped in a waterproof cloth, a motley eider for sleeping, and a pack to put it all into.

Skapti pothered around, counting everyone twice, furling and unfurling some ragged maps, and almost forgetting his own pack in the process. He insisted that Ivarr take the second position behind Gizur and fell in behind Ivarr after assigning the others their positions, which seemed to be in relation to their rank. Flosi brought up the rear, whence he glowered murderously at Ivarr.

Gizur stopped to dowse in the lee of a large fallen stone, with a small gold bauble dangling at the end of a string. It swung wildly as the wizard paced back and forth, then it abruptly stood still despite the icy blasts of the wind. The wizard pointed southeast. ''That's the direction of the old ley line. We'll follow it until it disappears. In other times, there were several lines that led straight to Dainn's door.''

''How does that thing work?'' Ivarr tried to get a look at Gizur's dowsing pendulum before it was whisked into his pocket.

''No one really knows anymore,'' Gizur replied, ''but we do know that Dark Alfar, dwarves, trolls, giants, draugar, and whatnot avoid certain hills, which makes it convenient for those of us who have no desire to be murdered.

Unfortunately, safe hills are becoming scarcer as the old sites deteriorate.'' As he talked, he studied the prospect before them, a desolate expanse of snaking black lava flows, bald sulphur coloured hills where geysers smoked and steamed, and towering blue fells much clawed by glaciers. Then the journey was begun in earnest.

The longer they travelled, the more tempers sharpened. Ivarr thought he could learn to like all the Alfar, even poor cowardly Finnvard who fainted if a butterfly lit on him unannounced, but Flosi was a different matter. He fanned the flames of every argument until it was positively blazing and, when there was nothing to argue about, he put rocks into boot tops and burrs into beards or dawdled along far behind. He tried to ignore the existence of Ivarr, except to bestow some disparaging remark or thinly veiled insult.

After several days of travel, the ley line faded away into oblivion. Gizur called a halt on the crest of a bristly fell where banks of snow still lurked in shadowy declivities. When Ivarr had left his own realm, winter had been approaching, but in the Alfar realm he found that he had somehow missed winter and was now advancing into spring, albeit somewhat slowly.

Gizur dowsed repeatedly into all directions. The gold pendulum swung fretfully and refused to indicate any line, while the Alfar argued about the best type of cheese to eat if one were suddenly provided then and there on the spot. Ivarr watched Gizur anxiously and shook his head as the squabble over the cheese waxed hot and furious.

"Hard cheese!" "No, soft!" "Mild!" "Aged!"

"Can't you think of anything but food?" Ivarr demanded, remembering Birna's excellent cheese a little too vividly.

"Whatever for?" Flosi replied airily. "What do you think we hired you and Gizur for, if not to do all the worrying for us? Say, Gizur, shouldn't we be starting a fire for a pot of something?"

Gizur looked around from his scrutiny of the landscape. "Why, of course, by all means let's build a fire. Don't you clodpates realize we're blundering straight over black dwarf mines and tunnels and halls? Right at this moment, right under our feet, some old wicked dwarf may be eating his soup or picking his teeth and waiting for the sun to go down so he can get out and do some mischief. Yes indeed, a fire would be an excellent announcement of just where we are for Lorimer and his dwarves. As a spy, Flosi, you have about as much natural grace a a blind cow in a hummocky pasture.''

''I do not!'' Flosi denied hotly.

''All right, less then, if you insist,'' Gizur said agreeably, striding away. Grumbling, the Alfar straggled after him, making much of their aches and blisters.

Ivarr caught up with the wizard on a knob of hill. The others, seeing that he had stopped, collapsed at the bottom to complain and quarrel.

''We're on our own now,'' Gizur said. ''The ley line has definitely disappeared.'' He nodded to Eilifir, who toiled up the hill and sat down on a nearby stone to listen as Gizur plotted over the map. ''I don't much like to go eastward or we'll run into Grjotgardr, which was once as agreeable a place as any on Skarpsey, but it's now overrun with trolls.'' He spoke as if trolls were no more annoying than an infestation of mosquitoes.

''But I heard just lately,'' said Eilifir, ''that a bad winter had reduced the trolls considerably, so perhaps Grjotgardr is not quite so objectionable these days.''

''Is that so? Well, that casts a new light upon the matter,'' Gizur said, and they went on to discuss the matter while Ivarr listened, feeling about as useful as an axe with two handles.

''So what do you think, Ivarr?'' asked Gizur finally, after he and Eilifir had bandied about a dozen unfamiliar names and places and various admonitions.

''Why ask me? I'm not much use to you, I fear,'' Ivarr said, squinting uncomprehendingly at the map and shaking his head. ''I haven't the least idea where we are or what the difficulties are, and what's worse, I don't even have a decent weapon of any sort, except this little knife. Birna

55

used it to clean fish with. I'm a poor sort of a hero if I can't even defend myself.''

''Why didn't you say something?'' Gizur glared at him exasperatedly. ''I thought you were quite bored with the entire prospect of being a hero, and here you've been suffering the same anxieties as I have about being lost, which we have been for three days now—''

''Lost?'' asked Ivarr. ''And you're just now admitting it?''

''Let's just say that I'm waiting for an alternate route to suggest itself. In a place as large as Skarpsey, there's bound to be more than one way to get to any specific place, don't you suppose?''

Eilifir interrupted gently, ''About a weapon for Ivarr—''

''Oh yes. I was thinking we could teach him some simple spells.''

''I don't think that's a very good idea,'' Eilifir said. ''He can use my sword for as long as he wants it. I much prefer my bow and arrows, and in a close pinch there's nothing like a hand axe.'' He unbuckled his sword as he spoke and presented it to Ivarr.

Ivarr took it, speechless with delight. It was a sturdy weapon of plain manufacture, but it glowed with the sheen of a quality instrument rendered more beautiful by long use.

''Thank you,'' he said rather gruffly as he fastened it around his waist, trying not to keep admiring the way it looked there, as if it were the first sword he had ever worn— which it was. ''It's a noble weapon, Eilifir, and I'll try not to dishonour it or its giver.''

Eilifir merely nodded and went back to his contemplation of the bristly landscape until Gizur gave the signal to march on.

The day got off to an abortive start, however. The first river they crossed, neither deep nor particularly swift, carried Finnvard off his feet and rolled him and his pack downstream like a huge round hogshead. By the time the others got to him, he was sinking like a scuttled barge. His face was blue with cold and he was shivering so hard his teeth rattled.

A hasty camp was made on the riverbank. Finnvard was clearly in a bad way, and no amount of blankets and cloaks seemed to help. Gizur ordered a fire built and tea was brewed, but Finnvard was not warmed until Gizur uncorked a small bottle and added a large dollop of the potion to a cup of scalding tea. Finnvard swallowed the scalding stuff without an eye watering and promptly stopped shivering.

The rest of the day was spent in drying out the contents of Finnvard's pack and all the clothing that had become wet during the rescue. Gizur grumbled and spent a lot of time studying their position and the map.

"I think Grjotgardr is going to take us a bit longer than I'd estimated," he said. "It looks as if we'll be spending at least three nights with the trolls." He felt the hem of his cloak and squeezed out another handful of water with a worried sigh. "Is Finnvard's stuff any drier than this? It's going to take the rest of the day to get it dry. And who can guess when the feathers in his eider will ever dry out?"

Their camp was in a rocky river bend, damp and unfavourable besides being so vulnerable to attack that Gizur insisted on a double guard that night. In addition, he scratched guardian rings all around the camp, which boded ill for anything wandering too close. Ivarr viewed these preparations with more anticipation than dread, quite satisfied that his watch was the first, when the trolls were at their hungriest.

The trolls of Grjotgardr, however, were hunting that night in a different quarter. He heard their distant howling and roaring and shivered with excitement and was secretly glad the trolls hadn't challenged him on his watch. But sometime shortly before dawn, a solitary troll blundered into camp, setting off two alarms before fleeing for his life, no doubt petrified by the flashes of light and the smoke.

Flosi bragged inordinately the next morning, since the invasion had occurred during his watch. Egills, who had shared the shift with Flosi, pointed out that Flosi had been sound asleep the whole time, as he usually was every time he stood guard. He, Egills, had seen the troll from the moment it crept out of the rocks some half-mile away—Egills of the one eye who as often as not burnt the end of his nose every time he tried to light his pipe.

After two fairly easy days, the terrain of Grjotgardr began to get rockier, breaking into flows of lava and lush little valleys hidden between. Ivarr began to observe increasing quantities of tracks in the mud beside the water—tracks like giant chicken tracks, with the claws plainly evident.

Gizur scarcely paused to take a look at the tracks, urging them to hurry on faster. "It's cloudy today, curse the luck, which means that it will probably get dark sooner than usual. I have a feeling the trolls won't overlook us again tonight, not this far into Grjotgardr.

As the day wore on Ivarr began to feel forebodings, and he looked around frequently at the cold bleak landscape, half-convinced he had just missed seeing something. They were climbing now, ascending into the foothills and high hidden valleys of Grjotgardr. Above, the towering fells were jagged with bared rock faces that seemed to warn them to keep out. Everywhere were signs of troll infestation—well-trodden paths covered with fresh tracks, stray bits of rag and bones and hair, broken crockery and other things plundered from unlucky travellers. In one place on the snow of a glacier they crossed, the snow was beaten down in a grimy circle which was strewn with a collection of well-chewed and cracked fresh bones.

Finnvard lost his nerve soon afterward and sat down on a rock, begging the others to leave him behind. "We can never escape from them," he said almost tearfully. "I simply can't go another step with my knees quaking the way they are. This is the end of the road for me, I fear."

With much exasperated cajoling they all tried to persuade him to keep going, but he was as adamant as the stone he sat on. Finally Ivarr walked away a bit and looked back over the way they had come. It was late in the afternoon and the shadows were beginning to lengthen. It had not been a pleasant day after Gizur dowsed at the strange hill. A creeping feeling had haunted him continuously. As he watched, a lone horseman rode across a little clearing scarcely a half mile behind them, vanishing almost immediately into a ravine.

"Gizur, I think I just saw Lorimer," he said as calmly as he could. "Following us, right up the same ravine we went up."

"I've known he was right behind us all day," snapped Gizur. "Did you dolts actually think it was the trolls I was worried about?"

"Lorimer!" Finnvard gasped, leaping up. "I'm ready to go on now. If there's one thing I'm afraid of, it's Lorimer."

"One thing?" Flosi snorted. "You're afraid of everything."

They scrambled up the last slope and found a level plain on the other side, leading right up to the foot of the great fell. Gizur halted and pointed eastward. "Do you see that tall pinnacle of black rock? That's Thor's Hammer, and directly behind it is the way into Blackfell, a narrow gill where a stream comes down the mountain. Follow the stream up to the top, where there's a deep, narrow gash. Go directly through it and you'll be on your way down. If you really race for it, you'll make it. I've spoken to Eilifir about fire bolts, in case the trolls catch up with you."

"Are you leaving us?" Skapti demanded, turning pale.

"Abandoning us to the trolls!" Finnvard cried in anguish.

"Oh, hush. You'll be perfectly safe if you keep moving. I'm merely going back to see what Lorimer wants. If he's following us, I'll try to deflect him considerably off the track. I'd like to deflect him right into Muspell's kettle and watch him melt. I shall probably catch you by the time you reach Thor's Hammer. Ivarr will take my place while I'm gone." He said it mainly to Flosi, garnishing his statement with a menacing stare. Quickly he shoved the map into Ivarr's hands and checked the contents of his satchel. His eyes gleamed with anticipation as he gathered his cloak around him and hurried away toward the ravine.

The Alfar complained and cursed their way through the

tortured terrain, which abounded in clawing stickery brush and scaling lava rock and crevices. The afternoon began to wane, and Finnvard began making ominous noises about sitting down. The sun sank lower, and Ivarr began to worry. Thor's Hammer was as far away as ever and their pace was snail-like. Their destination was hours away.

Then Finnvard sat down and folded his arms. "I'm not going another pace until Gizur catches up with us," he declared. "We need the rest, besides."

Ivarr glanced at Eilifir, who only shrugged and shook his head.

To everyone's surprise and disgust, Flosi also sat down and said, "I agree. We'll stay here until we have a competent leader." He glared significantly at Ivarr. "One whom we can trust."

CHAPTER SIX

"I'm doing my best to get us out of here," snapped Ivarr. "And I for one don't intend to sit here waiting for a pack of hungry trolls to find me. You can come or you can sit here."

As if on cue, a rock clattered down from the cliffs above. Skapti jumped nervously. "I'm not sitting around here while there are trolls prowling around," he exclaimed. "After all, Birna thought Ivarr was clever enough to help us, and what's clever enough for Birna is clever enough for me. I daresay she had more sense than you, Flosi, and you, Finnvard."

"We have perhaps an hour until the sun goes down," Eilifir said. "In an hour's time I'd rather be halfway up the ravine than sitting here."

"Right," Ivarr said, with a last contemptuous glare at Flosi. He set a course for the black tower that was Thor's Hammer. The rebellious elves trailed sheepishly at the tail end.

Skapti hurried up alongside Ivarr, very anxious. "You must forgive us all, Ivarr, we haven't a grain of courage among the lot of us, except possibly Eilifir, and he hasn't been with us long enough to become as cowardly as the rest of us, but I do hope you won't bear a grudge. We're all so dreadfully incompetent, you know."

"Yes, I know. You keep telling everyone so we can't possibly forget it for a moment," Ivarr said.

"As if we could," Skapti said gloomily.

They hiked as rapidly as possible over the twisted terrain, but soon Finnvard was stumbling and wheezing and whimpering. Flosi pushed him along from behind, encouraging him with threats and imprecations.

"Just leave me behind," he begged. "I can't go another step. I'll die here before going on." He sank down wearily on a stone and closed his eyes.

"Then I want your cloak and boots," Flosi exclaimed. "No sense wasting good equipment if the trolls are going to get you." He seized one of Finnvard's boots and began to tug.

"Let go, you fool! You're not getting my boots!" Finnvard kicked at him and leaped up with amazing agility. "I'm coming, I'm coming, drat you!"

The sun sank lower, and everyone began to stumble with exhaustion. To Ivarr's despairing eye, the pinnacle was getting no nearer. The setting sun bathed it in a menacing red light. Everywhere were distinct troll noises—long toenails scratching among the rocky clefts, growls and grunts from unseen caves where trolls lurked, waiting for the sun to vanish.

"We'll never make it in time!" Skapti gasped.

The same dreadful thought was in Ivarr's mind, but he said nothing, striding onward as fast as he could manage. He kept his eyes on the ground or glancing around at the cliffs and rocks. When he looked up again, Thor's Hammer did seem much closer. He could see the details of its craggy features and its long shadow pointing toward a black fissure in the wall of the mountain, which would lead them to safety.

"We're almost there!" He urged them on with praise and flattery. The sun was almost resting on the horizon. Behind them, the blue shadow of night was approaching with frightening speed. Ivarr imagined a wave of trolls rushing after them, just on the edge of the darkness. They all began to run at the same instant toward Thor's Hammer.

The sun sank with heartless rapidity. One moment it was hanging lazily on the horizon; then it was gone. Behind them sounded a croaking roar of gruff troll voices, echoed by whoops and bellows and screams across the tortured countryside.

Fortunately the stream bed up the ravine was sandy and smooth, an ideal place for running, and the moon cast ample light. They stood Finnvard upon his legs and encouraged him to run as he had never run in his life. The angry uproar of the trolls not far behind was even more encouraging. They ran and scrambled up the steep places, and the ravine seemed to extend before them for miles, deepening as they reached the top into a dark chasm. The frustrated howling of the trolls came echoing up the ravine as the escapees paused a moment to wheeze for breath. Finnvard started to sit down, but Flosi seized his arm and exclaimed, ''No you don't, you old donkey! The trolls are still coming!''

They stumbled down the other side, which was steeper, rockier, and lacking a sandy stream bed to run on.

''Stop!'' exclaimed Eilifir after they had careened down the mountain a short distance. ''Something has to be done to stop those trolls or they'll have us, very shortly. Get ready to use your powers.''

''They will anyway, with our magic,'' Finnvard protested weakly.

''We can manage it,'' Eilifir said. ''Come now, stand in a ring. Think about the third article of power. Recite it carefully in your minds, get all the parts in the right order, and don't forget any. Ivarr, you may join us if you care to. Concentrate as if you were moving a very great weight, balancing it, and pushing it finally over the edge so it falls.'' Their circle was joined quickly; the trolls were nearly at the summit.

''More power,'' called Eilifir sharply, and the elves squeezed shut their eyes and knotted their brows in terrible concentration.

''Good; now hold it,'' Eilifir said and began to chant a formula. ''There, it's done!'' he whispered excitedly. ''Quick now, take cover!''

Finnvard sighed gratefully. ''That's all we've got. I hope

it works, whatever you did. There's not enough left for two." He almost collapsed, but Egills held him up long enough so he could fall into the protection of an outcropping of rock. "At the moment, I don't think I have the strength to knock over a newborn kitten."

"Here come the trolls," Ivarr said, clenching his sword in both hands. "This time we'll make them pay in blood."

"Nonsense," Eilifir said. "They'll never get here."

Far above in the mountains there was an awesome cracking noise like thunder. Boulders began crashing down the slopes, leaping and exploding with trails of magnificent flame. The earth trembled, and an ominous rattling roar filled the night with its thunder. Boulders bounded from point to point, outlined with flame, and fiery splinters flew at each concussion. The entire mountainside seemed to be crashing and tumbling down, glinting with fire and shattering ice as part of a glacier joined the landslide. The ravine vanished beneath a thundering avalanche of stone and ice, plugging it neatly and forever.

When the last boulder had clattered down the mountain, the Alfar pounded each other's backs and hugged each other, all babbling nonsense and laughing deliriously. Flosi and Egills, arm in arm, began singing an Alfar battle song at the tops of their lungs. Skapti and Finnvard grinned dazedly, shaking hands with everyone about twenty times.

"I remember one time we made it rain spoiled milk on a frost giant," Skapti said, "instead of the spears we'd intended. Who would have dreamed we could do something this grand!"

"Magnificent!" Flosi said.

Eilifir cleared his throat. "It was a very near thing, actually. If we were better at magic, we could have done more to those trolls than frighten them and plug up the Blackfell pass. I suggest we all practice our drills until we can call out our powers instantaneously."

"Before long we won't need Gizur to lead us," Flosi said. "We'll have five times his power. We're already more than a match for a hundred trolls."

A distant shout cut through their jubilation, and instantly Skapti and Egills dived for cover. Finnvard went rigid with fright and Ivarr and Eilifir had to drag him to the shelter of a large stone. Peering over the top of the stone, Ivarr saw a glowing red orb atop a low hill swinging back and forth like a beacon, and again came the thin shout.

"It must be Gizur," Ivarr said gladly. "He's found us."

They swarmed up the hill toward the light and found Gizur cooking soup over a tiny fire. "There you are," he said. "I thought I'd have to eat all the soup myself. Whatever took you so long?"

Skapti threw down his pack and exclaimed, "Why, just on the other side of Thor's Hammer, which you directed us to, we stepped right on fifty trolls." They all clamoured at once about their adventure, with a quantity of exaggeration and contradictions. Gizur listened, but he kept darting skeptical glances at Ivarr and Eilifir.

"Is this really the truth?" he asked at last.

"More or less," Eilifir replied with a shrug. "And did you find Lorimer following us?"

"Most assuredly I did, and we had a very friendly chat," Gizur said. "Here's proof of it." He lifted one arm to reveal a huge ragged rent in his cloak. "Made by an ice bolt. But I blackened him properly in retaliation with a sooty blast, and then he offered to make me a bargain. If I would surrender up Ivarr to him he would stop interfering with your payment of the weregild."

Flosi leaped up. "Wonderful! When do we make the trade?"

Gizur glowered at him witheringly. "You imbecile, if we give up Ivarr we won't have a hair's breadth of a chance of getting the gold, unless you want to ask Elgebast for it."

"No indeed, he doesn't," Skapti said hastily; Finnvard and Egills were shaking their heads in vigorous negation.

"Ah well, I didn't suppose you'd agree to it," said Flosi with a sigh. Then he brightened. "Say, Gizur, did you happen to see what we did to the Blackfell passage? Plugged it up solid with the most smashing landslide, and we did it all

65

ourselves with our own power. What do you think of that?''

Gizur put down his cup of tea and feigned great surprise. ''Before long you'll make the Fire Wizards' Guild look like a pack of dirty little children playing with sticks and coals. Fafnir will take one look at you and expire on the spot, realizing the futility of resistance. Elbegast will kick out his right-hand advisers and hire you.''

''That's enough,'' Skapti said, cutting him short. ''But we at least are quite pleased and justifiably proud of our accomplishments tonight.''

The elation of their success carried them along for several days through some very unpleasant terrain. Blackfell was nothing but bogs and rocks and glaciers. By night they took refuge on the tops of rocky hills, and the trolls came in hunting packs to the very foot of the hill to snarl and slaver, until Gizur drove them away with fiery spells.

At last they reached a summit and looked down into a large valley, flanked on two sides by tremendous blue fells and silver-veined with a network of rivers and small lakes. Beyond were more mountains. To their mountain-weary eyes the prospect looked exceedingly depressing.

''Looks like prime troll territory,'' Skapti said with a sigh.

''And not at all like Dvergarfell,'' Flosi said. ''According to the map, this should be a busy mining area, with heaps of slag and tailings and smokey smelters and smithies and a thousand black dwarves. Well, Gizur, where are they? Or should I say, where are we?''

''No, you shouldn't say anything!'' Gizur growled, nearly enveloped in an unruly assortment of maps. ''Ivarr, hold this beastly staff so I can get some light on this map; the ink's faded abominably. Don't stand around gawking, you dolts; can't you dowse or use your powers to find out where we are?''

''Lost!'' declared Finnvard with great satisfaction. ''I knew it!''

''Then why didn't you say so?'' Gizur roared, grating his teeth together alarmingly. ''Someplace we've taken a wrong turn and we're not in Dvergarfell, as any lamebrain can plainly see. The last thing I am certain of was Thor's Hammer. We are either too far north or too far south—or something like that. How do you vote? Shall we go north or south? One of those is bound to take us to Dvergarfell and Dainnsknip.''

Skapti coughed anxiously, sidling away from Gizur. ''You mean you're just guessing which way to go?''

''We could do that much,'' Egills muttered. ''Why do you think we hired a wizard? You're supposed to know exactly which way to Dainnsknip.''

''Very well, I shall use a device to make the decision,'' Gizur snapped, rummaging in his pockets and producing a coin. ''Heads, north; tails, south. Fair enough? All right, then. Tails it is, so we're going south. Does anyone wish to complain?'' He glowered so fiercely that the potential complainers quickly closed their mouths and swallowed their complaints, hastily slinking back into their marching positions.

Ivarr tried to catch Gizur's eye, but what he managed to catch was a sly wink exchanged between Gizur and Eilifir. Gizur strode along in a fine humour, humming under his breath and watching the unhappy Alfar with an amused glint in his eye. For the next three days whenever someone ventured to complain, Gizur retorted, ''If you think I'm wrong, use your powers to find the right way, if you think you're that good.''

Ivarr watched Eilifir and wondered about that spell at the Blackfell pass, and who really had supplied the power for it. Eilifir assiduously evaded all questions, particularly ones relating to the true status of his power. Gizur probably guessed his secret, but he wasn't saying anything either.

After the fourth day passed in fruitless search, the chancy humours of the Alfar deteriorated even further. They settled into a silence which Ivarr thought far more ominous than their customary bickering.

''I've got blisters the size of lakes,'' Finnvard whimpered. ''I can't go another step. Just go ahead and leave me.'' He had said it at least twice a day since they began the journey, but now he seemed to be saying it with every other breath.

"I wish we could just leave you," Flosi replied. "We're all tired too, but we're not going to search while you sit and rest. Eilifir carried your pack almost all day besides."

Finnvard scowled stubbornly, sticking out his chin, which quivered with emotion. "I won't budge another step. I think that wizard has led us astray. You know they can't be trusted."

Gizur lifted his head from his perusal of the map. "Oh, is that so? You believe I'm plotting to sell the lot of you to Lorimer and I've walked two hundred miles over the worst terrain in Skarpsey just for the novelty of it? My dear fellows, you haven't paid me the slightest smell of a gold mark, nor even mentioned it. Now you have the daring to say you don't trust me?" His eyes flared and he gripped his staff.

"Well, where are we then?" demanded Egills. "I think we're lost and have been ever since we started."

"But the standing stones and ley lines—" Ivarr began.

Truculently, Finnvard folded his arms. "I say one rock looks very like another. I might believe it if I saw an actual line with my own two eyes. We're lost!"

"Lost!" echoed Egills gloomily.

"We never did look at this fellow's credentials, did we?" Flosi asked.

Gizur's cloak gusted furiously and he raised his staff threateningly. "Is that the way it is?" he roared. "Then perhaps it's time we terminated our agreement, if you find it so unsatisfactory. For your information, I haven't particularly enjoyed your company, either. Farewell!"

Gizur strode away in a cloud of belching smoke.

"Wait!" Skapti shrieked. "Gizur, we're sorry! We didn't mean it!"

"Then you shouldn't have said it," Ivarr retorted, yearning to grab Finnvard by the ears and give him a shaking. He raced after Gizur, but before he had gone five steps, the wizard gave his cloak a flick and vanished in a puff of sulphury smoke.

CHAPTER SEVEN

"Now we've done it," Skapti groaned. "This is just like the good old days. Blast you, Finnvard, this is all your fault."

"I'm not budging another step without a cup of hot tea," Finnvard said grimly.

In the long silence that followed, all eyes came to rest upon Ivarr.

"Don't look at me," he said. "I'm not going to be the leader. If you knew you needed Gizur so badly, why did you give him such a hard time? I'm leaving, before your bad luck rubs off on me. Now let's get the food divided up."

Skapti watched sorrowfully as Ivarr threw down his pack and began unloading surplus equipment.

"But you can't abandon us," Flosi blustered. "We made a deal, remember?"

"Please reconsider, Ivarr," Skapti said, tugging his ear worriedly. "Birna trained you and sent you here for a purpose. Years of foreseeing and spying and preparation have gone into getting you here at this moment."

"You can't kill Lorimer by yourself, you know," Egills growled.

Ivarr looked at their earnest contrite expressions and sighed. "Do you really think I can do anything to help you get that weregild? I certainly can't imagine it without the help of a wizard."

"Well, let's just summon another wizard," Finnvard suggested eagerly.

"Here? Now?" Skapti shook his head. "Lorimer would be the wizard we'd get, I'm afraid."

Eilifir nodded his head. "And you recall how long it took us to find a wizard who would consent to be hired. We simply don't have the time to burn a charm. Ivarr will have to lead us until we find a safer place."

The Alfar agreed with an abundance of sincerity, but Ivarr was still overshadowed by misgivings. Secretly he hoped Gizur would get over his temper and return. All Ivarr had for guidance was an old frayed map which Gizur had given him because he didn't want it anymore, and a general idea that Dvergarfell lay to the south somewhere, and that they had to find a single mountain called Dainnsknip. Ivarr looked consideringly at the inscrutable Eilifir, wondering if he would get any help from him.

Gizur did not return the next day. They waited for him until noon, their hopes growing more faint by the moment, and then they set off under Ivarr's leadership. Ivarr still nurtured a stubborn hope that Gizur would relent and come back but, by the fourth day by themselves, he had given up on ever seeing the wizard again.

Their camp at the end of the fourth day was set up in the lee of a large round hill. It was a wretched, rocky place to camp, and no one could get a fire to burn. A storm was brewing to the north, gusting at them with icy winds and frequently pelting them with drops of rain. All they had to eat was stale hardtack and cold water, which caused an undercurrent of grumbling and growling. To worsen things, Flosi began reporting that he had bad feelings about the campsite.

"Well, I have bad feelings about everything," retorted Egills. "The food, the beds, the blisters, the weather—"

"All we need is a good soaking," Finnvard grumbled. "I hope we haven't leaped out of the frying pan into the fire, taking shelter in this place. The only thing that reassures me is the fact that Flosi is the one who says he has a premonition.

Flosi wouldn't know a premonition from an eye wash.''

Flosi leaped to his own defence, and Ivarr moved away to watch the gathering storm clouds. His thoughts were filled with Lorimer and he could not shake the ominous feeling that Lorimer must find them sooner or later, and they would be almost defenceless without Gizur. Almost defenceless, except for Eilifir, who was becoming as big a headache as the others, in his own self-contained way.

The storm was fast approaching, and Ivarr began to observe the peculiar purplish hue of the rolling clouds and how they behaved more like clouds of belching smoke than conventional storm clouds. The lightning flashes were yellow and greenish, scuttling across the dark skies like monstrous spiders. The wind tweaked at the map he held across his knees, and he struggled to have one last look at it before he was defeated by the wind and the darkness. Rolling it up, he stood up and glared at the valley below them—a long narrow valley winding around the knees of rounded fells, and a river looping and meandering like a snake, widening into a chain of leaden lakes and ponds, very like hundreds of others in Skarpsey.

Sighing, he went down to pace around their dismal camp, where all but Eilifir were arguing bitterly over some trivial offence. Eilifir sat apart from them, idly swinging a pendulum.

Ivarr stared at him, then strode over and impulsively asked, "Will those work for just anyone? Sciplings, I mean? Or must a person have power?"

Eilifir smiled, as if Ivarr had just received a revelation. "Try it and see," he said. "I'm almost certain there must be a ley line or two going through Dainnsknip. Extend one hand before you like a pointer and swing the pendulum in the other. Think of the ley line and the standing stones. If the pendulum doesn't start to go in circles, try another direction."

Ivarr did as he was instructed, feeling slightly foolish. The pendulum ticked back and forth languidly in lessening arcs, so he altered the direction. Still no results. Closing his eyes

71

he concentrated hard, visualizing the stone which had been nearby when Birna died. The pendulum made no reaction. He tried again—and again—and again. In spite of himself, stray thoughts kept creeping into his mind. He caught himself remembering the day he and Birna had gone to visit the blacksmith of Hvitaness to treat a horse with the glanders. He could almost see the smith pounding at his anvil, and the sparks flying from his massive hammer.

"You've got something," Eilifir's voice said, betraying no excitement. Ivarr's eyes popped open. The pendulum was making tight, businesslike circles, and Ivarr's other hand was pointing across the little valley to a large fell with a very flat top and abrupt sides.

"Is that Dainnsknip?" Ivarr squinted through the gathering gloom. The Alfar had been watching, and they gathered around.

"There? It's a huge mountain," said Skapti. "And where's Dvergarfell?"

"How could we ever find Dainn's forge inside something like that?" Finnvard asked. "We could search for a year and never find it."

"That's it, I'm sure of it," Ivarr said, tingling with excitement. "Look how steep the one side is, and that overhanging knob on the other end looks just like the point of an anvil."

"By the beard of Odin and all its fleas!" Egills gasped. "It does look just like an anvil. I may have only one eye, but even a fool can see it. Tonight we may sleep in actual beds and eat decent food."

Flosi scowled at Ivarr and the pendulum. "I'm no fool, and I say it's stupid to rush over there and start scratching around just because Ivarr gets a phony reaction with a piece of string with a bead tied on one end. He's only a Scipling, after all, and he has no powers."

"You try it then." Ivarr threw the pendulum at Flosi's feet. "I'm going to pack up and move while there's still some daylight. Anyone who wants to come had better hurry."

Egills promptly began loading up his pack. Skapti and

Finnvard anxiously watched Flosi. The pendulum swung to a gradual halt. Flosi cast Ivarr a triumphant sneer. "See there? That fell is nothing. Anybody else want to try?"

They all looked at Ivarr uncertainly. He shouldered his pack, knowing for a certainty that a mysterious signal had passed from the pendulum to him.

"Say, you're not leaving, Ivarr," Finnvard said. "Be sensible now; you made a mistake, is all. The wind blew it, or your hand moved."

"If anyone wants to come, you'd better hurry." Ivarr started off.

"Wait a moment. I'll try it." Eilifir took the pendulum from Flosi. He extended one hand toward the flat-topped fell. The pendulum swung back and forth a long time before beginning to describe circles, which tightened and gathered in intensity.

"There. Are you satisfied now?" he inquired. "I'm going to pack up my gear and go with Ivarr." He put the device in his pocket and turned. Suddenly he froze, crouching, his eyes fixed on the valley behind them which they had crossed that day. "Great Hod, it's a troop of black dwarves!" he whispered. "Everyone down, and not a sound."

Ivarr flattened himself between two boulders and viewed their backtrail. Black-garbed dwarves were riding slowly across the valley, following a shrouded individual who rode apart, pausing often to study the ground. Ivarr was certain it was Lorimer and his renegades. From all appearances, they did not realize how close they were to their quarry. Quickly Ivarr signalled to the elves, pointing toward a brushy ravine. They stooped low, scrabbled their packs together and darted toward the ravine without a sound except Finnvard's fearful panting. Ivarr and Eilifir tumbled last into the ravine and peered through the scanty cover at the advancing dwarves. Their heads were up alertly now as they scanned the hillside before them, standing still and listening for the faintest betraying sound. The wind and the intermittent thunder screened the slight sounds of Finnvard's wheezing and the crackle of twigs underfoot.

"This won't hide us for long," Eilifir whispered. "They already suspect we're here somewhere. It's just a matter of time until they find us. What we need is a spell. Can you fellows remember fog?"

They linked arms in a circle, in spite of Finnvard's protest. Ivarr braced himself for the eerie sensation of Eilifir's power shooting around the circle. He felt as if he were flying joyously through a storm of thunder and lightning, like Thor himself. Then Finnvard began coughing and gasping and the giddy atmosphere suddenly dissolved.

"Nithling!" Flosi exclaimed. "You spoil it every time!"

"That was sufficient," said Eilifir. "Watch."

A rolling cloud of mist descended the hill in front of them, growing thicker and greyer as they watched. It overtook Lorimer and the dwarves like a mass of grey wool, obscuring everything. The shouts and curses of the dwarves drifted up to Ivarr and the elves as the searchers became separated and lost their sense of direction.

Ivarr and the Alfar held on to the hems of one another's cloaks and crept along the bottom of the ravine. The fog was so thick they could scarcely see each other. The dwarves were shouting furiously, trying to find themselves, but voices sounded muffled and strange in the fog; the dwarves went past each other and wandered in circles, shouting and calling. Once one blundered almost into the Alfar's path, his horse trampling around in terror as it struggled out of the ravine.

The ravine led the Alfar down into the valley on the other side, out of the fog. In half an hour's time they were searching along the foot of the fell with the mingled purpose of finding a suitable hiding place or perhaps stumbling upon Dainn's door. The fog spell was dispersing, and they could see the dwarves quartering the hillside, searching for their tracks. Then one gave a shout, and they all galloped toward the ravine.

Finnvard moaned, "No further, no further." He kept up a sort of chant as they hauled him along over the stones and

74

bushes. When they paused a moment to consider, they flung him down like a sack of grain and took him up again when it was time to go on. Everyone took his turn except Flosi, who advocated leaving him behind.

In one ravine, deeper and narrower than the rest so far, Ivarr called a sudden halt and redirected their course upward, splashing along in an icy streamlet and scrambling up steep little waterfalls. His heart began to thump with something more than exertion as they ascended.

"Ivarr, we've got to get out of this before it gets too steep," Skapti warned, across the inert mass of Finnvard.

"No further," added Finnvard.

Ivarr hurried along even faster, dragging Finnvard after him. He had no breath to waste on talking, not with the musty, moldery smell of earth strong in the faint breath that blew down the ravine in their faces. That cellary smell could only mean that there was a cave not far away.

They reached the end of the ravine, staggering and dropping Finnvard before the narrow opening. A little waterfall cascaded around the cave, soaking them as they crawled through, Finnvard especially, since he was almost too fat to fit. The moment they were inside, they heard the clatter of horses' hooves following them right up to the entrance. The horses milled around and the dwarves talked excitedly.

"Someone make a light," said the unmistakable voice of Lorimer, and immediately the gloom outside flared with a red glow.

"It is as I suspected," Lorimer said. "They've found a cave. We shall have to go after them."

The dwarves were silent. Then one spoke. "This hill belongs to Dainn the smith. It wouldn't be wise to trespass on him."

"Dainn is the one who should be fearful," Lorimer said. "When he knows it is Lorimer who comes searching, he won't dare try to hide them."

Grus laughed. "Then you don't know Dainn as we do. I wouldn't go into his tunnels, and you couldn't make me, Lorimer."

"You'll make food for the ravens yet, if you keep goading me," Lorimer snarled. "If you dwarves value your lives, you'll get down and go after them. I wouldn't like to blast you, but perhaps it is necessary."

Ivarr poked Skapti. "Get going. They're coming after us."

When they had felt their way along, very cautiously in the pitch blackness, far enough so no light would show behind them at the entrance, Eilifir produced candles and lit them without benefit of flint and steel or tinder.

"The black dwarves, of course, have no need of candles in their native element," he said conversationally.

The cave wandered crookedly, with passages splitting off on either side. Finally the main passage ended in a huge circular vault, and they searched in vain for another route, before backtracking desperately to explore side tunnels. Behind, they heard the clatter of boots and the rattle of swords and arrows.

"They've found us!" Skapti gasped. "Draw your swords, we'll have to fight!"

"After we're done running," Flosi said, shoving Finnvard along from behind. Being at the tail end, he would be of course the first one to have to turn and fight.

Stumbling suddenly down a rubbly incline, they stopped to untangle themselves and discovered they were in another roomy chamber. Desperately they groped around the walls for a tunnel.

"Dead end!" Egills puffed.

Above, a lurid yellow light suddenly burst over their heads, showering them with ice crystals. In its light, Ivarr saw about fifteen dwarves charging down the rocky slope, swords and axes in hand. He drew his sword and, behind him, Eilifir unslung his axe.

"If it's a battle they want, they shall have it," Eilifir said. "We can't allow them to capture you alive."

CHAPTER EIGHT

"Here's the way out!" shrieked Flosi, just as the first of the black dwarves reached the end of the slope, drawing his sword.

They turned and bolted toward a large doorway, barely visible in the light of the single candle in Flosi's quivering hand. A door slammed behind them with a resounding crash. Bolts and bars crashed into place even as the black dwarves began battering on the far side. The door was too thick to do more than vibrate slightly under the assault.

The elves sorted themselves out and relit their candles. Eilifir silently tugged the end of his cloak out from the doorsill where it had been caught. In awe, they held their candles high and stared at the massive door, bound with metal and covered with writings in runic.

"Well, they won't get through that for a while," Skapti said shakily. "Whoever shut and locked that door so fast is to be commended."

They all looked at each other expectantly. No one spoke. "Someone shut it, didn't they?" asked Skapti, his voice a whisper.

"I never," Flosi declared. "And Egills was ahead of me, because he tripped me up and ran right over me."

"I did no such thing," Egills snapped. "If you were foolishly lying in my path and I ran over you, I can't accept any responsibility for that."

"Then it was Eilifir," Ivarr said. "His cloak was caught in the door."

Eilifir only shrugged. "You may think so if you wish," he said.

"Let's go now, shall we?" Ivarr suggested. The runic on the door looked spidery and menacing. The black dwarves suddenly stopped their pounding and were silent.

"Probably looking for a way around it," Skapti said nervously, giving Ivarr a push to the front.

Holding his candle high, Ivarr led the way down the dark corridor beyond. Eilifir followed, superseding Skapti's place without a word, and no one made a complaint.

The walls of the tunnel were hand-hewn, and from time to time a large timber had been placed as a support; these were also inscribed with runic.

"Just what sort of a place is this?" Ivarr asked, after walking a considerable distance and growing colder and more uneasy at each step.

"It's a black dwarf mine shaft," Skapti said, a little testily, after scaring himself with his own shadow. "From the beginning, the dwarves have laid claim to the underground and its treasures, and the Alfar had the topside to themselves. This is probably an old mined out mine, full of rotten timbers and bottomless shafts. For all I know, we're on a direct course for Hel's kingdom of the dead."

"And Dainn's forge, if it is still here," Ivarr said, "is a relic of the old days when this was an active mine." He held up his candle and saw only signs of great age and decay.

Finnvard began to whimper. "It's probably a dead end and we're trapped here behind that haunted door. An old place like this is bound to be full of the draugar of dead black dwarves."

Even Flosi had nothing to say to that. They crept along in a tight group—partly because Finnvard's legs gave out and he had to be hauled along, moaning, "No further, no further."

And then, abruptly, their candles shone on the end of the tunnel.

"This is most curious," Skapti said, holding his candle aloft to illuminate yet another door. "I wish I could read runic half as well as I ought, but one does get out of practice."

Ivarr glanced sideways at Eilifir, who, he had the feeling, could have read the runic if he had been so inclined, but the contrary Alfar folded his arms and looked at the door with no interest.

"It looks locked," Ivarr said.

"Don't touch it!" Skapti exclaimed, as Ivarr extended his hand.

"It's only a door," Eilifir said.

Ivarr knew better than to expect any help. He grasped the handle of the door and pushed without much hope. Clearly the door hadn't been used in ages, judging by the buildup of dust.

The moment he touched the heavy panels, the door began to creak and pop and shudder. The Alfar leaped back. It grated open a foot or so and stopped.

"There's magic in this," Skapti whispered, punching Finnvard impatiently to keep him from fainting.

"I see a light," Ivarr said, peering through the narrow opening. "It looks like firelight. Are you coming with me or not?"

"I suggest you go see, then," Flosi said. "The door opened for you, so it's your problem."

"That's a good idea," Egills said quickly.

Ivarr slipped through the opening and peered into the cavern beyond. A soft glow partially illuminated roof timbers and pillars of natural stone. Tools, weapons, and other implements were hung around the walls on pegs, and one side of the vault was taken up with a row of stalls. It smelled of hay and horses and iron. Ivarr was stongly reminded of the blacksmith's forge back in Hvitaness. He crept forward, and a grey pony watched him curiously from its stall, chewing a wisp of hay.

As Ivarr approached, he heard a gentle musical tapping. Peering over a cart, he saw a man bent over a bench, tapping

79

away at a delicate gold cup. He was broad and stocky, with a white beard so long it was buckled under his belt with plenty to spare. His hands and face looked like old mottled leather which had wrinkled and blackened in the sun. He wore a leather apron which was so worn it was more holes than apron.

"There now," he said suddenly, after Ivarr had watched for quite a while. He held up the cup. "Good as new. You'd never know it had been mended, although Odin's expression has changed a bit—looks rather more handsome this time around. I wish the rest of us had the chance to be made over when we get old and broken and dull." He chuckled softly into his rather sooty beard and set the cup down. He bent his bushy gaze on Ivarr. "Come and sit down by my fire, my lad, there's nothing to fear, unless it's old smiths you've a disliking for."

"Then you are Dainn, the famous smith?" Ivarr stepped from his hiding place.

"If I'm not Dainn, then I have become him after all these years," the old smith said. "Perhaps he was my master at one time, or perhaps I am he, but it makes no difference. If you have come to see Dainn, then I am he." He eased into an old black chair with a profound sigh.

"I see—I think," Ivarr said, taking a stool.

Dainn gazed into the fire ruminatively. His eyes were so pale they seemed almost transparent. "There have been so many masters and apprentices. So many swords and cups and knives and helmets and breastplates, and they all seem to be inside my head from the beginning until now. I can remember the swords of light and power made for the kings of Snowfell, who always came to Dainn for their weapons. Swords without number, Dainns without number, and now I am Dainn. And now—" His gaze travelled back to Ivarr, dwelling on him in mild surprise. "—I suppose you have come for a sword." He began to scowl in concentration. "I am very old and tired, and I wonder if the magic has passed out of me. I think there is an apprentice here somewhere, but I can't remember him, if there is. It must have been years

80

ago. He has the power and I have the memory. Never mind, it will catch up to him some day, the impudent boy. He must be rather old by now, I think, the young devil. What a plague he was." His eyes focused on Ivarr again with another start, as if he had forgotten about him.

"I came about a sword," said Ivarr gently. "One which is already made and now it's buried in a barrow with the one it was made for. I was told that you knew where this barrow lies—the barrow of Elidagrimr."

"Elidagrimr, Elidagrimr," whispered the old smith. "Ah, that one, yes, I remember it now. It was a plain sword, compared to most I made at that time. Elidagrimr was in a hurry for it, so I neglected the usual embellishments. But it was not lacking in power. Glimr, that was its name, and I had the feeling it was a different sword from the others. It had secrets, even from me, its maker. It served Elidagrimr well, and when he died they hid him where no one could find and take that sword, Glimr. Yes, I knew it had to lie hidden for centuries before it was found again. I knew it would either do a great good when it was found, or a great evil, and evil is much easier to do than good. Much easier, much easier." He gazed thoughtfully at Ivarr with his transparent eyes.

"I want this sword Glimr for a very good purpose," Ivarr said. "A powerful necromancer has caused five of Elbegast's Alfar accidentally to kill the son of Svartarr, your king. Unless they can cover the otterskin with gold, Svartarr will take his vengeance upon the people of Elbegast. And it will take a great deal of gold. The otterskin is enchanted so it stretches larger and larger with each piece of gold put on it. This necromancer, Lorimer, is an evil creature and designs to kill the five outlaws before the weregild can be paid, so Svartarr will attack Snowfell. What I want the sword for is to kill Fafnir, the dragon who watches over Andvari's hoard. Without a sword of power, it can't be done. It will prevent the needless killings and burnings that are sure to follow if Ottar is not avenged in gold instead of blood."

Dainn's reply was a long and weary sigh. "It goes on

forever, doesn't it? Threats and killings and weregild—" He shook his head slowly and seemed to lose his thoughts in the fire.

"It could be the end of it for the Alfar," Ivarr said, "if Svartarr is able to destroy them all."

"I've seen a great many Svartarrs," Dainn said, "and they will never be able to destroy Snowfell utterly. As long as one Alfar lives, Svartarr will eventually meet defeat. And as long as Dainn lives, there shall be swords in the hands of heroes who are defending Snowfell against those who wish them harm. From the beginning, we smiths have sworn to protect those who fight against wrong and evil, and those who fear the Fimbul Winter when the sun perishes and the ice prevails. I am old, but I am fit for one more sword." He rose from his chair and walked to a wall hung with hammers of all sizes and shapes. He reached for the largest and heaviest and hefted it in his hand. "So heavy," he murmured, restoring it to its hook with difficulty. "Perhaps a lesser hammer—no, it would mean a lesser sword of lesser metal."

Ivarr followed him. "But what about Elidagrimr's sword, Glimr? If you would tell us how to find it, you would be spared the labour of forging a sword, and we would save a lot of time."

"Glimr is best forgotten." Dainn shuffled back to his chair and sat down heavily. "They made it nearly impossible for anyone to find it. Fire jotuns guard it, spells and dangers surround it, and the draug of Elidagrimr himself may not permit it to be taken. I always knew someone would covet that sword—but maybe it was meant to happen. Many have died in the search for it, I am told, but you are the only one who has come and asked me to tell you where it lies. That is a good sign."

Ivarr let out his pent-up breath. "You are wise, Dainn. I know you'll recognize a just cause when it is presented to you. I believe I was guided by powers I don't understand so I could find you here."

Dainn leaned forward, clamping a huge, black-seamed

hand on each knee. "Well then, perhaps the matter is in the hands of a larger destiny than we two puny individuals. You are a wayfarer far from your native land, aren't you? Neither dwarf nor Alfar, light or dark, nor are you a wizard or necromancer. How do you fare in this savage land of magic, Scipling?" He held out his massive hand to shake hands with Ivarr, and broke into an astonishing grin of welcome. "This is the hand that will draw Glimr from its tomb with Elidagrimr. A miracle, truly, standing before my eyes, that a Scipling should come from his own realm to lend assistance in the troubles between dwarf and Alfar. Tell me what you are called, and then you had better summon your friends from my doorway before they catch a chill."

"I am called Ivarr," he replied, wincing a little at Dainn's grip. "And I thank you with all humility. I hope I'll not disgrace a sword made by your hand, or those before you."

He hurried back to the door and called, "Skapti! Come on, this is it, and Dainn has promised to help us."

Skapti's feet came pattering down the tunnel outside. "Ivarr? We'd almost given up hope, and Finnvard began making a racket so we took him down the passage and gagged him. You're sure you're quite all right, and this really is Dainn's forge?"

"Come and see for yourself, you great numbskull," Ivarr said, giving him an affectionate shove. He could even feel charitable toward Flosi, in the mood he was in. He could scarcely keep from whooping and dancing in his elation.

"But are you certain we're welcome?" Skapti whispered, hesitating at the edge of the firelight. "Nobody finds Dainn unless he wants them to."

"Please be welcome in these humble surrounds," Dainn said from his old black chair. "I have always been a friend to those who come to grief with the king's laws, if their cause is just. Your leader has told me about your misfortunes. I believe I can help, if it's Elidagrimr's sword you must have."

"Thank you, you're most generous," Skapti said, and

they all bowed to Dainn, sitting like an ancient Thor beside the altar of his anvil.

Dainn sent for a tottery old servant, who produced enough chairs for everyone from dusty corners and cleared the tools and weapons off the table so he could set it with an array of plain, simple food in plentiful quantities. The grey horse nodded approvingly at the proceedings, and stretched out his neck to beg for tidbits from the table.

When all the pleasantries were taken care of and the remains of the food taken off, they sat with the stone flagons and talked about Elidagrimr's barrow to the merry tune of mead trickling down long-deprived gullets.

"The barrow," began Dainn, motioning to his fossil of a servant to fetch him a small carven box from a high shelf, "is located far to the south in Jotunsgard in the midst of the pernicious fire jotuns. These savage fellows will protect the barrow and its secrets to the death of the last one of themselves. They were made to believe that Dainn was the witness to Elidagrimr's death, and he laid an alog against the fire jotuns—which wasn't at all difficult to convince them of, since it is only natural for a man to put a curse on those who have killed him. So they buried him, believing if his barrow was robbed, Jotunsgard would be visited by terrible afflictions and strange signs in the sky. Not content with merely guarding the barrow day and night, the jotuns, who were giants in those days, built a tremendous Maze of mountains around the barrow. Their wizards wove much magic into the Maze, and there is only one way to reach the centre without harm. I understand it is a boggy place, sometimes, where necromancers work their vile experiments, or a tangle of trees or great stones. Those who wander in never come out. It will take a keen sense of magic to solve the riddle of the Maze, I fear."

The Alfar looked uneasily at one another. "That's a pity," Skapti said. "I fear we're all buffoons when it comes to magic. We had a wizard, but we quarrelled and parted company."

Dainn pursed his lips and scowled. "That is very

unfortunate. The fire jotuns protect the sword with unimaginable spells and curses. They are utterly untrustworthy rebels from the Fire Wizards' Guild, and you'll be in danger every moment you are among them. The Maze itself is like its creators—unpredictable and dangerous. Are you sure you want to take the risks that lie awaiting you?'' The box was in his hands and the key in his fingers, but he hesitated to hear their answer.

"Considering the alternatives," Skapti said reluctantly, "we have no choice but to go on without Gizur."

Dainn said, "Very well; then we shall look at some maps." With his huge blunt hands he lifted out several ancient maps made on crumbling leather. "There you see the Maze, although a mere map can't do justice to the size of it. Six concentric rings with an entrance on either side of each ring, twisted so you must spiral into the very heart of the Maze. All left turns or all right turns will take you to the centre. But the problem is, it may not be the centre you want, because right or left takes you to two entirely different places. And then you may not be able to get out again, if you have taken the sinister turnings."

Finnvard was shuddering, eyes squeezed shut in the effort of trying not to faint. Egills poured him a restorative draught and encouraged him to swallow it. In a faint voice he asked, "Is that the worst of it?"

Dainn's eyes rested upon him sadly. "Such a gentle soul has no place in such a dangerous venture. But I can foresee great rewards for you, my friend, if you persevere."

"If he lives to see it," Flosi said gloomily. "Can't you offer us any real hope of getting that sword?"

"Don't be discouraged," Dainn replied. "Perhaps tomorrow I can be of more help. I'm so dreadful old and not much used to guests." He bade them goodnight and left them to the direction of his cadaverous servant, who showed them to their beds—plain straw and coarse, clean linen, but very comfortable.

In the morning their tempers were mended somewhat and much cheered by Dainn's food. It was a pleasure to eat someone else's cooking, and to eat it at a table instead of shivering in the cold wind on a flinty fellside.

When they had finished, and the dishes were taken off, Dainn lit an old black pipe that looked much like his favorite chair—polished by much use and blackened by age.

"Now I see your group is divided and confused still," the old smith said. His weak and watery gaze seemed to see many things it shouldn't.

"We do have our differences," said Ivarr, looking hard at Flosi.

Dainn shook his head ponderously. "If you are to succeed, there must be no differences. Heroic deeds are performed by those whose minds are united with one purpose, allowing nothing to come in between. It is your responsibility to end this conflict between dwarf and Alfar while it still can be resolved gracefully. The more dead that pile up on each side, the nearer to impossible it will be to settle the feud. The cause of all our afflictions is Lorimer the necromancer, and nothing will be solved until he is removed. Do not look so downcast and grim; with Elidagrimr's sword all this will be possible."

His guests' gloomy expressions did not relent in the least. Skapti heaved a sigh and leaned on his fist. "Then we can't throw the whole mess at Elbegast. The murder of Ottar sits on our shoulders like a yoke."

Flosi, for once, had the good grace to make himself as insignificant as possible. Dainn's gnarled features smiled approvingly.

"I have taken the liberty of sending for someone to help you. He shall be a tremendous benefit to you in your search for Elidagrimr's barrow. I thought you should have a guide and a protector. I believe he will be arriving at any moment." Dainn settled himself to smoke his pipe and refused to respond to any questions from the Alfar.

Two pipefuls later, a furious knocking began on the heavy tunnel door. Finnvard gave a convulsive leap, looking wildly for a place to hide or to faint. "Black dwarves!" he cried. "And Lorimer!"

Dainn did not rise from his seat. He merely called, "Enter!" The door began to creak and rattle as its bolts shot back and it scraped open. A cloaked figure leaped through the opening the instant it was wide enough and came striding toward them.

"I just received your summons," he said, slightly breathless, folding himself in half in a low bow, "and I hasten to do your bidding, noble smith." He unfolded himself and his eyes lit upon Dainn's guests, while theirs fastened upon him with a mixture of hostility and disbelief.

"Gizur!" they all roared. "You deserted us!" "Curse your carcass!"

Ivarr and Eilifir rushed forward to shake his hand, and the others glowered at him in hot fury.

"This is our guide and protector? Why, he's already abandoned us in every pinch we've gotten into!" Flosi stood on his chair in a grand pose, pointing his quivering finger at Gizur in accusation.

"I always said you couldn't trust a wizard," Finnvard said with a rabbity scowl.

"Quiet!" Gizur snapped, his eyes blazing. "It so happens, I'd rather be boiled in Muspell's kettle than set one toenail outside this mountain with this lot— except for the Scipling and Eilifir, you're all the barmiest bunch of faint-hearted cowards and penny-pinching backbiters that I have yet seen outside Grjootgardr. All the way from Snaehavn and not a smell of a gold piece!"

The ensuing racket of argument and accusation was silenced by a gentle "Hem!" from Dainn. He looked at his guests sorrowfully and shook his head.

For a long moment they all glowered at one another in silence. Then Skapti sighed, "Won't you give us one more chance, Gizur? We'll all honestly try to behave better— especially Flosi."

Flosi scowled at Skapti, then muttered, "That's right. I'll behave myself better, if Egills will quit reminding me it's all my fault with every other breath."

Egills opened his one eye wide. "Do I do that? Well, I

don't mean anything by it. Shall we let bygones be bygones?'' He held out his hand, and after a moment Flosi took it.

"Well, for a while," he said gruffly, trying not to smile. "I don't really mean all those nasty things I say, either."

"Nor do I," Skapti declared, seconded by Finnvard. "Let's all agree to forgive one another for the stupid nithlings that we are, shall we?"

"Aye!" they all agreed heartily.

Gizur rubbed his nose, mostly to hide a smile. "After twenty miles on the trail you'll be at each other's throats and shrieking like a bunch of schoolchildren—but I'll give you another chance. A very long chance."

They swarmed around him to shake his hand and pound his back, as if welcoming the return of a long-lost brother. Ivarr shook his head, amused and vexed because he knew Gizur was right. Very shortly they would be murderously furious with each other again, and in the next moment the strongest of allies.

"I'm glad you've all decided to be friends again," Dainn said, rising from his chair. "The time, however, is drawing short. The lurking presence of Lorimer and his benighted followers is like a black cloud hanging over Dainnsknip. Gizur, you have maps. Bring them out and I shall mark on them the route you must take through Jotunsgard, and then I must wish you well on your journey.''

CHAPTER NINE

With a steady hand, Dainn drew in the route they would take. It was long and dangerous, straight into the heart of jotun country. First they would have to cross a long expanse of Svartarrsrike, with names such as Dunhavn, Draugarkell, and Vargrfell.

"You'll need all the strength of your luck and magic just to reach the borders of Jotunsgard," Dainn said in conclusion.

"The very commodities we're the shortest on," Skapti said gloomily.

They all leaned over the map to study the spot which Dainn indicated was the Maze. It looked woefully distant, lying far to the south not far from the coast, with few other symbols to show that mapmakers knew little about the region. The length of the mighty Drangarstrom was mostly unknown, drawn in only a few places with certainty. Ivarr traced a diagonal line to the northeast which would bring them into contact with the closest known arm of the river.

"I hadn't thought, somehow, that the Drangarstrom would be so big," he said, "or so mysterious. There must be thousands of waterfalls behind which Andvari could be hiding."

"I believe you shall find the right one," Dainn said. "You'll need a wizard's help. There simply isn't time to look behind a thousand waterfalls."

Skapti took a notched wand from his pocket and carved

another notch in it with his knife. "We have exactly two hundred and thirty-four days to get the pelt covered with gold. I hope that's enough time. It used to seem like forever, but suddenly it seems like next week. It's going to be terribly difficult, with next to no power among the lot of us."

"Perhaps it will come to you," Dainn said. "By the time you have taken Glimr from Elidagrimr and slain Fafnir and appeased Svartarr, I should think some sort of power would cling to you."

Flosi arose from his seat and leaned on the table. "But how does one acquire power when he hasn't already got it? I'm not even certain what it is, so how can we recognize it and hold on to it? Or what can we do to entice it to join us? Is it something you can cultivate, like good manners?"

Dainn could only shake his head. "When you encounter it, you'll know. I can't tell you how to capture it in words that would make any sense. It is a matter of reaching out and looking within to find something you know is already there."

The Alfar only looked more puzzled and downcast. Gizur said, "Don't worry about power. Just worry about following me wherever I must take you, and don't ask too many questions and don't get stubborn on me—and don't give up." He bent over the map to study it again. "Well then, it's Jotunsgard, come fire jotuns, come hot springs, volcanoes, geysers, and all that fiery sort of thing. Between ourselves," he added conspiratorily to Dainn, when the Alfar were volubly discussing the partition of the goods Dainn had generously supplied them, "do you really think we can make it, given our limitations?"

The ancient smith looked at Finnvard and Egills and Flosi and pondered. "Are there any acceptable alternatives?"

Gizur sighed and shook his head. "Death between here and there, death at Lorimer's hands, death at Svartarr's hands, or permanent protection by Elbegast, probably in a coal mine. No, compared to the alternatives, wandering around with the fire jotuns at least has the advantage that we might survive, by some gross oversight of our usual bad luck.''

Dainn solemnly shook the hand of Gizur, then Ivarr and Eilifir, and the others. They shouldered their packs.

"Good luck, my friends. May the elements be kind to you, and may the land-vaettir and the gods unite to confound your enemies. May your ears be quick and your eyes keen to approaching danger. Remember to be single minded and strong to your purpose. And now I bid you farewell.'' Dainn sat down in his chair and beckoned to his servant, who showed them to a small door half-hidden behind a pile of broken wheels and other metal objects awaiting mending.

"This little tunnel leads straight to the outside,'' whispered the servant in a leathery voice. "Farewell, heroes. Here's a lantern to light your way. Just leave it at the entrance and I shall fetch it later. Good luck to you.'' They all shook his hand and ducked into the low tunnel.

"Jotunsgard,'' he called after them, by way of farewell and admonition, his voice echoing down the tunnel.

A cold and windy dawn awaited them outside Dainn's tunnel. Gizur paused to study the aspect of the south, ignoring the icy wind parting and reparting his beard.

"We never did find Dvergarfell,'' Flosi commented rather acidly.

"That's easy to explain,'' said Gizur. "It wasn't here. Fortunately for us all, Dvergarfell lies further to the north. Do you think I would have trusted you on your own if I'd thought you'd go blundering into Dvergarfell, asking directions to Dainnsknip?''

Ivarr looked at the wizard suspiciously. "Explain yourself, please. Do you mean to say you left us deliberately?''

"Never inquire into the motives of a fire wizard, my boy,'' Gizur said testily, twitching a sparstone out of his sleeve and holding it up to determine the location of the sun. "You fellows are far too lazy with me around to make all the decisions. It was very good for you to be on your own for a while. I was fairly certain nothing would happen to you."

"Nothing would happen to us!" Ivarr exclaimed. "Lorimer almost caught us. That's not 'nothing.'"

"Anything, you mean. But he didn't catch you, did he? Isn't that what matters most?" The stone vanished, replaced by a large crust of bread left over from breakfast. "And you all did rather well. I had planned to meet you at Dainnsknip or thereabouts and show you where the entrance was, but by some mysterious quirk, you not only found the right mountain, you found an entrance, one which hasn't been used in centuries. A bit of a coincidence, I'd say. How did you manage it?"

"Without the least bit of trouble," Skapti butted in; he was walking very close to Ivarr's heels. "Ivarr dowsed for it and found it easily. It was a lucky day for us when Birna sent him to us."

"Bah," Flosi said. "It was just fool's luck. Eilifir dowsed out Dainn's doorway too, you remember."

"Do be quiet, Flosi," Skapti said cheerfully. "You're supposed to be reformed, remember?"

The reformation lasted nearly a week, and it was a great strain on everyone's disposition. The discovery of a ley line was somewhat reassuring, but tempers were still volatile from long and unaccustomed restraint.

At last their much-despised cordiality exploded into a tremendous argument, resulting in making camp near a half-fallen ring of upright stones in an area devoid of much cover. Flosi simply sat down and refused to budge.

"Very well," Gizur said. "This site offers us a splendid view of Draugarkell, at least. A thousand dwarves perished in that gorge in the mountains ahead of us, or so legend has it. I'm sure Skarpsey would be scuttled under the weight of all the draugar that are supposed to haunt it, so you needn't look so frightened, Finnvard. Any draugar that were here at one time have probably gone somewhere else to do their haunting."

Skapti attempted to encourage Flosi not to be so idiotic and stubborn, so they could move on to a safer place for the night, but Flosi was disinclined to be cooperative. Finnvard twitched and yelped at the smallest sound; when Egills noisily dropped a kettle, he leaped up and shrieked, "Draugar! Save us!" and sat down suddenly before he fainted.

"Oh tush, what a nithling you are!" Flosi exclaimed. At once an argument was spawned and all the Alfar leaped into it with great relief. Eilifir remained aloof, as usual, and strolled around their desolate camp, arriving by sheerest coincidence at Ivarr's side.

"I would like a look at that ring," he said quietly. "Shall we both go and inspect it?"

"Do you think there's something strange about it?" Ivarr asked, but Eilifir only shrugged.

They climbed up to the staggering circle, where the evening wind whistled sadly among the eroded stones, leaning at drunken angles or fallen completely. Nothing indicated that anyone had passed there within the past century or so, judging from the moss and lichens that had taken hold particle by particle on the stony ground. The hilltop seemed perfectly forlorn and forgotten by whatever powers it had once served.

"If we had gone just another half-mile, we could have camped in the lava flows," Ivarr observed, studying the terrain before them. "Or even in those low hills. I believe there's even firewood growing there. Doesn't it look like brush growing on the hillsides?"

Eilifir turned from his study of their backtrail and agreed that it did indeed look like scrubby trees growing on the slopes of the hills. When Ivarr inquired if he thought anything was wrong, Eilifir was noncommittal.

They returned to camp and at once Flosi confronted them. "I know what you're going to say. You're going to say let's move camp to the lava flows or the hills. Well, I say forget it. I'm not budging from this fire." He sat down beside the fire and held his hands out to it.

"Now that you mention it," Ivarr said, "it would be a good idea to move. Up on the hill we could hear every word you fellows were saying and our fire is visible for miles.''

"I had a bad feeling about this place," Finnvard said peevishly, "and nobody would listen to me, just old dumb Finnvard—"

"That's right," Flosi said. "We aren't moving."

Skapti looked anxiously from Ivarr to Gizur. "I think we're all exhausted and hungry and a night's rest will do us good. Perhaps we're just experiencing feelings that aren't quite accurate."

Egills snorted. "Bah on your feelings. I'm tired, and that's that."

Ivarr glared at Gizur, who sat on the stone lost in thought, absently biting the top of his staff. "Well, I'm going to keep a particularly close watch as long as we're here," Ivarr said, and he stationed himself in a prominent position and proceeded to look as pessimistically watchful as he could.

Eilifir relieved Ivarr's watch at midnight. Ivarr thought he had slept only a few moments when Eilifir's toe prodded him awake. "Dwarves," he whispered.

Ivarr leaped up instantly, demanding, "Where are they?" much in the same wild manner as Flosi when suddenly awakened.

Eilifir pointed to the north. "I believe it's the same group that followed us from Dainnsknip. I saw six of them ride over the horizon just a few moments ago. The only thing that suprises me about them is the fact that they didn't catch up with us earlier."

Ivarr looked in the direction Eilifir pointed, able to see quite well in the pre-dawn dimness. "They've got an admirable position behind that hill, haven't they? They could rush out on their horses at any moment and surround us entirely. Where's Gizur?"

He saw only a lump wrapped in a cloak. Closer inspection revealed a half dozen rocks draped in Skapti's unused cloak. "Gone!" whispered Ivarr. "Does he know about the dwarves?"

Eilifir nodded. "I think he's up on the hill at the old ring."

"Let's get the others awake." Ivarr gave Skapti a shake and used a staff to poke at Flosi, who leaped awake with a startled snarl, clutching the nearest weapon and ready to attack.

"Dwarves," Ivarr whispered, not without grim satisfaction. "Get your packs on; we've got to hurry."

"That wizard is gone again," Egills growled.

"Deserted again!" Finnvard moaned promptly.

"Not quite," said the voice of Gizur from a dark shadow on the hill. "Follow me quickly and you'll be as safe as the fleas on Thor's noggin."

Fortunately the packs were ready to go, a precaution Ivarr had insisted upon the night before. Grumbling, they hurried after Gizur, who took them straight toward the old stone ring, refusing to listen to any protests.

"I refuse to go up there." Finnvard declared suddenly, sitting down on a rock. "Go ahead and leave me if you must, but I simply can't tolerate those ghostly places."

Egills hesitated, too, and that caused everyone to stop. Flosi lunged at Finnvard and shook him by the collar in a fury. "You always say that! If I ever hear it even one more time—"

Something hissed through the air and struck a stone beside Ivarr with a flash of sparks.

"An arrow! Run!" Gizur shoved the Alfar past him, including a suddenly galvanized Finnvard, and stood with staff upraised as if shielding the others by offering himself as a target.

Finnvard reached the ring first and threw himself into the shelter of a fallen stone. Ivarr and Gizur were the last, standing behind two stones and peering out cautiously. Skapti ordered the elves to stand ready with their bows and arrows.

"If I ever hit a dwarf it would be an accident for both of us," Finnvard whimpered as he fumbled with the unfamiliar weapons. "I'd give anything to be back in my kitchen in Snowfell baking pastry tarts—"

A hail of arrows suddenly clattered against the hill around

95

them. and one struck a standing stone with a brilliant flash. Below, they heard horses advancing at an unhurried pace.

"Halloo!" came a shout from the gloom. "Gizur, are you there?"

"I'm here, Lorimer. What do you want?" Gizur lit his staff with a burst of flame and stepped from the shelter of the stones.

Lorimer's horse lunged halfway up the hill and halted, plunging around nervously. Lorimer laughed, saying "You must be mad, old fellow, even to be here. There's nothing in Draugarkell to interest anyone. Dainnsknip was far more fascinating, I'll warrant. Did you find the old curmudgeon? Was it a sword you wanted from him?"

"Questions, Lorimer, are impertinent at this time," Gizur said. "Why don't you take yourself off now to some nice dark cave, and stop trying to frighten honest people?"

Lorimer made a clucking sound. "Come now, Gizur, you can recognize a lost cause when you see it. These five numbskulls have no hope of paying Svartarr's weregild. It looks more as if you'll all perish at the hands of the fire jotuns, if you continue the same way you've been going. We've been following and watching since you left Dainnsknip. We know you're heading toward Jotunsgard. Why, Gizur? What is in Jotunsgard?"

Before Gizur could answer, the voice of Grus spoke from inside Lorimer's pocket. "A sword, a sword, you idiot! Haven't I been telling you? Elidagrimr's sword of power, which is hidden in his barrow. Dainn the smith is the last living person who knows where that barrow lies. I of course know, having all the knowledge of the dead."

Grus cackled horribly, and Finnvard moaned.

"Is it true, Gizur?" Lorimer asked. "Could you possibly fall for such a farce?" As he talked, about twenty dwarves assembled around the base of the hill. "Be reasonable, Gizur. I could make you very useful and very powerful. You know these Alfar are wretchedly outmatched by my dwarves. They are a hazard to you and a burden to Elgebast. And this Scipling you call a hero is only a young lad and

96

unarmed, except for a knife. What can you hope to accomplish?''

Ivarr touched Birna's knife. So Lorimer had noticed it and assigned some kind of value to it. "Vengeance, for Birna, at the very least," he called back boldly. "You're a coward, Lorimer, and a murderer. I haven't forgotten Birna, nor shall I ever. Let it be known that I have marked you for my vengeance."

"Upon my prophetic soul!" exclaimed the voice of Grus. "He means to kill you, Lorimer. I feel it in my bones. This is more exciting than I had ever envisioned, Lorimer, and I thank you for this charming entertainment. I wouldn't have missed it for the world."

"Bah on you and your visions," Lorimer growled, swinging around to signal to his dwarves. "A live and powerful necromancer of my abilities has no need to fear a dead Scipling. I fear he's not leaving this hill alive—just as a foolish precaution on my part."

The dwarves moved to surround the hill, taking care to remain just out of arrow-shot.

"We're protected up here," Gizur said. "If one of your dwarves lays so much as a hand upon any of these stones, he'll find himself nicely toasted in an instant. Dawn isn't far off either, so why don't you just call it a night, Lorimer?"

Lorimer turned his horse to ride downhill. "Is that your final answer, Gizur? You'd rather perish with these buffoons?"

"Any death would be preferable to falling under your power," Gizur said, suddenly raising his staff and shooting a bolt of fire into the midst of a knot of dwarves creeping closer to the hill. Lorimer's horse plunged away, and Lorimer replied with a shaft of his own, which Gizur deflected with a fiery spell. Two of the dwarves fell victim to Gizur's fire bolt. The rest retreated to a safer distance and began shooting arrows with a vengeance.

"Get busy, you fools!" Gizur commanded the Alfar, who had prostrated themselves in the scant protection of the fallen stones. Eilifir was returning arrows with deadly accuracy.

"What can we do? We're doomed!" Finnvard moaned.

"We need a spell," Flosi said.

"Oh, I can't, not now," Finnvard whimpered. "Not now, I can't even stand up, let alone—"

"Quit crowding me, you old jellybag," Flosi snapped, jabbing Egills with his elbow. "I'm not moving from this spot."

"Stop it! That was nearly my eye you jabbed with that arrow!" Skapti retorted, giving Flosi a shove.

Eilifir looked up from his arrow-shooting. "I think we can reactivate this ring if we bridge the gaps. I will stand in one; who'll take the other?"

The Alfar responded with a stubborn silence, hugging the ground with even greater determination.

Eilifir was unruffled. "Skapti, come over to this side and stand with a hand on each of these stones, bridging the gap. It won't harm you. It may do you some good, in fact."

"Not if I get skewered by an arrow, standing there like an idiot!" Skapti snapped.

"It will only take a moment, if this ring works as I think it will. If it doesn't work, it will all be up with us anyway, perhaps." Eilifir stood in the other gap with his hands outstretched to touch the stones on either side. "Now I want the rest of you to sit down and form a circle with linked arms. Concentrate on the fifth article of power, and you, Gizur, must be very careful or you may sizzle someone's brains. Ivarr, you'd be safer if you keep a little distance, in case something goes wrong. Ready, everyone? Begin!"

Ivarr watched for a few moments and saw no signs of any great magic. Skapti kept one eye open, anxiously watching the dwarves, who were milling around down below. Ivarr found them a much more compelling sight. The pale northern night served as a silvery background for their lurking dark figures.

Ivarr started to slither backward. Suddenly something seared his leg with tremendous heat. Whirling around wildly he saw that the standing stone closest to him was glowing red-hot at its base, and it had burned a hole in his pants leg.

He put out a hand to test the reality of what he was seeing, venturing to touch the stone's surface at a safe distance from the red glow. Instantly he jerked his hand back, but not before he received the impression that the stone had rocked under his hand. Also, it was scorching hot. He looked at Eilifir and Skapti, expecting to see nothing but incinerated heaps, but they were still there. A strange light radiated around them and their beards and hair stood out straight, crackling with energy. Skapti's expression was one of attentive astonishment; Eilifir had his eyes shut, concentrating. The air immediately outside the stone ring shimmered and glowed a pale orange, like a thin film of fire.

Finnvard was the first to collapse, but the flame remained. The others in the ring toppled one by one, leaving Skapti by himself. He opened his eyes, like a sleeper awakening from a refreshing nap, and gazed around approvingly.

A shout from the dwarves drew their attention. About ten of Lorimer's rebels were advancing at a purposeful trot. Ivarr unsheathed Birna's knife again, and it flashed strangely in his hand. He exclaimed, "Gizur, they're coming!"

"Don't worry about a thing," Gizur said, folding his arms composedly. "Just watch."

The first dwarves came flogging up the slope with murder on their faces. The foremost dwarf brandished his sword, selecting Ivarr as his target, and sent his horse plunging into the circle of stones. With a fiery crackle, horse and rider were knocked over backward, bowling over two other horses in a kicking, squealing tangle. Another attacker lunged at the thin film of flame and was rebuffed, fleeing with a blazing cloak. The remainder of the attackers turned and tumbled down the rocky slope helter-skelter, some thrown from their terrified steeds, some leaping to safety as their horses stumbled and fell.

Egills, Finnvard, and Eilifir had recovered and sat staring, open-mouthed, and Flosi was yelling and prancing, waving his sword and shouting threats and challenges. A volley of arrows came arching up at them, but each one burst into flame the instant it came into the fiery atmosphere surrounding the stones. Flosi cackled and strutted gleefully until Gizur forcefully sat him down on the ground.

The dwarves encircled the hill. No more rushes were made and no more arrows were wasted. Ivarr watched the southeast anxiously, knowing daybreak couldn't be much more than an hour away, when the dwarves would retreat from the sun. He could see them quite clearly in the early grey light—stocky, fierce little men clad in warlike attire with very efficient-looking forged helmets, breastplates, and swords.

"I bet they're waiting to see how long we can keep this up." Gizur chortled. "Let the sun bake their brains and turn them to steam—we won't budge."

At that instant, Skapti swayed and toppled face forward, arms outstretched rigidly. Instantly the nimbus of flame vanished. Eilifir hurried to turn him over and peered into his wide, staring eyes. "He's just overheated, I should think. Skapti, are you all right?"

Skapti blinked slowly several times. "Amazing," he said. "Simply amazing. More power ran through this worthless old carcass than exists in half the Alfar in Snowfell. I feel as if my bones are made of fire." He examined his hands, front and back, and rubbed them as if they tingled.

Ivarr's attention was divided between Skapti and the black dwarves. They urged their skittish horses closer, staring at the stone circle and gesturing with increasing excitement. They broke into a trot, holding their weapons at ready.

"The dwarves know it's gone," Ivarr reported grimly. "I think they may have lost their respect for us—what little they may have had."

"Everyone get down," commanded Gizur. Finnvard obligingly fainted, like one of his pastries with the steam let out of it. "Let them get a bit closer and I'll blast a few of them out of their socks. Skapti, what do you think you're doing? I said get down and stay down before Lorimer makes a pincushion out of you."

Skapti stood unsteadily, leaning one hand against an upright stone. Flosi yanked at the hem of his cloak from the ground. "You silly old fool, don't you hear? Gizur, his brains must be addled. Eilifir's old circle has made Skapti totally fearless."

Gizur did not take his eyes off the advancing dwarves, who had reached the foot of the hill. Smothering his exasperation, Ivarr scrambled toward Skapti, who was sure to catch an arrow any instant. Just as he grabbed Skapti by the arm, a tremendous burst of light blinded him, and a terrific jolt knocked him flat on his back. Dazzled, he shook his head and rolled over cautiously to see if Skapti had survived the blast.

Skapti still stood there leaning against the stone, with one hand still extended in a gesture to ward off evil. Below, the dwarves had scattered, except for the two who had led the charge and were now mere smoking heaps of rubbish. Lorimer retreated to a safer distance and sat fighting his terrified horse while he stared up at the ring.

"Ivarr the Scipling, I shall overcome you yet," he called in a voice gritty with rage. "You cannot come into our realm, a nobody, a nithling, and expect to thwart my plans. I will be the master of Svartarrsrike, and Elbegast and his Alfar will be exterminated. The very sun will perish. Yet you think, you puny creature, that you can stop me?" He laughed tauntingly.

"I can stop you!" cried Ivarr fiercely. "And I will, for Birna!"

Lorimer hesitated a moment, then let the plunging horse have its head and they went charging after the fleeing dwarves.

For a long moment no one in the circle could move, or do much besides gape at Skapti, whose astonishment bordered on shock. Gradually he lowered his hand. Suddenly everyone began chattering and laughing all at once and pounding on Skapti until he could scarcely stand.

"He's got power!" exclaimed Finnvard.

"How did you do it?" demanded Gizur for the tenth time.

"Why didn't I get to stand in the ring?" Flosi wailed enviously. "Why can't we all take a turn?"

"Far too risky," said Eilifir. "the next person might get burned into ashes. Look at the bases of those stones if you don't believe me."

The stones were still hot to the touch. Ivarr could now see that the sockets of the stones were quite different from the upright portion. The rock had a glassy texture, as if it had been melted.

Skapti sat down on a rock and mopped his face, chuckling to himself. "Who'd have thought it? Power at my age. I feel quite giddy. Whatever I think about, I can do. Light fires, find objects, levitate, cogitate—I believe I could even make myself invisible, or read thoughts, or change forms at the wink of an eye!"

"You'd better be careful," Gizur said. "We don't know what has happened to you or how long it will last or how much control you have, so don't disappear yourself or change forms until we're certain we can get you back."

Skapti nodded blissfully. "What a wonderful feeling. Competence at last. When we get back to Snowfell, I'm applying for a transfer."

Ivarr shook his hand. "Congratulations. You'll be a great help in killing Fafnir and getting the gold."

"Fafnir—ah, yes." Skapti looked slightly less competent for a moment.

"I don't expect it will last that long," Flosi said in a disgruntled voice. His expression was as sour as old beer.

In spite of their exhaustion, they were anxious to leave Draugarkell behind. With amazing energy and efficiency they strapped on their packs and trod in Gizur's footsteps with scarcely a complaint or a grumble. As they passed the charred remains of three horses and two dwarves they all were silent, and Skapti was rather pale. Gizur flicked his cloak away from the blackened earth and said, "Power is not to be taken lightly."

They chose their campsites with scrupulous care after that, although they saw not a sign of Lorimer. Skapti went through a period of thoughtful silence for several days until he adjusted to his new powers, which was a process beset with hazards. At first every small gesture caused some mishap, such as igniting little spontaneous fires or moving things in a most annoying manner, so that someone was tripped or something fell on his head. Gizur despaired, and the Alfar were furious at Skapti. He had to keep himself at a distance from the others for nearly a week, which gave him the opportunity to come to grips with his powers and get them under control. At the end of that time, he resumed his place behind Ivarr and did a great deal more speaking up when decisions were made.

They came into the region called Dunhavn, named after a fjord they could barely see to the southwest. It was a pleasant place, by comparison, with jagged black fells and green patches of grass or bracken scattered across the rocky earth, which was by far more lava than earth. It made Ivarr, in his more thoughtful moments, think of a giant beast they were climbing slowly over, a scaly and ridgy beast the moss and grass had begun to grow upon while it slept.

One morning Gizur announced, ''I've some good news for you fellows. How would you like sleeping on real beds again, and eating some decent food? According to the map, there's a house of refuge not far from here. If we grind out the miles today we can be there by supper time. Perhaps we'll even take a well-deserved rest for a day or two.''

''That would be splendid,'' sighed Finnvard. ''Last night I believe the rocks were doing a dance in the middle of my back all night long.''

''House of refuge?'' Skapti tugged on his ear. ''How do we know it's really a house of refuge still, or that its inhabitants are peaceable?''

Gizur snorted and rolled up his map quickly. ''Once a house of refuge, always a house of refuge. Travellers of all sorts have been stopping there for centuries and hanging their weapons on the walls. Besides, we need to buy more supplies.''

''You'll do the buying,'' Flosi said. ''We haven't got a

trace of gold about us. We'll make it up to you when we get to Andvari.''

"I can well imagine," Gizur muttered, mostly to himself.

Nearing dusk, they approached the house of refuge, halting on a hilltop to study it. A small farm was tidily situated below them in the folds of a green fell, where sheep and goats grazed. Egills and Finnvard greeted the scene with rejoicing, and even Flosi's permanently petulant expression brightened. "This is more like it," he said. "Why can't there be more pleasant little farms along our way? Get going, you old fossils, you can rest when we get there. There's real food and drink waiting for us down there."

Grumbling cheerful insults at each other, they shouldered their packs and descended slowly toward the farm. Ivarr started after them, feeling immensely restored by the sight of a regular decent little farmstead before him. It was enough to make him feel a few pangs of homesickness, even for the rude comforts of Fishless.

Skapti hadn't resumed his pack. He stared down at the inviting farm with a scowl on his face. "Stop a moment. I'm not sure we should go down there," he said. "I have a peculiar feeling—"

"Oh, nonsense!" Flosi retorted, without stopping. "You think you're practically a wizard, now you've had a little flash of power. You're just showing off, you old lizard."

"I know a warning when I'm warned, and a foreboding when it's foreboded. Gizur! Drat it, he's as blind as the others." Skapti eyed Eilifir challengingly. "Say, Eilifir, you were standing in that ring too. Did you gain any gifts of power? You haven't said a word about it. Do you feel any forebodings about this place?"

The recalcitrant Alfar nodded at his bootlaces to tighten them. All he would say was, "Perhaps." Then he closed his mouth with a snap and shouldered his pack.

Skapti and Ivarr had no real choice but to follow the rest.

CHAPTER TEN

The farmhouse was very ancient turf, with three gables, one for living, one for storage, and one to house the livestock. A flock of little goats grazing on the roofs greeted them with cheerful bleating. Smoke in generous quantities poured from the chimney and a glorious smell of roasting meat almost enthralled the hungry travellers. Gizur knocked at the window, which was more polite than knocking at a stranger's door, and at once an old woman appeared to welcome them.

"What a surprise indeed! Travellers, after all this time! Welcome to Nidbjorgsstead!" She was a pleasant old soul much like the old ladies near Fishless, with a very fair skin netted with innumerable smiling wrinkles and ruddy cheeks. She wore the customary black skirt and a richly embroidered bib tied at the waist and neck, and a stiff headpiece of which Ivarr had never seen the like. She smiled and beckoned them to enter.

Gizur addressed her in his politest manner. "We thank you most gratefully, gracious lady," he said with a low bow. "We have travelled far and we're sorely in need of a safe haven and a night's rest."

"Then this is the place for you," she said. "Nidbjorgs-stead is a house of refuge for travellers in this hostile land. Dwarves, Alfar, wizards, sorceresses, are all welcome in this house as long as they are willing to leave their quarrels outside our door. This is a house of safety for all who seek it."

Skapti hung back suspiciously, until he saw that Gizur retained his wizard staff as if it were an ordinary walking stick. Only then did he consent to hang his arrows and sword upon the wall outside and follow the others inside. A long table and benches occupied most of the space, all blackened and polished from years of use. A steep stairway led to the sleeping loft upstairs, and a door below led to the kitchen.

"My name is Thorvor," she continued, graciously overlooking Skapti's skittish manners, "and my two sisters are Solborg and Nidbjorg. I believe they're in the kitchen cooking something special for today. We just had the feeling we'd have company."

Ivarr inhaled the wonderful aroma of roasting meat. He was charmed to a lesser extent by the hall's carved rafters and other homely refinements; he was more delighted with the winter's supply of dried herbs and smoked meats hanging from the the beams. Most fascinating of all was the food on the table.

"Greetings and welcome. I am Nidbjorg," said the eldest of the three sisters, who wore a white gown embroidered in blue. "I hope you'll find your stay at Nidbjorgsstead pleasant and refreshing." She bade them be seated at the table, and more delicacies kept appearing from the kitchen while they ate. The three sisters sat down with their guests and chatted amiably about the surrounding country and other polite banter. Gizur inquired about routes to the south, and Flosi inquired if there was perhaps more gravy.

When all the customary topics seemed to be exhausted, and the food was nearly gone, the time for lighting pipes and asking more serious questions had arrived. Solborg, the youngest of the sisters, whose hair was still mostly black, turned to Ivarr. "We see that you are different from your friends. Far be it from us to ask prying questions, but you are a Scipling from the other realm, are you not? Pardon our curiosity, but we have rarely seen Sciplings so far from home."

They all looked at him with such compassion and good will that Ivarr didn't mind answering their questions. They reminded him of three rosy old apples, slightly withered by age but not at all sour or spoiled.

"Yes, I am a Scipling," he said. "From a place called Fishless because of its poor fishing. In all my travels in your realm this has been the most hospitable house I have encountered. I shall certainly hate to leave when the time comes." Ivarr suddenly did feel regretful—perhaps it was the generous supply of mead. He had a fleeting feeling that perhaps he wouldn't ever leave, but he shook that ridiculous idea out of his head and decided not to drink any more of the deceptively mild liquor.

As the evening progressed, the mead and food and cheery fire seemed to affect the others the same way. Even Skapti looked slightly less adamant. Flosi as usual waxed flamboyant and began to talk and boast too much. The three old sisters kept his cup filled and listened as sympathetically as any boaster could desire in an audience.

Ivarr suddenly became aware that Flosi was bragging fatuously about the events at the hilltop ring in Draugarskell. For all he knew, Flosi had told them everything about who they were and their plan to steal the weregild from Andvari. He tried to get up from his chair to get Flosi's attention, but his muscles seemed to have turned to pudding.

"Flosi," he said, "will you kindly pass the meat this way again? You've been talking so long it's getting quite cold. Besides, our kind hostesses are probably bored with hearing the same old story from all their visitors. Have some more of that excellent bread while you're at it."

Flosi, always sensitive to the slightest of rebukes, instantly bridled at Ivarr's veiled suggestion.

"It's been a long day," Gizur said hastily. "I suggest we retire early this evening. We'll spend tomorrow resting, and the morning after we must depart." He rose with a slight gesture in Flosi's direction which no one detected except Ivarr. Flosi instantly fell asleep.

"Pay no attention to Flosi," said Skapti worriedly, beckoning to Ivarr and Finnvard to carry Flosi away. "He's an incurable talker and will say any sort of nonsense after he's been drinking mead. Come to think of it, he's been a lunatic from birth too, so no one can believe a word of what he says. We're all so exhausted we don't know up from down, and as Gizur says, all we need is a good rest."

"Very well," Nidbjorg said. "Thorvor will show you upstairs."

Their sleeping quarters were in the loft. It was a cozy fragrant place with fresh straw ticks, clean floors, and windows in the roof peaks at either end. Three spinning wheels and bags of wool occupied one end, and a large loom boasted a beautiful piece of cloth, half-finished.

Flosi was dumped, still sleeping, on a bed and everyone sank down gratefully to sleep. Skapti, however, kept on popping up to peer around warily at the slightest creak or crackle of straw.

"What is the matter with you?" Ivarr demanded sleepily. "Those three old ladies aren't exactly dangerous, are they?"

Skapti scarcely heard. "There's a black cloud of mist surrounding this house. Nothing is to be trusted here, Ivarr; remember I said that, in case something happens. I doubt if I could sleep a wink in such a place. I'm going to sit here and keep watch." He scrubbed his eyes with his knuckles and tried to stifle a rending yawn. "I feel as if I'm floating on feathers. It must be that cursed mead."

Ivarr was too fogged by sleep to reply. The straw was as soft as a dream, after nights and nights of curling up between rocks. The mead left a sour taste on his tongue in spite of its smooth sweetness, and he was glad he hadn't drunk much.

A sound awakened him suddenly in the dark of the night. He sat up and listened, until he realized where he was. He almost chuckled, thinking perhaps the creaking sounds of the house had disturbed him with their unfamiliarity after sleeping out of doors so long. He curled up in the soft straw, but he was wide awake. Waiting to grow sleepy again, he

108

heard a sound downstairs as if someone had bumped a bench. Quiet footsteps ascended the stairs slowly and carefully.

"What do you think, sisters? Is this an opportunity not to be missed?" whispered a voice, followed by what sounded like a low cackle. Ivarr lay still, breathing softly so he could hear.

"Let's have a look at them," another whisper replied. "I still can scarcely believe these are the ones. Old fat cast-offs, one-eyed, inept—they're not what I expected Elgebast's spies to be."

"That only makes it all the easier for us to dispose of them," said the third, recognizable as Solborg. Her voice made Ivarr shudder. "Shall we begin at once?"

"Put that knife away! You fancy the sight of blood a bit too much, Solborg. We shall take care of them soon enough. The main thing is to make sure they remain here longer than they had planned, and the best way to do that is to arrange for an illness to befall one of their company. We may as well have a little sport before we kill them."

Ivarr's eyes flew open; fortunately, he was facing the wall and not the three sisters behind him. His sword was hanging downstairs on the wall, a token of his faith. All he had to defend himself and his friends with was Birna's knife.

Thorvor's voice whispered, "Do you mean hagriding them to death, dear sister? That would be a good way to prolong their misery."

"We shall see what happens. We'll take one to Svinafell tonight to the grand seidr. I am quite anxious to show the others my new shape-shifting formula. Solborg, you shall go with me because I don't trust you for a moment out of my sight, as long as there's a weapon in the house."

"I hope I shall get a turn at the seidr this year," grumbled Thorvor.

"You shall go tomorrow night with Solborg. And on the third night, perhaps we shall let Solborg stay here alone, with her knife."

Solborg made a chilling rattling sound in her throat. "I

wish tonight were the third night. Let's get going, sister. Which one shall we pick to hagride tonight? The Scipling?"

"No, stupid. He's the one we want to save."

"The sooner we get him under our power the better, Nidbjorg."

"No. What if he dies? I've never changed a Scipling over to a horse before and there's not much information about it in my books. I don't want to risk losing that sword. Let's take this one closest to the door and be done with it."

"It's that silent one," Thorvor said anxiously. "I don't like him in the least. I'm afraid he knows everything."

"Then we'd better get rid of him before he warns the others," Solborg said.

"I doubt if killing him while he sleeps is going to reassure the others that they are safe here." Nidbjorg said. "If you don't trust him, Thorvor, which one do you recommend?"

"This old whitebeard who has been so suspicious of us. It would serve him particularly right, wouldn't it"

"He reeks of power," Nidbjorg said. "Nothing but trouble, like that silent one. I can't reach into either of their thoughts."

"Well then, here's this one with the yellow pants, but I don't think he'd even get us there before he collapsed and died, let alone setting us back home. He'd be too fat and windbroken as a horse. How about this old fellow with the one eye?"

Nidbjorg replied, "I wouldn't trust a one-eyed horse in the dark, would you? And he's frightfully old. I wouldn't trust his knees."

"Well then, what's left? The wizard? I suspect he'd make a singularly vicious horse, not to mention all those powers. Nidbjorg, if you're going to change him over, you can go by yourself to the seidr. I'll stay home with Thorvor."

"I once hagrode Bursilafr." Nidbjorg said "It wasn't so very difficult, except when he tried to fall over backward."

"You're much too old for that sort of nonsense," Thorvor said. "We are none of us young and reckless anymore."

Solborg said, "So far we have managed to find fault with

every one of them. It's appalling what sort of spies Elbegast sends out these days. We should all be able to pick a horse and go riding.''

''Don't be hasty, Solborg. Here's the ideal subject for our spell, the youngest of the Alfar, the talkative one with the brains of a goose. I marked him from the first moment I saw him—strong as an ox and not nearly as smart. He'll take us to Svinafell and back and scarcely know the difference until morning.''

''Of course. Clever Nidbjorg. Here, grab an ankle and we'll haul him downstairs. Do you remember when old Gyrda put a horse through the ceiling when we were taking our lessons?''

Ivarr heard something being dragged across the floor, bumping softly down the stairs. He tried to roll over to wake up Gizur, but his muscles seemed paralyzed. He flexed his fingers and toes and managed to roll out of bed. Sitting up, he wondered if he could crawl over to Gizur and awaken him.

''What was that?'' one of the sisters downstairs asked. ''I heard somebody move.''

''Impossible. Your ears are getting old, Solborg. They all drank enough of that mead to knock a horse over. Are you going to help me with the chant or do I have to do it alone, as usual?''

They began chanting a spell. Ivarr slithered across the floor, feeling almost as strong as a sack half-filled with grain. He desperately hoped the floor would not creak. He reached Gizur's bed and tugged at his foot as hard as he could. The wizard continued to snore away without so much as a twitch. Ivarr pounded on his shin with his fist, which elicited a faint grunt. Mustering all his strength, Ivarr crept forward and gave the wizard a good shaking by his shoulders. The only observable result was a dramatic increase in his own light-headedness. Gizur made a foggy grunt of protest deep in his sleep. Ivarr eased himself to the floor before he fell, resting his forehead on the cool wood. He felt weak and sick, and the taste of the mead in his mouth was terrible. In spite of himself, he became suddenly sleepy, and he fell soundly asleep right where he lay on the bare floorboards.

He awakened in the morning when the others began to stir. His bones and muscles ached and he was cold, in spite of the fact he was lying in his bed with the eider pulled up to his chin. Astonished, he sat up and looked over at Flosi, who was sleeping soundly in spite of Finnvard sitting on the foot of his bed to pull on his boots. Skapti was puffing and snorting in a basin of water, like a seal, and Egills was arguing with Finnvard. Gizur was already gone, and Eilifir was looking out the window.

Ivarr was confused by the absolute normality of the scene he beheld. Finnvard prodded Flosi cautiously and was rewarded with a savage growl and a flurry of kicks. "Just go away and let me sleep," he grumbled. "If I don't feel like getting out of bed until tomorrow, I won't."

They left him in his bed and trooped downstairs. Ivarr hesitated, then tiptoed back to Flosi and tried to raise the covers for a look at his feet, which, according to legend, should be in very sad condition. But Flosi was in no mood to cooperate, and threw a boot at him.

Ivarr went downstairs, slowly accepting the idea that the events of the past night were nothing but vivid dreams. Certainly none of the strange limpness of his muscles troubled him now.

Nidbjorg, Thorvor, and Solborg gave no indication of a sleepless night. They had prepared a plentiful breakfast for their guests and were talking of roasting a lamb for evening. With a wince, Ivarr thought of Solborg and her knife, and he looked at her closely, as if to discern whether or not she was capable of murdering people in their beds, or hagriding unfortunate travellers to their deaths.

She smiled at him in a grandmotherly way and said "And you may help me kill and dress the lamb, if you wish, Ivarr, unless you don't care for blood."

Ivarr gave a great start and his heart beat wildly for a moment before he realized how ridiculous he was being. Hastily he agreed to help, hoping she hadn't noticed

112

anything strange.

After breakfast everyone dispersed to such activities as napping in the sun, oiling boots, and anything else that did not involve much walking. With much reluctance, Ivarr accompanied Solborg to the lamb pen and helped her select a victim for the evening repast. To his relief, it was quickly and neatly done. Solborg was an expert at killing and dressing meat—a trifle too expert, in Ivarr's opinion. He could scarcely take his eyes off her knife until she had wiped off the blood and sheathed it at her waist. Altogether, he was on the verge of instant flight one moment, and scoffing at himself the next.

When he was finished, he went in search of Skapti and found him sitting watchfully near the wall where the sisters had required them to hang up their weapons. Skapti made a place for him on the other end of his bench and went on brooding and scowling.

"I was wondering," Ivarr began, "if there are any of the evil sorts who needn't fear the sun?"

"Why, certainly. Fire jotuns, for one. They're descendants of the Ljosalfar, and there are many others who can tolerate the sun for the same reason. Dark Alfar have spawned an atrocious race of wizards, alfkonur—you'd call them witches—"

"Alfkonur?" Ivarr said. "Are they often the evil sort of hags who can turn travellers into horses and ride them all night until they almost die?"

Skapti turned pale, down to the end of his bright pink peeling nose. "Alfkonur! So that's it. I've had the horrors since we got here, and I'm sure that's the reason why. I'm going to tell Gizur we're packing up and leaving this instant. If he objects, we shall leave him, and I shall tell him so."

Ivarr seized Skapti's cloak and brought him up short, like a goat on a tether. "Skapti," he whispered, "I'm not at all sure we should mention it. We haven't got any proof. It may have been only a dream I had last night when I thought I heard them talking in the loft while we were asleep. They were deciding which one of us they would hagride to a seidr

113

at Svinafell. They took Flosi, and I tried to awaken Gizur, but I could scarcely move. I thought I went to sleep on the floor, but this morning I woke up in my bed. It could have been only a dream."

"If it wasn't," Skapti said, "who put you back in your bed? It had to be them."

"So they know I was awake," Ivarr whispered.

At that moment Gizur came striding into the hall and flung himself into a chair with a compelling racket. Skapti's chin jutted out as he stalked over to the wizard.

"Gizur, I've got something to say which you probably won't like. I know you won't like it, in fact, but I don't care. As the leader of these Alfar, I want to depart as soon as we can get ourselves ready."

Gizur raised his eyebrow. "By all means, then, let's get packing. But there is a slight problem."

Skapti eyed him warily. "What problem is that?"

"We shall have to take turns carrying Flosi on our backs for a day or two. The dolt got his feet wet yesterday and didn't stop to dry them out, so he walked them into a mass of blisters and bruises. I've put a poultice on his feet which will fix them up by tomorrow or the next day. We needn't be in any hurry to leave, need we?" He spoke loudly enough that his voice carried easily into the kitchen.

"Gizur," Skapti whispered urgently. "We've got to get out of here before nightfall. Ivarr and I are both convinced of it. These women are alfkonur and they hagrode Flosi. Did you ever know Flosi to get the least blister without complaining about it all the while?"

"They plan to kill everyone except me," Ivarr whispered. "I heard them talking last night when they thought the mead had knocked us all out. Or at least, I'm pretty certain it wasn't a dream," he added, seeing Gizur's brow knot into an incredulous scowl.

"Alfkonur, eh?" he murmured, nodding his head slowly. "Then that may explain why I've been feeling rather devoid of power. I thought I was just tired, but it must be their spells. I can't believe I'm not a match for the three of them, however. I'll rally my powers for a counterspell. Confound it, but I feel tired. Perhaps a short nap would help.'' He stretched his feet out to the fire and made himself comfortable. In another moment he was sound asleep.

Skapti pulled on his ear viciously. "Gizur! Wake up, you fool!" He gave the wizard a shake, but Gizur didn't stir. "I can't believe it. They've hexed him right before our eyes and he's powerless to resist. Ivarr, I'm beginning to have the feeling we're not going to escape from here without harm."

Ivarr sighed. "I fear the worst, Skapti."

When he left the house, Ivarr felt Thorvor's eyes on his back. By the time he was fairly outside, his hands were sweating. When he looked back, he saw Solborg ducking out of sight, as if she had been watching him.

Eilifir was strolling up and down idly. When he saw Ivarr and Skapti, he raised one hand to get their attention, and then pointed silently to the side of the house. "Gone," he said.

Skapti looked at the house and clapped his hand to his brow. "Our weapons!" he gasped. "They've taken them and hidden them from us!"

"I asked them about it," Eilifir said. "They said they thought it wise to put the weapons in a safer place because they believe Flosi is suffering from a disorder that causes him to walk in his sleep. He might do somebody a damage, they said."

Skapti clenched his fists. "And you accepted that as an explanation?"

"Shouldn't I?" Eilifir inquired.

"They're alfkonur!" Skapti whispered. "They've got Gizur in their power. We're trapped here, with no weapons, no wizard, and one by one we're all going to be killed, except Ivarr. I think we'd better tell the others to be on their guard, since we can't leave with Flosi in such bad shape, and Gizur is little better."

Eilifir shook his head. "There's no sense in telling Finnvard and Egills and Flosi what's really going on, or it's

115

going to be more difficult for us. The old women watch us so closely, have you noticed?''

Ivarr turned his head and glimpsed Solborg ducking around the door again. ''What are we going to do?''

''I suggest avoiding their mead,'' Skapti said grimly. ''I thought it had a peculiar taste last night. Eilifir, isn't there anything we can do to help Gizur fight their influence?''

Eilifir withdrew into his cloak. ''We can start by staying alive. We must be very careful, or Solborg's knife will put an end to any meddling.

They spent the rest of the day mending holes and putting grease on their boots, eating, sleeping, and in general relaxing as best they could. Gizur finally awoke from his magic-induced sleep, looking rather pale and weary. He glanced around narrowly a moment and looked up to make sure none of their hostesses were in the hall.

''My staff is missing,'' he whispered to Ivarr, his eyes blazing. ''They must have taken it while I was sleeping. Now I'm virtually helpless. Most of my power resides in that staff. Didn't you see them? Hasn't someone been here the entire time?''

Ivarr felt a chill of dread. He had been in and out several times, like everyone else. One of the sisters must have whisked the staff out of sight almost under their noses.

Before he could reply, Nidbjorg and her sisters came in and began to fuss over Flosi solicitously, listening to his complaints and growlings and offering him the daintiest dishes their kitchen could produce. As the sun began to sink, Ivarr stationed himself near Flosi, determined to stay awake all night. Skapti looked stiff and wary, and Eilifir was smoking quietly in a dark corner. After supper Finnvard challenged Ivarr to a chess game and beat him hopelessly in less than a dozen moves.

Flosi snorted derisively from his cozy quarters in the panel bed the sisters had offered him downstairs; his sore feet made climbing the stairs difficult, they explained. ''Scipling wits are no match for Alfar wits,'' he declared, and called for something to drink.

Ivarr mentally honed his wits. If Birna had taught him anything, it was how to play chess, and she had been a ruthless opponent, pouncing upon the slightest advantage mercilessly.

"I'm sure I can beat you," he said, setting up the pieces.

The game began with a large amount of spectator interest and copious amounts of the sisters' ale. Egills and Finnvard fell asleep almost instantly, but Skapti and Eilifir and Ivarr sat with full cups. Gizur pretended to sample the brew and went back to smoking his pipe.

The hall was silent with the peculiar crackling silence of an intense battle of wits—and the chess game was not the only battle under consideration. In spite of himself, Ivarr felt his concentration slipping as he began to tire. Several times he was certain he felt Solborg's cold pale eyes on his back and he itched to turn around. He knew there was a window behind him and it bothered him intensely. His pieces began disappearing from the board and Flosi began to look more smug. A sudden crash of burning peat in the hearth unnerved him to the extent that he uttered a small yelp.

"Some hot tea might be pleasant," Nidbjorg said, rising from her chair, "since no one wants the ale tonight."

When she returned with the tea, Ivarr smelled it warily and could detect nothing but the smell of tea. He watched to see if Gizur drank it. Gizur tasted a bit of it and nodded slightly to Ivarr, taking a larger swallow. Skapti took his cue from Gizur, and gulped his tea scalding hot until his eyes watered. Ivarr took a swallow of the tea mainly for the sake of politeness. To his great alarm, he instantly tasted the same bitter flavour as that of the ale. He put down the cup hastily and looked at Gizur, who gave him an apologetic little shrug as he leaned unsteadily on his elbows. His eyes looked dull and desperate, like the eyes of a trapped animal.

"It's your turn," Flosi said irritably after a long interval of alternately slurping tea and stifling yawns. "No wonder this game has taken so long, if you're going to sleep between each turn."

Ivarr rubbed his blurring eyes. He knew that Skapti and Gizur had dropped off to sleep.

"I can't keep my eyes open," he muttered. "The tea—"

"Well, I would have won anyway at the rate you were going," Flosi said. "I shall allow you to concede the game. You didn't start out too badly, but I could tell your mind wasn't on the game." As he talked, Flosi sagged until his head was resting on the gameboard among the pieces. "You've got to concentrate to—to concentrate to—win—" He fell asleep comfortably even as he talked.

Nidbjorg continued knitting at a great pace, glancing at Ivarr to assess the progress of the drugged tea. "You know you are beaten, so let me help you upstairs."

Ivarr shook his head, and nearly fell off his chair. He stood up unsteadily and took a stance against the wall bed, fumbling with wooden fingers for Birna's knife. Even so simple a task defeated him and he began to slide to the floor.

Nidbjorg clicked her tongue. "You'll catch a chill sleeping on the floor like that, but you may suit yourself. Thorvor, it's time you were getting ready."

Thorvor awakened instantly from a long nap under her knitting. "I wasn't asleep, sister. Solborg, are you ready?"

Solborg replied, "There's not much time, thanks to our troublesome Scipling friend. I think he knows, sisters, and has told the wizard."

"Bah on the wizard," Nidbjorg said. "We've got him under our thumbs and he scarcely knows what's happening to him."

Solborg and Thorvor began chanting their spell and Nidbjorg muttered and scratched around in the rafters directly above. Ivarr opened his eyes cautiously and looked up, wondering how Nidbjorg had managed to climb up there, at her age. To his amazement, he saw a huge cat with glaring yellow eyes. It hissed at him by way of greeting and crouched as if ready to spring. Ivarr rolled toward the woodbox to grab a stick to defend himself but the cat spat and hissed warningly. He stopped and looked at Gizur and Skapti snoring in their chairs. It would be useless to try

118

waking them, he knew, and the cat growled as if she knew what he was thinking.

Ivarr hesitated, then attempted a flying dive for the woodbox. He seized a stout club, jerked Birna's knife from his belt, and went lurching at Solborg and Thorvor with a roar of challenge. They stopped their spell and scuttled out of his way. Suddenly something struck him on the shoulders with great force, enough to upset his tottery balance and flatten him face-first on the floor. The cat gave a screech of triumph and dug its claws into his back, growing heavier and heavier until there was scarcely a breath in his body. Helpless, he heard the chant resume. He attempted to struggle, but the cat grew even heavier.

The spell ended with a murky puff of light and smoke, and the hags climbed onto the back of a jaded-looking horse and sent him lunging out the door with a clatter of hooves and the cracking of a whip upon his sunken flanks.

"Nidbjorg, do you hear me?" he wheezed.

"I do, of course," Nidbjorg's voice replied, with a purr. "I'm quite surprised you recognized me. I fear you're frightfully uncomfortable, though. If you'll throw that knife into the fire, I'll be glad to get off your back, and we can talk like two civilized beings."

"You may as well kill me, then. I'm not throwing away my knife."

"You're in no danger of being killed right away. We want you and that sword you're going after. Don't think we haven't heard about it. We could make good use of it, too."

Ivarr shook his head slightly. "I fear Lorimer the necromancer has already bespoken me for destruction."

"Don't you believe it for a moment. Lorimer wants that sword as much as anyone. Speaking of swords, by the way, why don't you tell me where your sword is? We've been trying to guess what on earth you're going to Jotunsgard for. Thorvar and I favour the idea there's a smith there you're going to hire to make you a sword, but Solborg has a very interesting idea herself, which she says she gathered from something Flosi clumsily hinted at. He said something about

119

a barrow. Now why did you groan just then? Am I getting too heavy? If you would just agree to cooperate and not say anything more to your friends, we would all be much happier. Think how much more power we possess than your foolish Alfar. We could help you rob Elidagrimr's barrow, and we could help you kill Fafnir. Then of course we would help Svartarr destroy Elbegast, after which we would destroy Svartarr and rule all of Svartarrsrike. It would be very pleasant for you to be on the winning side, would it not?''

Ivarr shook his head. ''Lorimer is more powerful than you are. You'd make a mess of it if you tried it.''

Nidbjorg dug her claws into him a little. ''That's a foolish thing to say in your position, young man. We don't care two sticks for Lorimer. We've got you and your sword right in our hands, practically. ''Now I do wish you'd throw that knife away. I don't want to sit here all night.''

''At least you won't be killing my friends as long as you have to sit on me.''

''Let's not talk this way, shall we?'' Nidbjorg said in a more pleasant tone. ''Killings are not a nice subject to discuss. Let's talk some more about that sword in Elidagrimr's barrow, since we're going to be here all night.''

Ivarr sighed and said he had nothing to tell her, and she baited him with more questions, spiced with a quantity of threats and promises. Ivarr wearily refused to answer or made up preposterous lies. It was the longest night of his life, but he kept a good grip on his knife. To his relief, Nidbjorg eventually tired of her questions and his answers and fell into a sulky silence, punctuated only by Skapti's snoring.

At last they heard the sound of horse's hooves plodding and stumbling into the dooryard. It was almost daylight and the old women hurriedly reversed their spell and carted Flosi into the house and dumped him into the wall bed. Nidbjorg leaped away, resuming her human form with an incantation, and she began grumbling and complaining to her sisters at once about their slowness in returning from Svinafell.

Solborg scowled at Ivarr. "And the Scipling hasn't missed a word of anything. What shall we do with him so he won't get the rest of them overly flustered?"

"What's done is done," Nidbjorg snapped. "If you don't want him to talk, you'll have to take him away somewhere, the stubborn wretch."

Ivarr raised himself to his feet with difficulty and hobbled to a chair. "That's right. As soon as I get upstairs I'm going to awaken my friends and we are leaving. You may do what you can to stop us, but we aren't staying here another night."

"You're talking rather mighty for one in your position." Solborg said. "I'll bet I could take you down a peg or two."

Nidbjorg cut her off sharply. "Enough talk. Upstairs with these fellows and be quick about it."

Ivarr watched in dull amazement as Thorvor and Solborg carried Gizur and Skapti upstairs with very little difficulty, reciting a chant over Gizur when he began making alarming signs of awakening. Then they seized Ivarr with uncommon strength and no great gentleness and dropped him in his bed with a fierce injunction to stay there.

Ivarr was only too glad to comply. His bones ached from their night-long grinding and his spirits were likewise depressed, in spite of his bold talk. He was so discouraged he fell asleep immediately and did not awaken until everyone else was already stirring. The sun was shining cheerily in the little window and the Alfar were in the best of spirits. Ivarr felt terrible, and remembering why made him feel even more terrible. He crept out of bed and Egills gave him a friendly buffet that made every bone cry out in sheer misery. In a hoarse voice, he croaked, "We're leaving this house as soon as we can get our packs together."

"Before breakfast?" Finnvard asked indignantly. "What kind of talk is that? I've never seen such pastries!"

"Where's Gizur?" Ivarr straightened his back by slow and cautious degrees.

"Downstairs checking on that young degenerate Flosi," Egills said. "Did you know he's got a feather mattress in that

121

wall bed? I wouldn't be walking in my sleep away from a bed like that. I wonder what's the matter with him?''

Ivarr shook his head, very haggard, and eased himself down the stairs. The scene that greeted him was anything but reassuring. Gizur sat on the edge of Flosi's bed, looking little better than Flosi. The three sisters stood primly behind him, holding a basin and bandages and various other treatments.

Nidbjorg said to Ivarr, ''Flosi walked in his sleep last night again and managed to do himself more harm. It seems we were all too sleepy last night after the chess game to watch him.''

Ivarr kicked a stool out of his way. ''What tripe! I've had enough of this sleepwalking business! We all know he was hagridden, and who is doing it. We've got to get Flosi out of here while he's still alive, or while any of us are still alive, for that matter.''

''Nonsense,'' Nidbjorg snapped. ''Just look at him. He can't be moved for several days.''

Flosi did indeed look bad. His face was grey with fatigue and from time to time he was wracked with shivers and twitches. Ivarr darted a sudden glance at Solborg, detecting a faint smile of satisfaction. He felt more afraid in their comfortable hall than he had on the hilltop surrounded by hostile dwarves.

''You don't look as if you rested well last night,'' Thorvor said solicitously.

''Well, I didn't, and you know very well why. Nidbjorg drugged us with the tea. Don't call me a liar, because I smelled the same substance that you put in your ale and wine.''

''Why, we put it in everything,'' Solborg said. ''It's only a flavour.''

''No, it's not,'' Ivarr said, abandoning all caution. ''The three of you are alfkonur, or witches as we Sciplings would call them, and I have seen you hagride Flosi two times. Where I come from, such an offence is punishable by death. And that isn't all. While I was trying to protect Flosi,

122

Nidbjorg changed herself to a cat and sat on me and nearly crushed the life out of me. I have simply had enough of your nonsense. Restore our weapons to us and let us go. I still have this knife and I'll fight with nothing more than this rather than allow my friends to be harmed any further." He drew Birna's knife and it flashed in his hand.

The sisters drew back with alarmed exclamations and such frightened expressions that Ivarr was startled and ashamed.

"This is a house of refuge," Nidbjorg said with dignity. "Nothing such as you describe could possibly happen here. I believe I shall recommend to your guardian Gizur to keep you away from our liquor so you won't continue in such extraordinary dreaming. If you don't improve such violent behaviour, I fear you'll spend the rest of your life locked away or chained to a wall."

Ivarr swallowed his anger, feeling another surge of uncertainty. Dreams often seemed more real than reality—but Flosi's condition was no dream. Sternly he demanded, "Then how do you account for Flosi's sickness and damaged feet?"

Nidbjorg replied, "Exactly that—a sickness or a fever which robs him of his rest and cause him to sleepwalk. Tonight we shall sit beside him and make certain it doesn't happen again. I hope everyone will sleep more peacefully tonight." She looked significantly at Ivarr and turned to retreat toward the kitchen, followed by Solborg and Thorvor.

"You shouldn't have challenged them openly," Gizur said in a weary voice.

"Then what are we supposed to do?" Skapti asked, creeping around the corner and glaring toward the kitchen. "Can't you exert yourself, Gizur, and fight back against their magic?"

Gizur sagged into a chair. "I'm almost certain Solborg is working a charm against me, using all the substances inimical to my power. I won't get my strength back until it is found and destroyed. I feel as if a good puff of wind would blow me right away."

"Then it will be up to me to get us out of here," Skapti said. "If it's a fight they want, let's give it to them. We didn't do too badly at Ringknip with Lorimer's dwarves."

"Yes, but now we don't have a magic circle to help us." Gizur said. "Nor do I have my staff. Eilifir might be able to do something, if you can get him to do it. And you, Skapti, I don't want you to try matching the three of them all at once. They are seasoned, practicing alfkonur. It will be no mean trick to escape them, unless I can find my staff."

Skapti tore off his hood and threw it on the floor. "Then we're right back to the beginning! We can't do a thing to save Flosi!"

Ivarr shook his head. "I've got an idea. Put me in Flosi's place tonight."

Gizur shook his head, and another voice spoke at his elbow—Eilifir had a habit of listening unnoticed until he spoke. "Too risky. If we lost Ivarr, all would be lost. Besides, you look nothing like Flosi. I'll go in Flosi's place."

"You mean you're volunteering?" Skapti demanded.

Eilifir smiled his rare smile. "There's nothing I would relish more than having two alfkonur at my mercy. I shall trade places with Flosi tonight, and we shall see what will happen. Givur, I trust you can arrange for a diversion of some sort, soon after dark?"

"I'll do it if I have to set myself on fire," the wizard declared.

Eilifir nodded. "That would be adequate. Be certain it is done out of doors, however."

"Are you sure you'll be all right?" Skapti asked. "I'll be standing by if there's anything I can do. If you wouldn't stand too close to them, I'd try a spell, but I'm not at all experienced—"

Eilifir was shaking his head. "I shall be perfectly all right. Gizur, will you guard the hall tonight?"

"Certainly, I'm still a wizard am I not?" Gizur snorted.

"If Solborg is left behind tonight," Ivarr said, drawing Birna's knife and testing its point, "I suspect she'll be wanting to reduce our numbers by other means. You'd better take care to stay awake tonight, Gizur, or she might carve you into steaks and chops."

"I've felt the eyes of a killer before," Gizur retorted, looking anxious nonetheless. He stuck out his hand to Eilifir. "Well, good luck, old fellow. We've got an element of surprise on our side, at least."

"We do?" Ivarr asked.

"Yes. Everybody will be surprised if it works. Now do your best to make up some convincing lies for me; I'm going to do some dowsing for my staff. Keep the witches in the kitchen if you can."

"Not I," Ivarr said with a shudder. "I can't even look at them, let alone talk to them."

Eilifir was nodding his head. "Not to worry, wizard," was all he said.

"Until tonight then," Gizur said with a mock salute.

CHAPTER ELEVEN

Flosi dozed most of the day, awakening only to demand peevishly something to eat or drink. Finnvard and Egills sat contentedly in the sunshine, swapping lies and trying to get Skapti to join in their good spirits—which were greatly augmented by some of the sisters' spirits. Eilifir planted himself in the kitchen and talked ceaselessly, to the amazement of all who beheld him, while Gizur prowled around dowsing covertly. Ivarr roamed around restlessly, waiting for—and dreading—the setting of the sun. He studiously avoided the kitchen, and Gizur shooed him away fiercely whenever he wandered too near. He had to admire the detachment of Eilifir, who visited amiably with the sisters as if the best of intentions existed on both sides.

The sunset, so long in approaching, deepened rapidly into night. Supper was made and eaten, the most tasty and elaborate meal served during their stay. Never were the three sisters more solicitous and charming. Gizur responded by taking up a harp and singing songs and reciting poetry for several hours, with the dubious aid of Finnvard and Egills. Skapti sat with his mouth shut like a trap, and Ivarr was glad he knew none of the songs so he could sit broodingly in the chimney corner. The sisters enjoyed the performance immensely, and Flosi watched wanly from his place in the wall bed.

At last the harp was hung up, the coals banked, and the

last cup of mead swallowed by Egills and Finnvard. Ivarr refused the drink rather curtly, saying he wanted no more bad dreams.

Gizur, Eilifir, and Skapti made their excuses more politely. Eilifir even accepted a cup of mead and, when no one was looking, he tossed it into the fire. The fire flared for an instant and then went out with a smoky snort, plunging the hall into darkness and a certain amount of confusion.

"Never mind," Nidbjorg said calmly. "I shall light a lamp. Solborg, the lamp is on that shelf above your head and a fresh wick beside it. If everyone will stand still a moment, I'll fetch a coal from the kitchen hearth, unless it has gone out too. I've never known our chimney to misbehave so drastically."

Solborg brushed past Ivarr in the dark, muttering, "I'll warrant it's some kind of portent, or magic of some sort." She groped around on the shelf and found the lamp. "There's no oil in it," she announced.

"Well then, go out to the kitchen and get some," Nidbjorg snapped. "You can see better in the dark than I can and your bones are far younger than mine, Solborg."

"You needn't go to so much trouble." Gizur said. "We were all going upstairs to bed anyway. I'm sure Flosi finds the darkness restful. Come along, Egills and Finnvard, there's no use in using the dark to conceal the fact that you're gulping down more of that mead; I can hear every swallow."

"All I hear are owls," Finnvard said, stumbling into a chair.

With much grumbling and scuffing, Finnvard and Egills were pushed upstairs to the loft, following Skapti, who carried the snoring Flosi. Thorvor appeared with a lamp, but Gizur assured her that they had made it quite safely and the lamp was not necessary. When she was gone, Ivarr slipped over to Gizur's cot, where the wizard was just beginning to breathe heavily, as a prelude to deep sleep.

"Gizur!" Ivarr whispered, and the wizard struggled to awaken. "Gizur, can't you fight them just for a short while?

Solborg is going to be here by herself tonight, and she's going to kill some of us. We need you, Gizur."

Gizur struggled to sit up, then abandoned the effort. "They're so powerful," he murmered, shutting his eyes. "I fear I shall die here."

"Nonsense. Gizur, get control of yourself." Ivarr gave him a fierce shaking. "You're a wizard, the best of the Guild. Collect your thoughts and concentrate on forcing the alfkonur poison from your mind and body. You can do it, Gizur."

"Can't," Gizur muttered.

"You must," said the voice of Skapti. "Have you forgotten the oaths you have taken to assist any and all in resisting the powers of darkness? Where's your Wizards' Guild sphere? Use it to summon help fron the Guild."

Gizur rallied slightly. "I doubt if the Guild would answer, and as for the oaths of the Guild, I never took them. I'm as good a fire wizard as the Guild ever turned out but, you see, I went to a smaller school of less renown which was significantly cheaper to attend and didn't require such a lengthy apprenticeship or such an exhaustive final examination. Much of the Guild certification is mere show and arrogance. And it's no secret that the old hide-bound Guildmasters are still suspicious of red-bearded wizards. I was determined to be a wizard, however, so I went to the Tulkari school."

"But why didn't you tell us this before?" Skapti asked.

"Because it wasn't important," Gizur said snappishly. "I didn't notice your group being too choosy when I showed up for the position. You almost begged me with tears in your eyes to help you pay that weregild and no mention was made of looking at credentials. If you prefer I could withdraw at this very moment, if you think I'm not good enough for your company." Again he struggled to rise, and fell back with a groan.

"No, no, I didn't mean anything of the sort," Skapti said. "Far be it from me to criticize your training, when I've had none. It's just that for centuries all we've heard about is

128

Guild wizards, and how there are so many shoddy and ill-advised schools of magic. We're in such a dismal predicament right now. I wish you'd waited until later to tell us you weren't a real Guild wizard.'' Ivarr was certain he was tugging on his ear in the dark.

Gizur replied caustically, "I assure you that Tulkari wizards are at least as good as Guild wizards, and I shall prove it if I perish in the attempt. You may think I'm sleeping, but believe me, I'm fighting—fighting for my—very life.'' He yawned and began to breathe deeply, breaths which lengthened into snores.

"Drat and blast!" Skapti shook him with no result. "We've lost him, Ivarr. We're on our own now, with Solborg.''

Ivarr looked toward Skapti. All he could see of him was a faint rim of glowing power outlining him in the dark. "You'll have to risk blasting her if she tries to come upstairs with that knife of hers. I'm sure you can do it.''

Skapti answered with a grunt. Ivarr could hear him munching on the end of his beard, a ritual he reserved for moments of particular stress. "I'll either blast Nidbjorgs-stead to Niflheim and us with it, or I'll just make Solborg madder. This is a splendid situation, just splendid, but I can't say I'm surprised. No real Guild wizard would stake his reputation on such a fool's venture as ours.''

He followed Ivarr to the head of the stairs, where they sat down, one on each side. They could look down and see the glow of the whale-oil lamp and hear the chorus of knitting needles clicking softly in their mufflers of wool. At intervals, a gust of wind buffeted the house, causing all manner of creaks and cracks and groans, for which Ivarr was grateful, considering their movements and whisperings in the loft.

"It's a windy night," Thorvor's voice said suddenly. "I'm not sure I care to go out if it's going to be unpleasant.''

"Suit yourself," said Solborg, "but I'm staying. I believe you owe me the charge of our captives for one night.''

"We may have no captives if we do," Thorvor said. "I've enjoyed our nightly jaunts to Svinafell. Nidbjorg, I think you should tell her that she can't kill them all."

Nidbjorg replied, "The wizard is mine, and you can't harm the Scipling. Aside from those two, I don't care what happens to the rest."

Solborg chuckled. "I'll be continent, dear sister, if you enjoy your hagriding so much. I shall save that one-eyed one for you."

"It's time to begin the spell, Thorvor. It looks as if we'll be without interference tonight, for a change. I expect our brave young hero was rather frightened and has decided to leave the fate of his companions to us. He's glad enough to be spared, I expect."

Ivarr heard the panels slide open and the eerie chant began. He leaned down so he could see further into the room, which was dimly lit by the guttering lamp. The incantation ended suddenly with a roiling of acrid smoke, and there stood the horse, a vast dark shadow in the centre of the hall.

"What did you do different, Thorvor?" Nidbjorg asked. "He's not the same colour. This time he's grey."

"Grey! Elbegast's horses are grey," Thorvor said with a shudder. "I can't imagine what I did to change it. A word in the wrong order, perhaps."

"I hope so. Perhaps you should do it over."

Solborg declared, "A horse is a horse and a hag is a hag. This will be the last ride for him at any rate. I hope you make it home." She bent for a look at the grey's low-hanging head.

"I suppose it's nothing," Nidbjorg said. "Solborg, help us up."

Grumbling, Solborg stooped down so her sister could use her as a mounting block. She opened the door and Nidbjorg twisted up a handful of mane and hammered her heels on the horse's ribs vigorously, sending the poor beast stumbling over the doorsill at a shambling trot.

Skapti sighed almost inaudibly. Solborg closed the door and came toward the stairs. She paused at the foot and drew her knife, looking at it admiringly in the lamp light. Then she took up the lamp and began to ascend the stairway as silently as a ghost. The wind gave a dismal shout around the corners of the house and went tumbling away across the fellside.

Skapti began whispering a spell and Ivarr drew Birna's knife. For a long moment Solborg hesitated on the stairs. Then she chuckled, a low and menacing sound.

"Are you there, Ivarr? I know you are, with that hateful little knife in your hand, hoping to do me a mischief if you get the chance. And who is that with you? Old Skapti, is it? How can I convince you your friends are hardly worth dying for? Perhaps you're not as stubborn as the Scipling, however, and might like to trade your life for some information."

"Never!" Skapti growled. He had armed himself with a club of firewood and stood waiting to strike the instant she came into reach.

"Like cornered rats," Solborg sneered, but she backed down a step, realizing she was at a disadvantage. "I could kill you without even thinking about it."

"But you won't," Ivarr said. "You want Elidagrimr's sword. And I think you're rather fat to be much of a fighter, anyway."

Solborg exhaled angrily. In the light of the lamp she held, her face looked evil, wrinkled, and droopy underneath the jowls and eyes. Her nose appeared as sharp as a hooked talon. "Fat, am I? Well, you'll think differently after you've starved for a proper interval, chained in our cellar. I warrant you'll become humbled by the time we're through with you, you haughty little vagabond."

Skapti replied with another insult. "You look just like an old black pudding bag, tied in the middle. Whoever heard of being afraid of a pudding bag?"

She made a sudden dive at Ivarr to grab his ankle, and he slashed at her with his knife, sticking the point into the wood staircase. She then seized his wrist while he was delayed in freeing his knife. Her fingers closed on his wrist with a grip of iron. He gasped, remembering her supernatural strength.

She laughed in an ugly manner and began to haul him

131

downstairs. "We shall put you away somewhere so you can't be a nuisance. Our little cellar is an agreeable place, if you like the dark and the bones. You're not the first tenant, of course."

Ivarr grabbed for a handhold, and Solborg retaliated with a hard yank on his arm. At that instant, something brushed past Ivarr's ear with a whirring, piniony sound, and a feathery mass struck Solborg in the face. With a screech, she fell over backward and went bumping down the rest of the stairs by herself. The jovial hoots of an owl came from the direction of the mantel. Cursing, Solborg righted herself and began beating at the flames lapping at the pool of spilled oil from the lamp she had dropped. The owl chuckled with sepulchral glee.

"Help! Fire!" shouted Solborg angrily, as the flames engulfed a wall hanging with a greedy roar.

Ivarr and Skapti were already shaking and pounding their companions into consciousness. Several dashes of water from the basin greatly assisted their efforts, and once the situation was explained to them, in one terrifying word, they scrambled around gathering up their possessions. Skapti bundled Flosi onto his back and dived down the staircase through the mounting flames. Ivarr hurled packs and clothing out the small loft window to the ground below and drove Finnvard and Egills downstairs like terrified sheep before him. By the time they had assembled outside and counted themselves several times, the front hall was filled with smoke and flame. Although the walls were turf, the fire found plenty of hangings, fleeces, and wooden beams, tables, and benches to burn. The floor of the loft also ignited promptly; the wood was very old and dry.

Gizur was the last to leave the burning house, carrying a sack over his shoulder, his satchel bulging, and with his free hand he conducted Solborg away from the flames, much against the wishes of Skapti.

"No, there's no need for that," Gizur said, putting down his burden of food rescued from the kitchen. "When Solborg hears what has happened to her sisters, I expect

132

she'll be quite anxious to go after them and attempt to render aid.''

"Let go of me, you red-bearded fiend!" Solborg snapped. "I'll cut all your throats unless you tell me what has happened to my sisters! Thieves, house burners, murderers! What ill luck rubs off of you!"

"I don't understand," began Finnvard, but she startled him into silence with a vindictive spate of more accusations and epithets.

"Where are my sisters?" she shrieked, pointing a finger at Flosi dozing on the ground. "You have tricked us! That other evil fellow is murdering my sisters!"

"I hope so," Skapti said. "Eilifir is an extraordinary Alfar. Gizur, what do you want to do with her? You're not going to let her go, are you?"

"Where's Eilifir?" demanded Egills. "Is he really murdering Thorvor and Nidbjorg? If he is, I'd call that a breach of hospitality, Gizur."

"No more than they deserve," Skapti said. "They nearly killed Flosi. They're alfkonur, and they were going to kill us all and force Ivarr into their service. While you two dolts were swilling down all the food and drink you could possibly hold, the rest of us have been fighting for our very lives."

"You should have told us," Egills growled resentfully. "You mean those dear old souls are really—" Finnvard stared at Solborg with dawning horror.

"Yes," Gizur snapped. "Finnvard, you and Egills attend to Flosi. Begin putting our packs together. Our charming hostesses have obligingly supplied us with a great many provisions. We should get well into Jotunsgard before we run out." As he spoke, he reached behind over one shoulder and withdrew his wizard staff from his belt at his back. Solborg uttered a small indignant cry and glared at him with furious resignation. Gizur flourished the staff, filling the air around him with sparks and glowing auras in various colours. "Yes, I discovered my staff where Nidbjorg had hidden it inside the wall panels of her room. It was rather clumsy of you to drop that lamp, Solborg, because you also lost something

133

out of your pocket which was burned in the spilt oil.''

Solborg slapped her pockets. ''The charm!''

''It was all I could do to change to my fylgja form for one desperate attack. I caught you by surprise, didn't I, my dear? You thought you could get the best of a wizard, just the three of you. A common mistake, so don't feel too badly. Skapti, if you're looking around for our weapons, I believe Thorvor ensconced them in a place of honour in the pig shed.''

At dawn, three dark blots plodded over the shoulder of the fell. As they came closer, it was obvious that Nidbjorg and Thorvor were limping sorely and nearly exhausted. They sank down on the wall when they reached their farmstead and stared dully at the smoking ruin that was their house. The roofs had fallen in on two gables, leaving only the stable.

''Well, what happened to you?'' demanded Solborg angrily. ''How could you have been so stupid as to make such a mistake? And why are you limping?''

Nidbjorg turned her eyes in Solborg's direction. ''If you speak one more word from that silly mouth of yours, I shall give you boils and plagues and fleas and lice until our injuries would be a pleasure. At least we didn't burn down the house, which you have managed quite nicely.''

Solborg shut her mouth quickly. She sat down at a distance from her sisters, glaring at Gizur.

Eilifir lifted a loaf of bread from Gizur's bag and took a bite of it, passing it to Ivarr solemnly. He then looked at Flosi, nodding with satisfaction at the salve on his wounded feet. ''He's healing quickly,'' he said, ''and sleeping soundly.''

Skapti could restrain his delight and curiosity no longer. ''Eilifir, you clever and audacious fellow, tell us what you have done to these hags. They're limping along as if they've walked a long way.''

Eilifir bent a considering look upon his captives. ''They've had a small taste of their own brew tonight. I changed them into old ewes and drove them all the way back

134

from Svinafell, at least as far as they could make it. I expect they got a bit tired and footsore.''

''A sorry trick if ever I saw one,'' Thorvor said, almost tearfully. ''Who would have thought a mild quiet fellow like that would be so cruel.''

''Would have such power, you mean, you old fool,'' Nidbjorg snapped. ''I offer no apologies or complaints. We were clearly bested in a battle of wits and power. Gizur, I concede the contest and we await your punishment.''

Gizur rested upon his staff a moment, then began pacing up and down. ''Well, your offences are grievous. Most wizards would blast you on the spot and be done with it, but I suppose compassion is a weakness of mine. I shall give you a chance to save yourselves, and also a warning that if we see you again, you will be destroyed on sight. I now adjure you to take yourselves to the Fire Wizards' Guildhall and submit yourselves to their judgment. If you do not present yourselves to the Guildmaster before thirty days have passed, I will initiate a search and a scouring for your three worthless hides, and the penalty for fleeing the justice of the Guild is indeed more stern than any measures I could take.'' He twirled his staff, showering everyone with sparks. ''Now get started on your journey, dear ladies—after you discard all your magical devices.''

Thorvor gasped and began to moan, but Nidbjorg silently tore the chains and symbols from her neck and waist and threw them to the ground at Gizur's feet. Solborg likewise divested herself of her tokens and assisted Thorvor none too gently with hers.

''Are you satisfied now?'' Solborg demanded when they were finished.

Gizur nodded. ''Except for that trifle in the corner of your pocket, you are ready to depart.''

Solborg hurled a small bundle of herbs at him, which he fended off with his staff. ''There it is, and may bad luck follow you!'' she snapped.

''Depart!'' commanded Gizur, gesturing significantly with his staff.

135

The three sisters hobbled away, muttering and glancing back with hateful expressions as long as they were in sight. They took a northerly course out of the valley, evidently knowing exactly how to find the Fire Wizards' Guildhall.

Ivarr looked thoughtfully at Gizur, who returned his gaze with a truculent expression. Ivarr said, "I was just thinking about what you told us last night. You don't really have any authority to send them to the Guild, do you?"

Gizur twirled his staff and appeared highly pleased with himself. "That," he said, "is the beauty of it." And he laughed triumphantly, winking at Skapti and pounding Finnvard on the back.

They moved Flosi into the cow stable, which the sisters had kept almost as clean as their own house, and they spent the rest of the day getting ready to leave in the morning. Flosi was recovered enough to be highly critical of the entire arrangement, resentful at having gone to sleep in a feather bed and awakened in the straw in a cow stable.

Ivarr watched warily, unable to believe entirely that the three alfkonur would allow themselves to be banished so easily.

"What have they got to come back for?" Gizur demanded as he was carefully destroying their tokens and herbs, handling them only with a pair of long-handled tongs. "I've destroyed most of their power, their house is burned, and if they try anything on us, we'll blast them. We have codes of honour in this realm which govern situations like this, and I promise you, Ivarr, we shall never see those three old hags again. They know when they've met their match."

Gizur remained in excellent spirit, inflicting everyone with his own praise and satisfaction. The mood was catching, and before long Egills and Finnvard were regaling each other with the most preposterous lies that either had yet uttered, always boasting that they had known all along that the sisters were alfkonur but they had found no cause for alarm in that minor inconvenience. Eilifir napped contentedly in the sun, resisting all efforts to question him about the night's activities.

136

In the morning Flosi's humour was at its most contentious, a sure sign that he was almost himself again. He complained about the food and lack of service and deplored sleeping in a barn, and worse yet, his feet were still in no condition to travel, despite the repeated anointings with all manner of salves and ointments from Gizur's satchel.

"Another day," Skapti groaned. "Gizur, I hate the idea of staying here much longer. Those alfkonur at Svinafell might be over here any moment and then where would we be?"

"In a reasonably good defensive position," Gizur said. "The walls of this barn are ten feet thick."

Ivarr shared Skapti's uneasy feelings. Routinely he cared for the livestock, wondering what would happen to them when they left. He milked the three cows and turned the lambs out of their pens to graze. The older sheep grazed high on the fell, but they were drifting further down each day with no one to chase them higher where the grass was thicker. There were also a few goats and various geese, ducks, and chickens.

"I hate to think of them starving when we leave," he said to Skapti. "I'll leave them their freedom and perhaps a few will survive."

"Not with all the trolls around here," Skapti said. "As soon as we're gone, they'll be down here tearing things apart and eating everything in sight. Or the alfkonur at Svinafell will come. Either way, I hope we're not here." He accompanied Ivarr on his rounds, worrying and making the gloomiest of prognostications.

Ivarr rounded the corner of the pig shed, and halted suddenly, in his tracks. There, almost within arm's length, stood a horse, snuffing hopefully at the bucket in his hand and swishing its long tail.

"Skapti!" he called softly, fearing the horse might disappear. "Look! Here's our means of leaving today!"

Skapti sidled around the corner warily. "Be careful, Ivarr, look at those great teeth. I've never liked horses much. They're an evil omen in magic, most of the time."

"Flosi can ride this horse until his feet are healed. That would be better than waiting here to be murdered by trolls or alfkonur." Ivarr rubbed the mare's neck and scratched her ears.

"It doesn't look like much of a horse to me," Skapti said. "Sort of old and broken down, like those horrid old women."

The horse waggled her ears and stamped a hoof, which caused Skapti to back away quickly. Ivarr fastened a bit of rope around her neck, saying, "Well, she might not look like much, but she'll carry Flosi. This is exactly the kind of horse I'd expect three old women to own—old and bony." He raised his eyes from the horse's knobby spine and exclaimed, "Skapti, look! There are two more! We might as well take them all, mightn't we? It would save us packing our own gear, at least. We could take turns riding, even."

Skapti eyed the other two horses, who stood at a suspicious distance, tossing their heads and lashing their tails. They were at least as old and knotty as the one Ivarr had captured, a bay much flecked with grey, and another rusty black whose face had turned almost white with age. The first black mare was almost handsome in comparison, very little greyed and sporting a white snip on her nose.

"Two black mares," Skapti said. "I don't like it at all, Ivarr. You must know about the Black Mare of Freyja, and how she can come charging down the fells and drive the animals mad with her neighing. Freyja is a great favourite with alfkonur, I'm told."

"That has nothing to do with these three old nags," Ivarr said. "I'm certain Freyja wouldn't have windgalls and oversized feet, however evil her intentions."

Skapti drew back as the other two came plodding up. The white-faced black mare nipped at the first one, who sprang out of the way and abandoned the last bit of grain in the bucket. With much flattening of ears and baring of teeth the three of them came up to Ivarr, making hungry nickers and looking at him with hopeful eyes.

When Ivarr led the horses into the dooryard of the barn,

Gizur leaped up with a grin of delight. Finnvard scrambled out of the way with frightened squeaks, and Flosi roared from the barn, "At last! We can go in style, as Alfar are intended. Other spies have horses, you know."

"Well, I don't want them," Skapti declared. "We've managed this far without horses, and we don't need them now. Think of all that meat to tempt trolls into attacking. From what I'm able to judge, they're far too old, besides."

"They look fit," Ivarr said, "and we're all tired of walking."

Skapti scowled as he watched Gizur inspecting their feet and legs.

"Old but sound" was the wizard's verdict. "I think they could take us easily to Jotunsgard. Finnvard, do you know what a saddle looks like? If you do, see if you can find any in the barns."

"Gizur, we're not taking these horses," Skapti said. "I have a bad feeling about them."

"Oh tush," said Gizur. "You're merely associating them with Nidbjorgsstead. You need to differentiate your impressions. These horses will be a great benefit to us. They carry all our packs, and one or two of us besides. Horses like this are extremely strong and willing to work, and their hooves are like iron. We can leave as soon as we get packed."

Flosi cheered from the stable and came limping out in fleece slippers to supervise everyone else as they prepared for departure. Even Finnvard was heartily in favour of taking the horses, although he was petrified of them and ran for safety at every snort or stamp of a hoof.

The horses stood as quietly as three large tables while Gizur, Egills, Ivarr, and Finnvard scrambled around, cinching saddles and tying their packs on and quarreling good-naturedly with Flosi, who sat on the wall supervising every knot and buckle. Skapti assisted grudgingly, wearing a morose and troubled expression. Flosi was boosted onto the back of the snip-nosed mare, who seemed the best choice as a saddlehorse, and all but two of their packs were fastened

139

onto the brown mare. The white-faced mare carried two packs, leaving space for a rider.

"We'll draw straws to see who rides," said Gizur. "We'll switch at midday so everyone will get a chance at riding for half a day."

Skapti looked even more unhappy. "Gizur, I want to talk to you. I simply don't feel safe taking the alfkonurs' horses. I don't trust them."

"A plague on what you think," Flosi grunted.

"It's better than staying here," Gizur said. "We can always turn them loose in a day or two if we don't like them." He held out the straws in his fist. "Now let's get this over with so we can get going."

Finnvard and Skapti drew out the shortest straws. Skapti only scowled and flung away his straw. "Nobody could ever get me to trust my neck to one of those beasts," he announced.

Eilifir, who hadn't said a word all day as he packed and provisioned, looked up at the sun and winked, and at Skapti with an amused expression. "Don't you like horses, Skapti?" he asked.

"No, and especially these three. They look sly," Skapti declared.

"Then I'll ride and be glad of it," Finnvard said, timidly patting the mare's white nose; she swished her tail amiably. They shoved him into the saddle and Gizur strode away without glancing back. From the rim of the fell he offered an irate shout to hasten them, waiting until the plodding train had caught up, and then went striding ahead again at a great rate.

Ivarr also exulted in the free wind and patches of sunshine. He felt as if he were hiking across the bald top of the world. Spring was foremost that day in the battle between sunshine and cloud, although at moments they were engulfed in brief flurries of snow or whipped by cold and whistling winds. They traveled along the rocky shoulders of fells to avoid the meadows and lowlands, which were extremely boggy. Melting snowdrifts offered little

140

resistance to their progress; if anyone's boots threatened to become mired, all one needed to do was to seize a horse's tail for a quick rescue.

In the evenings beside the fire, Gizur marked their progress on the map and gloated. He showed the others Dainn's markings on the map and how they were speedily drawing closer to Jotunsgard. Ahead of them waited the formidable barriers of the Thriningrstrom and the Thriningrfells. Ivarr stared curiously at the vast stretch of unknown land that was Jotunsgard. The last known venturer into that realm had been Elidagrimr, and he had not lived to return.

Nidbjorgsstead was many days behind, and they were beginning to forget the soft beds and fine food. Skapti said little about the horses, although he still refused to ride one.

"Have you noticed—" began Eilifir one evening beside the fire, after supper. Ivarr and Skapti looked at him in astonishment. It had been five days since anyone had heard Eilifir say a word, and five days ago he had asked for the salt, which was the first time he had spoken since Nidbjorgsstead. He nodded to them affably every day, but he didn't speak. Now that he had broken his silence, he was taking his time before continuing, as if reconsidering his hasty speech.

"I believe," he said at last, "we are being followed and watched very closely. A little too closely, I would say." He nodded westward, pointing out a small pinpoint of light gleaming in the shadows of a fell. Further southward there was another.

"I had thought it might be random fires made by trolls," went on Eilifir, "but for three successive nights they have appeared like beacons, as if single spies are tracking us and setting out lights to guide the main party toward us. It is not a good sign."

Ivarr asked, "Does Gizur know about the lights?"

Eilifir did not reply immediately. "A wizard keeps counsel with no one but himself."

"A good way to hide your mistakes," Skapti growled. "Drat and blast that Lorimer and his dwarves for such miserable persistence. I wager this time they'll keep their distance, though. They've seen that they can't kill us in a frontal attack. Now I expect they'll attack us by stealth, hoping to kill us all as we sleep.''

"We'll post a double guard," Ivarr said. "We'd better smother that fire; I'm sure they can see it much better than we can see theirs."

"Lorimer hasn't tried anything subtle yet," Eilifir said. "He has been too certain that he could overrun us without the least trouble. I would watch for clever tricks before I would worry about an attack."

Skapti shook his head stubbornly. "We'll prepare anyway, and if he tries something tricky, we'll be all the more ready for it."

"What do you think he'll do, Eilifir?" Ivarr asked.

"If I knew that," Eilifir said, "I'd be a better wizard than he is. But I strongly advise you to stay close to Gizur, whose power will protect you. Even Skapti or possibly myself would be better than nothing."

"Then you think he's after Ivarr," Skapti said. "We've known that from the start, Eilifir. If you've got any ideas or suspicions, you ought to share them with us so we can be prepared."

But Eilifir only wrapped himself in his cloak, as if his spate of words had quite exhausted him.

CHAPTER TWELVE

For the next several days, Ivarr could scarcely turn around without stepping on or running into Skapti, who had appointed himself the role of Ivarr's watchdog. Skapti's worried expression and perennial ear-pulling served to make Ivarr more uneasy than ever. It was not the first time Ivarr had dourly reflected what an unreasonable lot elves and wizards were.

He didn't think about it long, however; it was his turn to ride that morning and it was such a pleasant day that he soon forgot his worries and left Skapti protesting behind. He cantered ahead on the snip-nosed mare, who was the only one of the three who would consent to run. Before long they were further ahead than they should have been, so Ivarr stopped on a ridge to watch his friends toiling along below. They seemed to be moving so slowly, and the sun beat down on his back with such welcome warmth that Ivarr began to feel sleepy. Reclining on the mare's broad back, he shut his eyes for a moment, imagining how pleasant it would be to take a nap right there in the sun.

The next thing he knew, he was falling, and old Snip was lumbering away with snorts of alarm, elevating her heels from time to time and lashing her long tail in disapproval.

Ivarr leaped up to yell, "Whoa!" But the shout died with a faint croak of disbelief. Facing him, in a slight hollow, was a dark horse and a shrouded rider bearing a staff. A fleshless finger beckoned at him to approach, reinforced by a menacing gesture with the staff. Ivarr wanted to rub his eyes. It couldn't be Lorimer, not in bright daylight.

"Your eyes are not deceiving you," Lorimer's voice said. "And my eye has followed you for a long time as I waited for this opportunity."

Ivarr drew his knife in one hand and his sword in the other. "See if you think you can do anything about it, Lorimer."

Lorimer sighed impatiently. "If I wanted to kill you, I could dispatch you instantly in any number of interesting and painful ways, but we need you alive—for the moment, anyway. A dead carcass won't be able to wrest that sword from Elidagrimr."

"It won't do you any good to covet Glimr," Ivarr said. "The last ones to do so came out very much the worse for their efforts." He darted an uneasy glance down into the valley below to look for Gizur. To his consternation, his friends were nowhere in sight.

Lorimer chuckled dryly. "If talk made a man, you'd be the size of a giant, but the truth is, you're in a very bad situation. I've been following and waiting for exactly such a moment as this."

Grus cackled from inside Lorimer's pocket. "Won't it be a pleasure to have your company! Won't it be delightful inducing you to show us where Elidagrimr's barrow lies! Such torments will be a joy to inflict."

"I'll die fighting before I'll ever allow myself to fall under your thrall," Ivarr declared, making a brave show with his sword.

Lorimer shook his head ponderously. Nothing of his face showed except for his eyes, which glared balefully at Ivarr as he turned his horse toward his quarry and began to approach.

"All I need to do is shout, and Gizur will hear," Ivarr warned.

"Shout then, by all means," Grus said. "I'd like to hear you."

144

Lorimer raised his staff threateningly. A cloud had passed before the sun, blotting much of its light. "Hold your peace or I'll see to it you never make a sound again. Now throw down those ridiculous weapons. I assure you that I've far more power in my least finger than you'll ever possess in all your body. If, by some miraculous accident, you were able to kill me, I would not take long to restore myself with another body and my power would only be the greater for the experience. Ha, I see that startles you. What is the point in being a necromancer if one doesn't make plans to live a great many times?"

Ivarr stepped back, chilled with horror. "Then you're nothing more than a draugar!" He flourished his sword and knife in readiness.

Lorimer's horse paced forward without flinching. Lorimer raised his staff and began muttering the words of a formula. Ivarr abandoned his bold stance and dived behind a rock. Grus laughed in his muffled voice and shrieked, "It won't do any good to hide. He dragged me right out of my own grave and put life back into me. But I think he's going to take you to a barrow and remove the life from you, my friend."

Ivarr scuttled around another large rock, suddenly seeing his way clear to escape. Before him lay a rocky jumble where no horse would consent to risk his legs. Ivarr plunged into it, leaping over boulders and sliding down the faces of others. Exulting in his own ingenuity, he tumbled over a small ledge and dropped into a clearing among the stones—almost directly at the feet of Lorimer, who stood patiently waiting. With a swift movement, Lorimer bared a sword only inches from Ivarr's wildly pounding heart.

"It's senseless to try to escape from me," Lorimer said. "All routes of flight lead directly back to me, and that would be a good thing to get into your troublesome young skull. I expect we shall be travelling together for a considerable distance and I know you'll always be thinking of getting away. It would be more pleasant for us all if you are convinced of the futility of escaping before we even start."

"The futility lies in beginning," Ivarr said, "because I won't show you where that sword is."

"Come, it would be much simpler for everyone," Grus interrupted. "Much simpler for Svartarr, who would be quickly destroyed by his own armies. We could have it all resolved by the autumn Doom, when your friends are supposed to present their weregild."

"I won't do it," Ivarr said, his voice choking. His damp clothing made him shiver in the cold wind, which was spitting a few snowflakes.

Lorimer glowered at him with hatred. "I daresay you won't, either. But it is well within my power to seize someone who will be glad to tell me where the barrow of Elidagrimr lies—someone whose only concern will be to save his own dear skin."

At that moment a distant voice called Ivarr's name. Ivarr's eyes widened in swift comprehension. "Your quarrel is not with them," he said, "it's with me. It would be a nithling's deed to force one of them to tell you."

Lorimer pointed with his sword tip. "Sit down against that rock and be silent. It will take them an hour to work their way back in this direction. They travelled on for quite a distance before they missed you."

Grus was making revolting sniggering sounds within his pocket. "I wonder which one we shall catch. That fat fellow in the yellow trousers would be the most amusing."

"Quiet, carrion, and listen to what I shall tell you," Lorimer said. "I am going to the top of the ridge to watch for Gizur and his nithlings. You shall stay here and guard the Scipling. If he so much as moves to run away, you will shout for me."

He placed Grus on a rock, facing Ivarr and looking more shrivelled and grisly than ever in the wan daylight. Grus bared his yellow teeth in an unwholesome grin and fastened his eyes upon Ivarr. "I won't take my eyes off him," he declared. "If he tries to run away, I'll chase him for all I'm worth."

"Which isn't much," Lorimer grunted, giving him a

parting thump on the crown.

Ivarr leaned against the cold rock and felt sick with loathing for himself and his own stupidity. Eilifir had warned him not to get so far away from power and protection, but that was exactly what he had done.

"You mustn't feel too bad," Grus said, as if reading his thoughts. "Lorimer always gets what he wants. It would be far easier just to hand it over to him without all this flap; he's going to get it anyway. Take myself for an example. He always coveted my powers and hated me because I wouldn't allow him to use me, but he got around all that by killing me and using his powers of necromancy to force me to talk. But then again, I always liked to talk and got into most of my trouble because of it. You'd feel much better if only you'd start talking about almost anything, not the location of the barrow specifically, although that would save us the trouble of catching and torturing one of your friends—"

"Why don't you just shut up?" Ivarr said. "I'd like to give you a good toss as far as I could throw you."

"I'd yell first," Grus said. "You wouldn't have time even to get your feet under you and I'd yell my head off." He chattered on, but Ivarr didn't listen. He was too sunken in despair to have the slightest interest in Grus' family history of several centuries ago.

The day became gloomier and colder. Ivarr was glad for Birna's cloak and hood, which turned the wind and shed the raindrops as he waited. Occasionally he heard shouts, sometimes distant, but all too frequently closer and closer to his position. "It won't be much longer now," Grus said with a chuckle.

The shouts came closer. Ivarr knew that the last thing he wanted to do was yell and draw them straight into Lorimer's trap. He rested his head on his forearms and hoped they would not find him.

"Ivarr!" The shout was almost in his ear. He looked up and saw a huge, lumbering, flapping apparition bearing down upon him. It was Egills and Finnvard riding double on one of the horses with a great deal of jouncing and arm

147

waving, now that they had discovered him. They shouted and cursed at him joyously until the horse suddenly got a whiff of Grus. It was the old white-faced mare, a stiff dignified horse, but she suddenly stood on her back legs with a squeal of terror and sat down upon her tail, which dislodged her riders in a swearing heap. She then turned and galloped away, whinnying for her friends.

Lorimer appeared at Ivarr's side as soon as Finnvard and Egills untangled themselves, blaming each other and blaming Ivarr for their accident.

"It was the horse's fault," Grus said helpfully.

"Who said that?" Egills demanded, peering around, right over Grus.

"You dolts!" Ivarr said, "You've walked right into a trap."

Lorimer glided forward. "And your Scipling was the bait. You may cast your weapons over there."

Egills started dreadfully, and got another shock when Grus growled and snapped at his foot. "By the beard and hammer of Thor!" he gasped. "It's Lorimer!"

Finnvard only stared frozenly, as if he had fainted on his feet.

Lorimer strode up to him and glared into his face, demanding in a menacing tone, "If you want to live, you'll reveal the secret of Elidagrimr's barrow at once, or I'll release all the cold and evil spells I have prepared in anticipation of this day when we would meet, face to face. It is senseless to resist; I have all the powers of Hel's cold kingdom of the dead at my command."

"I'd recognize those yellow trousers anywhere," Grus added with gruesome gusto.

Finnvard swayed, his eyes wide and staring. He might have toppled if Egills hadn't put out a hand to steady him. Lorimer stepped closer, his baleful eyes glaring into Finnvard's glazed ones. Seizing Finnvard by the collar, he gave him a shake. "Speak, you fool, or I'll render you out for boot grease! Where is Elidagrimr's barrow?"

Finnvard responded with faint croaking sounds and

Lorimer gave him another encouraging shake, followed by a stinging slap.

"Say now, you don't need to hurt him," Egills said angrily.

Lorimer retorted, "I'll see your bones gnawed by rats in the lowest dungeons of Hel's nethermost regions. Unless, of course, you want to spare your friend agonies far more terrifying, and tell me where the barrow lies."

"I don't know," Egills said. "You'll have to ask Gizur, but I don't expect he'll oblige you with the answer."

"But that one in the yellow pants will," Grus said.

Lorimer gave Finnvard another shaking. "Perhaps I shall have to let my dwarves persuade him to speak. A pity it's not dark yet, isn't it?" He darted a venomous glance at Ivarr. "I wonder if a hero would consent to having his friends tormented by dwarves or perhaps killed, when he could save them by answering one small question"

Before Ivarr could answer, Egills stoutly declared, "He wouldn't tell if you were to cut us into a thousand pieces and feed them to the trolls. He's not afraid of you in the least way." He nearly stepped on Grus again and was rewarded with a fierce roar from underfoot.

Lorimer released Finnvard abruptly. "Is that so? Then perhaps we could arrange to put him to the test." He drew his sword and flashed it before Finnvard's staring eyes, snipping off a few hairs just below his nose.

"We could begin with his ears," Grus said.

Finnvard began to splutter and stammer, "Th—the—"

"Shut up, you fool!" Egills cried.

Grus growled, "It's not you who's going to be carved up, although it ought to be. Let him speak if he wants to."

Lorimer's sword snipped off a larger lock of beard, and Finnvard flinched. He was inordinately proud of his beard. "The—the—mm—" he gasped.

Suddenly Grus exclaimed, "Someone's coming, Lorimer. I feel a power, and I suspect it's Gizur. You wouldn't forget and leave me to his tender mercies, I hope?"

Lorimer hastily stuffed the troll's head into his pocket,

darting uneasy glances around. He gave Finnvard another shake, holding his sword before his eyes and snarling, "This is your last chance before I skewer your gizzard on this sword. Quick now, tell me and you'll come to no harm. Otherwise, all Gizur will find is a corpse. Or a pair of them," he added to Egills, who was still propping Finnvard up on his feet.

Finnvard's knees began to lose their rigidity. They quivered as Lorimer administered another severe shaking.

"Th—the ma—" he stammered, swaying.

"Don't say it, you fool! Gizur's coming! I see him!" Egills screeched, shaking Finnvard from his side.

Lorimer hissed furiously and took a swipe at Egills with his sword. Egills scurried for cover, and Finnvard tottered.

"Halloo! Is that you, Egills?" Gizur called, appearing out of a fold in the fell and riding forward on the brown mare with Skapti, Flosi, and Eilifir close behind.

Lorimer whirled to glare at him an instant, then pounced upon Finnvard as he finally toppled, bearing him to the ground. "Tell me this instant where that sword is or you will die!" he roared.

Finnvard's eyes rolled upward in terror. He made some gasping sounds, and suddenly Lorimer's hands were empty. He leaped away as a puff of grey smoke enveloped him.

"The escape spell!" he exclaimed, looking totally astonished for an instant.

Ivarr seized the opportunity to leap up and fling himself on Lorimer with a warning yell to Gizur. Lorimer promptly hurled Ivarr aside like a stuffed toy and grappled with him for possession of his staff, with Grus and Egills shrieking nonsense. With his supernatural strength, Lorimer swept Ivarr off his feet and tore the staff from his hands, staggering back and uttering the words of a spell. Before he could finish it, a sizzling zigzag of flame opened his sleeve from wrist to shoulder and jolted the staff from his grasp.

Gizur threw himself off his horse, hurling another bolt as he did so, which roared over Lorimer's head and exploded in a fireball of sparks against a boulder. Ivarr hugged the

150

ground, feeling an icebolt dart overhead with a whispery puff of frigid air.

Then Lorimer fled, whisking onto his waiting horse and spurring it away across the fell. Gizur sent one more bolt after him, and he vanished with a last defiant gesture.

"Finnvard! Where are you?" Egills called fearfully. "Finnvard, he's gone now, stop hiding from us. Did you tell him about the Maze? Finnvard, you did use the escape spell, didn't you? Finnvard?"

"Escape spell!" Gizur shook his head. "We'll never get him back."

"Don't say that!" Egills exclaimed. "Finnvard, if you can hear me, you'd better answer. You're giving me a terrible fright. Don't be malicious now."

The only answer was a peculiar moan.

"He sounds sick," Skapti said, searching around among the boulders. Suddenly he shouted, "I found him—I think! Look, look, everybody! It's Finnvard's fylgja!"

There was no portly Finnvard with yellow trousers and curling beard; it was a huge orange striped tomcat, blinking his green eyes in languid disapproval. He was an enormous cat with elegant whiskers, fastidiously white paws, and all the hauteur of generations of aristocracy.

Egills wheezed and cackled and slapped his knee. "Finnvard must have been terribly frightened at being shaken and threatened by Lorimer. It scared him right into his fylgja. But who would have thought—a cat—Finnvard—" He couldn't continue. He had to laugh, making noises like an old boat in a high wind.

Flosi ground his teeth in a paroxysm of envy. "Finnvard! What a waste! Look at him! He'd be more at home on a hearthstone with a belly full of cream than travelling to Jotunsgard looking for a sword!"

The cat favoured Flosi with a disdainful glare. He rose suddenly to his toes, stretching his back into a high arch, and showed all of his teeth and half his gullet in a wide yawn. He stretched each leg separately and spread out his claws, which were uncommonly large.

151

"Can he understand us?" Skapti asked. "I've never spoken with a cat before. Finnvard, can you nod your head or something to show you understand? That is you, isn't it, Finnvard?"

The cat turned his back and began switching his tail. Skapti bent over self-consciously to speak to the cat on his own level. "Finnvard, a cat is a fine fylgja form, but I hope you'll be more cooperative than some cats I've encountered. You'll be a great help, if you don't get distracted chasing birds and mice, that is. Can you change yourself back, Finnvard?"

The cat looked insulted. Egills cackled appreciatively. Gizur approached him gently and sat down on his heels. He scratched behind the cat's grizzled ears, which elicited a loud rumbling purr.

"There now, what an exceptionally clever cat you are, Finnvard," Gizur said. "You fellows must be careful about insulting his intelligence. When he's ready to change shapes he'll do it, so we can get going again, won't you, Finnvard?"

Finnvard groomed his fur in the most deliberate manner possible, ignoring everyone until he was finished. Then with stately demeanour, he advanced to Gizur and rubbed his ankles, purring his approval. Finally he stalked away, announcing his progress through the rocks and underbrush at intervals with a throaty, mournful yowl.

"I'll bet we never see him again," Flosi said, shaking his head. "Old Finnvard as a cat! I really can't feature his fylgja as anything else, now. A big, fat, stodgy old tomcat." He lost his pinched expression and began to grin. In a moment he and Egills were hooting and sniggering together like old thieves.

Skapti glared at them. "It's not at all funny, you numskulls. What if he can't change himself back?"

Egills grinned and said, "We may have lost a cook, but we've gained a cat."

Flosi doubled up and began giggling again, so Skapti turned his back in disgust, only to find Gizur trying to smother a grin.

152

"This will be good for Finnvard," Gizur said. "He has discovered the untapped depths of his instincts for self-preservation. I think he's been jolted into the realization of his power at last."

"I just hope it happened before he told Lorimer where we were going," Ivarr said.

It was an hour later when Finnvard, in his normal form, rejoined them. He was looking extremely smug; he treated their questions with dignified silence, refusing to discuss his new-found power.

At length Gizur forgave Ivarr, and Eilifir eventually broke his chilly silence. Ivarr kept close to the others, which satisfied Skapti. Of Lorimer and the dwarves they saw nothing except distant signal lights at night, as if they were following at a discreet distance and biding their time.

Ivarr studied Gizur's maps at every opportunity. They were drawing closer to the Thriningrfells and the great river that barred the way to Jotunsgard. The terrain was becoming more mountainous and difficult. Two days later, after the morning mist lifted, Gizur pointed and said, "At last— the Thriningrfells."

The far blue peaks rose sharply from a rumpled bed of foothills. From thousands of glaciers and snowfields the waters ran down and swelled into the Thriningrstrom, which eventually found its way into the Drangarstrom. Ivarr realized they were beginning to approach the goal of their journey, the dragon cave and the gold.

CHAPTER THIRTEEN

After an arduous crossing of the Thriningrfells and the Thriningrstrom, the travellers found smoother terrain, a series of high misty green fells, emerald valleys surrounded by black cliffs of lava, and cold rushing rivers studded with moss-covered stones. It reminded Ivarr so much of home that he continually searched the horizons for signs of the sea, sniffing the breezes eagerly for its ancient fishy smell.

When they stopped for the night, Gizur gleefully pointed out the red dot which Dainn had made on his map. It was only a few inches away on the parchment, across two large fells and a host of small fells and streamlets. "And I've got an important announcement to make," he said, as they were sitting around the fire drinking quarts of hot tea against the chill of the night. "Skapti will certainly be pleased, but I doubt if the rest of you will like it. I've decided to slaughter the horses tomorrow."

Skapti merely nodded his head, but Flosi and Finnvard were hotly indignant. "Slaughter them!" Flosi exclaimed. "What's the sense in that? There's not much meat on any of them that would be fit to eat!"

"It would be better than nothing, which is what we're getting down to," Gizur said. "If we don't kill them, they'll follow us anyway, begging for the grain which ran out yesterday, and attracting trolls. It would be a miserable fate for them to be abandoned here, especially with winter coming on. But chiefly, we need the meat."

"But they've carried us so far," Finnvard said. "Killing them seems like a shabby trick, Gizur. We can keep them at least until we get nearer some habitations of some sort, can't we?"

Gizur began sharpening his knife energetically. "No, Finnvard, we haven't any more grain for them and before long they'll be walking skeletons if we keep working them at this rate. It's no kindness you'd be doing them, nor us either, since we're nearly out of food."

"It's one of the risks of being a horse," Egills said gloomily. "The people you know and serve with all your heart may get hungry one day and decide to eat you. I'm certainly glad I'm not a horse."

"Well, Ivarr," Gizur turned on him, "I suppose you're angry too, since you found the horses and wanted them first."

"No; you're the wizard," Ivarr replied. "You should know best."

"Listen to him," scoffed Flosi. "Always flattering Gizur and agreeing with him. Ivarr, you'll never be a hero as long as you keep agreeing with everyone. Sometimes I wonder how we're ever going to make this business work, with a Scipling for a hero. And now they've decided to eat our horses rather than ride them to success and glory. Next we'll be eating our boots."

Ivarr stood up and peered around at the dark closing around their small fire. It was his turn to picket the horses to graze, and he felt reluctant to leave the warmth and light of the fire to stumble into the darkness and pound the stakes into the flinty earth.

The moon was a faint silver wedge tossing around with fleets of scudding black clouds. Ivarr dragged the stakes and ropes after him toward the brushy hollow where the horses had been tied earlier with short ropes. By the dim moonlight he could discern their dark shadows against the backdrop of bushes. Again he had the uneasy feeling they were watching him. The moon went behind a cloud and he could see nothing. He groped through the dark, barking his shins on

155

rocks and tearing his hands on stickery bushes. A cold prickly feeling began in the vicinity of his spine and bristled the hair on the back of his neck. He stood motionless until the moon sailed unconcernedly from its haven behind the clouds and again cast its uncertain light below.

Ivarr could no longer see the horses. He strained his eyes and listened for the flutter of a nostril or the swish of a long tail. Instead, he heard a soft cough behind him. Acutely conscious of his unprotected back, he whirled around.

They stood there, the three sisters, smiling and nodding to him as if to an old friend. "There you are at last," Nidbjorg said calmly. "We had wondered when we would again have the privilege of your company. Now we shall be together for a long pleasant visit as we journey, so we can all become fast friends, although we last parted in something less than true amicability. I assure you, our last parting still grieves me deeply, and I hope our next and final parting will be a more joyous occasion."

Ivarr recovered from his shock. "What are you doing here? Gizur sent you to the Guild for judgment. And what have you done with the horses? If you wish to avoid another drubbing, you can take those old nags and get yourselves out of here without Gizur seeing you."

"Nags, indeed!" Solborg said. "You were about to do them a very evil turn, weren't you? After serving you so long and so well, you'd simply kill the poor creatures, would you? What a fool you are not to listen to the advice of old Skapti. He knew all along there was something peculiar about those dear old nags, travelling and listening to your every word as they went. Haven't you figured it out yet, you dolt?"

"We were the old mares," Thorvor said rather proudly. "I've never heard of alfkonur maintaining a spell for so long and so well. We thoroughly deceived them, sisters."

Ivarr dropped the picket ropes and started to run back toward the fire, which looked very small and distant. Nidbjorg gave a shout, and Ivarr gasped in the sudden burst of numbing cold that overtook him like a great wave. His senseless feet caused him to stumble and fall, so he rolled up

156

in a shivering ball, his fingers too numb to close on the hilt of a weapon. Dimly he was aware of the witches approaching him and talking, but their voices were strangely garbled. Some vague hope lingered that if he lay perfectly still they would not find him, like a half-frozen, frightened rabbit cornered among the rocks. He heard the chanted words of another spell, then his consciousness faded away.

He awakened gradually to the familiar jogging of a leisurely trotting horse. Particle by particle, he came fully awake to his situation, which was anything but comfortable. He was sprawled along the shaggy neck of a horse, with his hands tied underneath its neck and his feet securely lashed together under its belly. Without raising his head, he ventured a glance around and spied Nidbjorg and Thorvor walking behind the horse, hurrying along spryly with their walking staffs. The morning was well advanced, and Ivarr's belly felt even more hollow when Thorvor hauled a large sausage out of her pouch.

"Solborg, stop a moment. I think he's waking up now," called Nidbjorg. "Perhaps a dash of cold water would help."

The horse halted abruptly and heaved a complaining sigh, lashing her tail in irritation. Ivarr turned his head and retorted, "I've been awake for some time now, so you can save your cold water. I would like something to eat, however, and then you had better explain what you're doing by kidnapping me from my friends."

"But of course," Nidbjorg said. "We have no intention of making you suffer. Sister, undo our friend's ropes and then share some of that sausage with him. It's very tasty—one I made myself last fall. I hope our meat and grain and all the other things you helped yourselves to have met with your approval."

Ivarr did not answer. Thorvor untied the ropes and obligingly cut off a generous portion of sausage. Ivarr slid off the horse warily, watching for the familiar kick old Snip liked to administer to her unwary rider's knee. He also checked to make certain his sword and knife were both gone, as he rightly suspected. With a sigh he sat down on a rock to eat the

157

sausage and look around him at the unfamiliar landscape.

"And what about me?" demanded Solborg's voice. Coming from the horse, it was enough to raise Ivarr's gooseflesh. "Why do I always get appointed beast of burden? I suppose you'll say I have to eat grass for breakfast."

"Certainly," Nidbjorg said sweetly. "What else would a horse eat? Come now, be patient for just a little while longer and you'll be rewarded. You know you're the youngest and strongest. Thorvor and I haven't many shape-shiftings left in us, I fear. We need someone to carry our provisions, scanty as they may be. Those wretched Alfar have eaten half a year's food in this short a time."

Ivarr looked at Solborg and shuddered. "Mares of Freyja! No wonder Skapti was so determined against you. We should have listened to him."

"Indeed you should have," Thorvor said. "Something about Gizur didn't ring quite true for a Guild wizard. For that reason we decided to forgo our journey to the Guildhall. It would have been rather pointless, considering he's no Guild wizard himself, and thus lacks the authority to send captives for judgment." She simpered at him smugly.

Ivarr munched desolately on the stale hardtack. "He still managed to escape from your spell, though. He'll blast you to cinders when he catches up with us." The threat sounded hollow even to his own ears. He sighed. "I suppose you want me to take you to Elidagrimr's barrow. I hope you're not expecting me to be very helpful."

"Still refuses to be sensible," Nidbjorg mused, shaking her head. "I'd hoped you'd changed your mind. I truly regret having to do what I must, but the alfkonur of Svartarrsrike must not allow a sword of power to fall into Lorimer's hands."

"What do you mean?" Ivarr demanded. "It belongs to me and I have no intention of letting Lorimer have it."

"Tush. You have no means of protecting it from him except one red-bearded wizard of questionable repute and five of the most inept and useless Alfar Elbegast has ever dumped into the spy league. It is merely a question of who

158

can seize you and your sword to use for their own designs.''

"Well, I will not be used," Ivarr said.

Nidbjorg only smiled a chilling smile. "You will not have any choice, any more than Grus has in Lorimer's pocket. You are in our pocket in much the same way, young Scipling."

Solborg swung her long face around to stare at Ivarr in displeasure. "I'd be glad to persuade the young moron to cooperate," she said. "I wager I could discover some means of subtle torture that would convince him that black was white and down was up, I could—"

"Never mind, Solborg," Nidbjorg said sharply. "Let's get going now if everyone is through eating. Now that it's daylight, I expect to cover some distance. Solborg, you shall carry us and the Scipling shall walk ahead where we can watch him." Her tone held a note of warning which was unmistakable.

Ivarr spent the rest of the day doing his best to keep ahead of Solborg, who nipped him sharply at every opportunity. He peered over his shoulder frequently, affecting a casual air, hoping to see some sign that Gizur was following. He never saw the least indication of a rescue attempt. Nevertheless, he took every opportunity to leave footprints in soft earth beside the streams they crossed and, whenever he could, he broke off twigs and branches.

"Very commendable," Solborg said, after half a day of these sly depredations. "You've nearly succeded in making it look as if an army had passed this way. Anyone could follow you except those dunderpates you're hoping to signal. A wizard worth his salt could track you without the slightest trace of a clue, so why don't you just give it up? It gives me quite a pain to see such pathetic efforts going to waste."

Ivarr glared at their backtrail, wondering where Gizur could be. He had expected to be overtaken almost at any moment, yet the day had passed somehow and he was still a prisoner.

At sundown they stopped in a protected pocket near the

summit of a large fell, commanding a good view of the country they had traversed that day. Thorvor sat down and began to knit, but her eyes were busy below, watching for signs of Gizur and Skapti. Nidbjorg faced the south, consulting some maps.

"We should be meeting some fire jotuns by the time we get on the other side of these fells," she said complacently. "I expect we shall be at the barrow within the week, if all goes well."

"I doubt it will," Ivarr said. "Lorimer was following us very closely, and when he discovers your shabby little trick, he's going to—"

"Hush! Don't mention his name in my hearing," Nidbjorg snarled, "or you'll be sorry in a thousand ways. You think we're just three creaky old women with bags of nasty little tricks for our own amusement, but let me tell you, young fellow, this is a very deadly game you've got yourself into. I wouldn't hesitate to wring your neck like a chicken's at a moment's notice if I thought it would further our cause."

She suddenly reminded Ivarr of an evil old serpent with her dry saggy skin and glittering eyes half-hid in papery folds. He blinked and looked away from her piercing, mesmerizing gaze. For the first time, it occurred to him that he was encountering a new sort of evil power, different from Lorimer's, and somehow more mysterious and threatening.

Ivarr stretched out and rested his aching head on a stone. Plans for escape floated through his mind, and Thorvor and Nidbjorg discussed knitting patterns. Solborg stood contemplating some inner visions of murder and bloodshed of her own, pleasurably waggling her ears and sighing.

Nidbjorg resumed their journey sometime in the middle of the night, snapping and snarling at everyone's heels with such intensity that Ivarr suspected that Gizur must be near. He tripped and stumbled along in the dark, hoping to delay them. He was also nearly blind and still tired, which added legitimacy to some of his tactics. For a while he held on to Solborg's tail, and she gladly led him into pitfalls and sharp

160

rocks and into cold little streamlets unawares, until he finally sat down and refused to go any further until he could see. After a lengthy discussion liberally sprinkled with threats, the sisters gave in and Thorvor grumblingly wove the spell to change herself to her fylgja form so Ivarr could ride instead of risking his neck in the dark.''

''This is madness,'' Ivarr grumbled as they jogged along, with him clinging to his uncomfortable perch on Thorvor's bony spine. ''We're all liable to break our necks. Why can't we wait and travel by day?''

Nidbjorg only showed her teeth at him very unappreciatively; and so the night proceeded. Ivarr managed to doze at intervals, which was almost more unpleasant than fighting to stay awake, since he invariably awakened as he was half-sliding off the horse's back, and that was a nerve-wracking way to wake up.

Dawn finally discovered them picking their way up the rough shoulder of a fell with a raw wind snapping at them. Ivarr was grateful for Birna's black cloak, which turned the wind and mist as a duck's feathers shed water. Nidbjorg's nose, he was glad to note, looked positively brittle with blue-ness. At the summit of the fell, the wind fell upon them full force, even mustering up a hail of hard snow pellets to pepper at them. Nidbjorg was not daunted, although the two horses sighed and groaned frequently and blinked their snowy lashes miserably.

The path descended into a sheltered valley away from the wind. The peaceful greenness lifted everyone's spirits to the extent that Nidbjorg called a halt to rest and eat. Ivarr would have liked half a day to sleep in the sunshine, but Nidbjorg was prodding him along too soon, once more on foot so Thorvor could ride the horse and rest herself. Ivarr wanted to know when he could rest himself, but his only answer was a threatening snap from Solborg's teeth. In an excess of good will, Nidbjorg admitted around midday that they would stop for the night in a house of refuge which lay in their way.

It was near sunset when they sighted their destination. Ivarr saw no smoke issuing from the chimney, nor was there a single sign of life about the place. As they drew nearer, he could see it was a cheerless ruin with a sunken roof and rotting doorposts. Dismayed, he gave up his fond notions of a warm fire and a respectable meal. At their approach, a family of owls flapped away with indignant hoots and hisses, as if they had not been disturbed in many a year. Ivarr looked after them eagerly, but they were large bulky grey owls, in no way similar to the small white owl he so hoped to see.

"This is a wretched place," he growled, profoundly depressed and irritated. "Only an alfkonur would think of stopping here. No roof, no firewood, and nothing at all to eat. At least the Alfar have a sense of comfort and propriety, incompetent as they may seem." He did his growling under his breath while everyone was busy setting up the miserable camp. Nidbjorg was a little deaf and the others weren't listening, so he felt free to add a few insulting epithets. Solborg had thrown off her fylgja form and was making undisguisedly nasty remarks about being abused because she was the youngest sister.

Ivarr managed to scratch together a pile of wood torn mostly from the crumbling turf walls where timbers had been used for framing. At least, he had a small fire, and he curled up in his cloak beside the coals with a weary sigh. The sisters amused themselves with reminiscences.

The reminiscences passed into a recount of various guests they had hagridden to death or otherwise dispatched, until Ivarr was too angered to think of sleep. Finally he sat up and glared. "You hideous old monsters! With a thousand murders on your hands, if you think I'll do the least thing to help you, you're mistaken. The instant I get my hands on that sword, the first thing I shall do is whack you all into pieces!"

Thorvor looked mildly alarmed, but her sisters exchanged a derisive snort. Nidbjorg muffled herself in her shawl and growled, "Do you really suppose we haven't thought of that? We have spells to guarantee your cooperation. Have you seen old Grus, the troll's head Lorimer consults for

162

advice? There are mysterious and amazing processes for rendering the dead sensible and seizing their powers and intelligence, instead of letting them rot away beneath the earth. The art of necromancy is a wonderful one, ordained to only a few. I am practicing to be one of those few, and I believe I could control you more easily as a draug—unless you change your mind and decide to be more cooperative.''

She stared at Ivarr as she talked, and he cringed from the venom in her tone. He hated looking at her, but something in her eyes held him and made him feel helpless and frightened. The more he struggled to convince himself that he must escape or perish in the attempt, the more Nidbjorg's force asserted that he not only couldn't escape from her, but the idea of leaving her questionable protection was far more frightening.

Unable to shake off her enchantment, he wrapped himself in his cloak and lay down beside the fire to sleep. Miserable and afraid, he watched them through one slitted eye. The sisters grumbled and whispered among themselves until they settled their dispute and left Thorvor to watch. She had her knitting for company, and watching her soon made Ivarr drift off into restless sleep. It was a sleep composed of uneasy dreams and fitful awakenings. Once, he awakened, or thought he did, to find Nidbjorg quietly measuring him with a marked stick; then she sat down to consult a fat book which she incanted from a hiding place in her sleeve. She turned leaf after leaf, reading and studying a moment, then turning another page, like a cook searching for a suitable recipe for some troublesome and unusual object. Ivarr had no doubt that he was the object, and the thought turned his blood into ice. He knew he had to escape, whether or not Gizur showed up to help him.

The next day as they travelled, he looked for opportunities, but the landscape was anything but conducive to escape. Their way led along the bottom of a deep ravine, weaving in and out between intruding knobs of hillsides. The rock was black and jagged, giving each hill a bristling crown or a set of sharp ears. Ivarr was oppressed

163

with a feeling of gloom—or doom, perhaps, which he feared was his own.

By nightfall they had descended from the fells into the lowlands, where clouds of mosquitoes hovered and hummed over acres of bogs and the air was cloyed with the smell of decomposing vegetation. Nidbjorg was sniffing with the gladness of a dog who is finally home.

"This is the place," she announced at last as the sun was sinking.

"You're not really going to try it, are you?" Thorvor murmured in anxious tone. "Remember how many you've ruined, Nidbjorg dear. It would be such a shame after we've come so far to get him—"

"Hush!" Nidbjorg snapped. "What chance do we have otherwise? He must be completely in our power."

Ivarr's heart began lurching nervously after overhearing their whispered conversation. He looked around attentively. They seemed to have reached the low point of all Jotunsgard. The ground was rank and soggy, and patches of reeds rattled in the wind like clattering bones. Not far off stood the remains of an old circular tower, crouching in the gloom like a slit-eyed beast waiting for them. Ivarr stopped stock-still when he saw the circle of stones, black and half-rotten with age, tilted at drunken angles.

He planted his feet firmly and declared, "You can't get me into that place. It stinks and it's evil!"

Solborg laughed harshly, suddenly seizing his arm in a vicious grip and twisting it behind his back with surprising strength. "Now come along, there's no such thing as evil. You needn't struggle, you can't get away, so you may as well meet your death with dignity, not kicking and squealing like a pig."

Ivarr gasped as she kinked his arm a notch tighter, pushing him toward the centre of the ring where lay a flat stone like a table, or an altar with a groove cut into it. Nidbjorg began chanting a spell, impaling Ivarr with her snakelike stare.

In the distance he heard Thorvor's nattering voice.

"Nidbjorg, I don't think I like this place. Are you sure you're in touch with the powers here? They seem dangerous and unruly, like necromancer's powers—"

"Hush!" Solborg snapped. Her hands felt like iron, and a great cold weight seemed to settle on Ivarr's chest, crushing him until he could scarcely breathe. Through it all rang the voice of Nidbjorg reciting her spell.

Ivarr struggled to resist the deadly paralysis of terror and Nidbjorg's spell. He could imagine Solborg and her well-worn knife—no, it was Birna's she was drawing from somewhere in her garments.

Then a shout, a shock of cold air, and Solborg flung herself away with a shriek, the knife clattering on the stone. Nidbjorg's spell halted suddenly with a shout, and the force of colliding powers sent Ivarr sprawling in the gummy grass. He gasped and gulped like a beached fish. Shakily he lifted his head to peer around warily. Solborg was lying flat on her back not far from him—dead from all appearances. Two heaps to his left may have been Nidbjorg and Thorvor. One of them was groaning. Ivarr forced himself forward to clutch Birna's knife. Then he looked around for his rescuer, his courage and spirits miraculously restored.

"Gizur! Where are you?" he demanded. "It certainly took you long enough to get here!" He spied the tall cloaked figure in the shadow of one of the stones when it announced itself with a familiar chuckle.

Ivarr at once recognized the leathery chuckle of old Grus in his pouch inside Lorimer's pocket. His spirits plummeted sickeningly as Lorimer stepped forward, still radiating a wave of icy cold air after making his spells.

"So it's you, Lorimer," Ivarr said with an attempt at defiance, still a bit unsteady from the effects of Nidbjorg's enchantment. "It was noble of you to rescue me at such an opportune moment. The Alfar realm was about to be short one Scipling, I fear."

Lorimer made a contemptuous sound. "Those meddling hags! I thought it would be such a pity if the job weren't done right. The place is right, but only the superior skills of an expert necromancer will ensure that the enchantment is a success. Grus can testify to that, can't you, old fellow?''

Grus cackled in reply. ''Who says you can't put an old head on young shoulders, or young on old? Better yet, one in each pocket, eh Scipling?'' He chuckled maliciously as Lorimer drew his sword.

Ivarr gathered himself for a desperate leap toward the old tower. Behind him, he heard Grus' chuckle break into a shriek.

''Silence, Grus, or I'll give you to the fire wizards for a door knocker,'' Lorimer ordered. ''Did you see where that Scipling rat scuttled off to?''

''Beside the old tower. I'd be careful if I were you. Some nasty murders have taken place here, and with any luck, yours will be the next.''

Lorimer stalked forward without glancing right or left. Ivarr crept around the tower as soundlessly as he could, Birna's knife in his hand. A narrow crumbling stair wound upward along the outside wall, scarcely as wide as a footstep. Hoping it wouldn't collapse and take half the tower with it and him beneath, Ivarr climbed upward as far as he could get and crouched on a rotten parapet, half-hidden by a weathered knob of rock and mortar.

Lorimer's measured footsteps sounded below. ''He's not here, you contrary lump of deceit and carrion,'' Lorimer's voice growled. ''Blast you, Grus, if he's escaped, you'll go into the bog.''

Lorimer sheathed his sword and bent slightly to peer at the ground by the faint light cast by the knob of his staff. Grus babbled a mixture of chagrin and defiance.

''He's here, I know he's here,'' Grus went on. ''Sciplings can't simply rise into the air and fly off—''

At that instant Lorimer realized where Ivarr was. His eyes looked straight into Ivarr's for a startled instant before Ivarr launched himself into the air and hit Lorimer full force in the chest with both feet. They went down in a tangle with Grus screeching and swearing. Ivarr made one plunge into the mêlée with Birna's knife and was rewarded with a terrible,

166

soul-chilling shriek. The knife was wrenched from his hand and he flung himself away. Tumbling behind the tower, he narrowly missed a wild blast that whitened the grass and stones. Two more followed, equally as wild, one in each direction as if to catch a fleeing fugitive. Then Ivarr could hear Grus moaning in the silence, and Lorimer muttering imprecations.

"I'm blind," the necromancer gasped, staggering over the uneven stones in the direction of Grus' voice. "That cursed boy has put out my eye and I can't see from the other for the blood. Do you see him? I'll blast him once and for all, and Hel may have that wretched sword. Speak up, Grus! I'll have your ears if you don't answer!"

"I'm right here in the edge of the streamlet," Grus chattered. "It's beastly cold and I don't know how to swim. If you don't save me, I'll drown." He ended in a series of blubbering snorts and gasps.

"Curse that Scipling. Curse the day he was born." Lorimer reeled in the other direction, mopping black gouts of blood from his face. Hearing a sound, he whirled suddenly and sent a ferocious blast toward the far side of the valley.

"Grus, you'll have to be my eyes for me until I get this bleeding stopped. Grus! Are you still there?"

"Blub—barely," Grus answered. "Come more to the left. Don't trip on those stones—didn't you hear me? Careful, you're almost in the water."

Ivarr moved quietly from the shelter of the tower while Lorimer fished around in the water for Grus, muttering and growling. With long cautious strides, Ivarr hastened toward the south end of the valley.

"There you are!" Lorimer cried, and Ivarr began to run. "Grus, I hear him! Quickly, look and see which way and I'll blast him!"

"I can't see upside down very well!" Grus wailed. "There—there he is! Straight south! Blast away!"

Ivarr leaped into a ravine with ice hailing down around him. He crouched behind a boulder and waited while Lorimer quartered the area with spells and ice bolts, hoping the necromancer wouldn't get lucky and drop one right on him.

167

CHAPTER FOURTEEN

Gizur looked up suddenly from his endless map study. The Alfar were dozing around the fire, except for Eilifir, and Skapti in his new and tender state of awareness. Skapti looked at Gizur in the same instant and they asked each other the same question:

"Where's Ivarr?"

They both leaped to their feet. Skapti dropped his cup of tea, which was cold anyway, and it splashed Flosi.

"Now look what you've done!" he snapped. "This was once a fairly respectable cloak!"

"He went to stake the horses to graze," Skapti said. "But that was quite a while ago. Too long ago!"

"Maybe he got lost in the dark," Finnvard suggested with a suspicious glance at the wall of mysterious darkness beyond the fire ring.

"We'd better go see." Gizur gripped his staff and strode away into the night, with Skapti and Eilifir following at his heels. Flosi trailed after them, growling at the inconvenience of Sciplings even existing. Finnvard anxiously moved closer to the fire, and Egills poured another cup of tea.

"I hope they find him," Finnvard said. "But I doubt if they will. He was such an agreeable sort, and always polite to me. I'll always wonder what evil being, troll, dwarf, hag, or—"

He broke off with a muffled scream as Flosi came plunging back into camp.

"The horses are gone too!" he puffed importantly. "Start getting our gear together, you old clodpates! I knew something like this was coming with that Scipling. You can't trust them a moment. He's a horse thief or you can hang me on the next tree!" It was a good oath—Skarpsey boasted very few trees large enough to be suitable.

Egills did not move. He cocked his head on one side and said, "I may be a slow thinker, but I don't believe for an instant Ivarr took the horses and absconded with them. No food, no weapons, and no map. If you ask me, I'd say you had all the brains of a bedbug, Flosi."

"Remind me not to ask you then," retorted Flosi, rummaging his pack together with a theatrical air of impatience and lofty disdain.

"Nobody would steal those old nags willingly," Finnvard said. "If some one did steal them, perhaps they have done some harm to Ivarr."

"What a fool's notion!" Flosi said.

Gizur stalked into the corner of the bustling and bickering and raised a hand commandingly. "Quiet, all of you. We must have a brief conference and I shall tell you what has happened. It appears that our three nice old nags were nothing less than our three nice old alfkonur from Nidbjorgsstead in their fylgja forms."

Finnvard gasped and looked for a soft place to faint. "And we rode on their backs and thought they were just horses! Why, I used to pet their noses and scratch behind their ears and say all sorts of fond nonsense to them. Whatever will they think of me for taking such liberties! I'll simply die if I ever see them again!"

"Finnvard, be quiet!" Skapti said sternly. "That's not important!"

Gizur continued, "I saw plenty of footprints which were not equine and definitely not Ivarr's. I also found a cold spot hovering over one area, as if an evil spell had just been worked there and the miasma was still lingering. It couldn't

169

have been an hour old. From the direction of the tracks, they've taken him on a southeasterly course into Jotunsgard on the back of our old friend Snip, with the distinctively smaller hoofprints and the crack on the near hind. About fifty yards from the scene of the ambush, the tracks vanished except for small traces which only a skilled magician can detect.''

"Then we're scuttled," Egills grunted. "We've lost him.''

Eilifir joined them after his search of the area. "They've used a spell to cover their tracks. Not a bent twig or disturbed crumb of earth to show where they've passed. It would take the eyes and nose of a ferret to see where they've gone.''

Gizur looked at him narrowly. "That sounds like shape shifting to me, Eilifir. Can you do it, or were you just using a figure of speech?''

They all looked at Eilifir, an unlikely-looking prospect with his scruffy beard and unassuming aspect.

"Of course he can't," Flosi snapped. "Can't or won't. What would he be doing here with us if he could—''

Eilifir made no other move except to snap his fingers twice, and suddenly Eilifir was no longer there. Instead, the black-masked face of a ferret peered at them from the top of a boulder.

"Gods in Asgard!" Finnvard exclaimed. "He did it! Drat him for a clever impostor!''

The ferret winked its bright little eyes and bounded the ground in a flowing leap, sniffing and running in questing circles. Suddenly he froze, with one paw in mid-air, sniffed deeply a moment, then whisked out of sight.

Gizur expelled a large sigh. "Well, he's yet to change himself back without damage before the spell is a success. Skapti, I shall leave you in command while I go after Eilifir in my own fylgja." He braced himself for Finnvard's wail of protest, but all he heard was a purring "Mmmrow!" Finnvard was rubbing against his shins and eying the mysterious darkness beyond their firelight with whisker-

170

quavering eagerness. "No you don't!" Gizur exclaimed. "Finnvard, this is far beyond your skills. Finnvard!"

The cat dived under a prickly bush and bounded playfully out the other side. With a series of loud yowls he rushed from cover to cover, pouncing and leaping at imaginary foes, until he caught up with the ferret.

Gizur prepared to depart, muttering about what he would do to Finnvard once he caught up to him. Skapti rubbed his hands together nervously. "Gizur, I'm ready to try the fylgja spell. I'm sure I've got the power if old Finnvard can manage it so easily."

"It can't be difficult, if that old crumpet can do it," Flosi said. "Come on, Gizur, you could help us if you only would."

Gizur shook his head vehemently. "I can't conceive of a more dangerous and volatile situation. It's likelier you'd blow yourselves to shreds. You'll need a lot more seasoning before you try these complicated spells, Skapti, or I fear you'll destroy the power you do possess. That would be a great pity, because it promises to be a very fine power. Just be content to follow by yourselves for a while longer." He patted Skapti's shoulder encouragingly. Then with a quick gesture, he vanished, leaving them with a series of chuckling hoots and hisses.

It was a long and discouraging chase, consisting of weary, forced marches and short halts to eat and catch brief moments of sleep. Gizur reported back periodically with no news except that the trail led southeast toward the lowlands of Jotunsgard, where a thousand bogs and fens could swallow up one lone Scipling. They stumbled on, with even Flosi too tired to complain.

In the evening of the third day, Eilifir returned in his customary form, looking very nearly worn out. He sat down on a rock and began applying his teeth to a stubborn bit of hardtack, until Gizur rejoined them in wizard form. The other Alfar clamoured around him for news. Egills was particularly anxious about Finnvard.

Eilifir held up one hand for silence. "Finnvard is directly

behind me," he said with difficulty, because of the extreme dryness of the hardtack. "And I found something I knew you'd all be interested in seeing, Gizur in particular."

He stubbornly refused to say another word until the Alfar had grumblingly broken camp and followed him. Eventually he led them into a dark little ravine which grew boggier with each step. Halting, he folded his arms and gazed ahead in silence. An old tower leaned sadly on its miry foundations near a half-fallen circle of stones. Standing disconsolately near the tower were two wretched old mares with sunken flanks and drooping heads. A third black horse lay on her side in a circle of blasted grass, trembling and moaning as if she might never get her legs under her again.

Gizur strode forward and seized old Snip by the forelock. She tottered and groaned, beseeching him with lusterless eyes. After studying the three horses a few moments, Gizur rejoined the Alfar at their safe vantage point.

"There's nothing to be afraid of," he said grimly. "They'll never do anyone any harm again. They've been totally devastated. Someone with a superior force has changed them into what they disguised themselves as— three aged mares. Nidbjorg looks in a very bad way."

"Good riddance, I say," Flosi declared from behind Finnvard.

"But what happened to Ivarr?" Skapti demanded. "It was Lorimer who blasted the three old hags, wasn't it?"

Eilifir gnawed thoughtfully on his hardtack. "Ivarr's tracks follow the ravine to the south. Lorimer's tracks incline east, where he joined his waiting dwarves. I'd say Ivarr is about four hours ahead of us. The wind blowing across a trail makes if difficult to judge its age closely."

"We haven't much time to lose," Gizur said. "Ivarr appears to be heading toward Vapnajokull. If we could all command our fylgja forms, we could easily catch him on the other side. Eilifir, Finnvard, you will go after Ivarr at top speed." Finnvard had already changed himself over, and was washing an imaginary dirty spot near the middle of his back and not seeming to hear a word. Only his tail twitched attentively.

"As for the rest of us," Gizur continued grimly, "we're going to work out everyone's fylgja, or a close approximation thereof. Skapti, you shall be first. It's fylgja or nothing, as we used to say in school."

CHAPTER 15

Vapnajokull reared from the lowlands like an icy giant. In ages long past it had enlivened the climate of Jotunsgard with belching clouds of ash and smoke and occasional spurts of molten lava, but for several centuries it had allowed the snow and ice to accumulate with no interference from its fiery inner nature. The great glacier which capped the mountain contented itself with capricious bolting, shearing off rock abutments and sending great blocks of ice crashing down rocky ravines far below the serene icy summit. Little vegetation consented to grow there, except lichens and other tough worty plants that didn't mind cold and wind and precious little soil to grow in.

By nightfall the party had crossed the glacier and descended the far side without catching Eilifir and Finnvard or Ivarr. They were too exhausted to go another step, and Gizur in particular was drained of strength. After nearly two hours of powerful concentration, he still had been unsuccessful at summoning the force sufficient to release the secret magic of Flosi's and Egills' fylgur. Skapti had finally, and with great difficulty, managed to coerce his elven form into relinquishing its natural form and taking on the shape of his fylgja. Somewhat to his mingled pride and dismay, his fylgja was a large white hare.

Gizur had struggled with Flosi and Egills, attempting everything from hypnotic spells to trances, and still nothing happened. Egills reported that his head still rang, and it finally developed into a severe headache, a warning that whatever magical capabilities he possessed were being tried to their limits. Gizur was also being greatly taxed, and Skapti watched anxiously as he sweated and toiled over his spells.

"I can't help them," Gizur finally confessed, sinking down shakily. "It will take something dramatic to startle the power into them. I certainly can't do it."

"But we can't make it this way," Skapti said worriedly. "You'll have to do something, Gizur. Put a spell on them of some sort."

Gizur sighed and rubbed his temples. "It's against the constitution of the Wizards' Guild for any wizard to exert his force over an ally to conjure him into an inferior form or to put him at a disadvantage. But if I wait much longer, I won't have the strength to put one foot before the other."

Mustering his powers to the utmost, he began reciting a formula to change the forms of Flosi and Egills, who couldn't help cringing and grimacing. The spell overcame their subtle resistance, however, and Gizur succeeded in changing them into two large black rats. The effort for Gizur had been supreme, and it was with difficulty that he took on his own fylgja, the white owl. He flew from rock to rock, waiting while the others caught up with him. Skapti raced ahead in joyous spurts with great energy, followed by two black shapes scuttling along with all the tireless tenacity inherent in the rat clan.

They met Finnvard halfway down the other side, paddling back to meet them, blinking resentfully at the snowflakes the wind was spitting. By this time the white owl was spending more time roosting on stones, beak parted, and wings sagging in weariness. Once safely down the glacier and the mountain, Gizur gladly released Flosi and Skapti from their spells and assisted Skapti and Finnvard back to the world of man-shaped Alfar. Eilifir was still ferreting ahead at top speed after Ivarr, certain that he would catch him presently and bring him back to the camp. Gizur

175

collapsed in exhaustion on the haphazard pile of packs and equipment that had accompanied them somewhat untidily in their respective spells, cleverly converted into mites or ticks or burrs that could cling to a small creature without hampering its progress.

The Alfar chattered in great excitement about travelling in animal forms, exclaiming over the advantages of being able to smell and hear things an ordinary man would not guess the existence of, and being amazed at the boundless strength and energy contained in the wiry sinews of small creatures whose very survival depended upon their wits and instincts. They marvelled that they had blundered along so obtusely and still survived, before learning of all the secrets available to the finely honed instincts of the animals.

Finnvard busied himself with the fire and the kettle, absentmindedly answering questions with an occasional "Mmrrow?" much to the merriment of his friends. Even Gizur smiled, gratefully accepting a cup of steaming tea.

Skapti watched Gizur and found himself munching uneasily on the end of his beard and tugging at his ear. "I know I'm a worrier by nature," he finally said in a quiet voice beside Gizur, "but I've never seen you so tired and weak—so devoid of power. The cat's head on your staff isn't even glowing, Gizur. I'm afraid you've taken more power from your reserves than you can spare."

Gizur shook his head. "I'm fine. All I need is some rest. Perhaps I have overdone it a bit, but I got us here at least, didn't I?"

"But what good will it be if Lorimer discovers us and you're unable to defend us?"

Gizur closed his eyes and waved his hand impatiently. "Just go away and let me rest. You're not helpless, you know. When the time comes to deal with Lorimer, I shall be ready, never you fear."

Dawn was not far off when Ivarr finally left the ravine. Since it led in the general direction he wanted to go, he hurried along in the gloom as fast as he could without tripping and falling. He paused frequently to listen for sounds of pursuit by Lorimer or his black dwarves, but he heard nothing.

When he finally crawled out of the ravine, the first thing he saw was a standing stone with a hole cut through it. His heart leaped with relief and he approached the stone more closely to study it. A sword had been carved into the smooth surface pointing to the south, followed by a batch of runic scratch marks which Ivarr could make no sense of, but he supposed it might say Jotunsgard or perhaps the Maze. The view through the hole showed him a notch cut in the shoulder of a large glacier-capped fell. From his constant peering over Gizur's shoulder at the map, he recognized what he thought must be Vapnajokull. Setting his eyes on the notch he began to climb, glad to forsake the lowlands for the safety of the high places. Soon he was climbing higher and higher, crossing ice-choked ravines and listening to the ominous grinding and growling of the glacier above. He crossed several of its prongs, driven deep into the ravines, and kept an eye on the notch to guide him.

From all appearances, Lorimer was not following him yet. The next most pressing problem was finding something to eat. He warily sampled some bright red berries, but the slightest taste of juice on his tongue set it to burning, so he quickly abandoned that idea. Bleakly he wondered if the notch would eventually direct him to a house of refuge, where perhaps he could wait for Gizur and the Alfar, or if perhaps the fire jotuns even possessed such hospitable establishments, which was doubtful. It was far more likely that the fire jotuns had had nothing to do with the upright stone and the notch. Grimly he plodded onward, following the line nevertheless.

At midday his hunger was the worst. He drank frequently from the little streams and pools he passed, and once he greedily ate handfuls of granular snow from a leftover snowdrift half-hidden beneath an overhanging bank. It did absolutely nothing for his hunger and made him thirstier than ever.

The glacier made alarming sounds throughout the day, and several times he saw huge blocks of ice tearing down the ravines with spectacular violence which he was too tired to marvel at. He crept along doggedly until he reached the notch, which was an icy, windy spot not far from the edge of the glacier itself. He didn't linger any longer than it took to ascertain that the far side was little easier than the way he had come up, and there were no signs of a house of refuge or any more marks made by human hands. He scarcely noticed the ice rumbling in the ravines on his way downwards. A single spiny ridge led him back down to the warmer climate of the lowlands. It was almost nightfall when he finally found a niche in a rockslide to rest in, although it was by far the least comfortable spot he could have chosen. He hoped the loose rocks would warn him of an enemy's approach. Feeling terribly sorry for himself, he put his head on his forearms and tried to sleep. After sleep finally claimed him, it was made hideous by repeated awakenings for no good reason. In the midst of a deep doze, something cold and moist deliberately touched his ear. He leaped awake and couldn't help giving a shout the instant his eyes registered on the dark cloaked figure sitting on the rock beside him.

"Hush! You're worse than Flosi," the self-possessed voice of Eilifir said.

Ivarr sank down weakly. "I can't believe it's you, Eilifir. Am I really awake? You can't believe what I've been through. I haven't eaten a decent meal or slept the night in three entire days. Where's Gizur? And how did you sneak up on me without making a sound?"

"Questions!" Eilifir murmured. "You think you've got the right to investigate everything, you Sciplings. Now come along quickly without being too noisy and I'll have you back to Gizur in less than an hour. What have you done with Lorimer, by the way? Is he close behind you?"

Ivarr paused in his cautious navigation of the rockslide. "I don't think so. I blinded him back at the old tower with Birna's knife. I didn't see a trace of him all day."

Eilifir walked in silence awhile then asked, "Whatever

possessed you to risk a physical attack on Lorimer? You must have taken him greatly by surprise or you'd certainly be dead by now, and all our hopes of a peaceful future along with you. Ivarr, you're no longer living just for your own benefit. If you should perish and the weregild were not paid, think what would happen to Skapti and the rest of us. Hunted down and murdered we'd be. Then great war between Ljosalfar and all the powers of the dark and ice would ravage Skarpsey from one end to the other. Thousands would perish and perhaps Snowfell would be utterly destroyed and the powers of darkness would prevail. I know you're thinking it's not fair for all that fate and destiny to rest upon the shoulders of a single young Scipling such as yourself, but you've got to show a little more responsibility, Ivarr. The truth of it is, you're much too incautious and precipitant.''

Ivarr scowled. A lecture, after his experience, was the last thing he expected or needed. He opened his mouth to defend himself several times, but each time he thought of a mistake he had made and shut it. ''I know you're right, Eilifir. I've had no real training for this. I'm only the second son of a second son who is a poor fisherman—poor in every way, meaning lazy and careless—so I'm not particularly brave or intelligent at all. Birna, the only person I admired or who taught me anything, was coldly murdered by that fiend Lorimer, and since then I've had the feeling I'm totally out of control of my own fate; and I wouldn't be able to manage it anyway, even if it weren't beyond me. But one thing is certain. I shall avenge Birna's death on Lorimer— somehow.'' He stomped at the clinging thorns and kicked rocks out of the way as he talked. By the end of his speech he was almost breathless and had nearly broken his toe on a large snag that refused to budge.

''The feeling of inability is common to anybody who is accomplishing anything,'' Eilifir said. ''But don't take horrendous risks to compensate for the feeling. I hope you'll take this as friendly advice, Ivarr, and not criticism. Your continued existence is a matter of great concern to me and all the Ljosalfar. What I fear most is that Lorimer is so offended and enraged by your attack on his person and subsequent blinding of his eye that his own personal interest in your feud with him will overcome his greed for power. He may be rather angry.''

''I'm sure he is,'' Ivarr said with a sigh. ''It looks as if I may have made yet another mistake. I'm not accustomed to the rules in the Alfar realm. We Sciplings attack each other quite frequently and rather enjoy it. But thank you for the advice, Eilifir. I shall try to remember I have a certain responsibility to stay alive until the weregild is paid.''

Eilifir nodded gravely and hurried on at a faster gait than ever. Ivarr did his best to keep up, but his feet were in an exhausted state after three days of walking and no rest. He stumbled often and felt as if he could hardly stand by the time they limped into camp shortly before dawn. The Alfar awakened and gave him a noisy greeting, and Finnvard began brewing a pot of tea while everyone asked a thousand questions. Finally Gizur roared, ''Quiet! All of you! Now let's do this in an orderly manner.'' He turned to Ivarr, who was ignoring them all and blisssfully gorging himself on such questionable delicacies as dry hardtack, hard cheese, and stockfish. ''Ivarr, the question of utmost importance is Lorimer. We thought you might have been taken by him, so how did you escape, and when, and where?'' He eyed the elves rather testily.

''How about why?'' asked Flosi quickly.

Ivarr darted him a cold glare. ''I hope it's you he gets next time, Flosi, and we'd see where your boasting and bragging would get you. I warrant you could no more escape from him than a cow could fly. Eilifir, you tell them everything. I'm far too hungry. And sleepy.'' He couldn't decide which was most imperative.

Gizur sat brooding beside the fire, wrapped to his ears in an eider. Ivarr began to notice him as soon as the edge was off his hunger. From time to time the wizard was wracked by shivering and his eyes burned with a feverish light.

''Gizur!'' Ivarr called, under the cover of Finnvard's mild

180

boasting about his fylgja form. "What's wrong with you? Are you sick?"

Gizur shook his head fiercely. "It will pass, it's nothing but an overstrain. Flosi and Egills have so little innate magic they're like lumps of cold tar to do anything with. I've never been so drained."

Ivarr looked at him in alarm. "Will you be all right in a day or so if you don't overexert?"

Gizur snorted faintly. "There's nothing to exert. My power is virtually nil. It will take awhile for it to build itself up again." He sighed heavily and shivered.

"How long will it take?" Ivarr asked, forgetting his exhaustion. "Lorimer can't be very far behind, and now I fear he's burning for vengeance worse than ever. I made the mistake of putting one of his eyes out with Birna's knife. I wish it had been his heart. Perhaps he'll bleed to death."

Gizur's cold hand grasped Ivarr's wrist like a claw. "You don't understand yet about Lorimer. I'm surprised Birna didn't tell you what he is."

"He's a draug," Ivarr said quickly. "He as much as admitted that to me when I got lost that day. But I thought draugar shunned daylight like the plague."

Gizur touched the knob of his staff and it flickered feebly. "Lorimer has been around for a long time. He spent a thousand years buried in a bog, waiting for someone to be foolish enough to release him. The name of that someone was Regin, one of Svartarr's wizards who had a necro-mancerous bent. He discovered the place where Lorimer had been staked for his crimes, after spending most of his life searching for Lorimer's powers and practices. Regin un-earthed the corpse, nicely preserved in our famous bogs, and did a truly miraculous job of restoring the natural body humours and blood and so forth. Thus was the draug Lorimer furnished with a body to assist him in his greedy machinations for power. It is a peculiarity of an evil draug that however many times he is slain, he returns more power-ful than before. That is, unless he is destroyed with a weapon of particularly pernicious power, such as Glimr in

181

Elidagrimr's mound.'' Gizur yawned and wearily rubbed his burning eyes. ''I don't suppose you saw any dwarves with him, did you?''

''No. Perhaps they've deserted him.''

''Not likely. They're far too fearful of him. It's possible—'' Gizur mused and muttered to himself as if he had forgotten about Ivarr, who was comfortable enough that he was almost asleep. Suddenly Gizur roused himself and gave Ivarr a shake. ''A world free of Lorimer would be a world cured of a vile disease. Whatever you do, Ivarr, and whatever becomes of the rest of us, you must destroy Lorimer.'' With that he fell asleep quite contentedly.

Ivarr too fell asleep, leaving Eilifir to arrange the night guard for the few remaining hours of darkness. When he next awakened, the sun was warm in his face and he could smell the breakfast Finnvard was assembling from their scanty stores. He was grumbling about it too, wondering how they were ever going to survive until the end of next week. Flosi and Egills were arguing languidly about some inconsequential subject, and Skapti was attempting to organize their untidy camp. Eilifir was sitting on a rock with his bow and an arrow across his knees, watching the surrounding fells with an attentive attitude.

Ivarr lazed in the warm sun awhile longer, then he sauntered through the camp toward Eilifir, noting as he passed that Gizur was still sleeping heavily. He looked very weary and drawn as he slept, clutching his staff in one hand.

Eilifir acknowledged Ivarr's approach with a short nod, returning his attention to the fells before them.

''Eilifir? Is something wrong?'' he asked.

Eilifir tipped his bow slightly toward the nearest fell. ''Look on the top there by that knob of rock. You'll see three men watching us. Quietly, don't make any sudden movements.''

Ivarr gasped. ''Eilifir, those aren't the only ones. Look over there!'' He started to point but Eilifir stopped him.

''Yes, I know. I've been watching them since they appeared just before dawn. If you'll look around calmly,

182

you'll see them on every hilltop.''

Ivarr tried to survey the opposition calmly, then exclaimed, ''But why didn't you warn anybody, Eilifir? You've been just sitting here for several hours? What if they'd attacked us?''

''I would have awakened you,'' Eilifir said.

Ivarr studied the figures on the surrounding hilltops, estimating there must be about twenty of them, two or three to each hill, clearly well-armed and ready for battle. They made no threatening moves, nor did they attempt to be particularly stealthy.

''Who are they? Fire jotuns?'' Ivarr demanded.

Eilifir nodded and made himself more comfortable on his rocky perch.

''Well, what do they want?'' Ivarr persisted.

Eilifir shrugged. ''We're trespassing. I expect they want us out of their domain, one way or another. Dead or alive makes no difference to a fire jotun.''

CHAPTER SIXTEEN

After a long and careful scrutiny, the fire jotuns abandoned their hiding places and rode forward to confront the intruders. Ivarr counted twelve riders approaching, armed with bows and lances and clad in dark muffling cloaks. They halted to study Gizur and his small band. Ivarr couldn't help admiring their horses—trim, slender creatures with small heads and fiery dispositions evinced by much hoof-pawing and head-tossing.

Gizur nudged Ivarr to follow him, and they cautiously advanced toward the fire jotuns.

"Just be calm and friendly," Gizur muttered. "Act a wee bit stupid. Keep your mouth closed and let me do all the lying."

One of the foremost jotuns kneed his horse forward with a plunge and a jingling of outlandish hardware. In a thunderous voice the jotun bellowed, "Stay where you are, trespassers! This is jotun land and we want none of your hunting and snooping. You're from the Guild, I can see, and if it's outlaws you're after, I'm here to tell you Jotunsgard protects its own!"

The other jotuns muttered a fierce accompaniment, looking very warlike.

Gizur raised his hands placatingly. "We're not hunting outlaws, or anyone else for that matter. I'm Gizur of Ravensend, and these fellows with me are merely hunting for treasure mounds, nothing more.''

The jotun chieftain nudged his snorting horse a few paces nearer. He tilted back the visor of his burnished helmet for a better look. Bright hawkish eyes bored into Ivarr and stabbed at the Alfar behind him. Thoughtfully the jotun smoothed his beard, which was braided into three dark plaits. ''Treasure mounds, you say? We've seen plenty of your kind—or rather, their bones, after the trolls or mischievous wizards are done with them. If you want to live to see your precious Snowfell again, you'd better turn around now and not look back. We jotuns are sworn to protect the barrows of the honorable dead. We shall escort you back to the mountains, and hope you have the good sense not to be seen here again.''

''Thor, listen to me a moment.'' Another jotun, a wizardous-looking fellow with very little flesh on his bones, joined his chieftain. He whispered a moment to the chieftain, who favoured the intruders with an increasingly sceptical glare.

''If I might explain—'' began Gizur, but Thor cut him off.

''Oho! Treasure seekers indeed!'' he boomed. ''My brother Bjarn has told me who you really are. You're the outlaws who murdered Svartarr's son, are you not? Gossip travels even as far as Jotunsgard.''

Skapti edged anxiously closer. ''It's not like you think,'' he began. ''We didn't actually intend—'' The jotun's face split with a tremendous grin of welcome. ''There's no one we'd be gladder to welcome into our hall. Svartarr is no friend of the fire jotuns. We'd gladly do anything to bollix up his plans. Jotunsgard is the haven for outlaws; there's room for all and no one dares to come after you.'' He beamed at the startled Alfar.

''Well, we're frightfully glad and grateful for your hospitality,'' Gizur said. ''As a matter of fact, we are almost out of provisions—''

Thor waved his hand. ''We'll supply you with everything you need. You've no idea how glad we are to help the slayers of Svartarr's son.''

"Then you'll permit us to continue our search?" Ivarr demanded.

"Certainly. We'll even help you. Nothing would delight us more than seeing Glimr once more in the right hands— the hands of the jotuns' allies. Herjolf, put our guests on your horses; honoured visitors needn't walk to Ulfgrimrsstead."

A bit reluctantly, the Alfar allowed themselves to be put aboard the unruly jotun horses. Thor insisted that Ivarr take his own black stallion, who instantly snatched the bit between his teeth and led the other horses in a wild charge homeward. Finnvard in particular was glad when the exhilarating ride ended at Ulfgrimrsstead before any necks were broken. They all dismounted and looked around in amazement at Thor's homestead. The sturdy turf buildings were gracefully built and the gables freshly painted. Ivarr marvelled at the lush hay tuns and the sleek cattle, sheep, goats, and ponies. Nothing was crooked, old, sick, or broken that Ivarr could see. It was a picture of serene perfection. Even the Alfar were properly awed into silence by the magnificent proportions of the main hall, with its stout mellow timbers and two enormous hearths.

Thor Ulfgrimrsson and his brother Bjarn made their guests welcome, in addition to several dozen more jotun neighbours who came to meet the strangers. Mountains of food were served, kegs of ale, and delicacies Ivarr had never seen before. Two harpists regaled the company with songs and poetry, and the jotuns never allowed a plate or cup to stand empty. The talking and jesting and singing filled the noble hall with a genial uproar.

Ivarr ate and drank to repletion, relaxing into sleepy contentment. He was certain he had never encountered such a hospitable host as Thor, and no one could compare to the jotuns for wit and generosity. Thor and Bjarn beamed at him with such fellowship and good will that he became impatient with gloomy Skapti beside him, who kept muttering and worrying until it was a wonder he didn't spoil the entire celebration.

"Jotuns aren't friendly without some reason for it," Skapti kept grumbling. "This is going to cost us dearly, I fear. I wish Gizur would get us out of here."

"Don't be absurd, Skapti. Didn't you hear Thor say he was going to help us find the sword?"

"Help us! We don't want their kind of help," Skapti groused.

Meanwhile, their packs were loaded with parcels and flasks, and new pairs of boots were pressed upon all the travellers. For two days they rested and acquired gifts of new shirts, breeches, belts, and they were forced to refuse courteously the offers of horses, exquisite jotun armour, and fine weapons.

"I simply don't know what to think of all this jotun hospitality," Finnvard sighed, patting his bulging waistline like an old friend returned from exile. "Sometimes I suspect it's rather too much, almost as if—as if—" His expression became remote and astonished. "Why, I believe I just had a moment of prescience. Somehow I thought—no, it's too silly. I couldn't have the power of prescience, could I?"

"It's more likely gas," Flosi remarked helpfully.

"What did you think you saw?" Eilifir inquired.

"Do you really want to hear?" Finnvard sighed when Eilifir nodded seriously. "Well, it seemed as if I saw this hall and farmyard from another viewpoint and it wasn't anything like what we see at all. It was rubbishy and ugly, and so were the fire jotuns. They were all smiling, but it was like wolves smiling behind friendly masks. Now isn't that ridiculous? Go ahead and laugh, all of you, I'm quite used to being made fun of. But I think I'll ask Gizur about it anyway."

"There now," Skapti said in glum satisfaction. "I've been telling you all along they weren't as generous and friendly as they pretended. You must know if Finnvard suspects something, it must be there slapping us in our faces."

Egills and Flosi refused to believe that Finnvard could see anything beyond his own cowardice and ate, drank and

187

enjoyed the jotuns' gifts and hospitality until the morning of departure arrived. Gizur started stamping around very early, examining everything twice and impatiently urging everyone to hurry. His expression was taut, almost anxious, Ivarr thought, and his power seemed to crackle around him in a nervous cloud.

"Now listen to me, you dolts," he said commandingly, when he had them all assembled. "We'll take our leave from our kind hosts in the dooryard. Since we're not troubling with breakfast, I believe they'll be meeting us there. I may as well warn you, I suspect they'll insist upon offering us more help than we want, so I want all of you, particularly Flosi, to keep your mouths shut."

Flosi opened his mouth immediately to protest, but Skapti muzzled him at once.

Thor and Bjarn were waiting in the courtyard, and beyond the barns and sheds there was a continuous snorting and stamping of horses, accompanied by the clatter of harness and weapons. The jotuns nodded and greeted their guests pleasantly. Thor was dressed in his armour and his eyes glittered with excitement. "We trust you've enjoyed your stay at Ulfgrimrsstead," he boomed. "Jotun hospitality is the most generous in Skarpsey, to those who are our friends. We invite you to stay as long as you wish in Jotunsgard, and after your dealings with Svartarr are finished, we would be honoured if you took land here and settled permanently. There's plenty of room for all of you to start your own homesteads, and we'd be glad to call you our neighbours. Since I am the chieftain, I'll see to it that the land will cost you nothing. Choice land, too, not all rocks and geysers. You know how rare good land is in Skarpsey."

Skapti muttered, "As rare as a jotun you can trust."

"That's very kind of you," Gizur said, with a glower at Skapti. "Ulfgrimrsstead is indeed beautiful—almost too good to be true. If I weren't absolutely convinced of your sincerity and honesty, I'd suspect you of putting a glamour spell over it. But of course we all know better, naturally. Such perfection couldn't be mere incantation."

Ivarr saw Thor's eyes narrow and his nostrils flare. Bjarn's hand tightened on his staff. Then Thor laughed. "A good joke, wizard. Glamour, indeed. But come, the day is advancing, and we have one last token of our friendship to offer you." He bestowed an ingratiating grin upon Ivarr. "I've assembled fifty of my best men and they're waiting now to ride with us to Elidagrimr's barrow. We can ride with you on the finest horses in Jotunsgard directly to the barrow and with fifty jotuns to protect you, Lorimer and his dwarves will keep themselves out of the way. It would be an honour for Ulfgrimrsstead to share a small part in the restoration of that sword to daylight. I've got fifty good men waiting right this moment to join you. What do you say, Ivarr, my old friend?" He even went so far as to drape a heavy arm across Ivarr's shoulders.

Ivarr politely extricated himself. "Your friendship is overwhelming, Thor, but a true friend wouldn't cause another's destruction. Dangers are waiting for us which I wouldn't dream of forcing you and your men to endure. I simply can't ask you to die for us, Thor."

"Who's talking about dying? With the jotuns you shall succeed," Thor declared.

"We can give you anything you need," Bjarn added. "Weapons, horses—"

"We're grateful to be sure." Ivarr glanced at Gizur's scowl and hurried on. "Elbegast himself has not seen fit to equip us with fighting men and horses, not wishing, perhaps, to lose them because he has little faith that we will realize our goal."

"We've come this far without help," Skapti said, with a shrewd, surmising glance at the jotuns, "and I believe we can finish the job without help. The seven of us draw far less attention and leave less of a trail than seven and fifty horsemen. Thus seven of us have a better chance at the sword and the gold."

"That's what I was trying to say," Ivarr said. "We thank you for your hospitality and your offer of assistance, but we must go on alone. We are outlaws besides, and if Svartarr

189

knew jotuns helped us, it would be mean trouble along your borders in the future.''

"Hang Svartarr and border troubles!" exclaimed Thor, his eyes glaring now with fury. "It's not assistance we're offering you! We're talking about an alliance which would put an end to Svartarr and Lorimer and whoever else tried to interfere with us. With the jotuns at your back, you could have all of Skarpsey, from sea to sea on all sides, and that would be the end of these petty disputes between the powers of light and dark and fire and ice. The island needs someone to come to the fore with indisputable power, and that someone had just as well be you, Scipling. The jotuns will back you all the way. You'd be a fool to pass by an opportunity like this one.''

Ivarr shook his head. "No. I don't want to be a king with indisputable power. I don't want the jotuns at my back, either.''

Bjarn regarded Ivarr coldly. "You fear for your back, perhaps?''

"Let's not start making accusations," Gizur said. "Suffice it to say that we politely refuse to take any jotuns with us on our journey, and that we have no interests beyond paying the weregild to Svartarr.''

"We also hope," Skapti said firmly, "that we can pass safely southward from here and that we won't be troubled by anyone's ill feelings at a later date. Not that we're afraid of a fight—our wits and powers have carried us successfully this far, so we're not nithlings.''

Thor clenched his fists and appeared ready to do battle on the spot. "An empire is in the making, and you're fools to pass up the opportunity. You're a sorry excuse for a wizard; where's your avarice, man?''

Gizur tapped his staff on the ground so it spat a few warning sparks. "Avarice is not one of the subjects Guild wizards study, nor do we of the Tulkari school.''

"Tulkari!" Bjarn gripped his staff. "If I had known that sooner you wouldn't be standing there in one piece now.''

Gizur's reply was a sarcastic bow. "A more skillful

magician would have known almost immediately. I'm glad to see that the jotuns' distortions of fire magic are in no way an improvement over the accepted practices. Just as your glamour spells are mere gloss over the ugliness within, your magic is a poor imitation of mine. That tough old mutton we ate last night will never be the tender beef you tried to disguise it as, and Ulfgrimrsstead under your glamour spells is still, and will always be exactly what it really is.'' He extended his hand and uttered several quick words. His staff flashed brilliant light, and with a huge rushing force a mighty spell was wrought whose energy blasted with gale force across the farmyard. Bjarn threw out a counterspell, but it was swept away, too weak and too late to be of any effect.

Gizur's spell stripped the homestead of its glamour like a wind ripping the leaves off a tree in autumn. Ivarr saw images of the hall and the barns and the animals flying through the air, disintegrating into nothingness like smoke images. When the wind and thunder passed, Ulfgrimrsstead was a changed place. The hall and fine buildings were replaced by crude muddy hovels, and filthy, ill-looking sheep peered hungrily between the broken and poorly mended bars of the fence. Mud and midden washed up to the door of the hall like a stinking sea, and the hall itself was reduced in grandeur to something more like a cow shed.

The jotuns were also changed with the removal of the spell of glamour. They were still tall, but divested of all hand-someness. Thor's beard and hair were matted and grey-streaked and his teeth reminded Ivarr of yellow tusks, which made his ingratiating grin all the more fearsome. Bjarn was a withered old stick with a pinched and peevish countenance, and one eye was screwed up in a vile squint, which may have been due to the rattling which he had received trying to counter Gizur's spell.

Clutching one wrist and grimacing, he snarled, ''Now you see us as we really are. Our pretty ploy didn't fool you, but if you think you've seen the last of us, you're mistaken. Jotuns have protected that sword for centuries, and jotuns must have it when it is brought out again. We'll get you too, my smart young Scipling.''

Gizur interposed with his staff. ''Begone, Bjarn, before I take pity on you and end your misery with one quick blast. The idea that you could attempt to fool my stomach with old mutton was your undoing.''

Muttering threats, Bjarn and Thor jostled each other toward the hall. The fifty waiting jotuns seized the opportunity to fling themselves on their scrubby nags and retreat at top speed, with tatters of greasy cloth flying. Thor bellowed after them furiously but not one even glanced at his chieftain.

The travellers departed quickly with many backward glances. No one pursued from the ill-favoured place. When they had put a safe distance between themselves and Ulfgrimrsstead, Gizur called a halt to study his maps.

Finnvard, who could never sit down without eating, began rummaging through the provisions with exclamations of delight. ''This is real enough. Pickled fish, more mutton, fresh hardtack—''

''I want someone to explain to me,'' Ivarr interrupted, ''what exactly, is glamour? How does it work, Gizur?''

Gizur was resting on a large flat rock viewing the terrain ahead. ''Glamour is the art of making something look like what it isn't—usually to make something as ugly as a troll's grandmother appear beautiful. I should have warned you fellows sooner, but I wasn't sure until last night and the mutton.''

''And you recall I had a premonition about it too,'' Finnvard said with pride. ''I knew it wasn't what it seemed.''

''Bah on your premonitions,'' Flosi said. ''And bah on glamour.'' He dug hastily into his pack for a look at the food parcels, then scowled critically at his new boots. ''Are these things real or will we find out later we're hauling around bundles of firewood? What about these boots?''

Gizur took the fresh hardtack from Flosi and bit into it. ''This is real,'' he said with satisfaction. ''A little coarse, perhaps, but it will do. Skapti, there's some cheese and something in a goatskin which we should investigate, I believe. If the jotuns thought they were coming with us, I suspect they outfitted us with the best they had. You're lucky you had me with you at Ulfgrimrsstead. I ought to charge you extra for that glamour spell, as a Tulkari speciality.''

The elves roared in protest. Ivarr listened and grinned, exchanging a wink with the silent Eilifir. It was good to be out from under a roof again and listening to his friends picking fights with one another and trading friendly insults. Egills always nudged Finnvard to make sure he was listening to his scathing retorts to Flosi.

''It was still a beautiful farm,'' Ivarr mused. ''My senses were certainly swayed by it. Someday I'd like to have a farm like that, only closer to the coast so I could fish and gather birds' eggs in the cliffs. I'd also hunt seals and run a few sheep and goats in the fells.''

''How dull,'' Flosi said. ''I'd rather be a spy forever than a farmer for two days.''

''Especially if you farm as poorly as you spy,'' Egills said, nudging Finnvard.

They travelled southward in the best of spirits for six days. On the morning of the seventh, Gizur stumbled upon part of an old ley line quite by accident and excitedly determined that it led straight to the Maze. With his maps unfurled in one hand, he pointed out the unmistakable landmarks which Dainn had described to them. Ivarr could almost hear his ancient voice saying, ''Look for a mountain with three great ravines, with glaciers in all three. To the east will be a mountain called Helkatla, which is a volcano, and a little cloud almost always floats on its topmost peak. You'll know it by the quantities of lava and cinders it has cast out. It is an old jotun myth that whenever someone comes to steal the sword, Helkatla will rumble to warn them of the barrow robbers.''

Ivarr stared at the three-pronged glacier and at the cone-shaped Helkatla until Flosi deemed it necessary to awaken him with a rude shove.

''You're not afraid now, are you?'' Flosi grinned

tauntingly, while Finnvard and Egills sat stiffly on a stone with haggard expressions and eyes glazed with anxiety.

Gizur ceremoniously rolled up all his maps and packed them away in his satchel with a satisfied manner. "Now we're on our own. Dainn got us here, but his advice ends at the entrance to the Maze."

"Then how shall we proceed?" Ivarr asked. "Dainn said that what we might find after all right turnings will be different from that with the left turnings."

"Let me do the worrying about that," Gizur said, pocketing a handful of devices. "Behind the Maze is a highly advanced magic, as ancient and mysterious as the giants who originally put the Maze together. It is something that I suspect a mortal mind cannot fully appreciate."

"My Alfar mind doesn't think much of it, either," Flosi said.

By the end of the day they had reached the entrance into the first ring of the jotuns' Maze. They camped beside the steep fell, silenced by the awesome size and abruptness of the great rock rearing up before them. It was so steep that nothing could cling to its slopes except tuffets of moss and trailing creeping vines. Looking through the opening, they could see a narrow twisting valley which curved away into the fells in both directions, a place so silent they could plainly hear the clatter of a freshet spewing down the back side of Helkatla into the Maze nearly a mile away.

In the morning they entered the Maze. Flosi tested the echoes with a whoop and found the result more than satisfactory. The Maze seemed to seize every sound and batter it back and forth from crag to crag until it was amplified a dozen times. After that, they spoke in whispers. Ivarr had the eerie feeling that every word they said was being funneled to the centre.

The bottom of the Maze was like the bottom of a deep narrow ravine. Uneasily Ivarr noted that they could not see ahead or behind much further than a good bowshot because of the jumbled rocks and scrubby bushes.

Gizur halted and looked keenly to the right and to the left.

He twiddled with a variety of devices, closely watched by Ivarr and the Alfar. Soon it became obvious that none of the instruments were working to his satisfaction.

"Is something wrong?" Skapti asked hesitantly, eyeing the wizard's fiery countenance and flashing eye.

"No, confound it!" Gizur roared, awakening all the echoes. In a quieter voice he continued, "Drat and blast it, I'm working on it, but this cursed Maze has a magical influence all its own which seems to confusticate everything I try to do. Fiendish, contrary magic calculated to drive a decent Tulkari wizard crazy." He gave his motionless dowsing pendulum a hopeful nudge, but the pendulum stubbornly refused to gyrate in the expected manner.

Gizur trailed away into musings and muttering and finally fetched up a glass sphere from the depths of his satchel. He gazed into it and tapped it impatiently with his finger. He spoke to it several times, shook it angrily, and finally began a series of spells to any power that happened to be within his range of influence.

"Can't raise a soul at old Tulkari's," he fumed, "and no one at the Guild seems to be listening either. Talk about infernal laziness. And these dratted globes are a ridiculous method of communication, but old Tulk insists upon us carrying them around so he can spy on us, mostly, when he hasn't got anything to keep him busy, the old boot. He still recommends—Hah! What's this? I've found somebody!"

The murky colours of the sphere swirled like roiling smoke. The Alfar stared at it as if fearing an explosion momentarily. Ivarr crept closer to peer over Gizur's shoulder at the globe. It mesmerized him almost instantly with its irresistible swirling colours and half-seen images. He thought he could see a face with lips speaking to him and he leaned a bit closer to see better. Gizur saw him and suddenly snatched the globe away, smothering it quickly in his satchel.

"Ivarr, you ninny! Don't you know you can lose your mind by gazing into one of these contraptions?" he roared.

Ivarr blinked his eyes and shook his head. "No, not until just now. Gizur, I saw a face and he was speaking to us. I'm sure he was saying 'Go to the left.'"

"Indeed! Are you certain?" Gizur demanded. "Did you hear anything?"

"No, of course not, but I felt it very strongly."

Gizur faced the left-hand turning. After a significant pause, he said, "That was exactly my impression also."

"Well, then, let's go," Flosi said. "What more do we need? Barrow spirits? Thunderclaps? I doubt old Elidagrimr will be issuing special invitations to come rob his barrow."

Skapti elbowed him aside. "Flosi, you've got no more respect than a pig. You shouldn't be talking that way in a place like this. What I wanted to say was that I don't think it's wise to be influenced by the face of a total stranger in the most important decision we'll be making. Begging your pardon, Ivarr, but it is true that Sciplings are highly susceptible to skillful thought controlling."

"Then I may have imagined I saw someone?" asked Ivarr. "Perhaps we should go to the right? Is that how you vote?"

"No, not at all. I don't feel comfortable even being here, let alone being able to make a choice," Skapti said.

"I have premonitions too," Finnvard said, "I wish we didn't have to go either right or left."

"We could split up," Egills said. "Send a scout each way, and whichever way nobody comes back from we'll know is the wrong way. I nominate Flosi for the wrong way."

After a lengthy discussion, they were still no closer to a decision. The only thing they were closer to was a bout of fisticuffs.

"Stop!" Gizur roared suddenly at the height of the confusion. "We could sit here until the moss grows on us, if that's what you want. Someone has got to make the decision and carry the responsibility for it. Even a wizard can't guarantee everything. Now stop bickering and get your packs on, or Lorimer will make the choice for us."

The mention of Lorimer in that place sent a shudder

down Ivarr's spine and effectively silenced the argumentative Alfar. Quickly they adjusted their packs and tightened their bootlaces.

"Which way?" asked Skapti.

"Left," Gizur said shortly, and strode ahead, punctuating every other step with a jab of his staff. Not daring to say anything lest it sound like a grumble, the others followed, keeping closer together than usual. Flosi trod upon Finnvard's heels or cloak several times, and Finnvard began to snap at him to keep back.

The end of the next day found them at the entrance to the second ring. They made another fireless camp, at Gizur's orders, and chewed on dried fish and berries and the jotuns' hardtack. To worsen everyone's mood, a slight drizzle had descended upon them about noonday, a curtain of mist that chilled the travellers to their bones. Still no one ventured a complaint, although Egills did casually observe that things were getting a bit dampish. Ivarr did not dare mention it, but the right-hand part of the Maze seemed to be under clear skies. The only other person who appeared to notice was Eilifir, who gave Ivarr an enigmatic shrug and burrowed deeper into his soggy cloak.

Contrary to Gizur's calculations, promises, and threats, the rain continued with wretched regularity throughout the night. The day dawned cloudy, and the travellers hastened onward into the second ring. The gloomy weather seemed to follow them. The only time Ivarr saw a break in the clouds was in the late afternoon when they came to the entrance to the third ring, but the left turning led them away from the blue sky and into more drizzly rain. They camped that night just within the third ring. Since they hadn't seen the sun all day, Gizur relented and allowed a fire to be built so everyone could at least have dry feet for the night.

The next day's travel took them to the entrance of the fifth ring. Gizur was jubilant; the elves were apprehensive, and Ivarr was silent and thoughtful.

"Tomorrow we will arrive at the centre," Gizur declared. "A place no man has seen since the old king was buried there centuries ago. And then we shall exit on the far side of the Maze and it's onward to the cave of Andvari and the treasure. The gold, the silver, the jewels—''

''The dragon,'' Finnvard added.

''The coins, the gold chains, the crowns—''

''And the dragon,'' Finnvard said, more pointedly.

''The sceptres, swords, arm bands—''

''The teeth, the claws, the fiery breath,'' Flosi interjected with great relish, delighted to see Finnvard shiver and moan. ''Ripping, rending, frying, bleeding—''

''Oh, shut up!'' Finnvard said, giving Flosi a shove and looking around to see if anyone else noticed his audacity.

''The dragon is Ivarr's project,'' Egills said. ''So we needn't worry about it now. I'm more concerned with avoiding consumption long enough to get to the heart of the Maze and out again with that sword. The dragon is a close second on my worry list at the moment.''

''This Maze is a very evil place,'' Finnvard said, his voice trailing away with a deep sigh. He shook his head with ponderous forebodings.

''More premonitions? Oh, bother!'' Flosi groaned and rolled his eyes. ''What a dirge you're getting to be, Finnvard. You were much more fun the other way, terrified of the least crackling twig. What a nuisance it must be to have powers. Always these nasty suspicions about everything; it's enough to take all the joy out of life. I believe a state of innocent ignorance suits me exactly, with none of these odious responsibilities—'' He went chattering on, but nobody listened. Least of all Ivarr, who was gazing eastward where he could see a patch of clear sky and the rays of the setting sun. For the hundredth time he drew the pattern of the Maze in the sand, six concentric broken rings. With a twig he dotted the line their course had taken them, and then for contrast he traced the course of the right-hand turnings. The centre ring should have two entrances, one on the north and one on the south. Their left-hand course would take them to the entrance on the north. Somehow this troubled him. The north symbolized the cold and the dark of winter, and he knew from Birna that the frost giants, Dark Alfar, and trolls ruled the north. But the Maze lay in the south of Skarpsey, he told himself, and such rules did not apply here. He scratched out the rings and stared at the ground, scowling and making a plan. Gizur would never approve, but he simply had to know what was inside the southern entrance.

In the morning he was awake before anyone else. Flosi was on guard, but he was sound asleep, clutching his sword and far more dangerous than he was wide awake. Well acquainted with Flosi's reflexes, Ivarr skirted him cautiously, stiff cold boots in hand. Gizur made no move, huddled beside the dead fire and sleeping heavily. Ivarr looked at him a moment, thinking that before Vapnajokull the wizard would have leaped up wide awake at the slight rustling sound of Ivarr's cloak brushing against Egills' pack. It was a grave revelation to realize that Gizur's powers were still depleted and dulled.

To let the others know where he had gone, Ivarr made an arrow from pebbles, lining them up in a large V with the point aimed eastward, to the right. He walked away quickly, losing himself from view among the rubble of boulders and underbrush.

CHAPTER SEVENTEEN

The centre ring loomed on his left, steep, impenetrable, and half-lost in mist. The ravine he was walking in had been the channel for a sizable stream at one time, gouging its way deeply between the sharp shoulders of the fells. Ivarr had to watch where he walked and frequently had to scramble up steep little waterfalls and detour around dark pools.

It took Ivarr only an hour's walk to spy the southern entrance ahead. From his distant viewpoint he gradually acquired a perfect view of the scene within. It was a pleasant little plain, surrounded on all sides by walls of black stone hung with moss and creeping plants. In the centre stood a longbarrow, ringed with stones to form the outline of a ship. Ivarr had never seen a place so utterly peaceful and protected. He had half-expected guardians of some sort, but the mound waited for him, innocent of all warlike appearances.

Ivarr hurried toward the last entrance, imagining everyone's astonishment and annoyance when he returned with the sword. He didn't suppose it would be too difficult to open Elidagrimr's barrow and find the sword. Elidagrimr himself would be nothing but dust, he told himself; it wouldn't be at all frightening to open a barrow in broad daylight.

The going became rockier and rather tricky with moss, so he slowed down to watch where he put his hands and feet.

When he looked up, the gate seemed no closer. In fact, it seemed to be receding into the shoulders of the fells abutting it. Ivarr hurried, feeling rather vexed, knowing he had been gone too long and Gizur would be beside himself with rage. Determinedly, Ivarr struggled on. The way was getting more difficult the further he went.

Finally he sat down and stared incredulously at the wall of the sixth ring. The gate had simply vanished. Ivarr shook his head, trying to convince himself he had accidentally missed it somehow. Before him, the ravine was rugged with monstrous boulders and clawing trees, and the prospect of going back was almost as bad. Sighing wretchedly, he turned around and began the descent. Looking over his shoulder, he saw the gate slowly reappearing as he descended, to tantalize him once more with a vision of Elidagrimr's barrow, serene and secure in its enchantment.

He was right about Gizur's wrath. The wizard had followed him and met him halfway. The return journey was one long harangue, and Ivarr listened meekly, realizing how dangerous it was to try reversing a spell in midpoint, which was what he had attempted by going against the Maze. He did not doubt that if he had persisted much longer, he would never have found his way back.

"I didn't think about the magical aspects of the Maze," he said contritely. "I just forgot it wasn't an ordinary series of mountains."

"Forgetting is a good way to get killed," Gizur snorted. "But the worst of it was the way you sneaked away from us. Finnvard and Skapti were convinced you had abandoned us to the wrath of Svartarr."

"I'm sorry," Ivarr said. "But at least I did get a glimpse of the south entrance and the barrow inside."

Gizur's face went grey. "You did?" he gasped.

"I couldn't get to it, of course, but—"

Gizur's fingers dug into his arm. "You're certain you saw the barrow by going that way?"

"Yes, I'm certain. I have very good eyesight and I'm not prone to idle imaginings. It had a ship ring around it, and the

201

top was flat like a king's barrow.''

Gizur turned away a moment and stared unseeing toward their camp, which was visible ahead. The elves were obviously enjoying Gizur's absence. They had a large fire going and were eating a sausage apiece, except for the circumspect Eilifir, who was standing guard.

"Does it mean something, Gizur?'' asked Ivarr.

The wizard's shoulders sagged and his knuckles were white on the hand grasping his staff. ''Yes, it means we must go back. Yes, we've got to go back to the very start and go the other way. But wait—perhaps we could switch over at the entrance to the third ring. The routes cross there. Yes I think we can make it yet if we can get back to that point. The faster we try, the sooner we'll know. And Ivarr—'' He stopped suddenly in his headlong scramble ''—forget that I ever chastised you for your side venture this morning. If you hadn't gone and seen that gate, our chances for retreat would have been nonexistent. Perhaps they are anyway, but you were right and I was wrong. There, it's not every day you'll hear a wizard admit that.''

The elves were aghast at the news, too frightened even to argue. Gizur explained that they had to retrace their exact course to the gate in the third ring in the hope of unwinding the spell, with no shortcuts. The elves broke camp in record time and half-trotted at Gizur's heels in their haste to leave the hateful place behind. Ivarr brought up the rear with Eilifir and Skapti just ahead.

Gizur paused at frequent intervals to cast about with various magical devices. Invariably he disclaimed all their findings and stuffed them into his pockets in disgrace. Ivarr thought he looked more concerned each time, but the wizard said nothing to relieve his steady oppressive feelings of doom.

The going became more rocky and brushy than Ivarr remembered, and the mist descended with a vengeance. They could hardly see the mountain walls on either side. The whole effect was sombre and threatening.

At last Flosi voiced everyone's growing conviction. ''This

202

doesn't look like the way we came, Gizur. I don't remember so many rocks jamming the way, and it's getting worse. Somewhere we took a wrong turn.''

Gizur whirled around and stabbed his staff into the ground with a burst of sparks. "We haven't taken any turnings, you idiot. How could we have taken a wrong turn? What I suspect is happening is this wretched Maze magic is working on us. All this is mere illusion and deception. No arguments, we're going on no matter whatever obstacles are planted in our way.''

"Illusion?" Finnvard murmured doubtfully as he studied a rockslide barring their way. "I've seen real ones that didn't look half so good.''

They clawed and climbed over the rockslide and on to more rugged terrain until it seemed they had been there forever.

"It shouldn't be much further," Gizur said for the tenth time. "Blast it, it's got to be here!''

But it wasn't. Egills began moving slower and slower, and Finnvard's wheezing proclaimed he couldn't go much further. Ivarr was about to suggest going back when Gizur spotted the entrance ahead. It had taken them the entire day to cover the same distance that had taken them only a few hours the day before. When they reached the gate, they sat down in dispirited silence to contemplate the forbidding sight of the fourth ring before them. Fog lingered over the surface of the ground, swirling inexplicably, and the smell was distinctly unhealthy. In the declining rays of the sun it looked even less inviting.

"We'll camp here tonight," Gizur said. "At least it's fairly dry here and we're not likely to sink in mud up to our collarbones.''

"I don't recall it looking that—that boggy, the first time through," Finnvard ventured. "But that just shows what a useless thing my memory is, doesn't it?" He attempted to laugh, and a hoarse croak echoed him from the fourth ring. Finnvard wasn't the only one to gasp in alarm.

"It's only frogs," Ivarr said after his heart quit pounding.

No one answered. All eyes were studying the gloomy path before them. For once, eating was no comfort. They all huddled around the small smoky fire which Gizur had started, not without difficulty, and gradually fell asleep, leaning on each other's shoulders. Gizur lingered by the fire, poring over books of ancient lore and wisdom, curtly refusing Ivarr's admonition to get some rest. Ivarr dozed, awakening several times to see Eilifir and Skapti watchfully awake. In the wee hours of darkness, Gizur was still there, turning the pages and reading endless pages of runic.

In the morning they struck boldly into the misty fourth ring. Before an hour had passed the footing became mucky, rapidly turning into stagnant water and slime.

"We will not go back to the centre," Gizur growled, glaring from side to side as he waded along, feeling the way ahead with his staff. "Whatever or whoever is perpetrating this hoax will be disappointed. Let the bog water cover our heads and bring on whatever monsters are lurking here, but we'll still go onward, backward of this miserable enchantment."

Finnvard slogged along, uttering wretched little moans. He held fast to the hem of Egills' cloak and kept his eyes screwed shut most of the way. He opened them in great dismay only when the group encountered a tangle of fallen trees obstructing their path, raising gnarled roots like claws to entangle and ensnare. No one bothered any longer to observe that nothing seemed the same as the first time they had passed.

Mercifully, the bog did not deepen. They slopped along until midday, but no one felt like eating. Shortly thereafter, Flosi descried a gap in the mountains, hailing it with a shout of joy.

Gizur stopped and frowned at it. "It can't be, not yet. The rings are getting larger and the gates further apart as we work our way outward. We haven't travelled very fast, either. That gate shouldn't be visible until at least sundown—or tomorrow morning, perhaps."

The Alfar looked at him uncomprehendingly. Then

Skapti said, "We could go past it. If we do, we'd have to make a full half-circle before we find another gate on the proper side. The next one, if we pass this one, leads back inside the Maze. Perhaps working backward has changed something, Gizur. I don't have a good feeling about this at all."

"To say the least!" Egills said, pulling one of his feet out of the swamp with a juicy slurp. "I say let's take the chance. I'm sick of this bog. My toes are growing webs."

Gizur looked at Ivarr and Eilifir. "Well? Shall we go for it?"

Eilifir nodded at once. "I think things could get worse with this swamp. Bogs, you know, are a favourite haunt of necromancers—Lorimer in particular. I wouldn't be surprised if this was the very bog Regin found Lorimer buried in." He spoke in a whisper, but they all heard.

The view into the next ring looked dry, at least. They advanced to the entrance, where a halt was called to rest and build a small fire to dry their sodden boots. By that time, everyone's spirits had settled into a state of silent depression. Even Flosi was too glum to start an argument. Gizur estimated they had several more hours of travel time before darkness set in, so on went the semi-soggy boots and they ventured into the third ring. It was a quiet, gloomy place which seemed to offer no opposition to their passage. They marched through it, alert and cautious, until the sun vanished over the jagged rim of the Maze. Since it was yet early afternoon, they had a long twilight before nightfall. Fortunately the way was smooth and afforded a good camping spot almost anywhere. The elves began to feel almost cheerful, and Flosi started making his usual critical remarks.

"Whoa!" Ivarr exclaimed suddenly, pointing ahead. "I can't believe it—but I see a gate!"

They halted instantly and stared ahead at the wall of mountains. The gap was distant enough to look blue and misty, but it was obviously a break in the mountains.

"No," Gizur said to himself, striding ahead a few paces.

205

"We simply can't be at an entrance—or an exit. That should be the way out, but you all know perfectly well it took us an entire day to get from the first gate to the second. Now we've encountered two in scarcely four hours."

Skapti bit at the end of his beard. "But what's to be done about it? There it is, right before us. We can't go past it, we can't stay here, and we certainly can't go back or we'll find ourselves at the centre again."

Egills grinned ghoulishly. "This must be the way the others perished—going around and around looking for the right gate and never finding it."

"Oh, hush!" Finnvard exclaimed, clapping his hands over his ears. "I can think up enough gruesome ideas without your help."

"Quiet!" Skapti ordered, as Egills was embarking upon the old argument that all their troubles were Flosi's fault because he had killed the otter. "Perhaps Flosi did disobey orders and kill the otter, but it's not fair to keep punishing him for it forever. Particularly since you're no better yourself, Egills."

Ivarr separated himself from the dispute and walked ahead to study the gate. He felt a sudden fascination for it, and a dreadful curiosity to see what waited beyond. It almost seemed to draw him forward, whether he wanted to go or not. He heard himself say, "Let's go have a look at it. That's the least we can do."

Gizur was close behind him when they at last came into view of what lay beyond the gate. In amazement they stared inward— not into the large outer first ring, but right into the centre of the Maze. In the gloomy twilight, the place looked shadowy and sinister. They saw heaps of grass-grown ruins, several long barrows, and many small round mounds. All around rose the towering walls, seeming to lean inward like muttering, conspiring giants.

"We're right back at the centre!" Skapti gasped.

Gizur whirled on the goggling Alfar. "Get back to the other gate, at once! Don't just gape and stare, get going!"

A delayed-action panic set in, and they raced helter-skelter for the last gate, which had been perhaps a half-mile away. Gizur pounded along in the rear, admonishing and prodding at any laggards—usually Finnvard, who began to puff and wheeze and struggle, stumbling every time he craned his head around to see if anything was pursuing.

The gate loomed ahead suddenly, unexpectedly, but it was on the wrong side. They halted at Gizur's sharp command while he stalked ahead to glare at it challengingly. "This isn't it," he said. "We'll go past and see what happens."

Holding his staff warily in both hands, he hurried the others across in front of him. Ivarr peered past him and saw that it was the same dismal scene they had seen through the opening they had just passed. Now it was even more gloomy and uninviting.

In silence they hurried on as fast as they dared in the deepening twilight. Mist rose from the ground and swirled around their knees. Gizur tapped the way ahead, muttering spells and imprecations that had no visible effect. A cold little moon shone over the mountain tops, peering indifferently down into the Maze.

Finnvard moaned tremulously. "I do think we're trapped, Gizur. The Maze wants us to go into that place where the ruins and barrows are. Some evil force is preventing us from leaving. We'll never escape from this Maze until we do what it wants us to do." Flosi started to jeer at him, but Eilifir cut him off, speaking quietly. "Finnvard is perfectly right. Whatever force has control over the Maze wants to meet us in the centre. Perhaps that is the only way we can get out. Once inside the centre, there will be two exits. If we take the other one and make all left-hand turns, we can get out on the far side of the Maze."

"And try again," Ivarr added, ignoring Finnvard's moan.

Gizur listened and nodded in agreement, his eyes beginning to flash angrily. "Whoever is attempting this miserable deception is going to pay for his interference! He's going to be darning socks in the lowest pits of Hel's kingdom with his own skin for thread. Forward, troops! We'll meet this treacherous scoundrel and teach him the meaning of a drubbing!"

They marched back to the entrance to the centre heavy-footed with exhaustion mingled with reluctance. Without hesitating, Gizur strode into the centre and halted at a respectful distance from the nearest barrows. The area was roughly a half-mile across at the widest point, Ivarr guessed, gazing over the barrows toward the entrance on the far side, which he could barely discern in the dimness. It was a doleful, silent place with rather more of a boggy nature than Ivarr cared for.

"Careful!" said Gizur sharply, seizing Ivarr by the arm and pointing to a yawning hole at his feet. "Looks like a mine shaft or an air hole. There might be more than one around here, so watch your step. Dark Alfar is my guess, judging from the sheer audacity of digging tunnels in Jotunsgard, not to mention in a place like this." He shivered suddenly with a different species of chill.

Egills, Finnvard, and Flosi stood in a tight knot. "We're not going any further," Flosi said. "This place is evil, Gizur."

"Listen!" Gizur held up his hand, and they all listened to the desolate silence for a long moment, huddling their backs to the cold wind. "Nobody here, or so it seems," Gizur continued, leaning on his staff. "Well, let's take shelter in one of the ruins and see what develops. I'm ready for him, whoever he is."

"Do you think it's Lorimer?" Ivarr asked, hurrying to overtake Gizur.

The wizard poked with his staff among the fallen ruins of an old tower, illuminating fire-blackened stones and old charcoal. All that remained of the tower was a shoulder-high wall, barely enough to provide shelter from the prying wind. Gizur looked around and deemed it satisfactory.

"I honestly can't hazard a guess, Ivarr. Not in a place like this. I confess, the powers in this place are well-nigh indecipherable. No doubt it is a place of great and malignant evil or it wouldn't have attracted the Dark Alfar. Perhaps it is the portal of Hel's kingdom of the dead."

"I've been afraid before," Ivarr said, looking around desolately, "but now I'm really afraid, Gizur."

"Nonsense," Gizur said without much conviction. "It's just an old burial ground—perhaps. No one could expect to feel exactly jolly about setting up camp in such a place, except maybe a fancier of old bones and rags. It's the dampness I object to. I can't seem to stop shivering."

They all crouched in the dubious protection of the ruin while Gizur strolled up and down like a sentry. Egills and Finnvard huddled back to back with drawn swords, like two old dogs baring their teeth and bristling their fur at strange noises, hoping nothing would frighten them more.

"Gizur, come in here and let's all wait together," Ivarr suggested after a while.

Gizur grunted, "Perhaps we'd better, I suppose." He stalked back to the ruin, settling down against the rough wall.

In a thin, nervous voice Finnvard said, "I feel a very definite premonition about this place, Gizur."

"A cabbage would have premonitions here," Flosi said through chattering teeth. "I feel it too. I think Lorimer and fifteen flesh-eating draugar are standing just beyond the corner of my eye."

Gizur lit his pipe, puffing clouds of fragrant, reassuring smoke. "Yes, I seem to discern Lorimer's presence nearby. If he is coming to issue us a challenge, he knows that he'll have to get rid of me before he can get to the rest of you. I may not be a Guild wizard, but mind you, what I lack in reputation and fancy degrees I make up in sheer determination. I confess I've made mistakes, for which I apologize. Sometimes I've gone beyond what I was trained for, but if Lorimer thinks he's going to possess that sword, he'll have to kill me first, and I don't believe he could do that very easily. I've never backed down yet from a challenge. I've always earned my pay, I'm proud to say."

Ivarr listened with half an ear. Something was murmuring at his subconscious, and it was becoming more insistent—louder and more distinct, like a sheep's bell tinkling as the creature descended a fell. The Alfar relaxed, listening to Gizur talking, soothing them, yet Gizur's eyes were darting around watchfully and his staff was ready across his knees.

Ivarr was not certain when the murmuring became an actual voice. Gizur heard it too, and had been listening to it long before Ivarr could hear it. Eilifir and Skapti heard it next and stared around in alarm. Gizur's story halted abruptly.

"What is that?" Skapti gasped, leaping to his feet. The widening eyes of the others signalled their awareness.

"He's here!" Flosi whispered, unable to move a muscle.

"Ivarr!" called the voice in whispery tones. "Ivarr, I've come for you!"

CHAPTER EIGHTEEN

Gizur and Ivarr lunged for the doorway, tangling briefly with Finnvard and Flosi, who were diving the other way.

"It's Lorimer, coming for Ivarr!" Skapti exclaimed, scrambling after Gizur.

Gizur blocked the doorway effectively, gazing into the dark beyond with the assistance of his flaming staff. "Lorimer!" he called. "I'm the one you want!"

"No," came the reply. "It's Ivarr who put out my eye, just as he would put an end to my plans for Svartarrsrike. No, he's the one I've got plans for. I'll get you later, Gizur." A darker patch of shadow drifted closer from the direction of the barrows, accompanied by a flickering blue nimbus. "It was I who led you here to the heart of the Maze, a hateful place of death and torment. What ironic fate it is that I should accomplish my greatest triumph on the very scene of my worst defeat, where my poor carcass was mercilessly staked in a bog by Svartarr's black dwarves. Swords and corpses; it makes one wonder what other curiosities are concealed in the swirling vortices of the Maze." He waved one eerie blue hand. "Send out the Scipling, Gizur, and I shall let the others go unharmed."

"Don't be absurd, Lorimer. You know we'll never hand him over to you without a fight," Gizur shoved Ivarr back twice and snarled at him, "Get down and stay quiet, you dolt!"

211

Ivarr snarled back. "Gizur, it's my quarrel with him. I'm going to kill him for Birna, and I won't let you stop me. I nearly succeeded once; this time will be the end of him."

"Hush! That's absurd! Until you actually get your sword, I'm still in charge here and I give the orders and you obey. When you become real hero, I will be forced to obey you, but not until, understand? Now, for the last time, sit down and be quiet!"

The darkness that was Lorimer uttered a dry chuckle. "I might remind you that you're in no position to bargain, Gizur. You have felt the predominating powers of this side of the centre of the Maze, and you know they are all in my favour. You have blundered into this place like flies into a spiderweb and you cannot escape until I release you. I could kill all of you except the Scipling, if I chose to."

Gizur snorted. "Not as long as I stand between you and them. We can easily depart from the Maze as soon as you are dead."

A sword flickered in Lorimer's hand now, and he drew closer. "Is that your final answer, Gizur? You refuse to surrender the Scipling?"

Gizur drew his own sword and stepped forward, holding it aloft. It beamed like a torch, illuminating his face and casting his eyes into shadow. "That's right, Lorimer. You shall take Ivarr over my dead body—then and only then."

"Then let it be as you have stated!" Lorimer raised his fist and hurled an icy blast at Gizur, who quickly countered it with a fiery spell of his own. The night was blanched by lightning and fire-bolts, and the echoes rolled away across the looming fells. The blasts met head on in rapid succession as the two wizards stood poised, knee deep in the roiling smoke and mist from the explosions.

Suddenly the blasts ceased. In silence the wizards regarded each other for a long moment, then Lorimer spoke. "That was a well done skirmish, Gizur, and I confess I'm astonished. They told me at Ulfgrimrsstead that your powers had suffered a great depletion and I shouldn't have much difficulty destroying you."

212

"Indeed! What obliging and charming jotuns at Ulf-grimrsstead. I'm almost sorry to prove them liars. Is it a duel with swords, Lorimer?"

Lorimer raised his sword, which cast a sullen blue light. Ivarr could see that his left eye had been replaced with a blood-black stone that glittered in the flickering of his sword.

"A duel then, if you think you have the power. Our best weapons at close quarters. No rules, all's fair until one of us is dead."

The swords touched ceremoniously, causing a bright waterfall of sparks. Then Lorimer lunged forward murderously, but Gizur parried his thrust with a crimson flash of light. With deadly speed the wizards dealt their blows, thrust, and countered, without relinquishing any ground on either side. The air was filled with acrid smoke and the grinding ring of metal clashing on metal.

The duel began to travel slowly when Gizur made the first strategic retreat. The brilliant flashes of light and sparks revealed the barrow mounds where the shadows leaped like skeleton figures dancing in satanic glee. Lorimer cast aside his cloak, which flitted away on the wind like a giant black bat and came to rest almost on top of the Alfar in their hiding place, giving them a moment of heart-stopping horror. Then Egills and Flosi attacked it with their swords and cut it into shreds, exulting savagely in their audacity.

The battle precariously skirmished around several of the deep mine shafts, and Lorimer fought with particular cunning, attempting to force Gizur to step into the black nothingness.

"Behold your doom!" Lorimer exclaimed, making a deadly thrust.

Gizur leaped to one side, instead of reacting instinctively and stepping back, which cost him a glancing wound on his left shoulder.

"I touched you that time!" Lorimer said. "I expect that wound will begin to tell upon you soon, and you'll make a fatal mistake, Gizur. But listen to me for a moment. Perhaps you'll like this idea." He lowered his sword in a show of equanimity. "Be my assistant, Gizur. Surrender now and swear your fealty to me and you shall live. Would not that be better than death? Or these horrible pits? You know what lies down there. Only a lengthy nothing descending fathoms into the heart of the earth. Not even the great Gizur could survive that. Wounded as you are, you've no chance to overcome me."

Gizur clenched the spreading black stain on his shoulder. "Oblivion would be a thousand times preferable to being your servant for a single day. Servant to a glorified draug, indeed! The shame would be poisonous for miles around. You belong back in your bog to rot and moulder away. Give me a stake and I'll see to it you walk no more!"

They both hurled their swords at each other at the same instant, raising their fists to call down spells of fire and ice. The swords tangled at midpoint at the summit of a gleaming arc with a thunderous report of combining forces. The earth trembled and rocks tumbled down in the ruined tower. As the sky turned a hideous sulphur colour, Ivarr saw the two wizards grappling over one of the swords. Then they vanished in clouds of smoke and mist, but not before Ivarr realized that Lorimer was forcing Gizur backward toward the edge of a mine shaft.

"Gizur's in trouble! We've got to help him! Skapti exclaimed, leaping to his feet. A tremendous explosion ripped the yellow sky asunder and flames climbed aloft. "Come on, you nithlings, this is our fight!"

Ivarr dived after Skapti, uncertain whether to drag him back or to join him in Gizur's defence. Another jarring explosion shook the old tower to its foundations and stones began to topple. The other Alfar scuttled to safety. Skapti seized Ivarr's arm and hauled him into the shelter of a barrow lintel. "If none of us survive and you're left alone, Ivarr, you've still got to get the weregild to Knutsbarrow on the plains of Hlidarend by Midwinter's. Promise you'll do it!" He had to shout over the explosions and roaring of flame and ice contending.

"I'll do it!" Ivarr shouted back. "Let's get to Gizur!"

The wizards still confronted each other, trading spells at close range. Before Ivarr and Skapti could reach Gizur, they saw his staff suddenly splinter and fly out of his grasp. Lorimer's ruby eye glittered as he raised his sword with a triumphant laugh. Before he could strike, Skapti boldly struck at him from behind, severing the arm that bore the sword so it went spinning into the depths of the shaft. With a terrible bellow, Lorimer whirled on Skapti and Ivarr. Gizur seized his own sword and thrust it to its hilts through the necromancer's body. Then he gave Lorimer a shove toward the waiting blackness of the mine shaft. Lorimer's ruby eye flashed as he spun about, teetering on the edge. His clawlike hands shot out, twisting themselves in Gizur's cloak even as Lorimer lost his balance and began to fall.

"No! Gizur!" they shouted in anguish and disbelief, rushing to the edge of the pit, but it was too late. Spells and counterspells thundered in the deep maw of the mine shaft for many moments, each fainter than the last, and then silence. Ivarr and Skapti stared at each other, unable to move.

Something came slithering toward them in the darkness, ending their state of shock. It was Eilifir, and the others were close behind, querulous and fearful.

"Are you all right?" Eilifir gasped. "Where's Gizur? And Lorimer?"

"Gone," Ivarr said numbly. "Down into that horrible pit."

Stunned, they all sat silently contemplating the black smoking hole before them. The moon shone disapprovingly through the clouds of lingering smoke, revealing the blasted turf where bolts had landed and the smashed ruin of the fallen tower. Finnvard wept unabashedly and Flosi attempted to comfort him.

"He didn't use the escape spell?" Finnvard asked, wiping the soot and tears off his face. "He's really gone forever this time?"

"I fear so," Eilifir said gently "We'll have to go on alone."

"We can't," Egills said desolately. "Without Gizur we're just a pack of fools."

Ivarr raised his eyes from the charred rim of the shaft. Small bits of turf and pebbles were still falling into the silent darkness, which smelled of scorched earth. "We must. There's no staying here. Gizur took Lorimer down with him, using spell after spell. I doubt there's much left of an old dried bog corpse like Lorimer. Gizur might have saved himself, but he chose to—to do what he did. We can't let him die for nothing."

Skapti was too upset even to pull his ear. "Lorimer would have killed him anyway, I could see that. I wish I'd been the one Lorimer had grabbed when he fell."

"No, it should have been me," Flosi said bitterly. "It was all my fault to begin with. I killed the otter."

Eilifir stood up. "It's no good talking this way. Gizur is gone and we can't blame ourselves. He knew he was risking his life when he agreed to help us. I think we'd better get moving, in case Lorimer's black dwarves are here waiting for him."

The Alfar silently sorted their packs from the rubble of the tower and walked toward the far entrance. The gate did nothing untoward; they hurried through it and halted on the far side in the shadows to decide on a course. Finnvard sank down on a stone, ostensibly to tighten his bootlaces. Flosi hovered behind him, waiting for his usual complaint. Finnvard shut his eyes, muttering and scowling to himself.

"Left, left," he muttered, opening his eyes in astonishment. "I'm certain we should go to the left, and that's remarkable, since I usually don't make decisions. I heard it as plainly as a voice speaking in my ear."

Flosi shook his head in disgust. "Finnvard, I think you've finally lost your mind, if you ever had one. Voices indeed. Just listen to him, talking nonsense like an old fool."

"No, Finnvard's right," Skapti said. "Left is the way to go. We'll be out on the far side and safe in three days. You forget—Lorimer is gone too. The Maze will work perfectly for us this time."

They travelled as far as they could into the next ring and wearily set up a rough camp. Eilifir volunteered to take the first watch, climbing onto a jutting rock while the others stretched out and went to sleep. No one seemed to sleep very soundly except Egills, whose exhausted snores sawed on the nerves of everyone else. Flosi muttered and thrashed around as if he were grappling with someone in his sleep.

When morning finally arrived, Eilifir took Ivarr aside and walked with him a half-mile or so back to the entrance to the ring. He pointed to the ground. The soft earth was churned up by the hooves of perhaps fifteen or twenty horses travelling to the right.

"In a great hurry," said Eilifir. "Perhaps they'll go around and find the other side. Perhaps they can't get out at all if they run into those bogs the way we did."

"Perhaps they're looking for the bogs on purpose," Ivarr said with a strange shudder. "But that's silly, isn't it? Lorimer is dead."

"But how dead?" Eilifir asked. "He has been killed before, you know. However, nothing burns better than a dried-up bog corpse. In some areas the supply of wood is rather scarce."

"What do you really believe, Eilifir?" Ivarr faced the Alfar and stared at him, eye to eye.

Eilifir looked back at him with his inscrutable golden gaze. "I believe we'd better hurry back or Finnvard will be prostrated with the fear that we're lost. Isn't it amazing how his powers of precognition are developing? Sometimes all it takes to jolt a slow learner is a crisis or an accident of some sort. And Skapti is amazing, isn't he?"

Ivarr shook his head slowly. "All right, I won't ask you any more questions."

"Good. What a relief. I wouldn't answer them anyway." Eilifir lapsed into a silence which lasted the rest of the day.

When they returned to their camp, they were welcomed with a watery soup of dried fish and flat tea. The Alfar were snapping at each other between long periods of moody silence.

217

"We're done for this time," Flosi said. "What can we do without Gizur? We're not clear of the jotuns yet. They'll grab Ivarr and his sword without the least compunction."

"Sword?" Egills grunted. "What sword? Do you see a sword? Maybe your eyes are playing tricks on you, Flosi. There is no sword, and I have my doubts there ever will be a sword."

"Nonsense," Ivarr said sharply "It's here; we're just on the wrong side. We'll have to go out and start over again so we can find the southern entrance to the centre ring."

Finnvard shook his head. "I'm not sure I can persuade myself to come back in here, once I get out. In fact, I'm almost certain wild horses couldn't drag me back in here."

So went the rest of the days and nights that they were in the Maze. The final camp was made just outside the Maze after sundown. In the morning, as soon as they could see, they left the Maze behind, with many backward glances. That day they took turns dowsing for a safe hilltop. Out of three dowsers, two were the most to receive positive indications, and the same person never received a positive twice in a row. It was frustrating and unnerving. Before the end of the day it was apparent that they were lost. They tried to retrace their path through the crags and pinnacles, but they could never recognize anything about the peculiar terrain. Even from their high vantage point, they could see nothing of the Maze and its massive convolutions.

"We'll never get back to where we were," Finnvard said, after several hours of unsuccessful backtracking. "I think this accursed country rearranges itself the moment you turn your back on it."

Smugly Flosi announced, "Or so it would seem when there's no real leadership. It doesn't make any sense to be led by a mere mortal in our own domain." He stepped closer to Ivarr and eyed him challengingly as he spoke.

Ivarr met his defiant glare. His patience was at the fracturing point. "Then feel free to leave any time you like," he snapped, giving the truculent Flosi a shove backward. "We've all been doing our best except you, and if you don't

218

want to follow me, as Gizur directed in case anything happened to him, then the black dwarves can have you. I intend to find Elidagrimr's barrow and claim that sword whether or not I have any help.''

Flosi's reply was a roar of attack. He charged head down like a goat and bowled Ivarr off his feet. They rolled head over heels in a tangle of pummeling arms and legs. Skapti and Eilifir waded into the fray and seized Flosi by the most convenient handholds and dumped him into an icy little pool beneath a waterfall.

''There, that should cool your temper a bit,'' Skapti said angrily. ''Flosi, I swear upon the hallowed halls of Snowfell and all our ancestors in their mounds that you're the most spiteful and ignorant young savage I have ever had the misfortune of encountering!''

''Now you'll have to build a fire so I can get dry,'' Flosi said bitterly as he hauled himself out of the pool with streams of water running from his clothes. ''The jotuns are sure to see it too, and that will be the end of this hopeless endeavor.''

''No fire,'' Skapti said firmly. ''You won't freeze.''

The Alfar looked at each other dolefully—except Flosi, who went stamping away to empty his boots snd wring out his clothes.

Finnvard heaved a sigh. ''Now we're lost for sure, I suppose.''

Skapti nodded his head. ''No Alfar should ever get lost. We're supposed to have enough power to dowse and foresee and perceive distant things. The problem is we simply don't have enough power to do all those things—yet, anyway.''

Egills shook his head. ''And I don't think I ever shall. Now Gizur's gone, it's easy to see what dunderpates we really are. Not an ounce of power among the lot of us.''

''Power!'' Flosi reappeared, still dripping. ''That's the solution, you dolts. We'll simply get more power, just as we did the first time.''

The Alfar glared at him in exasperation. Egills grunted, ''I think the feathers inside his head got wet, fellows.''

Flosi glanced at him impatiently and turned to Ivarr. His

219

defiance had turned to eagerness. "As I was attempting to say, we can get more power quite easily, and I don't mean for such nonsense as finding someone's fylgja form. I'm surprised no one has thought of it before."

"Then what is it?" Ivarr asked, anticipating another fiery clash.

Flosi folded his arms and looked insufferable. "It's easy. We'll summon another wizard to take Gizur's place."

Ivarr stared at him rather blankly. "Well, how do we go about it? I haven't seen too many stray wizards wandering around, let alone any 'Wizards for Hire' signs."

"Just leave it to Eilifir," Flosi said confidently.

Eilifir nodded in approval and rubbed his hands together as if to say he was anxious to get started summoning right away.

"This won't be like the first time," Finnvard said a little sadly. "We found Gizur at a house of refuge, almost as if our paths were fated to cross. He had heard of Ottar's assassination, and I remember how comical his expression was when he found out we were the famous outlaws. I wonder what he was laughing at? We're not so very much changed from those days, are we?"

Skapti patted him on the back and sighed. "I fear so, old fellow, in ways we couldn't suspect."

Eilifir began scratching around for firewood, impatient to begin. When he had the wood and bits of dry moss collected, he sat down to wait for darkness. When the right time arrived, he lit the fire and they all huddled around it, enjoying its warmth and hopeful light. Eilifir scratched a few runes in the dust and tossed a handful of small objects into the fire—bits of fur and feathers and bone, followed by a pinch of powder. The fire immediately flared and belched a cloud of acrid blue smoke. Sneezing and coughing, the elves moved back to rub their eyes and get out of the smoke.

"Is that all there is to it?" asked Ivarr.

Eilifir smiled and shrugged, making himself comfortable beside a large stone as if he intended to stay there quite a while.

"So we wait, I guess," Skapti said, tugging on his ear worriedly. "I wonder what we're to expect. Signals of some sort, I suppose, or perhaps the wizard will come to us. I wonder how long we'll have to wait? I hope this is a reasonably safe place to camp. I don't suppose anything is reasonable in Jotunsgard, though."

The night passed with many starts and alarms. Toward dawn, Flosi spied a large hare and leaped onto a rock, shouting and waving, certain it was a wizard in his fylgja; but the hare took one horrified look at Flosi and catapulted away with long leaps.

"Maybe it was just a rabbit," Egills suggested with a snicker.

The day dragged on, and Eilifir spent most of his time napping or casually standing watch. Periodically the elves asked each other if anyone felt any signals or impressions or vibrations announcing a wizardly approach. Flosi always wet one finger and held it up, reporting in a bored voice, "Nothing yet."

Toward afternoon, Eilifir sat up suddenly and cocked his head to one side, listening. After a moment, when everyone's eyes were glued on him, he stood up and began putting his pack together as quickly as he could. Ivarr scrambled to his feet. "Is this it, Eilifir? Shall we get ready and go someplace?"

Eilifir shouldered his pack and beckoned impatiently. Everyone began stuffing parcels into his pack and pulling on his boots in a great hurry. Ivarr began to feel a sense of urgency. "Which way?" he demanded of Eilifir, hurrying after the silent Alfar and silently cursing the strange fellow's aversion to the spoken word.

For an answer Eilifir pulled a dowsing pendulum out of his pocket and let it swing as he swept his hand in an arc as a direction finder. Suddenly the pendulum began to gyrate in tight circles when his hand pointed to the south-east.

"Is everyone ready?" Skapti demanded impatiently. "There he goes without waiting for the rest of us! Blasted, contrary fellow! Eilifir! Will you wait a moment?"

Eilifir hesitated a fraction of a moment until Skapti had heaved his pack into place and then he was off again, beckoning urgently. He led them down steep fells and over rocky, impossible places, like a hound following a hot scent. By sundown they had come down from the mountains into a misty valley of silent rock monuments and the pastel-coloured flaky hills where geysers lurked. Steaming pools and strange smells gave the place an unwholesome aspect which Ivarr did not care for at all. He kept his hand on Birna's knife and hurried after the wretched fellow, wondering what Eilifir was leading them into.

A pair of black towers loomed ahead like a sagging and dilapidated archway. Eilifir hurried through it and stopped suddenly, his hand extended, pointing to something that lay beyond.

"Well, will you look at that!" Skapti puffed as they clambered after him and gathered at his side. "What on earth can that be, if not a sign or something significant?"

"Bondscarp—Bondhol to some," Eilifir said, shutting his mouth again with a snap so no more useless words could escape him.

Below, in a flat misty valley, a sharp, purple-tinted spire rose like a needle from the ranks of lesser hills and glacial rubble.

"Bondhol?" Skapti mused. "From its name, there should be a cave somewhere near. I recall seeing the name on Gizur's map. This must be the right place. I'll wager a year's pay there's a cave and a wizard here someplace."

"A year's wages?" sniffed Flosi. "Why don't you make it worthwhile and wager something worth sneezing at?"

Eilifir was already clattering down the talus slope below them, his eyes upon the great crag as the setting sun softly shaded it with warm glowing colours. He halted only once when he espied a well-beaten path leading in the same direction. After a moment's consideration, he led them onto the path and struck out at a faster pace than ever. The path wound around the base of the crag, bending toward a deep blue fissure, where it unexpectedly turned into a flight of stairs hewn out of the stone.

"Amazing!" Ivarr said, looking up the flight of steps. "This looks exactly like the kind of thing a wizard would do. No one could climb these stairs if the wizard didn't want him to. Five or six defenders could stop an army of attackers."

The stairs led to a ledge, which in turn led to another fissure, and so it went up the side of the great crag, skirting breathtaking vertical drops. Sometimes it was scarcely more than a series of depressions cut in the steep side of the crag. Finnvard viewed each new challenge with trembling knees and small whimpers of terror, but he did not offer to balk.

The final ascent was up a very narrow chimney, almost vertical. Finvard hesitated, looking at the stairs and drawing deep breaths, like a diver about to plunge into a firth full of sharks.

"You're not afraid, are you?" Flosi taunted maliciously.

"I was born frightened," Finnvard said, "and it has preserved my life a thousand times. Anyone who isn't frightened simply isn't thinking clearly."

Nevertheless, Finnvard worked his way up the chimney in his own slow time, puffing and snorting with the effort. Flosi was elected to follow him and push if he got stuck.

By the time they reached the summit of the crag, the last bit of sunlight in the entire spiny valley was resting upon the pinnacle of Bondscarp, yet a good distance above their heads. The stairs ended on a wide ledge, with a sheer drop off to one side and solid cliff at their backs. Obviously, there was nowhere to go from the ledge except down. Everyone looked around in dismay—except Eilifir, who merely folded his arms within his sleeves and leaned patiently against the wall.

"Bollixed again!" Flosi exclaimed, the first to find his tongue. He tore his tattered cloak from his shoulders and stamped on it.

"That's not the least of it," Skapti said with an awful grin. "Listen below!"

Far below they heard the unmistakable clamour of hunting trolls hot upon the scent. Looking down into the shadows, they could see dark knots of trolls homing in on the base of the crag. A hoarse roar from below announced the fact that the trolls were probably in the act of climbing up after their quarry.

Finnvard sank down on a rock with a groan. "I don't mean to sound critical, Eilifir, but maybe you made a mistake."

Eilifir's only response was a shrug, and a rather airy one at that. Ivarr glared at the infuriating fellow and whirled around to inspect the ledge again. He explored every fissure, in case it led to a tunnel or more stairs, but there was nothing.

"At least we're in a fairly defensible position," Ivarr said, after a quick glance at the situation below. "It will take them time to climb up here. We'll be standing here with our swords to meet them."

Not far below, toenails scratched on stone. They all unsheathed their swords and positioned themselves in readiness.

Suddenly something whirled overhead, diving at the defenders and spinning away, only to come swooping back at them. It brushed at Ivarr with leathery wings and tilted crazily away over the void.

"A bat!" he said nervously. "Possibly a land-vaettir of the cliff."

"Ugh!" Finnvard shuddered. "Is it the biting variety?"

"How should I know?" Ivarr ducked as the creature dived at him again.

"It'll be a dead variety if it comes back," Egills growled. "Ha, there you are, you little blighter!" He lashed at the bat with the flat of his sword.

The bat cartwheeled and plummeted to the ledge in a small folded parcel, striking with a puff of yellow smoke. The puff suddenly mushroomed and burst into brilliance. Egills tumbled backward. A human figure materialized, carrying a staff with a glowing knob. By its bright light they could see someone in a long hooded cloak, a lengthy white beard, and an outraged expression on the old fellow's face.

"Brigands and murderers!" he shrilled. "How dare you think to assault me on my own doorstep? By all that's dreadful, I'll show you what to expect from attacking a wizard!" He raised his arms overhead in a furious gesture of impending destruction.

"Wait! You say you're a wizard?" Ivarr exclaimed. "Don't make any spells! Just listen for a moment!"

The wizard hesitated and lowered his arms. "Well? What are you doing here? I certainly wasn't expecting the likes of you." He surveyed their ragged clothing and packs with disdain. "Outlaws, most likely, or vagabonds. Perhaps you're beggars?"

Ivarr took a step forward. "No. We came here looking for a wizard. Our friend Eilifir seemed to be following a signal of some sort which led us to the top of this crag. From its name, Bondhol, we thought it must contain a cave where possibly a wizard lived. Are you the wizard of this crag, and is there a cave?"

"Is there indeed?" the stranger repeated thoughtfully. "I wonder about that myself, sometimes. These fellows with you are Alfar, are they not, and you yourself a Scipling, aren't you?" Not waiting for a reply he went on, "I think I've heard something about you. Got yourselves into a very unpleasant situation with Svartarr by killing his son. Yes, I'm sure it must be you. Lorimer has been pursuing you closely, has he not?" His bright eyes examined Ivarr minutely, looking in particular at the knife at his belt and quickly dismissing it.

"Lorimer has been following us until lately," Ivarr said. "I believe we've finally given him the slip. Did you receive the summons we sent out for a wizard's assistance?"

"Yes, I believe I felt something of the sort, but I can't imagine what led you to seek me out. If I had wanted to see you, I would have come to you." His bright eyes searched Eilifir next, and his black brows knit into a scowl as he looked at him.

"You signalled," said Eilifir, "and you know it."

"You must excuse him," Skapti added hastily. "He

225

doesn't speak often enough to be very civil. I daresay he won't speak again for a day or two, or perhaps a week. Very strange fellow indeed. If you're not the one we're looking for, we'll just take ourselves out of here. We're sorry to have disturbed you.'

"No, don't leave," the wizard said. "It's not safe with the trolls abroad. It looks as if they need some chastisement." He pointed his staff at the head of the stairway and Flosi and Egills leaped hastily out of the way. Almost at the same moment a troll flung himself out of the chimney with a terrible bellow, slathering and foaming around the jaws as he snapped his fangs. His anticipation was instantly quenched by the sight of the wizard; he froze almost in midleap with a despairing howl. With a single sharp blast, the wizard rendered him into a dozen lumps of stone, and two more trolls behind him met a similar fate. The stones clattered down the chimney, causing much confusion among the trolls coming up. With shrieks and howls they evidently made a reversal and began a noisy retreat down the scarp, with no regard for the groups on the way up.

"As I was going to say," the wizard continued, unruffled, "anyone who is an enemy of Lorimer is welcome in my home, which is indeed a cave inside this rock. Come with me and we shall descend to my home, where we can discuss this matter concerning Lorimer more fully."

"Thank you, but Lorimer is dead," Flosi said with satisfaction. "We saw him fall into a mine shaft and perish rather fierily."

"We shall see what we shall see," the wizard said. "Come along, and mind the steps. There are three hundred and twenty-two, and dear knows who repaired them last."

The travellers looked around in confusion. The wizard raised his staff and said a single word. Without a sound, a doorway appeared in the cliff, with elaborately carven doorposts and an ancient black door knobbed with tufts of moss. It opened with a welcoming screeching of rusty hinges, greeting the visitors with a blast of musty air.

"I shall go first and light the way," the wizard said.

"Never mind the door, it shuts itself."

Ivarr pushed a reluctant Skapti after the wizard, saying he would watch the rear. The others followed unwillingly, eyeing the dancing shadows cast by the wizard's glowing orb. The best of the steps were worn in their middles from centuries of use, a natural gathering place for puddles. Some steps were slick with moss and others were broken, which caused a lot of stumbling and muttering.

When the great door slammed shut with a sudden crash, the sound went echoing down before them like a hundred doors being slammed. Ivarr suddenly felt very uneasy at the thoughts of being locked inside a mountain with an unknown wizard. He distinctly remembered that the door above had boasted no handle on either side.

With quivering knees, they finally reached the bottom of the stairs. Another door opened of its own accord, flooding the gloomy stairway with firelight. The wizard ushered them inside and the door closed—again no handles on either side.

He sighed contentedly and rubbed his hands a moment before the fire. "I sent ahead for a fire. It's been awhile since I've been home, and I detest coming home to a cold and fireless house."

Finnvard lowered himself into a comfortable chair with a sigh. "Wouldn't it have been a better idea to make your door at the bottom of the Bondscarp, rather than at the top? All those stairs up, and then down—" He shook his head wearily.

"That would be too accessible," the wizard said. "Now make yourselves comfortable, my friends, and tell me your names and what has brought you to my door."

Ivarr was nudged forward as the spokesman, so he introduced them all by name and described their purpose in coming to Jotunsgard and the reasons behind it. The old wizard nodded as if he were already familiar with the story. He listened intently when Ivarr described the duel between Lorimer and Gizur and how they had both fallen into the shaft.

"Now you know all about us," Ivarr said. "We need a

227

wizard to help us and it seems that we were guided to find you, whether you wanted us to find you or not. It seems rather like fate, don't you agree?''

"We'll pay you," said Skapti, "as soon as we get the gold from Andvari, if that's what you're concerned about."

The old wizard pressed his long bony fingers together. His face was a study in wrinkles and folds and lines. Delicately he began, "I must first speak about Lorimer, and I have some unfortunate news for you which will not make you happy at all. Lorimer is not dead, my friends, and I can tell you that for a surety, because I was speaking to him today. That is how I know about his descent into the mine shaft. I was, in fact, mending the wounds he received in that battle and restoring him to his old strength and more besides. You may have guessed my name by now. I am Regin, the one who raised Lorimer from the bog."

CHAPTER NINETEEN

They all gaped at the old wizard in utmost horror. Finnvard sagged against Egills in the initial stages of a dead faint.

Ivarr clutched his knife. ''Then I suppose it will be only a matter of time before you surrender us to your master. Well, perhaps we won't submit quietly to our fate. What if we choose to fight?''

Regin clasped his hands together. ''I am sorry to have deceived you but I have no other choice. I know well that Lorimer is the greatest and most evil being living or dead that stalks the earth. As a black dwarf myself, I have made a study of the conflict of darkness and light, of ice and fire; thus I know that the forces of fire and light have also prepared an antithesis to Lorimer.'' He bowed slightly to Ivarr. ''As long as you exist, so does the possibility that Lorimer may be overthrown and finally destroyed, and all his plots with him.''

''He will be, if I can escape from you,'' Ivarr said coldly. ''We don't intend to wait meekly for Lorimer to arrive and destroy us.''

''Lorimer does not intend to destroy you,'' Regin said. ''Not yet, anyway, but these others—'' He sighed and poked a stick onto the fire.

''We're acquainted with his notions,'' Ivarr said. ''Even if he does succeed in his plan to seize Svartarrsrike from Svartarr, the black dwarves won't tolerate him very long. It was a black dwarf who sent us to the Maze to get Elidagrimr's sword.''

Regin nodded agreeably. ''That is very true. Svartarr's kingdom is standing on shaky ground and the dwarves are understandably anxious. Many are opposed to Lorimer, but they know there's nothing to stop him. They don't want to be too outspoken against him, you see, in case he actually does overthrow Svartarr. Lorimer could make them very miserable.''

''Not if he were dead,'' Ivarr said. ''Sooner or later you're going to regret the day you ever dug him out of the bog and restored life to him.''

''Oh, but I do already,'' Regin said quickly. ''I hadn't dreamed he'd be so greedy for power and so ungrateful to me for freeing him. I devoted my life to him, and now he expects me to be his slave. To put it bluntly, I am frightened of the creature I have re-created and loosed upon the world. Although I am a powerful wizard in my own right, I know I haven't a chance to oppose Lorimer.''

''We do,'' Skapti said. ''Ivarr has told you about Elidagrimr's sword. With that sword, Lorimer can be killed, permanently. If you have any wisdom to go with your power, you'll let us go so we can finish our errand. Once the weregild is paid to Svartarr, it will be Ivarr's turn to settle the score with Lorimer. He'll do it, too, mark my words.''

Eilifir shifted so his face came into the firelight. ''He'll do it, Regin. It's up to you to decide which side you prefer to be on when Lorimer is destroyed.''

Regin shrugged his thin shoulders. ''If he knew I had betrayed him, my life wouldn't be worth a mote of dust in a windstorm. How do you know this inexperienced Scipling can actually destroy Lorimer when we all know there's not a being in this realm who can do it?''

''Dainn the smith thought I could do it,'' Ivarr said. ''The old woman who was my teacher was preparing me for something and she believed a person was able to do almost anything he set his mind to. Lorimer killed her, so I have set my mind to avenge her death on him. This is her cloak I'm wearing, and this is her knife. These were the only things she left behind when she died.''

Regin rose to his feet and stood before the fire. ''I am only one wizard—albeit a powerful one—but I cannot oppose Lorimer alone. If I could undo the harmful work I've done, I'd undo it in an instant, but I'm the one who restored him. I know him too well. It's partly my fault that he is so invincible. I thought I could use his power to strengthen Svartarr and the black dwarves, but instead I was exiled and outlawed by Svartarr when Lorimer turned against him. It was a bitter revelation to realize that instead of helping Svartarr, whose father I advised for many years, followed by his son, I had actually created the ultimate engine of Svartarrsrike's destruction.'' His eyes flashed and his fists clenched and he seemed to be speaking to someone other than the Alfar and Ivarr.

''No doubt you were a wise and strong adviser,'' Eilifir said. ''But now the time has come for you to take the advice. Let us go, Regin. I don't believe you summoned us here to trap us for Lorimer.''

Regin stiffened and looked at Eilifir warily. ''Maybe, maybe so,'' he muttered. ''I suppose there's a treasonous streak in every loyal servant. But such talk is senseless and dangerous for me besides. If I turn you over to him, I know I'm somewhat safer, but—'' He hesitated, his face furrowed into deep creases of worry.

''But you know sooner or later Lorimer will do away with you,'' Skapti said slyly. ''He won't abide the competition. You know too much about him.''

''That's it exactly,'' Regin said with a sigh. ''I wanted to see you, to decide if you really could kill him.'' He and Ivarr eyed each other suspiciously. ''I've decided that it must be one of us who does it, you with your sword or I with the secret knowledge of Lorimer which I possess. The trouble is, I foresee complications. You need a wizard to guide you to the cave of Fafnir and Andvari, and there is a certain object I must have. Unless—without—'' He stopped to frame his words carefully, watching his prisoners with

231

doubtful, shrewd eyes.

"Unless without what?" demanded Flosi, who was regaining some of his natural brass.

"Unless I had this certain token of power, without which Lorimer could easily overthrow Svartarr, I wouldn't even think of betraying my present position of relative safety." He drew out the words with deliberation and thought. "But if I should lay my hands upon it, I assure you that Lorimer's doom would be virtually ensured, if you were there to back me up with the sword. But this is foolish talk, I fear. I daresay you wouldn't help me any sooner than I'd help you."

"Help you cut our own throats? No thanks!" Flosi retorted.

Eilifir's quiet voice inquired, "What is it you want from us, Regin? It almost sounds as if you're offering us a price for our escape."

Regin nodded almost imperceptibly. "My escape also. You are in need of a wizard to guide you to Andvari's cave, and I am in need of this small token to put an end to Lorimer. For a small price I will go with you."

"What? You go with us?" Skapti gasped. "As our guide, you mean?"

"You will need my advice and my maps. You will need my help if you are to get the sword out of the Maze, which I am familiar with." He gazed gravely at Ivarr, whose expression was stony.

Regin seated himself in the tall black chair at the head of the table and waited patiently while the Alfar discussed the matter with great agitation. They were as adamant as if someone were trying to sell them a horse which was blind, deaf, and lame on three legs. The general consensus seemed to be a resounding negative until Skapti pounded the table and roared for silence.

"Now that it's a bit easier to make myself heard," he said in the sulky silence, glaring at each of the elves in turn. "I shall say my say and sit down. I say it's a terrible risk to take Regin. We don't much trust him—"

"Not at all!" Flosi cried. "We don't trust him as much as

the width of one of his whiskers! I wouldn't sleep a wink if I knew Regin was there thinking his necromancerous thoughts and plotting his next resurrection of some evil bog carcass, not to mention the murder of each and every one of us and the theft of Ivarr's sword—''

"Silence!" Skapti roared. "As I was saying, we don't much trust him, but I don't see many alternatives. We need him and his skills and his power. We all know that the sum total of our powers is at best a tricky conglomeration of mismatches, mistakes, and mysteries, which is not likely to get us anywhere but into further trouble. Trouble far worse than anything Regin might possibly wish to do to us. He did say that he wants to destroy Lorimer also, and I see no reason for an individual like Regin to lie to nithlings, such as we are. I believe it would be far better to trust him than to remain here and wait for Lorimer to find us."

"Hear, hear!" Finnvard muttered, gouging Egills with his elbow.

"Very true," Egills said immediately, with a doubtful scowl.

Eilifir and Ivarr exchanged a glance, and Eilifir nodded slightly. Ivarr gripped the arm of his chair, staring at the old wizard coldly. Regin stared back at him, calculating and measuring him against his own invincible creation from the bogs. Ivarr suspected that Regin found him lacking the force necessary for killing Lorimer.

"Well," Ivarr said, "Let's take him along and hope for the best. What is your price, Regin?"

"It's very small, actually." Regin said. "I assure you, you'll not even miss it from the vast hoard Andvari has amassed. It's a ring, a plain gold ring with a few runes on it, and not as valuable as other rings you'll find in the treasure. Andvari himself wears the ring and he won't give it up willingly, but if I have it, I'm certain it will be the chief instrument in bringing about the downfall of Lorimer."

"Ord's ring," Eilifir said "Any necromancer would gladly perish for the possession of such a ring. It has the endearing ability to cause a corpse to speak if it is placed under its tongue.''

Finnvard shuddered. ''Ugh! There's nothing a corpse might say that would interest me that much!''

Regin smiled slightly. ''Wouldn't you like to know the future, my good fellow? How long you will live? If you will be rich when you die? If you will have a few friends or many? With a ring such as this, you would be able to find out the answers to questions such as these, and a good many others besides. I assure you I won't indulge in any necromancerous activities while we're travelling together. I have given up much of it, as a matter of fact.''

Ivarr stood up with a wry triumphant smile. ''But I've just thought of a slight problem, Regin. You are a black dwarf, you say, and we are creatures of the daylight hours. How can we travel together, unless by night? That arrangement certainly won't agree too well with us.''

Regin's fingers rubbed the wood of his staff, a rather new one with its ornamental knob yet uncarved. He then looked toward a shadowy corner, where another staff stood beside a cloak, and a satchel hung on a peg. ''There are several ways to get around the prohibition against light. One of the most difficult is simply called the Ordeal, by which all the darkness is simply banished from an individual's powers. Often it is necessary to undergo the Ordeal more than once, and occasionally the subject does not survive the test. Four times is the known record, I believe, for a necromancer who wanted to be purged of his evil powers.'' Regin did not go on any further, but looked into the fire silently. It seemed to render him almost transparent, so white were his beard and hair and meager the flesh that covered his ancient bones.

''Then we can travel together by day,'' Eilifir said.

''And you will help us find Elidagrimr's sword,'' Ivarr added, ''and help us take the treasure from Andvari and Fafnir.''

Regin nodded. ''I shall do everything in my power to help you, if you will assist me in the killing of Lorimer by giving me the ring Andvari wears on his hand. I don't believe you would be so foolish as to try and deceive me.''

"We won't," Ivarr said. "I especially want Lorimer killed—for Birna."

Regin inclined his head. "Lorimer and the ring in exchange for the sword and the treasure. Is that a bargain we are going to seal?"

"It's a deal." Ivarr said. He and Regin struck palms, followed by each of the elves, and the bargain was sealed with brisk enthusiasm.

Regin then permitted himself to offer the customary tokens of hospitality, suggesting that they clean out the larder and pack away what they would need for the expedition. They ate or drank whatever they could not carry, and made a merry job of it besides, for the most part. Ivarr kept watching Regin secretly, trying to see a shadow of deception or trickery in him. All his instincts cried out against trusting anyone associated with Lorimer.

They camped that night beside Regin's hearth, and in the morning everyone stuffed himself on more food, leaving the mice scarcely a crumb.

"Meager pay for all their years of occupancy," Regin said. "Now I believe we're almost ready to depart. But first—" He looked around thoughtfully, and Ivarr wondered if he were feeling regrets. Then Regin smashed a chair with his foot and violently overturned the table. He passed his hand along the wall, leaving a black streak of glittering ice. Pointing here and there around the room, he drove small ice-bolts at random, splintering the table and the benches.

Ivarr put his hand on his knife. "It looks as if your Ordeals have not quite purged away your ice powers, Regin," he said.

"It took twice before I could face the sun," Regin said, surveying his work. "Perhaps it will take twice more before I can no longer do this." He gestured, and a great bolt of ice shook the room to its foundations as it jarred the mortar out of the hearthstones. Ivarr and the Alfar took shelter under their cloaks.

Regin lifted his staff and touched an overhead beam.

Instantly it began to burn with a creeping blue flame. He touched other wooden things, burning places on the table, the benches, and blackening the stone of the walls. The rooms were thick with smoke and dust, and damp with the smell of shattered, melting ice.

"There, it looks as if a fearful battle took place." Regin looked around with approval. "And now, as a final touch, the sad evidence that Regin the faithful servant has perished in battle with his enemies—the melted remains of the poor old black dwarf." He took the cloak from the peg, scarcely glancing at its elaborate embroidery and fine cloth, and tossed it into the fire. When it was thoroughly charred, he pulled it out, stamped on the flames and poured water over it.

"What a mess you've made of a fine cloak," observed Finnvard, whose own cloak was so riddled that it was more holes than cloak.

"This will convince Lorimer and his dwarves," Regin said, dumping the contents of the satchel on the floor and smashing two glass spheres. "Regin the black dwarf, the necromancer, sorcerer of evil knowledge, servant of Lorimer, has ceased to exist." He cast the old staff into the fire, where it immediately ignited with a greedy crackling, issuing curls of odd-coloured smoke. For a moment he watched, betrayed only by a twitching of the muscles of his face. Quickly he turned away, drawing a deep breath and grasping his new staff firmly. He spoke to the door, then halted in midspell to turn to the Alfar.

"It would look appropriate if it were fire-blasted. I could do it myself, but if you'd like to have the honour, you are welcome to blast my door until nothing remains of it but cinders."

Skapti bowed solemnly after a moment of surprise. "Thank you for the privilege, Regin. Fellows, can we manage it without taking off the top of the mountain?"

Flosi and Finnvard looked uncertain, but Eilifir promptly said, "Of course we can. Start the formula, Skapti."

Before Skapti had finished reciting the spell, the door was

smoking, and upon the final word it exploded with a fiery bellow, just as it was supposed to; in a few moments the timbers had fallen from their iron bands.

Regin nodded and coughed admiringly. The Alfar put on dignified expressions and marched around the smoking timbers toward the stairs. Once out of Regin's sight, they chortled, chuckled, and congratulated one another on the splendid results.

Regin summoned a flame to the end of his new staff to light their way. "I suppose you'll be wanting to go back to the Maze as quickly as I can take you there," he said to Ivarr, who had been watching him in the dark.

"That was our agreement," Ivarr said.

"I didn't agree to going back into the Maze," Finnvard said. "I'd rather consider hanging myself up by the heels for fifty years. I think I'd actually expire and die if I have to go back into that awful place. I'd even wait here in this miserable place—no offence, Regin." His voice echoed dolefully.

Regin said, "Perhaps the others could wait outside someplace, while Ivarr and I go in alone for the sword."

Ivarr's suspicion sharpened. "So it would be just the two of us, Regin? I'm not sure I like that idea, with all those bogs."

"You'll have to trust me," Regin said, "if you really want that sword so badly. Here." He held out his lighted staff.

Ivarr took the staff without speaking and began the long winding ascent, wondering why anyone would willingly prefer to live in the dark and dank underground instead of above on the face of the earth. Regin's true character could also be dank and dark, he reminded himself.

The steps seemed endless, and Ivarr could hear Finnvard and Egills wheezing behind him. Flosi, as usual, was grumbling. Glancing upward at the shaft overhead, Ivarr thought he saw a shadow scurrying ahead of them on the stairs, about two spirals above. He watched more closely as he climbed, and became certain there were three individuals of some sort racing silently just ahead. He stopped, and Finnvard and

237

Egills collapsed gratefully on the slimy steps to catch their breath.

"Regin." His voice echoed menacingly. "Three eavesdroppers are just ahead of us. What do you know about them?"

The old wizard scowled and gazed upward a moment. "No. There are five of them, not three. I suspect they learned the secret formula to opening my door from Lorimer himself. I don't know how long they've been listening to us, but I do know that eavesdroppers perish miserably."

Gathering his cloak around him he uttered a spell. Smoke swirled around him, obscuring him for a moment, and then, with a sudden puff, Regin vanished. A large brown bat went winging silently into the void beyond the stairs, tilting upward out of the light.

The travellers hesitated, and heard nothing except the leisurely dripping of water. Ivarr looked uneasily at the flaming staff in his hand and slowly started climbing again.

Regin did not reappear. They climbed until they saw a light at the top of the stairs and Regin standing in the great doorway waiting for them. He was peering out and clutching his cloak like a thin old beggar looking at a hostile world. Hearing their approach, he pushed the door wider, revealing five dark stains at his doorstep.

"Black dwarves, going to Lorimer to tell him I had turned against him." Regin sighed and scuffed at the wet stains. "My own kind, yet I had to kill them. The world has certainly turned peculiar for this old wizard, has it not?"

With that observation, he locked his door with a large rusty key and hung it around his neck on a chain. Sighing, he made a downward gesture with his hand; instantly the cliff was nothing but rock. He accepted his staff from Ivarr, extinguished the flame, and began tapping the long and difficult descent of Bondscarp.

They reached the bottom of the scarp by midday, and by sundown they had reached an overlook with the Maze below, a welter of crags and fells wreathed in mist. The first entrance was directly before them. They all regarded it a moment in silence, remembering their flight from the Maze while still dazed with the shock of Gizur's death.

"We have an hour or so of light," Regin said, "Shall we camp tonight within the rings of the Maze?"

"No indeed!" several voices said quickly.

"Behind us is a safe little meadow with running water," Regin said. "I think that would suit us all rather better, perhaps."

"Quite so," Skapti said with obvious relief. "That's all right with you, isn't it, Ivarr?"

Ivarr nodded, still looking down at the Maze, and the others scrambled down the fell and started setting up camp. Finnvard scratched together a fire almost instantly and began rattling his cooking pots, while Egills and Flosi inspected and tested several spots for sleeping. Ivarr remained on the ridge, looking down into the Maze. Bitterly he thought of Gizur, with a mixture of sorrow and anger: Gizur should have known no death was lasting for a draug like Lorimer. Regin had evidently patched him up very shortly thereafter, and now he was stronger and more bent than ever on vengeance and destruction. Gizur had abandoned them to a worse fate—wizardless, alone in the Maze, and the sword as inaccessible as before.

A slight sound disturbed his unhappy reflections. It was Regin, seating himself on a stone behind him. Ivarr glared at him, but Regin only said mildly, "It does no good to punish yourself over the death of your friend. He believed he was performing the supreme effort for your cause. A wizard is not often called upon to surrender his life, but when he is, he dies gladly, fiercely."

"But it isn't fair that Lorimer is restored to life, and Gizur must be dead," Ivarr said. "Why couldn't you use your marvellous skills to bring back Gizur, instead of Lorimer?"

Regin shook his head quickly. "You wouldn't want that for your friend. Draugar are in torment until someone is able to stop their wanderings forever, and they're very malicious, evil creatures. Sometimes, however, we the living are able to benefit from them, and thus the existence of necromancers

239

and the dark, evil science of necromancy." He sighed as if the weight of that dark, evil knowledge were weighing heavily upon his shoulders. "I had no choice but to do as Lorimer commanded. I wanted to live to see his destruction someday; had I refused, he would have murdered me and perhaps enslaved another necromancer to do his bidding. He found me at my other home, Asraudrsbog, where I do most of my work—" He emphasized the word with distaste. "—And there I put the evil essence that is Lorimer into another form so he could go about his quest for Svartarrsrike and, incidentally, your destruction. Nothing will stand in his way."

"Where do you suppose your choice bit of handiwork is at this moment?" Ivarr asked. "I should think he's learning that unpleasant things happen to him whenever he tries to thwart us. It hasn't been overlong since someone was required to patch that eye I put out for him."

Regin drew his cloak around his thin shoulders. To Ivarr he looked ready for the barrow, yet Gizur, strong and hearty, was dead. Regin eyed him with a steady, hooded gaze as if he knew his thoughts.

"When Lorimer left me at Asraudrsbog, he did not see fit to inform his old servant Regin where he was going. Perhaps he has learned some caution and has given up on you. Perhaps he assumes you'll all perish quickly without Gizur to help you."

Ivarr snorted with black mirth. "Then he doesn't know we've hired you to help us. Or then again, perhaps he is delighted with our arrangement."

Regin began stuffing an old black pipe with dusty grey leaves. "Or perhaps he's gone back into the Maze to wait for you to come for the sword. It makes a lovely bait for a trap, Ivarr."

Ivarr suddenly felt cold, and his neck hair bristled at the thought of encountering Lorimer again in the Maze, this time accompanied by the very necromancer who had raised Lorimer first from his grave in the bog.

Ivarr looked down at his friends, where Finnvard was

stirring something in a large kettle and arguing vigorously with Flosi. "You won't talk me out of it, Regin. I will have that sword whether Lorimer is waiting or not. But I want the Alfar to stay here. You and I shall go into the Maze alone."

Regin puffed a few more clouds of acrid smoke. Then he knocked his pipe against the stone to empty it and put it into its pouch. Rising to his feet, he took up his staff and said, "Then we shall depart immediately."

"All right," Ivarr said grimly. "Immediately. I'll tell Skapti not to wait for us more than eight days. If we're not back by then, we're not coming back."

Skapti was not pleased by the plan, but Ivarr insisted that he stay and keep an eye on Flosi. The others were obviously relieved at not going back into the Maze; Eilifir, as usual, was noncommittal. Ivarr bid them all farewell and took a parcel of supplies in a small pack. Regin silently led the way toward the entrance to the Maze.

It was nearly dark when they reached the first gate, so they made a quick and comfortless camp just inside. Regin lit a tiny fire for light and a small pot of tea. They had not spoken since leaving the Alfar.

When the tea was gone, Regin arose and drew a ring around their camp, muttering spells to ward off evil and warn them of enemies. He sat down beside the fire and watched it die. When it was nothing but embers he spoke.

"I can only say I hope you won't be disappointed in what you find inside the Maze."

Ivarr made no reply. He curled up in his eider, wondering how on earth he could be disappointed, unless Lorimer waylaid him and killed him. After worrying about it for a considerable length of time he fell asleep with Birna's knife in his hand.

CHAPTER TWENTY

The Maze without the continual chatter and grumbling of the Alfar was a place of portentous silence. Regin and Ivarr spoke rarely, only when it was absolutely essential. The Maze itself presented no difficulties as Regin chose all left turnings. Ivarr was dubious; it was so easy that he was filled with misgivings until the third day when they reached the centre ring. They had kept up a murderous pace, and it was twilight when they saw the last gate before them. Ivarr slowed his pace as they approached. Fully expecting to see the wrong side of the centre with its multiple barrow mounds and treacherous mine shafts, he could scarcely believe his eyes when he finally gazed upon the lone barrow of Elidagrimr, shadowed in sombre twilight. He stopped, unable to believe it wouldn't slither away from him somehow and disappear, as it had the first time he had seen it. Falteringly he stalked the illusion, step by step, and arrived at the entrance without it escaping him. He stepped gingerly into the ring and still nothing happened. Three days of expecting Lorimer to leap out from behind every large stone had drawn his nerves tighter than harpstrings.

"Go on, it's not going to disappear," Regin said. "I'll wait here at the entrance and allow you to proceed alone with no unwanted advice from me."

Ivarr was so close to his dream fulfillment that he felt he could afford to forgive the cautious old wizard, who was forever scratching runes for luck and rings for protection and muttering spells to ward off evil. "Thank you, Regin. It's not that your advice is unwanted—it's just unnecessary. This is the moment I've waited for since this expedition started. This is the sole reason for my presence here in your realm. Everything we've struggled for is based upon that sword."

Regin's eyes were hidden in shadow. "I know you're impatient to be gone, but first I must burden you with more of my dreadful advice. As a fancier of old dead corpses, I know their peculiarities. One of them is the fact they don't like any living being taking anything from their barrows. They aren't mere dead husks, you know. The essence of Elidagrimr still lurks about those old dusty bones and rusted relics. Do you think he'll be pleased to see you making off with his treasured sword Glimr? It's more likely he'll lay an alog on you to curse you for the rest of your life. Are you sure you want to pay the price for Glimr, if it means being haunted by a barrow ghost for the rest of your life? Our realm means nothing to you Sciplings. Our battles are not your battles."

Ivarr shook his head. "You're wrong, Regin. This battle has become my battle. I couldn't turn my back on it now without shaming Birna's memory and making an absolute nithling of myself. Why do you keep trying to make it all the harder, Regin? Gizur tried to help, but you seem to want to put a stop to the whole enterprise. Don't try to confuse me, Regin, or change my mind. I came here rather indifferently, but all that is changed."

"Well," Regin said with a sigh, "good luck to you, then."

Ivarr nodded without looking back. All his attention was fixed upon the barrow before him. He walked steadily toward it, crossing swales and small rocky hilltops. It grew larger as he advanced, becoming the imposing burial mound that befitted a famous warrior king. By the time he reached the ring of stones encircling its base, the night was darkening around him, relieved only by the small smudge of light far behind at the entrance, where Regin had built a small fire as he waited. A sliver of moon cast a bit of pale light on the mound before him. As he looked, he thought he saw the shadowy domes of a dozen other mounds which he was certain he hadn't seen by daylight. His heart began to pound; the Maze was up to its old tricks again. He edged away cautiously, keeping his eyes on the strange mounds, then began walking quickly back to Regin and his fire, telling himself the day was a more salubrious time for breaking into a barrow mound anyway. He crossed two small hills, glimpsing Regin's fire each time from the summit; but when he crossed the third hill, he could see nothing of Regin's fire. He was fairly certain he had retraced his exact footsteps, but all he could see was an unfamiliar cairn of stone and more deep shadows which he didn't care to wander into.

"Regin!" he called softly, standing still a long moment, straining his ears to hear a cough or the crackle of twigs being fed to a fire. On such a clear, windless night, small sounds should carry quite easily.

He heard no sign of Regin, but what he did hear was a peculiar random clicking and rustling from the mound behind him. Whirling around, he realized with a shock that he had walked right into the midst of the spectral burial mounds. The scratching and rustling sounds were louder, all around him, as if some creature was industriously digging its way out. Ivarr hoped it was some burrowing animal and not something far more sinister. He edged his way back toward the large barrow, which seemed a long way off; but in a matter of moments he found himself climbing right up its steep side. The same restless sounds came from within. He stood still, thinking how the mounds reminded him of a large hall full of men, laughing and talking, with the plaintive notes of harp piercing the rumbling din at intervals. It sounded as if an army had gone with Elidagrimr into his mound, remaining in the barrow under the dear and familiar soil of Skarpsey to protect their king and his sword.

Ivarr drew a deep breath and began walking along the

back of the long mound, searching for the stone lintel that would denote its entrance. Beneath his feet, the murmurous sound of voices seemed to be getting louder.

But not loud enough to drown out shouts, he told himself. He could yell for Regin to come and help him, but he was reluctant to do so. A suspicion entered his mind that somehow Regin could be responsible for the illusion of the smaller burial mounds. He knew he possessed a keener sense of direction than to get lost in the dark only a hundred paces away from the entrance. Losing Ivarr in the Maze would be an easy way for Regin to dispose of him.

At the end of the barrow, he stopped to search for the entrance. Below were six round barrows, their tops barely visible in the mist and moonlight. He drew back with a shudder, not liking the looks of the view. Suddenly a flash of light arrested his attention, and for a moment he thought it must be Regin coming to look for him. As he watched, feeling more relief than he liked to admit, the pale flash of light spread into a mass the size of a bonfire, blazing with a cool blue light. Ivarr was frozen by the sight, but some analytical part of him noted exactly which barrow the light was coming from, reminding him that old legends about treasure usually mentioned a blue light showing in the dark.

The blue light grew brighter, expanding until it became a ring burning around the mound. It lost its early blue cast and became a hedge of dancing, orange flames. Ivarr's heart accelerated as he warily stepped closer, expecting to feel a blast of heat. Although the fire crackled menacingly, it shed no warmth. Ivarr walked toward it slowly and stood looking at it when he could go no further. He cautiously put out his hand and touched it—nothing. His hand was not even warmed. The flames parted like a curtain, showing him something beyond. It was a ship, clinker-built, with two tall prows carved with shapes that seemed to dance and writhe in the firelight. The ship was laden with cargo, fine gold and silver vessels and the quiet forms of other offerings—cattle, swine, hounds, and a horse clad in the trappings of war. Under a rich canopy lay the bodies of the dead king and his

245

wife and the servants who had chosen to accompany Elidagrimr on his voyage of death. Not a trace of decay had touched any of them. He could have been present at the original long-ago funeral burning of Elidagrimr after his death in battle with the fire jotuns. It was the lavish burial of an honoured king and his slain warriors, performed by his surviving followers with the victorious fire jotuns skulking around laying their plans and spells so no one would ever discover the resting place of Elidagrimr and his sword.

Ivarr stepped further within the curtain of flame for a closer look at the slain hero. He lay stately and calm in his armour with the firelight gleaming on his golden beard and helmet. One hand lay across his breast, and under his hand was the sword, vigilantly bared as if ready for its master's hand to seize it at any moment for the defence of Snowfell. Its silvery metal twinkled in the firelight, enticing Ivarr to take another step forward so he could feast his eyes on as much of it as he could see. He crept up to the side of the ship, touched it and found it as substantial as a real one. Marvelling at his own audacity, he climbed over the side and crawled to the side of the king's byre. He crouched there until he was so stiff he could hardly move. He memorized the intricate design of the hilt and the patterns etched into the slender blade, which was partiallly sheathed in a scabbard of elegantly simple workmanship. Several times he extended his hand to touch the sword, but withdrew it each time to reconsider. A single touch of Glimr could mean an instant and fiery death, or the awakening of an ancient curse, or a hundred angry draugar who were sworn to protect Elidagrimr's barrow from thieves.

Light-headed from holding his breath, Ivarr at last touched the metal with one finger. It felt cool, like water. He sighed, steadying himself, and took a grip on the hilt. Gently he withdrew the sword from Elidagrimr's grasp, drawing it past the golden helmet with the utmost concentration. Suddenly it was free and in his hands, and then he saw that the shining blade was broken off short, with the other piece extending from the sheath.

Ivarr sagged onto one of the ship's benches to sit and stare at the broken sword in his hand. Bending or breaking a hero's sword was usually part of the funeral ritual. He wondered why it had never occurred to him until now, with such a shock, that the sword might be ruined deliberately so another hand could not use it.

After a long interval of agonized thinking, Ivarr arose, holding the sword irresolutely. Slowly, regretfully, he started to put the sword back into its rightful position. Something about the ashy features of the corpse suddenly reminded him of Birna. He knew with a surety Birna would have mocked him and snorted indignantly if she could have known he would leave the sword behind, after coming so far to get it. There was nothing she despised like a wasted effort. He took another long, calculating look at the sword. Now that his shock and disillusionment had worn off somewhat, he wondered if perhaps it could be reforged and mended. Even if it couldn't, he would keep it as a talisman to bolster his courage. This, after all, was the sword everyone said could not be taken from Elidagrimr's barrow.

He slipped the sheath and the broken piece of sword from Elidagrimr's grasp. He looked at Elidagrimr for the last time, wondering if the ancient hero would bear him a grudge for taking Glimr. He saluted with the broken sword and backed slowly away, cautiously climbing over the edge of the ship. Almost the instant his foot touched the earth, the ship and its contents burst into hot, crackling flames. Ivarr tumbled backward. In an instant the fire vanished and the ship with it, leaving not one ember or blackened stone behind. Glancing back frequently he hurried toward the entrance, skirting the base of the long barrow. The thin moon shed its light more generously, showing him exactly where he wanted to go and what he wanted to see. The small barrows were gone and he could no longer hear the stirrings of the dead in their mounds. Straight ahead burned Regin's tiny fire, an obvious beacon visible for half a mile.

Regin was standing beside the fire when Ivarr returned. Before Ivarr was within the ring of firelight, the wizard inquired eagerly, "Did you find it? Have you got it with you?"

Ivarr did not answer until he sat down on a stone beside the fire. Looking at the wizard, he knew Regin knew the sword was broken. He laid the sheath across his knees and said, "Of course I have it with me. I wouldn't have come so far for nothing. I'm sure you knew all about the sword, yet you didn't tell me it was broken. Was there some reason you wanted me to go wandering in that burial ground all alone in the dark?"

Regin sighed. "I could have told you but would you have believed me, and that my intentions were honest? Never in a million years. Whatever I advise against, you are most determined to do. In all my days I've never encountered a creature more perverse than a Scipling. But perhaps that is why you've managed to survive on Skarpsey for as long as you have." He looked at the sheathed sword and shook his head in wonderment. "I saw the vision of Elidagrimr's ship shortly before I took the first Ordeal, and I realized then that there was no lasting future in the ways of darkness, once the broken sword was mended. Tell me, how did you get through the flames to the ship without being burned alive?"

Ivarr looked up from his silent contemplation of Glimr's hilt. "I simply walked through them. There was no heat until the ship burst into flames and vanished. I almost decided not to take the sword, since it was broken."

Regin gasped. "In all my days I've never seen such perversity. A sword of power is practically placed in your hands and you almost decided not to take it. Whatever made you think you had a choice?"

Ivarr's reply was an ill-humoured grunt as he began searching in his pack for something edible. Wearily he leaned against a rock and closed his eyes, stretching his feet out toward the fire. Beyond its small rim of light waited the silent dark heart of the Maze, but now it seemed curiously empty and robbed of all mystery. Ivarr stared toward the long-barrow, thinking of Elidagrimr and his men and their burial long ago, and how Elidagrimr had waited for centuries to give his sword to someone who would continue the battle against the dark powers which had overcome him. Ivarr feared no jealous retribution from Elidagrimr. What awed him was the size of the mantle he had assumed when he had taken the sword. It was now his responsibility to get the sword reforged and to use it as Elidagrimr himself would have used it.

"It must be reforged," he said. "That's the next test, right? Can you do it, Regin?"

Regin's eyes flew open wide with horror. "Oh, no, not I! I wouldn't dare even to touch that metal, being born a black dwarf, a creature of the darkness by nature. I will never be purged enough ever to venture to meddle with a sword of power made for the Alfar."

"It was made by Dainn, who was a black dwarf," challenged Ivarr. "Why can't you touch it?"

Regin's hands fluttered. "Dainn had creatures like myself in mind when he forged it. I'd wither away like a dead leaf in the flames, or burn like a moth that flies into a candle. I have great and amazing powers, but nothing great enough to unravel Dainn's spells. If you find the power to reforge that sword, Lorimer will fall at your feet. You'll be able to command almost anyone you want to."

Ivarr studied the sword. "I'll get it reforged, somehow."

"I don't doubt that," Regin replied.

Ivarr lay down and tried to sleep. He kept his hand on the sword, as if it might dissolve before his eyes. If he slept at all, it was between frequent fitful awakenings. Always Regin was crouching there like a seedy old raven, opening one red-rimmed eye to look at him a moment, then shutting it quickly again.

In the pale hours of early morning they started the journey out of the Maze. Ivarr stalked along, following his own tracks he had made on the way in, as tense and wary as ever.

"I assure you," Regin said, "we're not going to wander into any bogs or find our way blocked, so you can stop scowling at me. You can't forgive me for not being able to mend your sword, is that it?"

"I suspect that you might if you only would," Ivarr said. "Lorimer certainly doesn't want it mended"

"And neither does Fafnir, but that doesn't mean I'm a defender of dragons. I've severed my ties with Lorimer and bound myself to you and those Alfar—rather a strange trade, if I were interested in living long."

"Then you'd reforge the sword, if you could?"

"Gladly. You can't fight a dragon with a broken sword. There's nothing you can fight him with, as it stands now."

Ivarr's spirits descended into a cloud of gloom for the rest of the day. He said nothing until they had made camp and eaten a wretched little meal of stale hardtack and boiled dried fish. In spite of it, Regin settled down to doze beside their fire, as if slumber were preferable to dwelling upon his stomach's outrage at such a meal.

By sundown the next day, they were within hailing distance of Skapti's camp. For once, someone had been standing watch properly. Flosi sounded the alarm, and Finnvard began stoking up the fire, as if he intended to roast an ox in its entirety.

Flosi came clambering up the hill to meet them, demanding, "Did you get it? Where's the sword?"

"Later, later," Ivarr said, suddenly almost too exhausted to keep his legs under him as he stumbled into the camp. He flopped down on someone's pallet and closed his eyes.

Flosi capered around in a fit of impatience, shouting at Egills and exchanging insults with Skapti. Eilifir and Skapti looked expectantly from Regin to Ivarr and back to Regin.

"Well, what happened?" demanded Skapti, tugging on his ear and threatening to start munching on his beard.

"We're very tired," Regin said, sitting down carefully on a rock, as if he were a hundred years older than he was. "Let us rest for a few moments and then Ivarr will tell you all of it."

"All of it?" Skapti looked at Ivarr keenly. "Is it bad news, then?"

Everyone was suddenly still—even Flosi, who was angrily shoving Finnvard aside so he could have the best view.

"No, not exactly," Ivarr said, sitting up wearily. He began relating the experiences of his trip with Regin to the centre of the Maze. He spoke flatly, omitting nothing, not even his suspicions of Regin's motives. The old wizard did not flinch or protest. Ivarr described the barrows and the fiery funeral ship and the lavish preparations and the beautiful armour on Elidagrimr's corpse. The Alfar hung on his words, enthralled, and Finnvard neglected to stir his soup as waves of gooseflesh rolled over him.

At last Ivarr removed the sheathed sword from its hiding place within his cloak, concluding, "This is Glimr, the sword of Elidagrimr, upon which all our hopes rest, and the symbol of our power and success." They started to applaud; then Ivarr pulled the broken blade from the sheath with one swift yank. The Alfar gasped in horror, their faces instantly turning a sickly shade of grey.

"Broken!" Skapti exclaimed. "We're doomed! Snowfell will be destroyed by Svartarr and Lorimer!"

In the silence of black despair, Eilifir suggested, "Perhaps we can use our powers to reforge the sword."

"Hah! Not likely!" Egills growled, shaking his head. "We had only the slenderest of chances before we knew the sword was broken. Now, I'd say our chances are downright emaciated, if not starved to death."

Flosi broke in angrily. "I'll wager old Dainn is snickering up his sleeve right now because he sent us after a broken sword—not that he even expected us to get here alive, of course. We should have realized all black dwarves will stick to Svartarr like a pack of leeches." He glared furiously at Regin, who gazed back at him calmly as he smoked his pipe.

The Alfar stood a moment in profound silence, except for the plopping sounds of Finnvard's soup. At length Regin broke the silence by knocking his pipe against the rock and putting it away in his pouch. He arose creakily and said, "Someone had better go on watch. We'll discuss the matter of the sword further when we've all had some much-needed rest."

Sighing and grumbling, everyone began stirring around.

251

Finnvard offered to serve the soup, but no one was interested.

In the morning Ivarr called a council. "The question seems to be, how will we kill Fafnir with a broken sword?"

"A very good question if you ask me," Flosi declared.

"We've had ample opportunities to be killed," Ivarr went on. "I believe there must be a plan and a purpose behind this mad scheme and, if we persevere, we'll make it. Somehow we have escaped, when it seemed for certain we'd be murdered, hagridden, or eaten by trolls; if we keep up our momentum, I believe we will continue to escape. I'm certain that something terrible will happen the moment we give up and decide we can't go on. As I see it, at this moment we have only two choices before us. We can't really give up and go back to Elbegast and beg for his help, much as we might like to. Our only choice now is between death and survival—by survival I mean going onward toward our goal. Right now I want to propose a vote. All of you who wish to die raise your hands."

The Alfar stared at him in astonishment. Even Regin's eyes opened a notch wider. Everyone's arms remained hugged to his sides.

"No one? Then how many wish to live?"

All hands shot into the air at once. Ivarr ceremoniously counted them, adding himself also. "Well, that's encouraging, but if you want to continue living you're going to be very uncomfortable for a while. It means no more complaining, lagging behind, or eating or sleeping more than our share. It means staying awake on guard duty and following orders exactly and promptly, without arguing. It means acknowledging as your leaders those with the most power. As I see it, Regin will be first, followed by Eilifir and Skapti and myself."

Skapti raised his hand. "Not to argue, Ivarr, but I must beg to differ with you. Regin and the rest of us come after you, not before. Broken sword or no, you are still the hero who directs his Alfar and wizards to do your bidding. You may not be magical, like Regin, but you have a certain power of your own. No one but a real hero would come unarmed into this realm to undertake such a desperate cause with only the assistance of a bunch of nithlings like us. You are the leader, Ivarr, not Regin or any of us. I think everyone else will be in agreement with me." He looked around sternly, daring someone to disagree.

Even Flosi was silenced. Everyone nodded solemnly. Skapti continued, "Good. Ivarr, we're right behind you all the way. We're ready to follow you into the very jaws of Fafnir himself."

Everybody nodded, looking rather unhappy at the mention of Fafnir's jaws. Ivarr was pleased and a little alarmed at the success of his council. Egills and Finnvard sat down at once to sharpen their swords, discussing which vitals of the dragon they would go for in the coming attack. The merry music of whetstones soon filled the encampment to accompany some truly fearsome discussions about the best way to slit a dragon's weazand.

Regin opened his satchel and took out a long, slender map tube. "I suggest we chart our course for the Drangarstrom in this area which few men have seen." He described a triangular area between Jotunsgard and Svartarrsrike. "I believe this is where Andvari is hiding. The more inaccessible and dangerous the area, the more likely it is. After all, you can't conceal a huge pile of treasure and a fully grown dragon just anywhere. Now I realize much of the Drangarstrom isn't shown on my map, because hardly anyone has seen it and lived to tell about it. But I am confident we shall find the Drangarstrom if we persist in a northeasterly direction. If you'll look at the map a moment, you'll understand why I am so sure this must be Andvari's hideaway. Upriver you have the plains of Svartarrsrike and Hlidarend, the most famous battle and burial grounds in all Skarpsey. Every year when the sun returns and the snow starts to melt, and perhaps a volcanic fissure opens somewhere under a glacier, a series of great floods sweep this plains area. Barrows are broken open and lost warriors' scattered bones and bits of gold ornaments are swept into the tributaries and headwaters of the Drangarstrom. All old Andvari needs to do is wait, and sooner or later the rings, the coins, the gold helmets will come tumbling down into his hands. Imagine the hoard he must have gathered by now." Regin's eyes glinted coldly.

"And imagine the dragon, guarding each little bit," Finnvard added.

Ivarr felt much better about the broken sword when they were under way, bearing to the northeast. Their course took them through some of the most sinister terrain he had yet seen. The fiery centre of the earth seemed too close to the surface, with pools and springs of scalding water, steaming geysers, and threatening rumblings beneath the surface of the earth. In some places the bogs were burbling, boiling cauldrons of muck. Two mountains trailed murky smoke over the land for miles, so the sun glowered through it like an angry red eye. In its sullen light, Ivarr felt uneasy and kept glancing around to see if they were being followed. If only the light were a bit stronger, or his imagination weaker, he could be sure if something or someone was following them.

On the second day in Muspell's Cellar, as the fire jotuns liked to call that delightful area, Ivarr finally caught sight of someone following. Horsemen rode parallel courses along distant ridges, in small clusters at great speeds. They all vanished in the same direction and only a few seemed to be following the intruders and marking their progress.

Regin studied them through a rickety old spyglass. "Fire jotuns," he said with a fatalistic sigh. "They aren't going to allow the robbers of Elidagrimr's barrow to depart unchallenged."

CHAPTER TWENTY ONE

The Alfar grouped around Ivarr and Regin, looking anxiously at the distant horsemen.

"This time we're in for it," Egills said with gloomy satisfaction. "There must be a thousand jotuns waiting for us in those mountains. And all for a broken sword that isn't any good to anybody."

"Hush!" Skapti snapped. "They seem to think it's worth fighting for, anyway."

Ivarr turned to Regin. "You chose this course, Regin. If we are attacked, it will be mainly up to you to defend us. The Alfar aren't extremely fireworthy, if you know what I mean."

"You might be surprised," Regin said, raising one black brow. "These Alfar have more ability than even they suspect."

"We do?" Flosi eyed Finnvard and Egills doubtfully.

"Well, whatever the case," Ivarr said, "you'd better have some spells or blasts ready to fight off those jotuns when they attack."

Regin replied stiffly, "I shall be prepared, never you fear."

The mountains steepened around them and seemed to be funneling toward one break in their rugged ranks where centuries of glaciers had ground out a path leading into the lower plains on the far side. A score of streamlets running down from the high fells formed a considerable river which thundered away down the rocky nadir of the deep gloomy valley. Far below, after many miles and the induction of another score of streams, the river would pour into the vast churning waters of the Drangarstrom, finding its way by devious paths to the sea.

Ivarr did not lead them far into the depths of the valley. They halted behind a bulwark of rock and rubble to look ahead at the scowling crags where the jotuns lurked.

"Jotuns before us and jotuns behind us," Ivarr observed grimly. "I don't see how we can get out of here by natural means. If we could all change to fylgur we could have a chance of slipping past under their noses, but there are three of us for whom it would be impossible. Remember how Gizur exhausted his powers taking you over Vapnajokull. We're not going to risk that with Regin."

The position of the jotuns could not have been improved. They positioned themselves around the only passage out of the valley, where the cliffs drew closer together and the valley narrowed and deepened into a rugged gorge. The jotuns plugged it very effectively with a group of archers on each side, with a small knot of riders covering it from below. A shout from the cliffs warned the jotuns of the approach of their quarry, and the jotuns took up their positions and fitted arrows into their bows with the unmistakable deadly clatter of smoothly polished instruments honed for battle.

The intruders shielded themselves as well as they could behind their rocky outcropping. After a few moments, three riders came forward slowly, holding their weapons aloft as a peaceable gesture. Two were clad like wizards, and one was Thor of Ulfgrimrsstead, riding a skinny wretch of a horse that looked as if its last good meal had been two years ago.

"Halloo, grave robbers!" Thor called in a booming shout. "Have you got Elidagrimr's sword with you, thieves and deceivers?"

Ivarr raised his head warily. "We have it, Thor, and we're not about to give it back, if that's the purpose of this murderous trap you've set here. It'll go the worse for you if you try stopping us."

Thor lolled confidently in his saddle—a motley thing of many mends and tag ends of cracked leather. "Is that so? My wizards tell me they suspect you of a lie. We've proof that your wizard friend Gizur was killed inside the Maze. Who is your protector and adviser now? There are no Guild wizards in Jotunsgard, only necromancers and jotun wizards, who are not likely to be of much assistance to you. Who is that small fellow in the black cloak, and where did you find him? Speak, stranger, if you have any regard for yourself."

Regin motioned Ivarr to be silent. "Don't mention my name, or a great advantage over Lorimer will be lost. I've had plenty of experience in dealing with fire jotuns; may I take over this discussion?"

Ivarr nodded, scowling. "Just don't make any bargains with them, however great your experience is."

Regin darted him a reproving glance, then called back to Thor in a surprisingly strong voice, "You there, Thor of Ulfgrimrsstead! Yes, I know all about you and your household. I also know there's no love lost between you and the other jotuns of your quarter. The only reason the others are here is to keep you from stealing the sword yourself, and the main reason you are here is to make certain none of these others steals it. You're all nothing but a pack of thieves and deceivers yourselves, with your lying and your glamour spells, so we can all do with a bit less of your name-calling."

Egills chortled and patted Regin on the back in congratulations. "You tell them, you old fox!"

Thor flourished his lance and tried to force his horse forward, but it merely shuffled dispiritedly and tried to steal a mouthful of grass. Furiously, Thor turned to his wizards for a whispered consultation. Then Thor bellowed, "It's me who has the power to issue threats, not you! If you don't surrender that sword, we'll kill you all like so many gnats. But if you'd rather live awhile longer you miserable traitors and thieves, send out the Scipling with the sword and I shall let the rest of you escape. I, Thor Ulfgrimrsson, have spoken!'' He yanked at his poor horse's reins and kicked it forward a few paces.

''Hah!'' Egills muttered to Regin. ''Wouldn't Thor, that greedy old tub of guts, like to have the power Glimr would give to him!''

Ivarr shouted over the barricade of stones, ''Never, Thor! Neither the sword nor I will be surrendered. Attack us and you'll get a firsthand taste of Glimr's power!''

Thor and the wizards whispered together again. Then Thor rode a bit closer, pummeling his horse's sides before it would move. ''Show me the sword!'' he challenged.

''No,'' said Regin. ''If you come another step forward we shall blast you with fire.''

Thor leaned back in his saddle. ''Who will? Those feeble inept Alfar? Cowards and nithlings, all of them, or you may well blast me where I stand.'' He uttered a bray of laughter that echoed off the cliffs.

''You have been warned!'' Regin cried.

Thor drummed his heels on his horse's ribs and beckoned to his two advisers, who lowered their weapons and rode forward at a purposeful trot.

Thor was still smirking when Skapti rose on one knee and levelled a blast at the three of them. ''Nithlings! Cowards! Inept!'' he shouted, and with a final word, he mustered the force to summon a flash like lightning and a terrific jolt of thunder that made everyone's ears ring. The three horses sat on their haunches and tumbled their riders off backwards. The stunned riders scrambled to their feet and took to their heels with Thor pounding after them, glowering over his shoulder as he ran.

''Beautiful! Magnificent!'' Flosi exclaimed, thumping Skapti on the back. ''It was perfect! I'll bet they thought lightning had struck them! Look, they haven't stopped running yet!''

''Probably on their way for reinforcements,'' Regin said chidingly. ''That was very well done, Skapti, but I wish you'd leave the blasting to me for a while, I can handle these

258

clumsy oafs without a particle of exertion. I'd hate for you to make a mistake with your new power.''

Skapti nodded, but he still looked pleased with himself. ''It was rather good, wasn't it? With a little practice I could singe the whiskers off their chins at forty paces.''

''I don't doubt it, but it's far more pleasant to practice on something that can't fire back at you,'' Regin said.

Ivarr watched the ignominious rout of his enemy Thor. His defeat seemed to rouse the other jotuns into a fury. They gathered around him with shouts and waving arms. In a moment, another leader leaped into his horse's saddle and began gathering volunteers. A dozen finally assembled themselves and rode out to a safe distance to study their foes and capture the two stray horses. The third horse, Thor's ill-favoured mount, had seized the opportunity to depart from a life of woe and scanty portions and had expired where it had fallen. The new leader rode boldly as far as the unfortunate creature's carcass and began stringing his bow importantly.

''Do something!'' Flosi cried repeatedly, administering urgent pokes to Regin's ribs.

Regin remained impassive to Flosi's assaults and watched the jotuns advance. ''We'll give them plenty of rope and then we shall hang them all,'' he said calmly, but his eye sparkled at the prospect.

The jotuns shouted insults at their foes and to each other for encouragement until they reached arrow range, where-upon they released a volley of arrows to hail down upon the grave robbers. Regin made a spell at the twang of the first bowstring, and the arrows burst into flame the instant they reached a certain height, so nothing descended except a few bits of charred wood and the melted points. The jotuns jabbered excitedly and a few whirled their horses around to start a hasty retreat, which the new leader halted with a few well-chosen threats. Again they readied their bows and skirmished forward to release a second volley.

This time Regin released a puff of powder that drove the arrows straight back at the jotuns. With shouts and howls, they dived for the earth, a few with minor wounds which seemed only to infuriate them to greater feats of daring. Exchanging their bows for swords and axes, they milled around in an ugly mood, working up the proper wrath for a third attack. With a roar of fury, they charged the hilltop where their quarry waited, swinging their weapons to the peril of anything within range.

Regin stood directly in the path of their furious rush. A black-bearded jotun was bearing down on him like a reaper about to scythe an old dry reed; but just as Regin was within a sword-swipe of being cloven in twain, he raised his arms and pronounced a spell.

Ivarr recalled no thunderous report or fiery concussion, but the attackers were repulsed, much like a clot of flies suddenly swotted by a massive hand. The black-bearded jotun with the gleaming sword vanished, and Ivarr found himself lying flat on his back, blinking dazzled eyes at the sulphurous sky overhead.

"Get up, Ivarr, quickly!" Regin ordered, "This is no time for resting! One of those wizards was Bjarn Ulfgrimrsson, a master of illusion. If I know anything of him, there's worse to come."

"Send them all out," Flosi said smugly. "We can deal with them, can't we, Skapti? Thirty or three hundred makes no difference to us."

The vanquished jotuns limped back to their fortifications by sorry twos and threes. Although several had to be carried, no fatalities were apparent. This recent disgrace seemed to content even the most audacious of the jotuns. No more boasting leaders stepped forward, and Thor Ulfgrimrsson and his kinsmen maintained a sullen silence.

At last the fourth wave of attackers appeared. Three long-bearded jotuns came walking slowly across the valley towards the bastion of the barrow robbers. At a safe distance, they stopped. One lifted a hand in greeting.

"Show us yourself, sorcerer," he called. "We don't know who you are, but your power seems highly creditable. Why don't we settle this dispute sensibly among ourselves instead of blasting and killing one another?"

"You sound very sensible and fair," Regin replied, taking care not to present himself for a target. "Sensible enough to realize that if you attempt to obstruct us you're likely to meet with misfortune. Nothing or no one is going to stop us from continuing through this valley to the lowlands beyond. I advise you to step aside or you will be destroyed."

Another wizard stepped forward, and Ivarr at once recognised the lengthy withered frame of Bjarn of Ulfgrimrsstead. "Our patience is growing short," he said in his grating voice. "You refuse to show yourself, as a wizard of repute would not hesitate to do, yet you bluster and threaten as if you were weaned on brimstone. I'm curious as to what sort of wizard you really are in addition to turning traitor against Jotunsgard. We've seen some blasts and tricks, but you've done nothing truly impressive yet. Perhaps you are more mouth than magician. I dare you to prove to me that you can kill something more than a sick old horse and a pack of cowards in flight. Here, send a blast at me. I'm offering you the chance to kill me right now, if you can." He held out his arms to show that he would not resist or even defend himself.

"Blast him! Do it!" Flosi cried excitedly. "Now's your chance!"

Regin stepped from the shelter of the rock, holding his staff in one hand. Ivarr snapped, "You haven't a chance against three of them! Blast one and the other two will get you! Don't be a fool Regin."

Regin ignored him. He leaned on his staff and for a long moment the wizards all stared at each other calculatingly.

"You needn't make such a spectacle of yourself, Bjarn Ulfgrimrsson," Regin said. "It would take a real nithling to blast such a buffoon as you. I understand that you had the Scipling and his Alfar and their wizard all in your power at one time, and you let them walk away from you. I hope you live never to forgive yourself for that mistake."

Bjarn gripped his staff. "Who are you? You have the look of a black dwarf. Isn't it treason to ally yourself with the killers of Svartarr's son?"

"I am a necromancer and we live as a law unto ourselves and trouble Svartarr as little as he troubles us or anyone else who cares to meddle with us." Regin kept the beak of his hood drawn well over his face as he spoke.

"A necromancer!" Another of the wizards took the foremost position. "Why have you betrayed Jotunsgard, which honours necromancers and their science? For centuries we've waited for someone to unravel the mysteries of Elidagrimr's sword and lead us to our destiny as rulers over Skarpsey, yet you prefer to allow this low-born Scipling to seize the power that rightfully belongs to the jotuns. We could make you a king. You have been deceived. How much gold have they promised you for your service? I'm certain we could double the amount."

"Only one small ring from Andvari's cave," Regin replied calmly, "and that is all the payment I desire. These Alfar have not threatened to make me a king or to burden me with a lot of unnecessary riches or quantities of unwanted power, for all of which I am most grateful. Nor am I overfond of talking. Since you persist in goading me into a display of my skill, you leave me no choice but to resort to a challenge. Either clear off entirely and take every single jotun with you, or I shall challenge the three of you to a decisive duel to see whether we pass or not."

"The three of us?" Bjarn demanded, and the wizards exchanged a startled glance, as if disbelieving their good fortune, a look which rapidly deteriorated into suspicion. "Just you against the the three of us?" Bjarn began to grin wolfishly.

"Certainly you have ears to hear," Regin retorted, "And if you have any power I suggest you use it."

For an answer, Bjarn levelled his staff at Regin, sending an icy blast toward him like a miniature thunderhead. Regin countered it easily and fired a blast at the jotun wizards. They stopped it with a spell of their own and returned a shower of icy needles. Regin raised a hedge of flame with a wave of his hand, melting the ice with a sizzling hiss. The rain that fell from the melted ice blackened the grass as if it were poison.

They continued to bat spells back and forth as if for exercise or a display for the benefit of their audiences. From time to time, the opponents complimented each other on a particularly adroit spell or counterspell. The Alfar began to make comments and give cheers and call out encouragement to Regin as if the whole show were nothing but an afternoon's amusement for a group of friends.

But suddenly the nature of the duel changed as the three jotuns released three spells in quick succession. Regin averted them and retaliated with fiery spells of his own, one after the other, but the three wizards were unscathed. They drew a flickering blue ring of flame around themselves, as if to remind Regin they knew all about fire magic too.

The next spell was cast by the wizards and seemed to fall short by about fifty feet. It smoked and swirled a moment, then suddenly burst into life. Five white wolves charged at Regin, fangs gleaming and eyes glaring. Regin destroyed them, exploding them like pitchy logs.

The wizards called for a moment to rest and confer, which Regin graciously granted. He sat down on a rock to catch his own breath and look around at his companions. "Not too bad for an aging novice," he said wryly. "If I hadn't been purged of almost all my black dwarf magic, those fellows would be fifty feet underground by now."

"We'd better help, hadn't we?" Skapti asked, pulling on his ear worriedly. "Some of those ice bolts were awfully close."

"When I need help I'll ask for it," Regin said with asperity.

Ivarr watched the three wizards, who were sitting down comfortably and passing around a small flask. He shook his head and observed to himself that no decent Scipling battle would progress so leisurely, with intervals for rest and refreshment.

Regin took his place again, nodding formally to Ivarr, who was scowling almost as suspiciously at his defender as he was at the jotuns.

"Are you ready to begin again?" Bjarn called, with a slight bow.

Regin returned the bow. "I am ready. I hope you have saved your most challenging spells for the last. Very pretty, these simple ones, but simply not enough to frighten me, my friends."

"We're sorry to hear that," Bjarn replied, and for the next half hour the wizards batted spells back and forth much as before. Then the jotun wizards cast a smoky pall which hid them from view. Instantly Regin was on guard. Everyone watched the smoke cloud anxiously, except Finnvard, who had a maundering expression on his face.

"I have a peculiar feeling," he said musingly, and turned to look up the valley, back the way they had come.

"I think our retreat has been cut off."

"Hush, Finnvard," Flosi snorted. "What would you know about fighting tactics?"

"Only that it would be good for the jotuns and bad for us if someone got behind us," Finnvard insisted stubbornly.

"Let Regin do the worrying," Egills said.

"But I'm almost certain—" Finnvard began.

Regin cut him off with a noisy gust of power that shredded the screen of smoke and sent it swirling wildly. Everyone leaned forward to see what the wizards would do next.

"Look!" Finnvard exclaimed in a voice quivering with doom, and everyone whirled around to gape at the apparitions rising before them. Three columns of fire swirled and took shape, blocking the valley.

"Fire giants!" Regin shouted over the roar and crackle of flames, positioning himself between his companions and the fiery monsters, brandishing his staff aloft and hurling bolt after bolt.

Ivarr dived into the shelter of a large rock and peered around one corner, squinting into the glare cast by the giants' glancing eyes. They were shaped like jotuns, twice as tall as the highest tree Ivarr had ever seen, and they were covered with armour that gleamed like the sun. Their faces were likewise brilliant and their hair billowed like the flames

264

of a bonfire. With a thunderous roar, one raised an arm and hurled a firebolt at Regin, who seemed dried and fragile enough to be blown completely away with one fierce puff.

Regin countered the bolt and returned three of his own, exploding with smoky greenish concussions. Compared to the might and brilliance of the fire giants, Regin's efforts looked as puny as sparks popping from a hearth log. Flosi began calling for a retreat, desperately scuttling out of the way of a disintegrating firebolt which pelted them with flaming particles.

"Don't panic!" Regin's voice called through a pall of black smoke so dense they could not see him. "Remember, fire jotuns are masters of illusion and deceit. Hold your positions—" An explosion ended his speech abruptly, and Ivarr looked at Skapti in horror.

"I think they got him!" he gasped.

Skapti recoiled as a scrap of burning fabric lit on his hand like a black butterfly. "Then we're doomed! Get back to the others! Get everyone together!"

They crawled backward through a storm of firebolts and black smoke to the hollow where the others crouched. Soot had blackened their faces, and coals rained down frequently, causing a flurry of swatting and beating until it was extinguished.

"We think Regin was blasted!" Skapti slapped desperately at a coal which was burning a hole in his sleeve. "We've either got to retreat or surrender or do something to retaliate. Those giants are going to roast us like a handful of chestnuts!"

"We'll retaliate first and then run for it!" Finnvard gasped. "Go ahead, Skapti and Eilifir! Do your best for poor old Regin!"

They began a formula, but stopped in midword. A hoarse voice penetrated the roaring and crackling of fiery spells. "Poor old Regin isn't finished yet by any means. I'm much too tough for roasting."

Regin crawled into their hollow, rather the worse for a severe singeing. He still clutched his staff and satchel under one arm, using his free hand to brush away the hot coals and soot the fire giants were spewing down on them. Skapti and Ivarr seized him and hauled him into the relative shelter of their hollow, where Finnvard and Egills attempted to pound some of the soot off him. He struggled to his feet, exclaiming, "There's no time for that now; those jotuns are almost upon us!"

Raising his arms, he chanted a spell which called down a sudden deluge of rain. The smoky air cleared somewhat, filling with mist as the fire jotuns sizzled the moisture into vapour. Regin instantly darted a series of firebolts at them, which they brushed away easily as they ponderously advanced. Then by some fateful quirk, a firebolt glanced off one giant's breastplate and ricocheted overhead to fall into the midst of the embattled defenders. The globe of explosive fire rolled to a halt between Flosi's feet and sat spluttering and quivering as if it would explode at any instant. Everyone froze, transfixed by the inevitability of their doom. Then Egills lunged forward, hand outstretched, and at the same instant Flosi bent to do the same thing. Together they seized the deadly globe and hurled it over their barricade of rocks. It exploded before it struck the earth, bursting high into the air overhead and showering them with hot sparks.

Regin rose from the ground where he had flung himself. Incredulously he stared around the circle of shocked faces. "Is everyone all right?" he gasped. "It must have been a flawed spell. One in every thousand or so fails to explode properly." With shaking hands he wove another spell to slow the steady advance of the fire giants, looking over his shoulder at Egills and Flosi anxiously.

They still sat there staring at each other in disbelief. Their hands and forearms gleamed with an afterglow from the firebolt, and their beards and hair stood on end with crackling energy. In a few moments the peculiar manifestations were gone.

"Great flaming salamanders!" Skapti was pale with fright. "Regin, what happened to them? Will they be all right?"

"I don't know," Regin said, blinking his red-rimmed eyes. To Ivarr he looked more like an ancient rusty black crow than ever. "I've never seen anybody simply pick up a firebolt that way. Fellows? How do you feel?"

Egills slowly shook his head and looked around at the singed grass. "A bit shaky," he croaked, looking at his hands which were still pink and healthy. "I can't figure out why I'm not dead. Not even a blister," he marvelled, shaking his head again and sighing.

Flosi ignored them all. He held up his hands, fingers outspread. At the tip of each long finger glowed a miniature fireball. When he moved his hands around, it looked as if he were writing with flame. His expression was enraptured. He pointed at the fire giants, who were belching soot and coals again, and a huge hissing fireball streaked across the meadow and burst against the breastplate of the centre giant.

"Flosi!" Skapti exclaimed, indignant with astonishment.

Flosi favoured him with a beatific smile. "I've got power. I've never been so frightened as when that firebolt stopped right between my boots. It felt as if lightning were about to strike. I felt each atom of my body come to life at that moment and I realized how infinitely precious all those atoms were to me and how much I wanted them to continue in their present state of coherence. I realized I would have to do something extraordinary. And I did it."

"We did it together," said Egills. "I think I've got it too, and I'm amazed. I thought I was far too old and rusty." Solemnly he levitated Finnvard a few inches into the air to convince himself of the fact, and shook his head resignedly. "Now I suppose we shall all be forced to battle with those wretched fire jotuns."

The fire giants' fetid smoky breath was darkening the sky. They loomed directly ahead, withering every bit of green within range of their awful heat. Their fiery glances ignited strips of dry grass and bushes into flame. Regin's blasts and spells halted them briefly, but they came stalking closer and closer until there was scarcely any air to breathe.

''Concentrate!'' shouted Skapti over the rumbling and crackling of fire. ''A spell! Anything! Article ten, if you can manage it!''

Concentration was the last thing Ivarr wanted to think about when he was choking on soot and gagging on smoke. He glanced up with streaming eyes to the cliffs, which had been lined with watching jotuns. Now they were pointing up into the sky, evidently much excited. Ivarr looked upward in spite of himself. Regin seized his arm and pointed.

''Those mad Alfar!'' he gasped. ''They're going to destroy us yet!''

He shoved Ivarr to the earth, trying to screen him with his own cloak. Ivarr glimpsed a black spot ringed with flame growing larger and larger in the sky, hurtling toward the earth with terrifying force. As Ivarr opened his mouth to shout a terrified warning, the fiery thing roared overhead, dragging a tail of fire that cut a black swath across the earth straight toward the fire giants.

CHAPTER TWENTY TWO

A resounding explosion jolted the earth, and Ivarr, smothered as he was under Regin's cloak, was dazzled by a blinding flare of light. The impact shook rocks and boulders from the cliffs, which came clattering down noisily in the sudden silence.

Regin leaped to his feet, holding his staff in readiness as he glared around. Ivarr peered warily around a rock, seeing nothing of the fire giants except swirling dust and smoke and blackened earth where they had stood, no more than fifty paces away. The defenders of the pass were rapidly dispersing on horseback and by foot, since a large number of horses had bolted madly. In a matter of moments, the battlefield was deserted except for the seven travellers, who were cautiously creeping from their hiding places like sooty lizards.

"Well, that was a spectacular demonstration," Ivarr said. "Truly, Regin, you're to be congratulated if that's a sample of your abilities."

Regin shook his head impatiently. "Don't blame me for that debacle. I was doing my best to put the brakes on you wretched fellows. I could have discouraged those fire giants with no help from you Alfar."

Flosi grinned through his soot. "You were taking too long at it."

Skapti exclaimed in distress, "We were only trying to aid

your spell. You mean that thing, whatever it was, wasn't your conjuration?''

''Certainly not,'' Regin said. ''I believe it was a comet. I didn't have much time for a judicious inspection of it.''

''Astronomy was one of my favourite subjects,'' Flosi said. ''I wanted to see if we could call down a falling star on those wretched jotuns and blow them all to smithereens, and we almost did it, didn't we? Perhaps it was a trifle high, but it served its purpose.''

''You missed by about five miles,'' Regin said angrily. ''A direct hit would have turned this pass into a crater and us into nothing. Who do you think you are, messing around with dangerous phenomena like falling stars? Plenty of fools like you are destroyed every year by overstepping the bounds of their power, and I can see you're a prime candidate unless I give you some very valuable advice, young man. Come with me this instant and the two of us shall have a private talk.''

''What about?'' Flosi glowered suspiciously.

''About power and magic and the rules that govern responsible practitioners.'' Regin took a firm grip on Flosi's arm and led him away, talking very forcefully.

Flosi was rather quiet for the next two days, much to Ivarr's private amusement. Regin must have put some sense or fear into him, which no one else had been able to instill. Ivarr knew Flosi must be itching to boast and rave about his new-found powers, but not a word was said about it. What's more, Flosi did not even flaunt his new skills and never mentioned a word about shape-shifting, although he must have been dying to discover his fylgja. The change was as admirable as it was peculiar. His former headlong heedless attitude was suddenly pocketed with moments of actual silent contemplation. He addressed everyone with a little more courtesy, and Regin he regarded with outright respect.

The change in Egills was less striking. His main pride was the working of a hundred little tricks and pranks, like a small boy with a wide streak of mischief. When he finally decided to come to grips with his fylgja, he went away alone and sat on a large rock for several hours. The change was a long time in coming, but at last he managed it—immensely enjoying Finnvard's shock when a large black goat rubbed his curling horns on his friend's back as he was cooking breakfast. With a wicked bleat he trotted away and returned in his own shape some time later, looking very satisfied with his accomplishment.

A week of travelling in the unknown region between Svartarrsrike and Jotunsgard returned everyone to a semblance of routine. Ivarr watched Regin closely for signs of betrayal. Their discovery of an ancient ley line was somewhat reassuring, but it was almost obliterated by time. Regin remarked that most of the links in its chain of power were broken and dead, which was not comforting knowledge in troll terrain. A thousand little valleys and ravines made it prime skulking territory, although Regin repeatedly assured them they were quite safe, since the trolls were bound to be rather scarce due to the lack of travellers or settlers to prey upon. The region was also foggy much of the time, and occasionally Ivarr was certain he could smell the sea when the wind came from the east. On the sixth day the fog lifted for a few hours, and they saw the dim blue forms of a chain of mountains to the east, beyond which was rumoured to lie the fabled caverns of the great Drangarstrom. For the next three days they plodded toward the Drangarfells without seeming to make much progress, but by degrees they discerned clumps of trees growing in the sheltered folds of the mountains. Spires of rock bristled from the shoulders of hills where the winds and rains had gnawed on them for centuries.

On the eve of the tenth day, they camped in a steep dark valley of the Drangarfells. Distantly they heard a deep thrumming murmur, as if the river were a mighty harp-string vibrating in its deep chambers.

Two days of climbing up and one of climbing down finally brought them to their first sighting of the river. From a high ridge they looked down into a steep, lava-cluttered ravine where the river boiled and churned among house-sized boulders, not merely content to eat its way through a mighty mountain range like the Drangarfells; but forced to gnaw at the very vitals of the earth. An outside crescent of black sand bore a hedge of battered driftwood to show where the high water mark lay.

"How could anyone ever cross that?" Flosi asked in a hushed voice. "It looks like half the rivers of Skarpsey poured into one. Listen to the ugly sounds it makes."

Regin shook his head. "Let's hope we never have to cross it."

"Which way do we go from here?" Ivarr asked. "Upstream or down?"

Regin pointed upstream and refused to elaborate when Ivarr attempted to question him about his means of arriving at that decision. All he would say was, "If Andvari's cave lay to the south, the jotuns would have plundered it by now. Nothing lies ahead of us except the unknown."

He led the way with no maps and only a few cryptic devices which he would not permit anyone to investigate. Ivarr trod at his heels, watching his every move. Their route wound toward the river, and that night they camped in the coarse black sand chewn from the lava rock of Skarpsey. Egills was particularly dissatisfied with the selection of camp sites and kept muttering about flash floods, ground seepage, and aching joints.

Regin outlined their path, impressing upon them what a vast labyrinth awaited them. The river continually carved new channels for itself, leaving necks and islands in its course as it twisted along in its braided channel. Regin would lead them along the old dry river courses, climbing over the necks at each bend to save distance. It would be faster in the long run than hacking a path through the rocky slopes above, where there was no guarantee they would be able to climb down to the river level again.

The high gloomy walls of the river canyon oppressed everyone's spirits. The gorge narrowed in places until it was scarcely two arm-spans wide, and so deep it was like descending into midnight, with only a distant crease of light

272

far above. Finnvard desperately hated the narrows, and several times he was nearly stuck in the small apertures carved by the water. The large boulders plugging the way had to be scaled, not without difficulty, and frequently they encountered deep pools.

Everyone grumbled about it. "At least the walking is easy," Skapti declared firmly, over the grumbling chorus of everyone's fears.

"And we're not so visible," Ivarr added wearily.

"Except from above," Finnvard said with a knowing air. "We'd be like cornered rats."

"Above!" hooted Flosi, whose confidence was returning, minus much of its nastiness. "Are you worried about big birds, Finnvard?"

Finnvard smiled a cryptic smile. "There are other things that fly besides birds, Flosi."

Flosi opened his mouth for a sharp retort and closed it without speaking. In a moment he said, "You don't mean the dragon, do you?"

Finnvard pretended to be far more interested in sitting down for a rest and finding a bit of dry fish to munch on. His expression was decidedly sly. "Dragon? Who said anything about dragons?"

"You were having a whale of a nightmare last night," Egills said. "It was quite diverting the way you were throwing off your cloak and eider and shouting that we were all burning up. What I suggest is that you stop putting so much pepper in everything you cook."

"Or perhaps your feet were too close to the fire last night," Flosi said with a grin.

Finnvard ignored them and spoke to Eilifir, who hadn't spoken a word for several days. "Mark my words, Eilifir, I dreamed of a dragon last night and it's not going to be too much longer before we see one."

Eilifir nodded profoundly, and Egills and Flosi tittered. Egills snorted and said, "I have no doubt tonight we'll see a flaming case of indigestion flying overhead, or perhaps a badly singed stocking."

They climbed three steep necks that day, picking a cautious way upward through a jumble of stones to the sandy top and down the other side to the riverbed. By evening, no one remembered Finnvard's warning except Ivarr, who was on the first watch and trying hard to keep himself awake. He studied the sky, which was clear and filled with stars, and he neither saw nor heard anything suggesting a dragon. When his watch was finished he told Eilifir to keep a close watch for dragons and gladly went to sleep. In the morning he awoke to Egills testily chiding Finnvard for his silly dreams. Finnvard was undisconcerted, and stirred away at the morning-broth, trying unsuccessfully to get the lumps out.

Four difficult necks were crossed that day before everyone became too exhausted to continue, although several hours of daylight remained. They made camp in a small sandy side canyon, where a cold trickle of water came down from higher land to merge with the river. Before them lay a pasture-sized expanse of wet black sand and skeletal heaps of driftwood. In the wee dark hours of morning, Skapti awakened Ivarr to take the second watch. He sat shivering and yawning at the moonlit expanse before him, listening to Egills' whistling snores behind him and the scrabbling and twittering sounds made by river rats in the rocks above him. Ivarr sat still, peering upward to catch a glimpse of the creatures. When he looked down again, Regin was standing beside him as if he had appeared out of nowhere. Ivarr controlled a wild urge to shriek, and pretended to yawn instead.

"Oh, hello, Regin, you startled me," he said coolly.

Regin studied the cliffs above the river and looked up and down the channel. "A goose walked over my grave, and now I can't sleep."

Ivarr caught Regin's sense of foreboding. "I've seen nothing except river rats and some owls. But you can sit and listen for yourself, if it will make you feel better."

"Thank you, I shall." Regin seated himself not far away and buried himself up to the ears in his cloak. His eyes searched the darkness, and his staff was across his knees in readiness.

Ivarr sniffed the musty smell of Regin's damp cloak and suppressed a shudder. The wizard smelled as if he had been shut up in an old trunk in a cellar too long. Ivarr found himself thinking of the night he had attacked Lorimer, remembering the smell and feel of the necromancer's leathery hide, pickled in bog water and peat for centuries, and now preserved in a brine of hate and vengeance.

He jumped at a slight crackling sound as Regin stretched one leg.

"Stiff," the wizard muttered. "Just like an old deer leg the dogs have chewed—" He halted, listening intently. "Do you hear that?"

Ivarr heard nothing and promptly said so.

Regin lifted one finger for silence. "You'll hear it in a moment. At least my ears aren't getting old."

Ivarr began hearing a sound. It was like water rushing, or an immense kettle boiling. Regin seized him by the arm and began running back to the camp. The rushing deepened to a roaring. To Ivarr's amazement, the sky began to glow as if the sun were rising. The Alfar leaped up at Regin's shout of alarm, scrabbling their gear together in confusion, then hastily abandoning it in favour of racing for the cover of an overhanging bank. Flosi delayed to wait for Regin.

"Ivarr! This way! It's Fafnir!" Regin shouted, giving Ivarr a shove toward the overhang. In the sudden upheaval, his possessions had been thrown around rather carelessly, and Elidagrimr's sword had vanished.

"The sword is gone!" he yelled, able to see clearly in the light cast by the approaching dragon.

"Bother the sword! Run, run!" Regin shouted as the dragon swept into sudden view, barely clearing the walls of the canyon. It was as fiery and dazzling as a comet and fully the size of a viking longship, with tremendous wings like sails. A small deadly head at the end of a long sinuous neck preceded the full-bellied, glowing body, followed by a long barbed tail snapping along behind. The sound the creature made was a combination of a huge bonfire burning out of control and a smithy clashing with hammers and tongs, punctuated by sharp flapping cracks from the great wings. The huge apparition thundered by overhead and banked suddenly, as if sensing the intruders, and swooped around for a second fly-by of the ravine.

Regin pushed Ivarr toward the river. "Run for the water!" he cried, indicating the shallow arm of the river curling into the dry channel. Ivarr began running across the wide stretch of sand.

The dragon came thundering down the channel, its wings barely missing the walls on either side. Ivarr could see its head darting from side to side, searching, and he knew the precise instant it spied him. All his blood seemed to turn to ice and his legs felt as if they were hardly moving. He heard Flosi's horrified shout then he glimpsed Regin running down the channel to his left, taking a stance and making menacing gestures at the dragon. A firebolt bounced off the monster's scales, drawing its attention to the small defiant figure below. The dragon was almost directly above Ivarr, illuminating the earth with giddy orange light and belching clouds of acrid black smoke.

The next thing Ivarr knew, he was face down in several inches of cold water with all the breath knocked out of him. Something heavy flattened him in the water and wouldn't let him up. The orange glare of the dragon flashed over him and continued up the riverbed after Regin. The wizard hurled another firebolt, and suddenly a tremendous gout of flame seared the ground with a loud steamy sizzle, and the small form of Regin vanished. Ivarr gaped, gasping like a fish. All he saw of the wizard was a black tatter flying away in the holocaust of flame. The dragon proceeded up the riverbed, uttering shrieks and smoky belches.

Ivarr heaved the weight off his back and sat up, staring into the shaggy, wolfish face of a large hound. Its face was sharp and sly, and its mischievous golden eyes were Flosi's.

"Flosi, is it you? What a spectacular fylgja," Ivarr said. "I never dreamed your soul contained such noble heights. I thank you for saving me. A pity you didn't have time to save poor old Regin." Grimly he turned toward the blackened spot, and the hound responded with a disconsolate whine.

The Alfar returned warily, hugging the shadows and jumping at the least sound. Immediately they began to gabble with relief at finding Ivarr alive, breaking off only when Finnvard exclaimed, "By the wizard's gizzards, Flosi's a hound! How shall my cat fylgja ever stand him? Not to mention a hare, Skapti. What a vicious-looking brute! Uff!" he added, sitting down suddenly as the hound put its paws on his shoulders and began licking his face with malicious glee.

"Where's Regin?" Eilifir asked, breaking his long silence.

"Dead," Ivarr replied heavily, and everyone's spirits plummeted. "He ran out to distract the dragon from me, and the next thing I knew, Flosi was sitting on me in the river. In another moment, the dragon blasted Regin, instead of me. It seems to be my fate to be the doom of wizards, I fear."

After a moment of silent shock, Flosi's voice said sadly, "He was the only teacher I ever liked. I could have learned a lot from him."

They began collecting their belongings and looking around for another shelter in case the dragon returned, while Eilifir and Flosi made a quick and fruitless search for any charred remains of the wizard.

CHAPTER TWENTY THREE

First they regrouped their scattered belongings and retreated to a tiny rocky cave downriver a short stretch, which was exceedingly damp, due to a small spring running through it; but otherwise they were grateful for its protection. Ivarr found the sword with no difficulty and kept its scabbard in his hand in the cave, where no one was comfortable enough to think about sleeping. Scarcely were they adjusted in their miserable quarters when Fafnir returned, screaming along the clifftops, more brilliant than before, gleaming in every scale from nose tip to tail barb. He circled their deserted camp and blasted it once with fire. Then he flew to a large crag in the middle of the river and perched there, with the tip of his tail flicking at the black water with hissing jerks. His head swivelled around warily, and jets of flame came from his nostrils as he sniffed the air. The travellers hardly dared to breathe aloud.

The dragon sounded a piercing shriek that echoed up and down the river, drowning even its endless bellowing. Then Fafnir spoke in a huge and thundering voice that turned Ivarr's muscles to jelly.

"I am Fafnir, the strong and the mighty! Whoever dares tread upon my domain shall perish! This river and all its gold belong to me and none other! I am the strongest of the strong and the mightiest of the mighty! Hear me, earth, and tremble!"

The Alfar trembled, if the earth didn't, and Finnvard stuffed a wad of Egills' hood into his mouth to keep from whimpering out loud.

Fafnir posed on his crag a moment longer, making heaving, hacking sounds that were like monumental coughing. Then he launched himself with heavily cracking wings and much metallic clamouring and quantities of black, choking smoke.

"He's gone," Eilifir whispered with a sigh.

Finnvard indulged himself in a wretched moan.

Ivarr pounded his fist against the rough stone. "And me with a broken sword to fight him, and Regin and Gizur dead."

The only reply was gloomy silence. After a long interval, Eilifir cleared his throat. "I think we can use our own power to reforge Ivarr's sword."

Skapti shook his head impatiently. "Eilifir, you're dreaming. We can't do anything like that."

"We conjured a comet," Eilifir said. "We can melt a sword."

"We nearly conjured a crater, is what we conjured," Egills said. "What if we messed it up and it wouldn't work? We'd only have one chance to test it. If it failed, we wouldn't have Ivarr to try it a second time."

"I can't begin to imagine the spells that must be woven into that blade," Skapti said with a shudder.

"Maybe we can steal a sword from Andvari," Flosi suggested. "I mean, maybe Ivarr can."

Eilifir shook his head. "There won't be anything like Glimr, and Glimr is the sword Ivarr was sent here for. It must be Glimr or nothing."

The Alfar looked at Eilifir uneasily. Ivarr looked at the broken sword in its sheath. "I suppose you could try, couldn't you?"

"Ivarr, you know us," Finnvard said anxiously. "Something is bound to go wrong. We'd hate to fail you this close to the end. Wouldn't it be safer just to grab a sword from Andvari?"

279

"No, the safest thing would be to steal the gold when Fafnir's not at home," Skapti said. "Part of us will divert him, and the rest will get the gold and stuff it into packs for all they're worth. There's no limit, almost, to what a good Snowfell backpack can hold. I had an uncle who carried around his entire household, including six fishing barges and a knarr—"

The discussion dissolved into an argument as to whether indeed an Alfar could get a knarr into a backpack or a satchel. Sleep seemed out of the question anyway, so they sat up until dawn, talking and chewing on hardtack, which of course called for some hot tea to wash it down.

As soon as the sky was light, there was no way they could leave the place fast enough. That day they came upon a waterfall, rather a small one, and spent several hours climbing down to it to see if a cave were behind it. There was no cave, and all they gained was a thorough soaking from the spray. However, no one complained. They resumed their upriver trek with grim, steady resolve. As the sun declined to the west, Ivarr found himself watching the sky, a habit he had acquired from Finnvard.

"Will Fafnir be back tonight?" Ivarr asked him directly.

Finnvard half-closed his eyes and gazed upward. "Yes, I think so. He knows he's being invaded."

For the night they found a low cove and crawled back into its deepest point until they could go no further. Then they piled up stones to make a screening wall which would hide their fire, and also protect them from much of the force of a direct snort if Fafnir discovered them.

Eilifir was standing guard when Fafnir appeared. Ivarr awoke suddenly to the spine-chilling scream of the dragon upstream. Fafnir came swooping down the river canyon with a fiery roar, passed their hiding place, and continued downriver. After a long, silent moment he came back, snorting and rumbling and creaking. He made several passes overhead, with more snorts and screams each time as if frustrated at not being able to find the intruders. He settled on a cliff and limbered up his voice by screaming for half an hour, then delivered his thunderous speech:

"I am Fafnir, the strong and the mighty! Whoever dares tread upon my domain shall perish! This river and all its gold belong to me and none other! I am the strongest of the strong and the mightiest of the mighty! Hear me, earth, and tremble!"

He sat coughing and grumbling a while longer, then lurched away upriver with ponderous flapping. As soon as they were sure he was gone, Finnvard lit a fire and brewed tea, sighing about the lamentable lack of pastries.

"Nothing like a butter tart to strengthen a fellow's courage," he declared, along with a lot of other nonsense calculated to cheer up his companions.

"The sword is what worries me a great deal," Ivarr said, resting his chin on his fist. "In my dreams I can see myself challenging Fafnir, and when I draw my sword, it's this one, broken off short. Or I find it's nothing but a toy in my hand, and Fafnir just laughs at me and comes after me with his claws and fangs. Maybe my dreams are prophetic too."

Eilifir shook his head and spoke thoughtfully. "We are Alfar of the highest order, endowed by power and proven by ordeal. I say we can reforge that sword for Ivarr."

"Highest order?" repeated Egills. "We're not any order at all, are we?" He was practicing a host of annoying little mischiefs on Finnvard: tweaking his nose, dropping pebbles on him, and changing his spoons into snakes, all of which Finnvard endured in silence.

"We need Regin or Gizur more at this moment than any other," Ivarr said, stabbing the broken sword into the sand and glaring at it. "For this, Gizur died, and Regin died trying to distract Fafnir from me. Now what's the use of it? I'll be the cause for all of us perishing. Perhaps I should be the one to go into the cave first and die first, if that's to be our fate."

Eilifir shook his head, and Skapti said, "Absurd, Ivarr. Just be patient and let things develop. You don't see Finnvard worrying, do you?"

Finnvard was sleeping peacefully now, using Egills for a brace.

Ivarr stood up. "I'm going outside. Fafnir might return and somebody should be watching." He knew Fafnir wasn't likely to come back after delivering his speech of defiance. It was probably part of the dragon's routine, which he had repeated every night for countless years.

Sighing, he climbed a large rock and sat down in a shadow, contemplating the stars and his own disappointment in the sword. His thoughts turned to Lorimer and he became uneasy. Lorimer would not leave his thoughts, no matter how hard he tried to evict him. He tried to convince himself Lorimer was nowhere near; he was probably at Asraudrsbog, or maybe he had given up. The black feeling of hopelessness persisted until Ivarr ruefully wondered if some of Finnvard's prescience had rubbed off on him.

He was even less assured when he finally returned to the cave and Finnvard was the only one awake, waiting for him by the dying fire.

"Ivarr, it's most peculiar, but I've been thinking of Lorimer," he said at once. "I simply can't stop wondering where he is and what his next move will be."

Ivarr sat down heavily and stared at his broken sword. "I don't believe we'll be long in finding out," he said. "You're the seer, why don't you put your powers to work and figure it out?"

Finnvard solemnly replied, "I shall try." He went out to watch.

Ivarr unsheathed Birna's knife and put it beside his head when he lay down to sleep. Finnvard's stout figure planted watchfully outside their cove was somehow reassuring.

The next day the only comfort Ivarr could draw from their ordeal was the fact that Lorimer would have had great difficulty following them, even with the assistance of his dwarves. The dry channels were tortuous, and a drizzling rain settled itself for a lengthy stay on the shoulders of the fells. Spirits sank accordingly.

By sundown they were poking into every crevice and

crack, looking for a place to sleep which also offered cover from Fafnir. They finally crept under a large overhang and made a miserable camp among the rocks. They were weary to the bone besides being wet. Another waterfall had been inspected and found lacking dwarf, gold, and dragon, although there had been a rather promising cave.

As Ivarr gulped the stockfish stew, he thought of Regin and the feast they had made of his provisions the night they left Bondscarp. He felt slightly guilty for letting Regin know how he had distrusted him. In retrospect, he could see that Regin had taken a tremendous risk in turning against Lorimer, with so little to gain by it.

Ivarr shivered suddenly, not liking to think of Lorimer in such dismal surroundings. The Alfar were dispiritedly attempting to dry their clothing and no one was saying much. They all looked discouraged by the sheer enormity of the task before them. The rain showed signs of staying forever to further cheer them.

"Throw a little more wood on that fire," someone said. "I'm soaking wet and mortally cold."

Finnvard automatically threw some sticks on the fire. Then he gasped, "Who said that? Who spoke?"

The Alfar peered at him resentfully from the cloaks and blankets they were wrapped in, but no one spoke. Finnvard turned his head by slow degrees, fearful to look behind him. Ivarr whirled around and beheld a tattered figure leaning on a staff. Instantly Birna's knife flashed into his hand. The Alfar leaped to their feet, grabbing various weapons and making a variety of signs to ward off evil.

The ragged figure raised his staff warningly. "This is a nice welcome," he said. "I've been forgotten in only two days, after nearly getting fried defending you."

The travellers gaped at the apparition. "It's Regin!" they suddenly clamoured, throwing off their cloaks and blankets jubilantly.

"Great gollups, man!" Skapti cried. "You look terrible! What's happened to you?"

"We thought you were dead!" Finnvard added.

"Maybe he is," Egills said. "Who could look that bad and still be alive?"

Regin sat down wearily on a cushioning blanket. His cloak and the clothing underneath were little more than charred scraps, and his long beard and hair were singed away to almost nothing. In places, his skin had a shiny puckered appearance, like a healed scar. His eyebrows were burned away, except for a few stray tufts, which gave him a fierce, startled expression.

"Thank you for your kindness," he said as Finnvard presented him with a large crock of fish stew. "I've been blasted by a dragon at close range, and I've been trapped in an escape spell for two days. If I hadn't used it, poor old Regin would be nothing but a heap of charred bones by now. Escape spells, as you know, are a catch-as-catch-can affair and I regret to confess it took me a while to unravel it. My clothing didn't fare particularly well, as I was crawling around for two days in the air shafts of a Dark Alfar gold mine, but by and large, this old wizard is still intact and immensely grateful for it." He tapped his staff on the ground to bring attention to its charred spots, and ruefully combed the stubble on his chin which had been his beard.

The Alfar could hardly wait long enough to allow Regin to consume his feast before peppering him with questions. He put down his bowl and began filling his pipe. When everyone's suspense was almost intolerable, he began answering their questions.

"And as for the cave of Andvari and the dragon," he finally said, "I believe we're getting very close. Tonight, just before sundown, the clouds parted a bit, and for a moment I could see a great distance upstream to the mountains which mark the end of the lowlands and the beginning of the highlands—the highlands which Svartarr eventually calls Hlidarend. Descending the sheer face of the cliffs was a misty veil of water, almost concealed in the clouds. I saw it only for an instant, but I'm almost certain it is the end of our search for Andvari."

The Alfar whooped, pranced, pounded on each other, and

284

executed leaps and dance steps that would have done credit to a troupe of acrobats. Poor food, tattered cloaks, thin boots and exhaustion were all forgotten in an instant. To celebrate, everyone was served double rations of fish soup.

Fafnir appeared near midnight, roaring and shrieking in a fine fury. He blasted fire twice as he circled above them, no doubt knowing exactly where they were and trying to decide how to get at them. After swooping overhead several times, he alighted on the opposite side of the river. For a long time he sat hissing and coughing before delivering his usual roaring boast, word for word. The elves watched his furious display with less fear, although Finnvard chewed nervously on the end of Egills' hood.

Fafnir blasted flame until his scales glowed a dull red and black smoke spurted from his mouth and nostrils. Finally the flame came at wider intervals, and Ivarr could hear his sides heaving like a hundred pairs of old squeaky bellows.

"Thieves!" Fafnir grumbled. "Bah! Robbers, bah! Cowards!" He ended with a fit of smoky choking, and it was some time before he finally got himself airborne again.

The Alfar crept to the edge of their overhang to watch.

"I don't think he sounds healthy," Egills said. "I had a great-uncle who coughed like that, and before he was a hundred and ninety-two there was nothing left of him but skin and bones."

"Fafnir is an old dragon," Regin said. "It sounds like his passages are about destroyed after so many years of blasting fire. He used to wreak a lot of havoc on the white dwarves upriver. Lately nothing much has been seen of him. I suspect the most he does is fly up and down the river and make a lot of noise where he's sure no one can hear him."

Skapti tugged at his worrying ear. "A dragon is a dragon, no matter how old or smoky. It's still going to be a miracle if we kill him."

Ivarr watched the red spark that was Fafnir vanishing into the dark. He knew there would be no question about killing Fafnir if he had a reforged Glimr. He glared at Regin resentfully, and Regin looked inscrutably into the fire.

285

In the morning, Regin was stirring around before dawn, building a bright crackling fire and boiling water for tea. In response to Egills' grumpy query he said, "If we get an early start we might make it to the waterfall today."

Flosi yawned and shivered. "And I suppose Andvari will cheerfully welcome us and invite us to dine on gold dishes and sleep on feather beds." He gave Finnvard a shaking and rushed around nervously, making a nuisance of himself.

"This is more like real spying," Skapti said, rubbing his hands briskly over the fire. "Spying upon a dragon has to be the ultimate assignment. This will be our finest hour."

"Unless we're Fafnir's finest meal first," Egills said dourly, sorting his boots out in the dark.

That day they travelled quickly, stopping only to rest a few moments, and talk was sparse. They hurried eagerly toward each new bend or obstacle, certain the waterfall would be on the other side. The river channel now was a wide concourse of massive tumbled boulders, with the river growling in a deeper channel in the centre. Every ledge held a clammy pool and everything was wet and cold. Feet slipped, fingers got pinched and raw, and tempers wore thin. The bellow of the water prevented any talk, but Ivarr knew everyone must be worrying about finding a place to hide where Fafnir's fiery breath could not reach. Ivarr smiled wryly as he futilely tried to warm his cold blue hands.

By late afternoon they were barely moving. They were edging along an exposed ledge above the roiling water and fervently hoping the ledge would not peter away to nothing. It was already uncomfortably close to disappearing, although it had begun promisingly. With their noses against the stone, they inched along cautiously, angling upward toward an unguessable destination.

Ivarr was leading the way. The ledge hadn't diminished further, mercifully, and he thought he could see where it was leading them. Above were more rocks, but they looked like the understructure of a plateau of some sort.

The ledge ended in a little pocket in the lava, barely big enough for all of them to crowd into. Straight above, the afternoon sun glinted through a narrow crack about thirty feet up a steep chute. The Alfar boosted Ivarr up to the shaft and he wedged himself there a moment, looking at the blue patch of sky above. Bracing himself with back and feet, he worked his way up until he could put his head out. He saw the scoured back of a huge lava flow, grown over with tuffets of moss and clumps of grass. Raising his eyes, he beheld the face of a cliff, hundreds of feet high, hidden on all sides by more cliffs so that the sunlight did not linger long on the spot where Ivarr was peering from the fissure. His eyes lifted, searching, and he saw the waterfall, spuming over the face of the cliff and thundering down in a wall of white feathery foam. Curling cascades frayed away to mist before ever touching the bottom of the chasm. Beyond that deceptively airy curtain was the dim outline of an opening.

Ivarr finally became conscious of impatient shouts from below. He crawled all the way out of the shaft and lay gazing at the waterfall.

"We made it!" he called down into the fissure, adding a long, reverberating whoop. "It's Andvari's cave!"

CHAPTER TWENTY FOUR

When they crept to the edge of their pedestal of lava, they looked down into a sandy cove surrounded by black cliffs of lava smoothly worn into gloomy facades. The waterfall thundered down into yet a deeper pit, as if pounding itself straight through the earth. It had gradually hollowed out a deep bowl for itself, below the level of the cave. Mist billowed up from below, filling the sandy cove with moisture as the hissing silver sheet plummeted past.

Climbing down from the lava flow was a matter of moments. Still somewhat dazed at their success, they walked to the lip of the cauldron and looked down at the foot of the falls. It was fifty feet below, and the rock was black, streaked with green slime. The roiling of the water had carved an exit into the main riverbed, leaving a bridge arching over the spouting water. The bridge led to a narrow ledge, which gave access to a wide shelf behind the foot of the falls. Crudely chiselled hand and footholds led up to the main cave.

They looked at it only an instant before realizing what they were seeing. Andvari himself could have been sitting there, and might have seen them anyway from the mouth of the cave. They scuttled backward hastily, beating a retreat for the lava cliffs. In a crevice at a safe distance, they began to cackle and wheeze and pound each other in high glee.

Looking back, Ivarr saw something he had been a fool to miss. Half smothered in sand were two huge weathered wooden doors—more wood than a Scipling would burn in a month. Moss had covered them over, and they stood half-open and forever mired in several feet of black sand. But it was not the doors that caused Ivarr to shudder at their stupidity. It was the long drag marks of the dragon's tail in the sand. The track led from the stone pedestal, where they had climbed out of the river chasm, and disappeared inside the doors. They had stepped right on it without seeing it. For all they knew, the dragon could have been watching behind those doors.

"Down, you fools, and quiet!" Regin ordered. "If they haven't seen us it's a miracle. Dragons are notoriously ill-tempered if anyone disturbs their sleep. Fafnir could come roiling out of that cave at any instant!"

They wedged themselves deeper into the crevice and held their breath, listening and waiting. There was not a sound to indicate that anything was aware of their presence, although they waited until the sky was blood-red with the sunset.

"I don't believe he's coming," Ivarr said with a sigh, stretching his stiff muscles. "I guess that means we're safe for a few hours, but not in this little crack. We've got to find a better hiding place than this. While you're doing that, Skapti, Regin and I are going to take a look inside the cave."

Flosi leaped up eagerly. "I want to go too, can't I, please?"

Ivarr had never heard Flosi say "please" for anything. He was so astonished that he granted Flosi permission to accompany them. Immediately he began having second thoughts and wished he hadn't spoken so hastily, but the words couldn't be unspoken now. While Flosi tightened his boot laces and inspected his sword, Ivarr and Skapti agreed upon a place to meet after looking into the cave.

Regin led the way across the black sand to the massive doors. They warily skirted the cove, hugging the walls, and approached the doors from one side. The doors were immense and thick and elaborately carved beneath the moss.

The passage beyond the doors was dimly lit from an opening beyond, and it smelled of a peculiar combination of smoke and decay. The walls were ornamented with faded etching and carving. The sand and rubble beneath their feet sloped gently upward, as if at one time it might have been a flight of steps. The sand muffled the sound of their feet as they walked upward toward the dim light.

The passage gave way to a lofty cavern buttressed by columns of natural stone. At the opening of the cave, the water hissed downward, muting the light to a pale, watery glow, now dyed pink from the setting sun. In the faint light they could see ruined carvings and crumbling balustrades. A rubbly stairway led upward to another set of massive doors. Ivarr took a step in their direction, but Regin nudged him sharply and nodded toward the cave opening, making a sign for silence.

A small hunched figure crouched on the edge, gazing into the sheet of falling water. Long white hair and beard streamed down his back and over his drawn-up bony knees. His limbs were gnarled and knobbed, and he stared at the water as if hypnotized. All at once the creature straightened somewhat and scuttled toward the chiselled handholds in the cliff face. In the blink of an eye he had vanished from sight.

In a few moments he came climbing back, dragging himself into the cave with his long thin arms. He sat down on his haunches, water streaming from his hair, beard, and tattered garments as he examined his prize. It was a gold armband, the likes of which Ivarr had seen only in ancient collections.

Andvari wrung out his beard skillfully and trotted over to a small heap of gold coins, a sword hilt, and other small oddments he had gleaned that day from the river. Then he sat down again like a miserable old beggar to stare at the water thundering down before him.

The spies did not move or speak. Finally the sun dropped behind the wall of the cliffs and the cave darkened. Andvari rose, stretched, and stooped to gather up his discoveries of the day. Tottering under the load, he limped away into the darkness and began ascending the broken stairs. Without conferring, the spies swooped after him like shadows and peered after him through the crumbling balustrades.

The stairway terminated at the wide doors, which had huge rings for handles. Andvari struggled to open one wide enough to squeeze through, emitting a crack of orange light like firelight; then it was quickly closed.

Ivarr shadowed him almost to the door. He pushed on it, deciding it would open when he wanted it to. Carefully, he edged it open a crack. Flosi knelt to peer through the crack a moment, then signalled Ivarr to open it further.

The chamber they looked into was a picture of ruined magnificence. Hangings drooped from the high ceiling like old rotten rags, the walls were greenish with damp, and the furniture lay in smashed wreckage in heaps against the walls. All this Ivarr's eye took in at a glance. What riveted his attention was the scene in the centre of the hall. A mountain of glittering gold towered over the tiny figure of old Andvari, who was sitting on a rickety seat amidst a clutter of fabulous gold things thrown on the floor. He was eating a raw fish and huddling a ragged dirty cloak around his shoulders. In a moment he rose, poked at some crudely made little arrows and a tiny longboat, and looked toward the door as if expecting someone.

"Is that you, Imp?" His bare feet came pattering toward the door. The spies nipped inside and hid behind a hanging. "I thought I shut it. Nothing like having a young sprat around to make a fellow feel old. Should have let the river have him, you old fool. No, no, no, not my little Imp, the precious plague, bless and drat him. Yes, we're glad we saved him, usually."

The old dwarf shut the door and glared at it a moment. Ivarr stared, revolted and enthralled by the ugly little creature, whose face was distorted by wrinkles, scowls, and hairy moles. One eye was nearly obscured by a permanent squint and the other was open wide in bitter indignation. After an uneasy moment of poking around in the clutter near the door, the old dwarf grumbled away, his bristly brows drawn together.

"Just getting old, I suppose," he growled. "I say, it's precious cold in here." He poked at the gold heap as if it were a bed of coals. In a louder voice he roared, "I said, it's getting cold in here! Fafnir! Are you deaf, you old kettle?"

The gold stirred again and a scaly head lifted itself and yawned appallingly. Smoke curled from the dragon's nostrils and trickled from his throat behind a yard or so of pink tongue and a ferocious fence of sharp yellowed teeth. Fafnir stretched himself, extending his clawed forefeet almost to Andvari's toes and arching his back until it nearly touched the ceiling, raking the gold with his villainous barbed tail.

"What do you expect me to do about it?" he inquired, admiring the claws on his left paw.

"If you can't at least keep the place warm, you've got to get out," Andvari snapped. "What's the good of a dragon if it doesn't put out some heat? That's the only reason I let you stay here, although you've been getting terribly lazy this past century or two. Oh, I get plenty of smoke, but very little fire these days. I think you're getting old, Fafnir, too dreadful old."

Fafnir shook himself, dislodging a hail of gold coins caught between his scales. "Not nearly as old as you are. I give off heat until this room is smothering, like a furnace, and your tottery old bones still have ice at their marrow. The Imp leaves the door wide open until I'm nearly frozen, and then you wonder why the cave's not warm."

"That's another thing. I know I shut it." Andvari looked around into the gloom, illuminated only by the muted glowing of Fafnir's scales. "There may be thieves in here this very moment. A fine job you do of protecting the treasure."

"Tush. I didn't see anybody last night. I tell you I blasted the scuttling, snivelling creatures to cinders, or at least a few of them. If they're out there tonight skulking around, I'll throw the fear into 'em."

Fafnir dragged his heavy belly toward the door, clanking

like a pile of battle armour. The spies slipped out of his way until he had passed.

Andvari scurried after him, crying in a shrill angry voice, "You arrogant lump of old soot and ashes! You find those thieves and keep them away from my treasure. That's right, I said my treasure, because that's just what it is. I'm the one who dives into the river after every single bit of it and I'll throw it all back into the water rather than let anyone take a single piece of it. And that includes you, most particularly!"

"You'll die one day, old dwarf," rumbled the dragon with a hateful flirt of his tail as he lumbered toward the door. Then he stopped and began sniffing loudly. The spies froze behind their barrier of old chairs.

"I used to know what an Alfar smelled like, and I thought I just smelled one. It wasn't your precious Imp, either."

"Bah! Your nose couldn't smell fifty wizards if they were sitting right on it. Bah! Get yourself out of here, you old kettle!"

Andvari slammed the door in a rage and stumped back to his wretched chair and miserable meal, growling balefully under his breath as he shivered in his dirty old cloak.

Quietly Ivarr pushed open the door. Then they raced down the stairs and through the cave. When they reached the outside, Fafnir was puffing and blasting and rattling his wings. After a tremendous effort, he heaved himself into the sky with a thunder of wings. An awful cloud of choking smoke and fire surrounded Fafnir as he rose like an eerie black and red sun and went winging down the river chasm looking for his prey.

When he was out of sight, Eilifir signalled from the nearby ridge. Taking care to remain out of sight lest Fafnir return, the spies scrambled up the cliff to Eilifir's hiding place.

All the elves were crowded into a small fissure, waiting impatiently.

"Well, did you see anything? Any gold?" demanded Skapti.

"Gold! I should say! Heaps of it!" Flosi exclaimed exuberantly. "A regular mountain of gold, with Fafnir curled up on top of it like a cat in a basket; old Andvari was sitting in the midst of it, guarding it with a pile of old swords. It's a lovely set-up indeed. If we stole it piece by piece from under the nose of Andvari, whose eyesight is as sharp as that of fifty eagles, I estimate it would only take us a century or so. Not to mention Fafnir, of course, who is at least the size of a longboat, with claws like hay hooks and teeth like knives. I'd never really thought he'd be so tremendously huge. His eyes are the size of shields, practically."

"Tush, you exaggerate," said Regin, who was calmly stuffing his pipe. "Fafnir is a very old dragon. You can tell by the quantities of smoke. In old age they lose much of their flame and get very sooty, like an old chimney. He won't be especially difficult to kill."

Ivarr shook his head slowly. "He's got metal plates half a foot thick over every inch of his body and a great poisonous barb on the end of his tail, besides his claws and an excellent set of teeth. It's not going to be easy at all to kill him, especially without Glimr. Perhaps we could all attack him while he's sleeping and kill him that way."

The Alfar looked aghast. "But it takes power to kill a dragon!" Finnvard gasped. "We may have some power, but certainly not that sort!"

"Enough to conjure a comet," Ivarr said. "Why not enough to kill a dragon?"

Skapti shook his head vigorously. "Killing dragons is the province of heroes, not middle-aged Alfar who have barely discovered the vague outlines of their powers. You're the one the fates selected, Ivarr. It has to be you."

"Then the fates had better get busy reforging this sword, if they really want this weregild paid," Ivarr retorted angrily.

Everyone sat in gloomy silence, chins in hands. Gradually all eyes came to rest upon Regin, who was smoking his pipe and gazing into the waterfall.

"Then it's up to Regin to think of something," Skapti announced decisively. "If he wants Ord's ring so badly, then he'll find a way."

Regin sighed. "I'll do my best. Right now I'm as flummoxed as anybody else."

Eilifir stirred and spoke. "We could reforge Glimr." No one seemed to have the energy to disagree with him again.

They camped in a small cave in the cliffs. It was crowded and smoky, but at least it was dry and out of Fafnir's sight. Ivarr stood the first guard, watching Fafnir's fiery course in the sky and smelling his vile exhaust. Finally the dragon came flapping back to the waterfall, plummeting to earth with a terrific thumping flop. From his hiding place, Ivarr could hear Fafnir gasping. For a long time the dragon lay in a heap, panting and groaning, glowing scarlet as if his scales were red-hot from over-exertion. Ivarr wished he had a sword; it would have been an ideal time to attack Fafnir. The dragon finally heaved himself to his feet and staggered off to the cave. The spray from the falls hissed on his overheated scales as he passed. For the rest of the night there were no more disturbances.

The next day they held a conference, while the might and fury of Fafnir was fresh on their minds. After a great deal of arguing, Regin finally stood up, clutching his staff and glaring around with smoke-reddened eyes.

"I can see there's only one thing to be done," he said. "Elidagrimr's sword must be reforged somehow. It's the only sword that can kill the beast. I swear I shall do it if it kills me!"

"No!" Skapti and Eilifir said at once. Skapti rose and paced, tugging on his ear. "Eilifir says we can reforge it ourselves. I don't know if we can, nor if we can't. We don't want to cost anyone his life working on it, meaning Regin. One wizard spent is enough. Well, what are you fellows waiting for? Flosi, you're supposed to be Regin's pupil; tell us what's to be done to heat a forge hot enough to melt Dainn's metal."

Flosi looked around the circle of intent faces. "Do you really think we can do it? Do we have the discipline? After all, I was so lazy and undisciplined as to kill the otter, against orders."

295

Ivarr drew Glimr's pieces from the sheath. "I think you can do it."

"And so do I," Regin said. "I won't be able to help you, but I know you have the power."

"Then we'll do it!" Finnvard declared fiercely, wringing Skapti's hand and slapping palms with everybody. Even glum old Egills was almost beaming and rubbing his hands as if he couldn't wait to begin.

"The first thing is to translate the runes," Regin said. "Eilifir, are you any good at runes?"

"Tolerable," Eilifir said, taking the pieces and fitting them together so he could look at the runes.

Flosi inspected their cave and declared it would be as good a forge as any, and the others accepted his judgment readily. "We might get blown to smithereens," Flosi said cheerfully, "or we might suffocate from the heat, but at least one of us must survive long enough to give the finished sword to Ivarr. This may be the last thing we do, but I swear by Odin and Asgard it's going to be the best."

They all went down into the forge except Ivarr and Regin, taking the sword with them. Regin could scarcely sit still. "I wish I were pure enough to help, but I'm sure the blade would snap if it had any of my spells in it. What's taking them so long? They've not got a fire yet."

After a long silence with no fire in the cave, Regin became almost too impatient to keep from rushing inside. "It's been hours!" he said, looking anxiously at the declining sun. "Surely they should have finished their spell by now. It can't be such a long one as that, Ivarr. I fear something has gone wrong!"

At that moment, a weak red glow began lighting the rocks of the cave. It strengthened into a deep ruddy beam of light that poured from the forge and defied the gathering darkness. Even Fafnir gave it a wide berth that night as he began his nightly scouring.

Toward dawn, Skapti prodded Ivarr awake to tell him the sword was poured into the mold and was now cooling. The next day the hammering began and went on for five days without stopping. When one Alfar tired, another took his place until the sword was hammered to amazing thinness, perfectly straight and deadly sharp from tip to hilt.

At noon on the sixth day the Alfar came out of the cave, sooty, singed, and jubilant. Skapti presented it to Ivarr, sheathed.

"You're to be the first one to draw the new Glimr," he said. "I feel I should make a speech of some sort, but I'll do us all a favour and just forget it. But here it is, Ivarr. It's a bit shorter than the original and we haven't engraved it. After you kill Fafnir we'll engrave a dragon on it and write the legend on the blade. Draw it out and test it, Ivarr."

Ivarr slowly drew the long slender blade from the sheath. It was beautiful in a simple, sober fashion, like a beam of sunlight dancing with motes. The hilt was the same as when Elidagrimr had owned it.

"And it won't break," he half-questioned, around the lump of delight and fear in his throat. It seemed like a fragile reed in his hand, it was so light and easy to handle.

The Alfar all looked sootily smug. "Try it and see," Egills croaked with a mirthful wheeze.

Ivarr raised the sword in both hands dreading and hoping. It whispered as he brought it down, and it spanged against the boulder with a loud, clear note. Rock chips flew and Glimr did not shatter or bend. There was not even a nick in its perfectly honed edge, but the rock was reduced to rubble.

The Alfar did not explode deliriously; they merely grinned and nodded as if they were not in the least surprised. Regin solemnly shook each one by the hand, offering his congratulations and admiration.

"But that isn't all," Flosi said. "You'll also need a shield to protect you from Fafnir's breath. A shield that will not melt or burn." He produced a glimmering shield of light-weight metal and bowed modestly. "I made it myself," he added while Ivarr admired it.

Finally the inevitable moment of silence arrived. They all looked at Ivarr, a little fearful, a little impatient.

297

Regin asked the question they all avoided. "Well, when do you propose to challenge Fafnir?"

Ivarr had thought about little else in the past hours. "I shall meet him at sundown when he comes out of the cave."

"Tonight?" Finnvard asked with a quaver in his voice.

"Yes, tonight," Ivarr said. "The sooner, the better. Now if you don't mind, I want to be left alone until the time comes."

CHAPTER TWENTY FIVE

Ivarr left them at the cave and walked down into the sandy arena beside the falls. There would be no place to escape from Fafnir; one side was steep cliffs and the other was the deep rocky chasm of the river as it spewed angrily from the confinement of the cauldron at the foot of the falls. Ivarr thought briefly that he would be forced to choose between fiery death or watery death if his weapons failed.

He stationed himself where he would be the first thing the dragon clapped eyes on when he emerged from the cave. Watching the sun crawl slowly toward its destination in the west, he held Birna's knife in his hand and thought of all the adventures that had led him to this point. He also thought of his parents back in Fishless, wondering if they had missed him from Birna's hut, realizing that probably the people assumed some misadventure had befallen him and Birna—a dark night and a deep crevice in the lava, or murdering outlaws, perhaps. He also thought of Gizur.

His vigil was not a long one. The dragon appeared as soon as the sky was black. He was coughing and snorting soot, blinking his luminous eyes painfully. Groaning, Fafnir hauled himself out of the cave. For a moment he rubbed his eyes with the backs of his scaly paws. Experimentally he belched out a cloud of flame and fell to coughing until Ivarr hoped he was about to choke. Stuffy black smoke rolled from his dull scales.

Ivarr drew the sword and stepped from his sheltering rocks. "Good evening, dragon."

Fafnir gave a snort of surprise and opened his eyes. Not fifty feet away stood a small creature making menacing gestures and standing upon his very doorstep to insult him. Fafnir rumbled deep in his chest and flicked his deadly tail back and forth.

"Do you know who I am?" he thundered. "I am Fafnir, the strongest of the strong and the mightiest of the mighty! The earth trembles when I speak! How dare you trespass on my domain? What do you want, anyway?"

Fafnir struck a formidable pose, wings half-extended and claws hooked, and his neck was arched so his head was tucked almost against his chest.

"We want the gold," Ivarr replied, holding the sword before him. "It rightfully belongs to the Alfar dead, or at least in the possession of living creatures who will use it for benign purposes. We wish to take it to ensure the peace between the Ljosalfar and the black dwarves."

"So you think we'll just hand it over for the benefit of people we care nothing about?" demanded the dragon with another rumble.

"It would be easier that way than killing you," Ivarr said, flicking the sword. "But killing you is exactly what I shall do if you attempt to stand between us and the gold."

"I suspect it would be a rather one-sided battle. I could kill an insignificant thing like you with one blast so easily it would be absurd."

Ivarr brandished the sword until it hummed, a low purring song of confidence and power. "The battle would not be as one-sided as you think. This sword belonged to Elidagrimr and now it is mine, given to me specifically for this challenge. Are you going to defend the gold, Fafnir, or are you going to allow us to take it peacefully?"

Fafnir relaxed his defensive posture. "Well, perhaps it isn't worth dying for after all. Let old Andvari die for it, since he's willing to risk his life jumping into that icy river after each little bit. You can take it right now if you want to. Call

all your friends down from their hiding places and you can
begin hauling it away.'' The dragon turned his back with ill
grace, giving Ivarr a view of the spikey armour on his spine.

"I believe my friends will have the good sense to stay in
hiding," Ivarr said. "None of us are so foolish as to believe
the word of a dragon. You attempted to kill us without so
much as bothering to inquire what we wanted or who we
were, which is the reason why I doubt if you'll surrender the
gold without a struggle."

Fafnir glanced over one shoulder. "It's nothing to me but
dross metal. I care nothing at all for it except as a bed to sleep
on, and not a comfortable one at that. All I want is to be left
in peace, so summon your friends down at once, if you really
want the gold."

"No. I don't trust you. This is between the two of us,
Fafnir. Depart or die; I don't care which you choose."

Fafnir heaved a smoky sigh and raised his wings as if he
intended to take off. Then, with a move as quick as
lightning, his vicious barbed tail snapped around, murderously armed with his deadly sting. Ivarr barely had time
to strike at it and leap aside. The huge barb was neatly
severed with a gush of blood and poison. The dragon gave a
screaming roar and whirled around, blasting fire and
smoke. Ivarr deflected the fire with Flosi's shield, leaping
forward to hew at Fafnir's huge hind leg like a terrier
snapping at a horse's heels. The heavy, plated scales were
pierced with a single thrust, severing the tendons, and Ivarr
scuttled away as Fafnir spun around to snap at him. Thus
disabled, the dragon was slowed but definitely more furious.
Fire and smoke boiled from his jaws, and his scales gleamed
cherry-red with rage. Each of his attacks was repulsed,
earning for himself several major wounds and a host of
smaller ones. He struck at Ivarr with his claws, losing several
in the attempt.

Ivarr crouched behind the shield as the flames billowed
around him. His eyes streamed from the smoke and one arm
was slightly burned, but it was nothing of consequence.
Fafnir was leaking smoke badly from several gaping wounds

as he backed off to pant and wheeze and glare at Ivarr. He was dismayingly tough. A chest wound sure to kill him only spouted a small geyser of fire and he showed no signs of weakening.

After two more clashes, Ivarr wondered what it took to kill a dragon. Fafnir only laughed at the wounds dealt him, snapping at the sword with his teeth. Ivarr was careful not to let him grab it and jerk it away. Nothing would remain then but the choice between death by the dragon or the river. Several times Fafnir attempted to press Ivarr toward the river chasm, but Ivarr evaded that ruse determinedly and drove Fafnir backward in a bold rush. The sword seemed to battle of its own accord, as if Elidagrimr himself were wielding it. Ivarr knew his leaden arm was not controlling it entirely.

Fafnir paused again, hissing and boiling, and ventured a quick glance over his scaly shoulder at the river chasm. Instantly Ivarr understood the dragon's greatest fear was the water. Fafnir's eyes were hate-filled slits as he glared at Ivarr and snarled, ''This is the last contest, my thieving, cheating friend. You and that cursed sword of yours will both find a grave in the Drangarstrom very soon, I believe.''

Ivarr made no reply, and the dragon bellowed fire at him until the shield was almost too hot to hold, but he refused to drop it. Holding it before him, he advanced. Fafnir was between him and the river.

Fafnir perceived his intentions at once. He charged full ahead at Ivarr in a furious rush, raking with his claws and snapping with his teeth in a desperate frenzy. Ivarr stood his ground, aware more than ever that the strength behind the sword could not be his own, marvelling at the speed and dexterity of the sword as it countered Fafnir's attacks.

In the end, it was Fafnir who retreated. He made several more murderous lunges, which were all repelled as Ivarr advanced. Finally Fafnir stood on the edge of the gorge, roaring a final challenge and lashing his tail in a rage. The water churning below leaped up to sizzle and hiss on his scales like water on hot coals, which seemed to further enrage

302

Fafnir. He reared into his defensive pose and belched flame without ceasing, more flame than Ivarr would have believed possible. Flames rolled over him in waves, searing his exposed skin. His hand holding the shield suddenly became very hot, too hot to grasp the handle, and he saw that the shield was melting. Dropping it, he poised the sword like a javelin and threw it at Fafnir's bellowing jaws. It flew straight, piercing the fiery gullet, and Fafnir shrieked and reared aloft, clawing at the sword in vain. The glowing point had pierced his spine and passed through the scales to the outside.

With a final great roar of flame, the dragon toppled over the edge of the chasm. With a tremendous roaring shriek of hot metal meeting icy water, the dragon was gone. Billows of acrid steam rose into the night air. The following silence was profoundly empty.

The Alfar rushed down from the cliffs and found Ivarr on the edge of the chasm, stretched out senseless and blackened.

"But not dead," Regin whispered, still trembling. "Carry him into the cave behind the waterfall. We must treat these burns at once."

Ivarr awoke at the first rays of the sun and lay for a long time watching the sunlight playing on the waterfall outside. The Alfar were still asleep. Regin was sitting on a mossy rock, staff in one hand, and his satchel at his feet as he gazed into the darkness of the cave.

"I lost the sword," Ivarr said, and the words sounded even more hollow and miserable in the cave, with its drippings and echoings.

Regin looked desolate, as if he had aged ten years in the night. "It doesn't matter. At least you're still alive. In another instant the fire would have overcome you. The shield simply dissolved in your hand."

Flosi was awake, looking much the worse for wear. "Perhaps we could recover it from the river," he suggested without much hope.

"No," Regin said, shaking his head. "The river boils like a cauldron down there below the falls. Anyone trying to

303

swim in it would be drowned.''

"Then Fafnir is dead, isn't he?" Ivarr asked to assure himself.

"Dead as last year's coals," Skapti answered. "It was a masterstroke on your part to drive him into the river, but when the shield melted, I was certain that was the end of you.''

"And the sword is gone too. You'll never etch your dragon on it now, Skapti." Ivarr could scarcely bear to think of it.

"But the dragon is gone," Finnvard said, with a yawn, and his eyes sparkled with excitement. "Now the only obstacle is Andvari. An old dry stick would be more of a problem. How are you feeling, Ivarr? Are your burns quite healed enough to go on?"

Ivarr looked at his hands. Instead of the charred, blistered claws of last night, they were pink with restored health and free of pain. Wonderingly he held them up and looked at each of the Alfar.

"I don't know how you did it," he said. "But this is the finest Alfar magic you have performed yet, and there simply aren't words to thank you fellows.''

The Alfar looked pleased. Eilifir snorted gently. "Tush. Let's be getting on with it, shall we? Finnvard and Egills and Skapti are almost perishing for a look at the treasure.''

The great doors to the inner chamber were closed and evidently locked from within. This proved no great hindrance; the Alfar scratched some runes in the sand and recited a formula, and the doors burst open wide with protesting shrieks. The watery light rushed into the treasure vault and set it gleaming.

"Halloo! Is anyone here?" Skapti called.

A shabby figure edged out of the shadows like a suspicious old crab.

"How—how d'ye do?" Andvari croaked with an uneasy grimace. "I suppose you're the fellows that killed the dragon. I'm most grateful, really; he was getting to be such a frightful nuisance. Now that he's dead, what do you propose to do with me? Poor old Andvari won't do you any harm." Wringing his hands, he tried to grin ingratiatingly, but the result was awful.

"I'm sure you know what we want," Ivarr said, looking around at the treasure.

Andvari nodded glumly. "I knew it. Well, take it then, there's nothing an old wretch like me can do to stop you. It belongs to your dead ancestors and ill luck has followed me since I first began to collect it. I hope the same ill luck will follow you," he added in a mutter as he skulked away.

The Alfar began gathering up the treasure into their Snowfell backpacks, which swallowed it all without getting fat or heavy. When they were finished, the sun was setting and their backs were aching. Their packs and Regin's satchel were now bulging dangerously.

Andvari crept around the empty chamber, his eyes gleaming slyly. In a doleful voice he said, "That's all of it, every single piece. The work of hundreds of years is all stuffed away into your packs and not a bit left for poor old Andvari. Not even Fafnir is here anymore, poor beast, lying dead on a sandbar somewhere with that sword sticking through his throat. You haven't left me one flake of gold to comfort me, have you?"

Flosi hoisted his pack to his back with a grunt. "In several more hundreds of years you'll have just as much, and no dragon to share it with. We've done you a great service, actually."

Andvari hissed, watching Regin strolling around the cave looking into every crevice. "Why don't you leave now? Just take my gold and go away with it. Gold and dragons! I'd like to be shut of them, but I see that's not likely. All this gold will eventually come back to me, tumbling down the river from your battles and barrows to the north. It's frightfully unlucky, this gold. Take it away, take it away before I go mad!" He clenched his weedy hair in his fists and almost shrieked the words, his eyes fastened wildly upon Regin. He tried to scuttle away, but Regin ordered Flosi to grab him. The old dwarf screeched and kicked, but

Flosi was more than a match for his spindly struggles.

Regin scowled at Andvari. "There's one more piece of gold, and I want it. Give me that ring on your finger."

"Eh? This little ring?" Andvari blinked his one good eye innocently and put his hand behind his back. "It's just a bauble. You couldn't be wanting it, could you? Look at all the treasure you've got already. There's rings in there with stones the size of birds' eggs."

Regin shook his head. "I must have that ring you're wearing."

Andvari began to scowl. "I warn you, this is too much to be endured. I am old and crazy, but I know a few things. This ring won't matter as much to you as it matters to me. Can't you leave me just one small piece of gold to comfort me in my solitary old age?"

"You know as well as I what that ring is," Regin said. "It's Ord's ring and it has a mission of destruction to perform. Hand it over."

Andvari kicked Flosi and began to shriek and struggle. Flosi took a firm grip on him and shook him until the poor creature rattled like a bag of bones, but Andvari remained stubborn, screeching defiance. Flosi seized the ring and pulled it off, after nearly pulling the finger off also. He presented it to Regin, and Andvari scrabbled away, hissing in a fury.

"What a greedy lot you are!" he sputtered. "Not even one gold ring! But I have something else for you, my friends. As the defeated, I declare upon you this alog. I curse this treasure for you and for everyone who puts a hand upon it, so misfortune will follow its possessors as long as it is in their hands. Ill fortune will follow the wearer of that ring until all of this gold is back in my possession, and that will be a very long time indeed if I have to wait for the barrows to be carried away again. You may also beware of dragons as long as you own that treasure. There now, I lay this alog against you in my own name, Andvari, and may you never forget it. Blasts and fogs upon all of you! Faugh!"

They left Andvari screeching and shaking his fists in a

state of rage. The Alfar shrugged off the alog, since the gold was for Svartarr and would not be in their possession for long anyhow. Regin kept Ord's ring on his finger, where it gleamed in the sunlight as he smoothed his map on his knee and looked northward, upriver. He charted a course for the plains of Hlidarend, with a stop at Asraudrsbog for supplies. All the while he was plotting and discussing the route with the Alfar, Ivarr's attention kept straying toward the waterfall, where he could see the stooped form of Andvari lurking within the shadows, watching. After they started on their upward course around the falls, Ivarr glanced back and saw Andvari dive into the water below the waterfall with a singular flash of silver just before he struck the water, like the scales of a large fish. Ivarr stopped to look back a moment at the sandy cove where he had fought and defeated Fafnir. With a pang of despair he thought of the sword Glimr, probably lying in the deep black maw of the river or tumbling along with the current to wedge between some underwater rocks somewhere, forever lost.

Their course over the mountainous ascent to Hlidarend was a harrowing near-vertical climb up giant scarps and crags. The view was breathtaking, watching the Drangarstrom unwinding below them with all its tributaries funneling into it like threads in a skein of wool. They stopped frequently to appreciate the view, since the packs were heavy and awkward to carry. In places they hoisted them up with ropes, after sending one of the more agile fylgur scampering up the difficult spot to toss a rope down. The gold, they discovered, refused to accompany them through a shapeshifting—perhaps the first of the ill fortunes Andvari had wished upon them, thought Ivarr uneasily.

Ivarr watched for misfortune intently, worrying over each small difficulty lest it mushroom into an insurmountable one, but the Alfar were in great spirits. They laughed and joked and sang scalds as they climbed and played malicious tricks on each other. Regin, however, pressed the pace mercilessly, as if he could not be rid of the treasure soon enough to suit him. He did not participate in any of the

Alfar's silliness, and Ivarr, in his gloomy mood over the loss of Glimr, found his morose society quite refreshing.

The cliff they were climbing ended at last in a jumble of lava rock and scrubby bushes. They arrived at the top just in time to set up a hurried camp before the last traces of light disappeared. Too exhausted even for tea, the Alfar collapsed against their heavy packs and fell asleep except for Eilifir, who posted himself to watch. Ivarr too slept fitfully, plagued by dreams of old Andvari shaking his fists and screaming his dreadful curse. The dream was so vivid that Ivarr awakened, startled to find himself lying on a mountaintop in the moonlight instead of inside the cave. He listened to the river grinding away in its rocky channel. If he stood up, he could see the water hurling itself out into space to descend past Andvari's cave to the black cauldron below.

Ivarr rose quietly, after failing to convince himself getting up to get a drink was too much trouble. A small streamlet trickled down past their camp from a snowbank atop a nearby fell. Shivering, he had his drink and noted that dawn was not much further off. He was hurrying back to his warm eider when he saw someone climbing over the edge of the cliff from below. He was about to raise a shout of alarm, thinking instantly of Lorimer, but then he recognized the bent and scuttly form of Andvari. The old creature was less than twenty paces away, muffled about with a ragged cloak and a parcel of some sort. He saw Ivarr a second later and dived away into the brush with a croak of alarm. Ivarr leaped after him, but came to a standstill a moment later, wondering why he should bother about a wretched old white dwarf. He went back to the camp and awakened Finnvard, who was supposed to be watching, and told him about Andvari in case the fellow was skulking around hoping to steal back some of his gold. Then he tried to go to sleep again, but he kept bolting wide awake, thinking he heard mocking laughter, as if Andvari were relishing his curse.

In the days to come, they passed through the last of the unknown territory, and nameless fells on the map gave way to fells which had been viewed by someone at least once at the time of their naming. The river vanished underground several times, allowing them to cross and alter their course somewhat eastward toward Asraudrsbog. From there they would go straight north into Svartarrsrike.

Ivarr saw no more of Andvari, but that was not enough to convince him the old dwarf wasn't following. Regin also seemed ill at ease in the flatness of Hlidarend, broken only by rivers, the barrow mounds, and the low rolling hills. Ivarr was glad to detour around the barrow mounds and the ruined hilltop fortresses which surveyed the once-embattled domain with suspicious slit windows. They stopped for the night uncomfortably near one of the old crumbling hillforts, the only spot which offered any concealment.

Regin volunteered to stand watch. Long after the others were sleeping he paced around their camp, peering into the dark and listening. His restless prowlings awakened Ivarr, who silently joined him.

"A goose walked over my grave again," Regin said in a low voice. "Lorimer is looking for me and I know he will demand the gold and the sword and you to wield it. I fear it will come to a duel with him, and my new powers aren't quite ready for a challenge of that magnitude."

"The Alfar can help you. They've grown confident in their skills."

Regin thought a moment. "If it comes to a battle, some of us would be killed, perhaps all of us. If we were captured, there's always the possibility of escape, but one seldom escapes from death."

Ivarr left the wizard to his mutterings and lay down to sleep. With Regin on watch, however, his fears and suspicions warred with his common sense. He knew Regin had done nothing to indicate treachery; on the contrary, he had nearly killed himself several times for their sake. Still, Ivarr distrusted him.

Ivarr closed his eyes and began to drift off to sleep. Suddenly a stealthy scratching sound startled him awake. He caught Regin in the act of drawing a ring around him with the tip of his staff and muttering spells under his breath.

Ivarr relaxed; he was accustomed to Regin's fussy guardian rings and spells to ward off evil. The spell was more lengthy than usual and Ivarr began to feel sleepy. By the time Regin was finished with his ring, Ivarr was almost asleep, but a wakeful part of him was watching Regin. The old wizard leaned on his staff and nodded approvingly.

Shortly before dawn Ivarr awakened, not without reluctance. It was cold and frosty, reminding him that the short summer season was drawing to a close. He yawned, wondering why Finnvard wasn't rattling about with the morning tea yet. Raising himself on one elbow, he looked around to see if any of the others were stirring yet. He saw only frost-grizzled lumps and the grey ashes of the fire. Regin was nowhere to be seen, and, upon a second inspection, neither were the packs that contained the gold.

Ivarr leaped up with a shout. "The gold! It's gone!" He pummeled the unconscious elves, looked back, and saw no one moving. He snatched away the ragged cloak Skapti always used and saw that no one was there. The camp had the look of being hastily evacuated, with only the important things taken. There was no sign of Regin or the Alfar.

CHAPTER TWENTY SIX

The desolation of Ivarr's situation filled him first with panic, then numbness. He climbed a hill for a look around at the landscape, but that only served to reinforce his aloneness. For lack of a better plan, he gathered up the scattered possessions of the Alfar—several old cloaks, a cup, a pot, the dull knife Flosi used to stir his tea, and a small pouch with hard cheese and stale hardtack inside. He absently nibbled the hardtack and examined his situation more critically.

The first idea that presented itself for consideration was that Regin was somehow responsible. He might have put a spell on them and transported them by magic, leaving him alone with no food and few weapons, knowing he would not long survive by himself.

Next, the absence of signs of a struggle made him think of another possibility so shocking he had to sit down suddenly to wrack his brains for proof. Perhaps the Alfar had simply abandoned him after getting the gold they wanted, since he was no longer useful to them. But they were his friends, he told himself. They wouldn't be that fickle, would they?

Ivarr walked around the camp, mulling over several sets of equally impossible alternatives. If Lorimer had seized them during the night, why had Ivarr been spared, and why hadn't he even awakened? He knew Finnvard would raise a terrific uproar under such circumstances. He stood gazing for a long time at the spot where Regin had scratched rings around him. Then he walked up the hill to the stone where Regin had sat guarding them. He walked around the stone several times looking at the ground for signs of anything that would give him a clue. Nothing. He leaned against the rock, feeling beaten. The only hopeful sign was the sun coming up, melting the frost on the black stone.

Suddenly Ivarr's eyes focused on some unnatural scratch marks on the stone. As the frost melted, letters appeared until he discerned a complete message in Regin's spiky runic script: "Asraudrsbog—east." An arrow pointed. As Ivarr stared at the writing, wondering if he were imagining things, the letters slowly melted like the frost in the sunlight.

Ivarr shook his head. Was it Regin's writing? Might it not be Lorimer's, perhaps? Lorimer would be suspicious of his absence, suspecting Regin of concealing him somehow. The writing could be directing him right into the clutches of Lorimer. Or perhaps it was a message Regin left to Lorimer—Ivarr shook his head and abandoned such speculations. The message was his only clue, so he would follow it.

Making a light pack of improvised materials, he noted several landmarks to the east and set off at a steady pace for Asraudrsbog.

Three days later he knew he had arrived when he parted some rank bushes and stepped into mud over his ankle. Freeing his foot, he slipped back into the bushes to peer around for signs of his destination. Regin must have a hall or a tower he occupied—his laboratory, he had called it. Ivarr dodged from bush to bush, advancing further into the boggy terrain until he saw what looked like the ruins of an old fortress sinking into the mire. A crumbling dike of earth and stones attempted with little success to hold off the advance of the bog and offered a reasonably dry approach to the round tower which was the last of the buildings to remain habitable. The bog had risen around a large hall, another tower, and a cluster of smaller turf huts. A host of frogs was tuning up for its nightly chorus, and clouds of hungry mosquitoes hummed hopefully over Ivarr's head as he studied the round tower. A red glow showed in one narrow window, and he smelled a trace of smoke. He crept nearer the causeway and sat down to wait for dark.

When he deemed it safe, he rose, determined to risk everything for a glimpse in the lighted window. Poised for a fast, silent dash across the causeway, he was just on the point of launching himself when a door opened suddenly, spilling red firelight almost to his feet. A large shadow blocked the doorway, and Ivarr tumbled back into the shadows, certain the maker of that silhouette could be none other than Lorimer.

Lorimer peered out into the silvery dusk a moment and stepped back into the tower. He reappeared, dragging a large bundle, which he hauled to the centre of the causeway, where he dumped it and stood back regarding it.

The bundle unfolded itself a bit, rather stiffly, revealing itself as a much-dishevelled Regin, with his hands and feet bound. He looked more than ever like a disreputable old crow, wounded and captured by enemies, but fierce to the last.

"Have you anything more you wish to say, Regin?" Lorimer demanded. "I've given you every chance. I wasn't deceived long with your ruse in Bondhol. I could have seized you and destroyed those wretched elves long before this, if I'd wanted to."

Regin shrugged with as much dignity as he could muster in such a position. "Nonsense. You wanted the treasure and you wanted Ord's ring. Well, now you've got them, but you'll never get Ivarr and Glimr."

Lorimer made an impatient sound. "Yes, but I've got those five Alfar. I'm sure I can force one of them to tell me where the Scipling is hiding. I hope that's a thought you'll dwell upon as you're dying in the bog. It won't be pleasant for them, I assure you."

"You'll get nothing from them. I'm the only one who knows where Ivarr is, and it seems I'm going to be dying very shortly, so you'll never find out until one day when he slits your weazand with his sword."

Inside Lorimer's pocket, Grus cackled appreciatively.

"And I shall be there to see it! Bless the Scipling and bless the sword!"

"Silence!" Lorimer snapped. "I ought to throw you in after this other traitor. In spite of you all, I shall have Svartarrsrike one day soon—much sooner than you suspect."

"Your sceptre is much more likely to be a blackthorn stake through your heart," Regin said. "I only regret I shan't see the day it happens."

Grus exclaimed, "Now there's a wizard after my own heart, and I do mean that literally."

Lorimer snarled furiously, seized Regin roughly, and shoved him off the causeway into the sucking mud of the bog. With his staff, he gave Regin a few pokes to make sure he could not somehow flounder ashore. Then he turned and hurried back to the tower, accompanied by Grus' mocking laughter.

When the door was closed, Ivarr edged forward, parting the bushes to see Regin sitting calmly in the bog, his hands bound behind him, already sunken in the mud up to his waist.

"Regin!" he called. "It's Ivarr! Don't struggle or it will pull you down faster. I'm going to get you out of there, if you can hang on long enough."

Regin gasped slightly. "Ivarr, get out of here immediately. Lorimer could come out of the tower any moment and catch you. Don't risk yourself just to save my worthless old carcass. I can well imagine what you must be thinking. You probably think I put that message there to lead you into Lorimer's hands. I didn't imagine he'd be coming here with us. He's holding the Alfar at an old hall south of here. Help them escape so the lot of you can work at getting that gold back. He's got it there in my tower. Fly now, what are you waiting for?"

Ivarr removed his cloak and his boots. "I'm going to crawl out and cut the ropes on your hands so you can help pull yourself out of here. You saved my life from Fafnir, and you kept Lorimer from capturing me also, so I'm going to save your life whether you want it or not."

314

Regin sighed. "I shall be very angry if you get yourself caught, Ivarr."

"I won't get caught," Ivarr shuddered as he wriggled into the warm water in a prone position so the bog would have less chance of trapping him. "How did you manage it that night Lorimer captured the rest of you?"

"A concealing spell, so Lorimer simply didn't see you. That and a spell to keep you still. I doubt if you heard a thing. Those Alfar were not easily overwhelmed, the mad fools."

Ivarr gasped as he sank deeper into the mire, but he quickly freed himself. It stank of dead rotting things and slimy vegetation. He reached Regin and began sawing at his bonds with Birna's knife.

"It might be less bothersome merely to die," Regin grumbled. "I'd somewhat comforted myself with the fact that I wouldn't have to worry about that cursed weregild any longer."

"Don't be an idiot," Ivarr growled. "Where would we find another wizard now? I doubt anyone would want to fill your job." He removed the end of Birna's cloak from its moorings in his belt. "Now take hold of this cloak and I'll pull you out."

He crept back to solid ground with the hem of the cloak between his teeth. The hard rocks and dry soil felt wonderful under his feet. Bracing himself against a stone he began to pull.

"It's not any use," Regin said after a while.

"Hush! Pull on that cloak and don't let go. I've wrapped it around a stone so you won't go any deeper, if the fabric holds." Ivarr wished for a good stout rope, along with a good stout pony.

The grip of the bog was no easy force to argue with. Regin pulled until the cloak had stretched into a twisted rope and still he did not seem to make much progress. Then suddenly the suction was broken with a loud, resentful slurp, and Regin hauled himself ashore hand over hand.

They shook hands, grinning and dripping mud. "Now we've got to get out of here," Regin whispered. "He'll know

I've escaped tomorrow. Follow me, I know of a place we can hide.''

"But what about the gold?'' Ivarr demanded.

"What about it? Do you think the two of us are going to march up to Lorimer and demand that he hand it over? He's got a pack of renegade black dwarves prowling around here with him; and besides, I've seen enough of Lorimer for a while.''

"Regin! Do you know how many days it is until Svartarr's Doom? Only five more days. We don't have time to waste.''

Regin sighed. "Would you at least consider waiting until dawn?''

Before Ivarr could answer, an uproar started in the tower. They heard the voice of Lorimer bellowing and cursing, and suddenly the door opened and black dwarves began rushing out, weapons in hand. Ivarr and Regin dived into the dubious shelter of some small bushes and continued to eavesdrop.

Lorimer strode out last, still shouting and lashing around with his staff. To do the black dwarves credit, they were all agile enough to avoid having their skulls cracked. They dived out of the way skillfully and hurried down the causeway, almost treading upon Ivarr and Regin without glancing at them once.

"Don't return without the Scipling!'' Lorimer roared, in the midst of a long list of threats and curses. "If we don't have him, we might as well surrender ourselves to Svartarr and meekly accept whatever punishment he gives us. Curse that Scipling! I'd kill him barehanded but for that wretched sword. Bah! Get going, you miserable maggots of Ymir!''

After they were gone Lorimer continued to stalk up and down on the small bit of stable earth before the tower. Finally he barked "Goti! You lump of laziness, are you watching that gold? Andvari could steal it from beneath your nose. It wouldn't go well for you if he did.''

Lorimer stumped back into the tower and slammed the door. Regin sighed, shivering. "Come along now. We've definitely got to move before they trample us, don't you agree?''

''There's only two of them in there,'' Ivarr said. ''If we had the Alfar here we could rush them.''

''Hah, and we could all perish in the attempt.'' Regin seized him by the arm and hurried him away from the tower, along the edge of the water. ''Plenty of dwarves tramping about,'' he muttered. ''Two more sets of tracks won't be noticed, particularly when they disappear here.'' He stepped into the water and beckoned impatiently at Ivarr. ''Don't dawdle, I know my way around here perfectly well. There's an old path here under the water, made of stones. Just follow me, quickly now, but don't splash.''

They waded through a stand of reeds, which screened them from the tower, toward the ruins of the old hall where it lurked saggily in water and muck halfway up to its eaves. Regin climbed in at the window and disappeared into absolute darkness. Ivarr peered uneasily after him, shivering in his sodden clothing and smelling rotten wood and turf.

''This isn't my idea of a good place to hide,'' he muttered angrily. ''Regin! Where are you?''

A slight splash from the darkness, and Regin answered, ''We'll climb up into the loft so we can watch them. There's a bit of a ladder there in the corner. When I was just a young fellow this used to be quite a jolly place in the early days of Svartarr's takeover. None of us then suspected that Asraudrsbog would indeed become nothing but a bog and a lot of sunken buildings.''

''It makes an ideal haunt for a solitary old necromancer, though,'' Ivarr said, hoisting himself through the window. Reluctantly he eased into the black water beyond, not liking at all the strange combination of house and swamp. Suddenly his feet slipped into a hole on the oozy bottom and he went in to his neck, flailing and kicking.

''Quiet, can't you?'' Regin warned. ''Don't get so far from the walls. It gets rather deep in the middle.''

Ivarr spat out a mouthful of swamp water and struggled

317

toward Regin. They found the ladder, what remained of it, and climbed into the loft. The floor was ominously bowed and creaked a great deal under their weight, but the small window afforded them a perfect view of the front of the tower.

"Now what?" Ivarr growled irritably. Some of the bog muck had washed away, but he still stank of it.

"Rejoice that you're hiding in the one hiding spot the black dwarves won't think to look in," Regin replied. "Come early morning we'll nip out of here and go looking for the Alfar. I expect Lorimer's got them under guard in the ruins of the old hill fort. It has an excellent dungeon."

"Dungeon? How—" Ivarr began, but his question was interrupted by a long, quavering cry from the other side of the swamp. It was the kind of cry that bristled hairs on backs of necks and made hands turn clammy.

Ivarr grabbed Birna's knife, wishing he hadn't given Eilifir his sword back so hastily. Although it was no comparison to Glimr, it would have been greatly reassuring.

The door to the tower was flung open with a crash that made Regin wince. Lorimer stepped out, his sword in hand, gleaming with a pale blue light. He looked up and down, then shouted, "Show yourself, you coward! I won't have you howling around me! Begone before I blast you!"

The howling started again, and Ivarr shivered. Gradually the dismal yelling turned into words howled out dreadfully.

"It's my goooold! Give it back, Lorimer, or you'll rue the day! The river will take it back! Goooold and dragons, Lorimer! Aaalog is upon you, Looooorimer!" Andvari's horrible howling sounded as if he were down in a well where his voice echoed hollowly.

Lorimer answered with a savage howl of his own and began darting ice bolts around in the dark. Andvari stopped his yelling.

"I got him," declared Lorimer. "Goti! Are you still watching the gold?"

"For all I'm worth," a rather mournful voice replied. "I wish you wouldn't shoot those bolts around so wildly. Some

318

of my men might be returning with the Scipling and they could be killed. I can't imagine why you're so worried about one scrubby old white dwarf. I do wish the old blighter would have chosen to haunt those Alfar instead of us, however."

"Goooold! Goooold! Not enough gold for Ottar!" came the dreary voice.

Lorimer whirled and listened. He took two quick strides to the end of the causeway. "You're talking nonsense!" he thundered. "Who is Ottar?"

"Svartarr's son, you ninny," came the conversational response from across the bog. "It wasn't those misguided Alfar who killed him. It was you, Lorimer. I saw what I saw and I know what I know."

Lorimer drew in his breath with a hiss. "Then you have sealed your own doom, old dwarf. I will not rest until I have killed you too!"

Andvari laughed mockingly. "Won't you try to buy my silence with gold? Give me back my treasure and I won't tell Svartarr that his son is still alive and healthy. I found him, Lorimer, and I didn't let him die as you had planned on the cruel rocks of the Drangarstrom. Give me back my gold and Svartarr will never know."

Ivarr was transfixed. Then he shook Regin fiercely. "Did you hear? Did you hear? Ottar's not—"

Regin silenced him instantly. Lorimer's reply was a resounding roar of fury, and he began blasting the surrounding bog with ice bolts. Several burst against the turves of the old hall, making the structure shudder and shaking down lumps of broken turf. Then Lorimer darted into the tower and shut the door with a crash.

Andvari continued to howl sporadically throughout the night, punctuating his soliloquies with malicious chuckling. Several times Lorimer leaped out the door to riddle the area with blasts, none of which daunted Andvari in the least.

Regin was gleeful. "Lorimer's luck is going sour on him, Ivarr, just as I knew it would the moment he took Ord's ring from me. Now Andvari's curse is on him."

Lorimer sent another bolt into the darkness, then moodily

stalked around the tower, a black shadow against other shadows. Then he hurried down the causeway to the place where he had left Regin. With the end of his staff, he fished around in the water, probing for a body. After a few moments he rushed back to the tower, glaring around angrily. "Regin!" he roared. "I know you're here! Who helped you escape? Was it your treacherous kinsmen, the dwarves? The Scipling? It won't do you any good, do you hear? I have the gold! With it I shall buy war and kingdoms! Death to anyone who tries to stand in my way!"

After fuming and bellowing around awhile longer, Lorimer shouted, "Goti! How long is it until dawn?"

"A couple of hours," answered that individual. "Why?"

"It's time to be going," Lorimer replied, with a lowering glance around the bog. "Besides which, I have had an idea which may be the salvation of this scheme yet. You will be obliged to carry the gold."

"By myself? Begging your pardon, but it can't be done by a single black dwarf. And what about my men? We can't simply desert them."

Lorimer laughed harshly. "I don't expect to see them again, not unless they capture the Scipling, and that isn't likely. He was here and not long ago, I'm certain of it. Regin's not in the bog; someone pulled him out. All I found was a bit of muddy rope. I've come to doubt, somehow, the loyalty of my devoted black dwarves, who have taken to a certain amount of grumbling and even desertion, if you will recall that last unfortunate wretch and what befell him. Come outside a moment, Goti my friend, so we can talk properly."

Goti edged out into the darkness. "We're all still loyal to you, Lorimer, but things have been going rather badly of late, particularly since the Alfar have escaped. It is rather a good idea of yours to avoid them, if we possibly can, but I don't see how the two of us can move all that treasure."

"Indeed!" Lorimer said, raising his arms and reciting a formula. Goti whirled around suspiciously, but the spell was complete. When the cloud of mist cleared, Lorimer was fastening a rope around the neck of a large stout horse, who was rolling his eyes around in a panic. Lorimer chuckled and fastened the rope to a ring set in the side of the tower for that purpose. He began tying the packs to the horse's back.

"Regin! Are we going to let him escape?" Ivarr whispered.

"He's got my satchel and staff. Are you going to stop him by yourself? We know where he's going to take it anyway, so we may as well let him take it there. We'll all come together, Lorimer, you, me, the gold, Svartarr, and the outlaws, in about five days at Svartarr's Doom on Knutsbarrow."

"What! Why would Lorimer do that? I doubt if we'll ever see him or that treasure again if we let them go."

"Nonsense, Ivarr. An ordinary person might be content with a king's ransom in gold, but not Lorimer. We'll give him a small start and follow close behind. He can't travel very fast with that poor horse as burdened as it is." He nodded out the window. The early light showed them the horse with his legs braced as Lorimer tied Regin's satchel on the top of the load. He gave the entire business a shake to test it, which nearly staggered the poor beast. Then he untied the rope and led the horse down the causeway.

"Well?" Ivarr jogged Regin impatiently. "When do we follow?"

Regin sighed resignedly. "As soon as we find Skapti and the others. Lorimer's dwarves were holding them in a hill fort not too far from here."

"You used a spell so I wouldn't be captured, didn't you? I didn't even wake up when Lorimer's dwarves took the others. I'm—I'm grateful, Regin," he added stiffly.

Regin drew his soggy hood over his ears and shivered. "Someone had to be free to rescue us, didn't they? Right now I want to get out of this place before the damp gets to my joints. Don't worry about the gold; it's going to bring us all together whether we want to be drawn after it or not." He sighed and gazed after the retreating figure of Lorimer and the treasure, wobbling to and fro on the back of the plodding horse.

321

They waded out of the swamp in the early dawn light. Ivarr watched warily for the return of the black dwarves, but Regin strode boldly onto the causeway, beckoning impatiently for Ivarr to hurry. He flung open the door to his tower and peered inside, ignoring Ivarr's protests.

"Hah! Here it is!" Regin cried with sudden exultation. "My staff! I suspected he'd forget about it in his rush to escape, and here it is, just where he left it." He grasped it in both hands, his eyes shining triumphantly. Then he began ransacking the room, which looked as if someone else had already done a thorough job of it, and came up with several loaves of black bread and some mouse-gnawed cheese.

"Let's be going now," suggested Ivarr for the fourth time as Regin continued his search of his old quarters. "Regin! We're wasting time. The longer we wait the more lost the Alfar are likely to get. Can't you leave this until later?"

Regin rolled up some maps quickly and stuffed them into an old battered satchel exhumed from a moldy trunk. He snatched up small instruments, examined them critically, and either tossed them away with an impatient grunt or shoved them into his satchel. Finally he gave it a last shake and peered inside with a scowl and a regretful sigh.

"These are tools I threw away ten years ago as worn-out and useless," he said, slapping the satchel shut. "I hope there's one or two more spells in them so we won't be going to the Doom totally unprepared."

"That's somewhat better, I suppose," said Ivarr, "but are you sure—"

Something hissed past him where he stood just within the doorway, holding the open door with one hand; before his startled eyes, an arrow appeared in the wood of the door, its point well-buried and its grey-fletched shaft still quivering. With astonishing presence of mind, he slammed the door shut and barred and bolted it before uttering a great shout of alarm.

"Regin! We're under siege!" He dived toward a slit window and peered out cautiously. "Blast! And not a bow or arrow to defend ourselves with!"

CHAPTER TWENTY SEVEN

A few more arrows thunked into the door or shattered against the walls outside. Ivarr could glimpse nothing of the attackers; each time he presented himself at one of the windows, several arrows glanced off the stones, dangerously near.

Regin crept beneath a window and ventured a sidewise peep. In a gruff voice, he shouted, "Who's there, and what's the idea of attacking a wizard in his own home? Speak and identify yourselves and your grievance or I shall be forced to return your arrows with firebolts."

After an interval of silence, a voice called out, "Hello the tower! Is that Regin, the former necromancer, in there?"

"It is indeed. Who are you?" Regin demanded, motioning Ivarr to stay down. Ivarr had discovered a tremendous and fearsome old lance and was taking a position just inside the door.

"Who else is in there with you?" returned the spokesman of the attackers. "Is it Lorimer?"

"Certainly not," Regin replied, glaring out the arrow slit. "If you ruffians are black dwarves looking for your master, I'll tell you where he has gone. He's going to Knutsbarrow with the gold because those five outlaw Alfar have escaped and he's properly terrified of them. I'm certain they're on the way to this spot at this very moment, determined to slaughter any black dwarves they find in their way."

"Is that so? We're not afraid of any outlaw Alfar. Regin, you dragon-blasted old rogue, it's me, Skapti! I was just making certain it really was you and Lorimer wasn't anywhere near." Skapti stepped out from the cover of an old broken wall. "How did you escape? And what has become of Ivarr?"

Ivarr opened the door and stepped outside with his rusty lance. "I fished him out of the bog where Lorimer was baiting toads with him. What do you mean by nearly scaring the life out of me with that arrow?"

The Alfar leaped out of their hiding places and dashed across the causeway to surround Ivarr and Regin and pelt them with questions and shake their hands and buffet them around in an excess of good will and delight at finding them again.

"Stop!" Ivarr cried over their chatter. "I've got tremendous news for all of you, and Flosi most particularly. Listen, all of you. Last night while we were spying on Lorimer and his dwarves, we heard Andvari shrieking and moaning around here about his treasure—and about Ottar. Lorimer was shouting back at him, and I heard Lorimer himself say that he was the one who conspired to kill Ottar. He took the boy and deserted him somewhere along the Drangarstrom to die where no one could find him; then Lorimer arranged it so you, Flosi, seemed to be the murderer. But someone did find Ottar and rescued him. It was old Andvari. I heard him say so himself. You remember what we saw in the cave, Regin and Flosi. Toy boats, and small arrows made from driftwood."

Flosi sank down slowly. "And so Ottar isn't dead? It was just an ordinary otter I killed? Then it was Lorimer who convinced Svartarr we'd killed his son. And all this time I've been feeling like a murderer for no reason and suffering untold hardships and risking death almost daily, all because Lorimer needed some dummies to take the blame in his murderous plot. Worse yet, I've had to watch my friends being miserable, which was bad enough when I thought it was all my fault, but now that I discover it was all for

324

nothing—'' He clenched his fists, his eyes flashing fire. ''Lorimer is going to pay and I don't mean just the weregild. We'll go to Svartarr and tell him Ottar is still alive and we owe him nothing. But first, I'd like to catch Lorimer and tie that weregild around his neck and sink him in the Drangarstrom at the first opportunity.''

The Alfar seconded his idea with warlike gusto. ''Our honour is at stake,'' Finnvard said pompously. ''We can't allow Lorimer to steal our gold—even if we don't want it.''

''Perhaps Andvari will trade Ottar for the treasure,'' Skapti said excitedly. ''Then we can take Svartarr his son and say 'Bah!' to that cursed otterskin!''

''Then we'd better get busy and go after Lorimer,'' Egills declared. ''We've still got our weapons and our powers. We can do it, fellows.''

Regin watched the Alfar, shaking his head. ''Knutsbarrow is where Lorimer will go, sooner or later. As I said before, the mills of fate are beginning to grind very fine now. We'd save time and miles by just going there now.''

''No. We get Lorimer and the gold first,'' Flosi said grimly, and the others agreed.

When all the questions had been answered to everyone's satisfaction, they set out on the trail of Lorimer with Regin in the lead, using his sharp eyes and discerning spells to trace Lorimer's footsteps where the ground was flinty. As they walked, Flosi described for Ivarr's benefit their rather fiery escape from the dungeon of the hill fort and the subsequent flight of the black dwarves. Finnvard added his own comments when Flosi's descriptions became a bit florid. Eilifir wasn't speaking, but he looked decidedly pleased.

Near the end of the day it became apparent that Lorimer realized he was being followed. He took greater care to hide his tracks and practiced subtle deceptions that would lead his pursuers off the trail. Regin was not deceived by the false tracks and traps which Lorimer left behind, one of which Finnvard almost succumbed to—a harmless-seeming hare entangled in a snag, which would have made a tasty stew.

''Don't touch it!'' Regin commanded, just as Finnvard

was about to grab the creature. "We have no idea what sort of a spell it might be."

Finnvard leaped back in horror. Egills remarked comfortingly, "Never mind, Finnvard, it's probably tough."

They made a hungry camp that night, dividing the three loaves of stale bread and washing it down with cold water.

The next day, their quarry took a turn toward the north, and the Alfar began preparing themselves for the confrontation with Svartarr. Regin assured them his influence in their behalf would not be inconsiderable.

"Even though Lorimer holds all the tokens in this game?" Ivarr inquired.

"Lorimer doesn't have Ottar," Regin replied. "Only Andvari knows where to find him. But I was adviser to the old Svartarr. My words should carry more weight than Lorimer's."

"However," Eilifir pointed out, "you did raise the curse of Lorimer from the bogs of Jotunsgard, and that will not cause Svartarr to look upon you with much favour."

"Not to mention the fact that you've renounced your black dwarf magic in favour of Elbegast's magic," Ivarr added.

Regin shrugged in the cold autumnal wind. "Perhaps, perhaps. But I have to try, in spite of all the disadvantages against me. If Svartarr is unconvinced when I get through with my arguments, it will be because his own heart is evil and greedy for revenge rather than justice."

Later that day Lorimer's trail took a decided bend to the south, and the Alfar became even more grim. With so little time left, they could not allow Lorimer to escape to the unknown regions of Jotunsgard with the weregild. That night they sharpened their weapons and put new strings in their bows. Finnvard and Flosi attempted half-heartedly to amuse the others by exchanging insults, but Ivarr felt only a brooding anxiety.

"We've still got two days," Skapti said encouragingly. "A great deal can happen in two days. We can catch Lorimer and get the gold from him and still make it to Knutsbarrow. According to the map, Knutsbarrow is only about twenty miles from here, which is scarcely a day's hike.''

Regin nodded, but he still looked worried. ''Flosi, fetch my satchel, would you? I'd like to take another look at the map.''

Flosi was sitting on the other side of the fire, facing Regin and gazing past his shoulder with a blank expression on his face.

''Flosi?'' Regin said, more loudly, and Flosi continued to gape. Regin suddenly whirled around, grasping his staff, causing everyone else to leap up and seize their weapons also.

''Great fires of Muspell!'' Skapti gasped in a whisper. ''What can it be, Regin?''

The flat northern horizon seemed to be blazing in molten, angry red flame. A thick pall of smoke rolled upward, blotting the early stars and dyeing the rising moon the colour of blood.

''Svartarr's Doom,'' Regin said in awe. ''Svartarr's dwarves light thousands of fires on the barrows to summon the outlying settlements on the night before the law-giving.''

''Then my calculations must have been two days off!'' Skapti wailed, whipping out his notched stick to begin swiftly counting the notches.

Egills sighed gloomily. ''I never liked the idea of a law-giving being called a Doom. I hope this Doom isn't our own personal doom.''

They climbed to a vantage point in some rocks and watched the sullen fires far to the north. Every fell and barrow was lurid with flame.

''Now is the time to decide,'' Regin said, ''whether to go to Svartarr and ask for his judgment and show him the true mettle of Elbegast's men, or to begin a lifetime of hiding from Svartarr's wrath.''

After a despondent silence, Finnvard said, ''My mettle is more like kettle metal, but I think we must go and face Svartarr like proper Alfar.''

"While Lorimer vanishes into Jotunsgard with the gold," Flosi added gloomily.

The fires burned all night; in the morning the northern sky was still black wilth smoke. Resolutely, they marched northward, arriving in the region of the barrows at sundown, falling in quite naturally with a throng of black dwarves who were on their way to the Doom. The added spectacle of the payment—or nonpayment—of the weregild ensured Svartarr a good turnout for his reading of the law. The black dwarves were a merry group as soon as the sun was out of the sky, singing songs and passing around their earthenware jugs as amiably as any group of Alfar. They pitched their tents and picketed their ponies around the barrow mounds, except the immense Knutsbarrow. Svartarr's soldiers made their camps around the king's barrow. Atop the barrow, Svartarr's tent glowed blood-red in the reflected light of the many fires surrounding it.

The outlaws skulked uneasily from one group to the next with their hoods pulled low, as a shabby band of wanderers who had assembled with the rest in hopes of a free meal or finding a master to serve. Ivarr expected at any moment to be seized roughly and taken captive, although the general atmosphere around Knutsbarrow was festive and carefree.

Regin stalked around, summing up the situation, and finally beckoned to one of the fighting men sauntering around the jolly scene. He whispered in the guard's ear a moment and sent the fellow hurrying off toward the barrow, darting many glances behind at Regin and his companions.

"I've told him we have a message for Svartarr," Regin said, "and we wish to deliver it in person. Does anyone wish to change his mind? This is positively the last chance for escape."

"Not I," said Flosi, who had not ceased scowling with the wrath of the falsely accused the entire day.

"I guess no one does, if I don't," Finnvard said in a small voice.

In a moment the guard was back with a pair of his friends.

They eyed the outlaws with steely interest; the Alfar eyed them back without fear.

"Svartarr will see you at once," the first dwarf said with stiff courtesy, leading them toward the tent of Svartarr with the other two dwarves following in the rear.

They climbed the steep side of the barrow amid a growing flurry of excitement among the spectators. More fuel was added to the fires, making the top of the barrow bright with firelight.

Svartarr emerged from his tent. He was a stout, handsome dwarf with a luxuriant black beard, and his clothing was rich almost to the point of dandification.

"So you're back," he greeted them, striding forward. "I never thought you'd dare show yourselves again. Where's the gold? I can't believe you'd come so boldly without it."

Skapti advanced a pace. "Well, we have, and you needn't treat us like outlaws or murderers. We've done nothing to deserve your wrath. Ottar is not dead; he's with Andvari, the old white dwarf of the Drangarstrom. His true murderer dumped him there to die, but Andvari saved him."

"It was only an otter I killed," Flosi declared, "and not a fylgja. We demand to be freed of your outlawry. Lorimer is the one you should banish for all his scheming and plotting."

Svartarr's truculent features betrayed no astonishment, and his eyes glittered with suspicion. "My son is alive, you say? A plausible tale, if you ask me. I could search the Drangarstrom forever and still not find him. Someone must be punished for this crime, so the inhabitants of Skarpsey will know Svartarr is a dwarf to be respected. No doubt it was this cunning old traitor Regin who thought that one up for you. It won't work. Produce either my son or the gold, and perhaps I'll listen to you."

"It's the truth," Regin said. "But I can see by your aspect that the news of Ottar's rescue is not news to you, and now the peace of Skarpsey is being auctioned off to the highest bidder. What is the price you are going to pay, Svartarr?"

Svartarr glared at him resentfully. "Have you forgotten

that I am the king of the black dwarves now, Regin, and not the small boy you taught lessons to? I demand a small measure of respect, if you think you can muster it.''

Regin folded his arms. ''I can't. Not while you're being such a fool. What are Lorimer's terms, Svartarr?''

Svartarr replied haughtily, ''Terms? He has demanded no terms. Svartarrsrike will be enriched with this treasure and I will have my son returned to me, and Lorimer will remove himself from my kindgom. Can you beat that bargain, Regin? Otherwise, somebody must pay for Ottar's kidnapping.''

''And Lorimer will come out of it as something of a hero,'' Regin said. ''A very clever scheme. But I don't understand how you think you can get him out of your kingdom. He covets Svartarrsrike and he won't give it up willingly.''

Svartarr shrugged his shoulders. ''So I'll give him a piece of it, an inconsequential bit of land to the north of Snowfell. I needn't account to you for it, Regin. Even if you did advise my father, you no longer advise me.''

''What else does Lorimer want?'' Regin demanded.

''Oh, nothing of any lasting importance,'' the young Svartarr said, his eyes sidling nervously in Ivarr's direction. ''I never quite believed all that rot about Elidagrimr's sword. Why should a mere Scipling be the only one destined to use it? A sword is a sword, isn't it?''

Regin's countenance blackened with fury. ''And you think we'll just hand over Ivarr and the sword, and that will be the end of it? What do you think Lorimer wants that sword for, if not to eventually conquer Svartarrsrike?''

Svartarr glared at him furiously, and turned to stalk back and forth. ''Perhaps not, Regin. You always were such a gloomy old stick. Lorimer might be content away to the north. He'll have Snowfell to contend with, after all. Confound it, he's got the gold and Ottar; what could I do beside agree to his terms? Svartarrsrike can defend itself, most assuredly, and I believe Lorimer realizes it would be futile to attack me, even with that troublesome sword from the barrow.'' He raised his voice slightly and kept darting uneasy glances toward his tent.

Skapti could scarcely restrain himself. "Since you felt free to dispose of Ivarr so easily, what do you intend to do with the rest of us? No doubt Lorimer has done that bit of thinking for you also, hasn't he?"

Svartarr's fine disdain was beginning to wilt, and his eyes looked frightened. "Perhaps you'd better ask him yourself."

The flap of the tent was parted by the glowing knob of a staff held in a hand bearing the plain gold ring of Andvari, and Lorimer stepped into their midst. "I've been listening," he said in his cold, dry voice. "Svartarr, you've done well. The day will come when you're thankful for your loyalty to me. As to this last question, I intend to answer it with this." He drew his sword and held it gleaming before their eyes. "The Scipling and Regin I shall require. The rest of you have fulfilled your purpose in helping the Scipling find the sword. I can't think of a reason why you should be permitted to encumber us any longer."

The Alfar quickly armed themselves with ready spells and swords. Ivarr said, "I can think of several reasons, Lorimer. One is Birna. You killed her and I resolved to make you pay for her death."

"And Gizur," Skapti added. "You won't be easily rid of us, Lorimer."

Lorimer replied, "I expected some resistance. Will you all come at me at once, and get it over with? Where is your famous sword, Scipling? It's time you learned that I can master even Glimr's power."

"If you're so powerful," Ivarr retorted, "you'd know I lost the sword in the battle with Fafnir. It's somewhere at the bottom of the Drangarstrom."

Lorimer hesitated a moment. "Lost!" he snarled. "Cursed Scipling perversity! I ought to keep the gold and let Ottar become Andvari's successor. Why else do you think I came here?" He took a menacing step toward Svartarr.

"A bargain is a bargain!" Svartarr exclaimed, taking a step back. "It's not my fault he lost it; you can't blame me.

331

At least if you can't have it, no one else can either. Here's your captives, do with them as you like, but you must give me back my son—and the gold. I'll give you more land to compensate for the loss of the sword. Your freedom from outlawry is worth much, Lorimer, I hope you'll remember that.''

"And you have already claimed Ord's ring from the treasure," Regin said. "It's as valuable as the sword. Call it even with the ring, and let these others go. My worthless old carcass won't do you much good, but I'll surrender myself to whatever fate you think proper or amusing.''

Lorimer's answer was a contemptuous snort. "What do I care for land or outlawry? Even your killing would be a useless pleasure. What I want and intend to take—''

A doleful voice in the dark beyond the bonfires halted him in midsentence. "Goooold! Goooold! The curse of the gold is upon Lorimer! Someday I'll get it all back, to the least finger ring, and the river will gnaw your bones Lorimer!''

Svartarr whirled around, listening. "Is it him? Is it Andvari?''

"Yes, it is Andvari," Lorimer said, cocking his head to listen a moment. "I directed him to come here with Ottar to turn him over to you, but it looks as if his journey was wasted.''

"That's a lie!" Flosi said, but Skapti and Eilifir quickly pushed him out of sight and silenced him. Svartarr seemed scarcely to have heard in his agitation.

"Don't send him back, Lorimer! We can still bargain, can't we? You can name almost any terms and I'll agree to them! What do you want? More gold? A title?" Svartarr whirled around wildly as Andvari began howling from another direction, ignoring Regin's attempts to calm him.

Lorimer appeared to deliberate. "Make me your chief adviser and I'll take you to Ottar and the gold tonight.''

"Done!" Svartarr cried, slapping his palm. "These dwarves are my witness. Now let's be off!''

Regin snatched at his sleeve. "Don't you realize what you've done? If something should happen to you, you've just handed Lorimer your kingdom until Ottar is of age, and what do you think would become of your son in the event of your death? Svartarr, you can't agree to this—"

Svartarr paid him no heed. "And what do you want done with these captives? Name their fate and it shall be done. How far is it to Ottar and the gold? Shall we take horses?"

Lorimer returned the Alfar's glowers with interest. "We shall walk; it isn't far. As for these outlaws, we shall take them with us. I can do a better job of watching them than these buffoons." He poked his staff at one of Svartarr's dwarves, who leaped back with alacrity. "Command them all to remain here until we return."

Svartarr gave the order to the chieftain of the guard, who could not have looked unhappier. As Lorimer directed his prisoners toward the riverbank, Ivarr looked back at the chieftain, who was shaking his head and arguing with several of his men.

The river cliffs were not distant; they could hear the thunder of the Drangarstrom from Knutsbarrow. Lorimer watchfully drifted behind with his staff glowing in his hand. Andvari's howling served as a beacon, leading Svartarr down a twisting path toward the water below, a path which was scarcely more than a narrow shelf in places with an unpleasant expanse of nothingness below.

Lorimer stopped when they were nearly to the bottom and pointed ahead to a sandy cove nearly hidden under a great scarp of rock. Advancing slowly, the captives recognized the Snowfell packs and Regin's satchel, opened so the gold cascaded out onto the black rocks, twinkling and winking coldly in the pale moonlight. Ivarr heard Svartarr's gasp of admiration.

Svartarr examined the gold articles in a cursory manner while Lorimer looked on like a motionless pillar of shadow. Svartarr dropped a jewelled crown and straightened to speak to Lorimer.

"Good enough, Lorimer. There's enough gold here to buy the North Quarter. Produce my son and you'll buy the perpetual rights and privileges as my first adviser. Come,

Lorimer, what are you waiting for? It was a cruel enough trick, stealing Ottar and making me think he was dead—for which I'll gladly forgive you as soon as you restore him to me." He ended on an uncertain note. Lorimer's cloak billowed in the windy breath of the river. The air was full of the spray spuming from the rocks that tore the river's silken black surface with foaming white wounds. Lorimer chuckled, a dry, chilling sound.

"I don't possess Ottar to give him to anyone. You have allowed yourself to be deceived, Svartarr. How easily you fell into my nets. It will be a simple thing to toss all your lifeless carcasses into the Drangarstrom, and I shall take command at Knutsbarrow. I doubt if many will attempt to protest. As for Ottar, he can remain where he is, eating raw fish with old Andvari, unless I can find him and kill him."

"No!" Svartarr drew his sword, and the Alfar drew theirs. "I see now I was a fool for Ottar's sake, but no dwarf dies without resisting to the last instant."

"Why didn't you listen to me?" Regin demanded bitterly.

Lorimer laughed and raised his sword. "It wouldn't have helped him, Regin. You know nothing can stop me from taking what I want, except one sword which lies at the bottom of the Drangarstrom. Perhaps your bones and the sword of Elidagrimr will one day share the same cold and comfortless bed among the stones—"

Beside Ivarr's ear, Eilifir swiftly drew his bow and released an arrow. It struck Lorimer full in the chest and burst into flame. The necromancer staggered back, startled more than damaged, and began slapping at the flames. Svartarr seized his opportunity and bolted for the trail. The Alfar took cover and continued to hail arrows upon Lorimer, which did little more than annoy him. He sent back a fearsome bolt of ice and darted one up the cliff trail after Svartarr. Regin and Flosi conjured a magnificent firebolt, which Lorimer countered. He began stalking toward the trail, batting arrows and firebolts aside with ease. In the short intervals of silence, they could hear him chuckling humourlessly as he advanced.

"He's not even slowed down!" Skapti exclaimed. "We're going to have to retreat if we don't want ice bolts down our throats!" He ducked as another deadly blast whitened the rocks around them.

Suddenly from above, a fusillade of arrows descended upon Lorimer, forcing him to take cover. The Alfar sprinted up the path as a voice bellowed from the cliff, "We're here, Svartarr! It's Boggvir and fifty good men on the cliffs! Come up the trail to us!"

Ivarr grabbed Regin's cloak. "Svartarr's not ahead of us, Regin."

"There he is!" Finnvard said, looking back. "He's lost the path! He's going along the riverside!"

"I'll go after him," Ivarr said, brushing off Regin's protests. "What does it matter now if I'm killed? We've got the gold, and the sword is lost forever. I'm the most expendable member of the group."

"That's not true!" Finnvard said. "We'd be devastated if anything happened to you! Regin, don't let him go!"

But Ivarr was gone, leaving the trail and climbing down through the rocks as the others advanced to challenge Lorimer. He leaped down to the sand and crouched behind a rock to watch a moment. More dwarves on the cliff were shooting arrows and hurling spears, but Lorimer was undaunted. A group was holding the bottom of the trail, with the fierce and fiery magic of the Alfar successfully holding Lorimer at bay.

Ivarr hurried away up the narrow spit of black sand, feeling his way through the shadows. Occasionally he stepped in icy little runnels, and several times he had to skirt boulders dangerously close to the edge of the river.

Sooner than he had expected, he met Svartarr edging his way back along the bottom of the cliff. Halting, Svartarr demanded, "Who's there? Is it you, Lorimer?"

"It's Ivarr, the Scipling," said Ivarr. "We came to rescue you from Lorimer. Boggvir and the Alfar are holding him off at the bottom of the trail long enough for you to get up the cliff."

"Scipling! Came to rescue me? Did you now, after I

treated you so shabbily? I expect I've been playing the fool since Ottar disappeared. Come along, lad, we've got to hurry before some of my men are injured or killed holding the trail. What a dolt I was to miss it. Just plain scared is what I was—me, if you can imagine, the king of the black dwarves, so frightened I couldn't see straight on a moonlit night.'' He scuttled along the river cliff with ease, hauling Ivarr after him over the difficult spots, remarking what skinny creatures men and Alfar were, compared to the ideal, squat burly shapes of the dwarves.

''There he is, the evil beast!'' Svartarr whispered suddenly, whisking Ivarr into the protection of a large stone as they came into view of Lorimer, who was still countering every fire spell sent at him and replying with deadly ice bolts.

''I believe we can make it up the rocks to the path from here,'' Ivarr said, pointing to the spot where he had come down.

They reached the place without attracting Lorimer's attention and began to climb. Suddenly Lorimer spied them and sent a blast in their direction. They flattened themselves in their narrow niche, then began scrambling upward again. Another blast separated them; Svartarr dived out of the way and continued climbing upward, but Ivarr ducked down to a ledge to wait for the blast's icy fury to abate. Looking up, he saw Svartarr reach the safety of the path, as did half a dozen of his men, but Lorimer seemed to have singled out Ivarr for special punishment. Ivarr scrambled for another hiding place and Lorimer followed him with blasts and ice bolts, ignoring the arrows that showered him and pausing only to rebuff the firebolts. Hiding places became fewer in the steep cliff, and Ivarr's dodging only led him to an eventual descent to the spit of sand along the river. Ivarr drew Birna's knife, retreating slowly.

Facing Ivarr, Lorimer laughed again. Sheathing his sword, he raised his arms and began chanting a spell. Ivarr knew only a few puny signs to counter an evil spell, but he knew they would trouble Lorimer about as much as gnats on a walrus. Backing away, he knew he had reached the point of no escape or deliverance.

CHAPTER TWENTY EIGHT

Lorimer finished his spell with an icy blast, and Ivarr was rather astonished to find himself still crouching behind his sheltering rock. Peering out warily, he saw that Lorimer had conjured a frost giant to battle with the dwarves and Alfar at the foot of the ascent. The frost giant was like a towering blizzard, scything at the cliffs with his deadly gaze and breathing withering gusts of ice-laden wind upon his attackers. The howling and gusting of the creature was deafening in the narrow river channel. Arrows and firebolts vied with icy blasts and bolts until the fury of the battle must have carried as far as Knutsbarrow.

Ivarr dodged to another rock as Lorimer began to advance. Blue flame curled from the gleaming blade of the necromancer's sword.

"And now we will settle the question of Birna's revenge," Lorimer said contemptuously. "It will give me great pleasure to see you perish. Somehow, you puny creature, you have destroyed my perfect plans and defeated my un-defeatable power. I never forgot the eye you cost me, nor the humiliation at Ringknip in Draugarskell, and least of all that fall down the mine shaft in the Maze. For your countless insults and offences, I shall end your miserable and interfering existence. Your presence in the Alfar realm is an offence, and I shall not rest until that offence is rectified by your death."

Ivarr noticed how rapidly he was running out of the room to retreat. "You are the offence to the Alfar realm," he retorted. "There will be others who will come after me, until one discovers another sword which will destroy you. You're already half-defeated, Lorimer, since Regin renounced necromancy for Ljosalfar magic. He has sworn to destroy you, and if I die, I die with the knowledge that someday Regin will find the way to put you back into the bog with a stake through your heart."

Lorimer swung his sword angrily, with a vicious humming sound. "I shall keep your head and preserve it so I can listen to your threats and insults every day and laugh!"

Ivarr looked at the river, thundering by almost at his feet. Again he would have to choose between two deaths, and he knew which one he would choose.

Lorimer seemed to read his thoughts at the same instant and lunged forward with a furious assault, determined to kill or seriously disable him before he reached the river. Ivarr leaped across the hissing torrent to a large flat rock surrounded by boiling foam. He turned to see what Lorimer would do just as Lorimer leaped after him, sword in hand. Ivarr flung himself in the direction of the next black slippery rock, managing to gain a toehold long enough to seize an outcropping and hold on. Then his feet slipped suddenly and he felt the powerful drag of the river trying to tear him from his precarious hold. The water was as cold as death and a thousand horrible images flashed into his mind of waterfalls and the thunderous maws where the river descended underground to do its damage in the dark, and he even saw Andvari discovering his clean skull and studying it with a gleam of recognition in his fishy eye.

One of Ivarr's hands slipped from the ledge. Lorimer howled his fury and exultation and the river answered with a mindless bellow.

Suddenly something closed around Ivarr's wrist with a grip of iron. He felt hands tugging and pushing, and then he was hauled out of the water onto the rock, where he gasped and spluttered, half-choked by the spray he had breathed when his hand slipped. When he opened his eyes, he was staring into a round boyish face with plastered-down hair.

"Are you all right now?" his rescuer panted.

"Yes, fine, I think," Ivarr wheezed. "Who are you?"

"No time for questions!" croaked a hoarse whisper at his elbow. It was Andvari, his white beard streaming like pale weeds in the water. "Take this and get yourself ashore before that heap of bog-carrion escapes us!"

Cold metal glimmered in the water and flashed when he grasped it.

"The sword!" Ivarr gasped. "Andvari, you found it!"

"Wasn't hard, with a dragon's carcass stuck to it," the old dwarf grunted. "Now get going after Lorimer. We'll be right behind you."

Andvari dived off the rock, hitting the water with a splash and a twinkle of silver scales. Ivarr glimpsed the tail of a large fish, and a sleek otter shape dived after him.

Ivarr struggled to his feet and faced Lorimer across the millrace of inky water. Lorimer had seen nothing of Andvari and Ottar, since the rescue had occurred on the far side of the rock after Ivarr was nearly swept away.

At the sight of Ivarr, Lorimer uttered a triumphant shriek and raised his sword to leap across. Ivarr raised Glimr over his head, gleaming and sparkling, and Lorimer was transfixed. Then he whirled around and leaped back to shore and began hurrying back to the frost giant. Ivarr leaped after him with a challenging shout. Lorimer glanced back and didn't hesitate. He rushed past the frost giant, which was half-melted and sagging badly as it blustered and blasted flurries of ice and snow at the defenders of the trail. They gave a shout at the sight of Lorimer and doubled their energetic attacks on the frost giant. A great fiery spell that threatened to singe the beard of every dwarf on the cliffs finally dissolved the frost giant into a large black puddle. Lorimer batted away several arrows and a fire bolt and didn't halt his flight toward the sandy cove where Svartarr had examined Andvari's treasure.

Ivarr stopped long enough to assure his friends that he was

unharmed and to show them the sword triumphantly. The dwarves came pouring down the path, rallying behind their king and their former captives, whom they now regaled as heroes and comrades. The entire axe-waving assembly poured into the little cove, intent on seizing Lorimer so Ivarr could put an end to him. In their enthusiasm, they would have rushed right into the pool of shadow where the scarp overhung the cove, but Ivarr halted suddenly. The gold was not where Lorimer had left it, scattered rather carelessly around on the sand. Drag-marks led directly into the shadows under the cliff.

"Lorimer!" called Ivarr. "Now I'm ready for the holm-gang you challenged me to just moments ago. Come out and face your doom, Lorimer, and reconcile yourself to the bog once more!"

The only answer was a peculiar stirring sound, followed by a hiss. Regin hurried to Ivarr's side, crowding between Svartarr and Boggvir.

"Ivarr, I think we should retreat," he whispered urgently. "You know it's not like Lorimer to hide, unless he's plotting something. I have a most sinister feeling."

"Retreat? Dwarves never retreat," Svartarr said with a glower.

"We'll do as Regin says," Ivarr replied, motioning the dwarves to move back. "You too, Skapti. This battle is between Lorimer and me."

Protesting and muttering, they all backed away, leaving Ivarr and Svartarr standing alone—Svartarr in spite of Regin's protests and Ivarr's urging.

"Yes, I know I am a king and therefore somewhat valuable," he said with a fiery gleam in his eye, "but Lorimer had damaged my honour. If I don't help you kill him, I'll never have the proper faith in myself again. The honour of all Svartarrsrike is at stake. If it was known that I hid myself away like a coward and let one young Scipling fight for me—"

A movement at the corner of his eye caused Ivarr to whirl around. Something long and sinuous was snaking through

340

the sand toward them at a deadly speed. Before he could react, the thing twined itself around the leg of Svartarr and yanked him toward the cave under the outcropping. Ivarr leaped after him and severed the tentacle with one swooping blow. With a scream, a huge roiling mass poured out of the darkness, a small wicked head poised to strike. Svartarr lunged out of the way, but the creature's jaws opened with an evil hiss, spraying a cloud of poison.

"A lingorm!" Regin shouted. "Ivarr, run!"

The lingorm advanced and darted another writhing tentacle toward Ivarr, who summarily chopped it off and backed away slowly. Svartarr staggered, gasping from the effects of the poison and struggling to wipe the burning stuff from his skin. The lingorm's cruel little eyes followed him as the creature swayed, snakelike, poising for another attack. Regin shot a firebolt at it, which it instantly countered with a spell of its own.

"Lorimer!" Ivarr gasped, and the monster turned toward him and parted its jaws in a hiss.

"Lorimer it is," said the voice of the necromancer, chuckling dryly and writhing his sinuous coils in a menacing manner. "I heard your challenge to a holmgang, Scipling. Prepare yourself to die either suffocated in my deadly coils or choking from my poison. I think your courage is beginning to fade a bit, isn't it, in the face of this magnificent fylgja?"

Ivarr parried a lightning flick of a tentacle intended to ensnare him. Glimr snapped it off with a vengeful whine, faster than Ivarr dreamed his hand could move. The lingorm's head dived at him, spewing poison, and he leaped back before he inhaled any of the deadly stuff. Lorimer also withdrew, hissing scornfully, to hide himself in the cave.

Svartarr's dwarves pounced on their king at once, dragged him to safety, and began anointing the blistering burns caused by the poison.

"I hope your fine sense of honour is satisfied now," Regin scolded. "You'll have some very noble scars to boast of when this is all over."

"The honour of Svartarrsrike is at stake," Svartarr

grated through clenched teeth. "I shall not rest until that monster is dead and cut into a million pieces!"

"Well, we can't allow it," Boggvir said firmly. "We'll tie you up to a rock if we have to, begging your noble pardon, of course. We simply won't allow you to do anything crazy. Here, you two fellows, I'm putting you in charge of watching the king," he added, beckoning to a pair of burly dwarves.

Ivarr and the Alfar held a conference before the cave. Finnvard and Egills were shivering and grinning with the heady excitement of imminent danger.

"Someone's got to go into that cave after him," Flosi said. "I mean, somebody besides Ivarr. We can't let him go in alone. I suggest I do it, since I've got excellent vision in the dark."

"You're not leaving me behind!" Skapti exclaimed indignantly.

"Nor me," Boggvir added, insinuating himself into their conversation. "Never let it be said the black dwarves go out of their way to avoid a fight with a lingorm." He had already festooned his armour with one of the severed tentacles of the lingorm, which would no doubt become a family treasure until it disintegrated.

Ivarr shook his head. "I prefer to go alone. I want everyone else to stay out of harm's way in case the monster comes back out. You'll have excitement enough if that happens."

"We'll all go," Egills suggested. "We've all got a score to settle with Lorimer. You needn't be selfish with your glory, Ivarr. We're going to need plenty of glory so we can decently retire when we get back to Snowfell."

Knowing it was futile to argue, Ivarr sighed and gave in without a quarrel. Boggvir ordered up some torches; while they were waiting, someone suddenly exclaimed, "Svartarr's gone!"

Boggvir whirled around to stare at the cave. "What fools we were! He must have slipped away while we were chattering!" He sprang toward the cave with his sword drawn, with Ivarr and the Alfar on his heels.

"Eilifir is missing too," whispered Skapti as they paused

at the entry into the cave. "He must have gone after Svartarr."

The cave was not deep or extensive; it was more like a grotto among the massive rock formations of the cliff. The floor was rough and muddy, as if water had once run out of the cave. They crept from one jumble of rock to the next, peering into the gloom by the light of Boggvir's torches. Ivarr smelled fresh air and he began to move with less caution, suspecting that Lorimer might have used another opening to escape.

Rounding a bend in the passage, they were startled by an unexpected burst of light in the blackness. Ivarr fell aback, shoving the others behind him. When he ventured to peer around the corner, he saw a dim chamber lit from a large opening above where the moonlight shone through, and further illuminated by brilliant flashes at sporadic intervals. He recognized the unmistakable acrid smell of firebolts, and the waves of cold air must have come from ice bolts. Looking more closely, he could see Eilifir and Svartarr crouched in the scanty shelter of some large boulders. The lingorm was cornered in a further extension of the grotto, where its snaky head darted out to blast poison or ice bolts. Almost immediately, the lingorm caught sight of its new attackers and uttered a shrill scream of challenge.

Lorimer's voice thundered in the cave, "So you've all come to die together. What fools you are! Regin, you especially disgust me. You could have gone far as my assistant, and even the Scipling and his sword could still have possibilities, if you'd only realize your purpose is to be used as tools for great ones such as I."

"You're going to die, Lorimer," Regin said. "And quite soon, I should think. This is your moment, Ivarr. Don't go for his head; you'll find it's not particularly vital to a lingorm. What you want to pierce is his heart if you want to kill him quickly."

Ivarr looked at the sinuous heap of writhing black coils and wondered where on earth the creature's heart might be located. He advanced, with his friends at his back, until they

343

approached Eilifir and Svartarr, who both looked very pleased to be rescued.

"I have the gold, Scipling," Lorimer said. "I know how a Scipling loves gold. We can share it, if you'll only turn your sword against these dwarves and Alfar so we can escape. Gold such as this will make you more powerful than Svartarr in all his greed ever dreams of being. I can promise you anything you'd ever want, Scipling—gold and power."

"Where is the gold?" Ivarr asked of Regin, not taking his eyes from the lingorm.

"Swallowed it, more than likely, hoping to carry it away and hide it," Regin said. "But that gold must go back to the river and Andvari."

"Never!" the lingorm shrieked, lunging from its hiding place. The Alfar raised their weapons and took a step forward. A black tentacle shot out at Finnvard, and Ivarr leaped forward to hack the murderous thing off short. Dodging the flailing limbs, he managed to strike a blow at the lingorm's main body before twisting away from the creature's violent lashing and spitting of poison.

"You've weakened him!" exclaimed Flosi, who had helped Finnvard defend himself and was still prancing and preening. "Get him, Ivarr! We'll make a hundred pairs of boots out of his skin and a tankard out of his skull for you to drink from! And with his eyes and teeth—"

Lorimer interrupted by lunging out of his grotto, tentacles lashing and poison swirling from his jaws. His attackers retreated from the poisonous fury of the monster, knowing they could not risk getting close enough to him to do any damage. Ivarr retreated last, keeping just beyond the clouds of poison the creature blasted at him, tantalizingly close to the whipping tentacles, most of which had been reduced to stubs and clubs by Ivarr's sword.

Suddenly the creature's head darted through a screen of poison and Ivarr looked straight into Lorimer's murderous blazing eyes for an instant. Then he dealt the lingorm's head a staggering blow with Glimr, which would have killed an ordinary creature. The lingorm made a strangled screech

344

and flailed backward, enabling Ivarr to strike another telling blow. It writhed away with amazing speed, and Ivarr counted the seven bulges in its sinewy sides that were the packs and the satchel stuffed with gold. Then the lingorm slithered up the rock wall of the grotto toward the opening above.

Ivarr gave a shout of warning. "To the cliffs, before he escapes!"

They raced from the cave, startling the waiting dwarves into a hasty retreat up the path to the top of the cliffs, where the dwarves who had seen the lingorm emerge from the cave were most eager to relate their discovery to Ivarr. The monstrous creature was slithering across the cliffs, heading eastward when Ivarr overtook him, with the Alfar and Regin close behind. The night was almost spent, and Lorimer's fylgja in the dim dawn was a hideous spectacle.

Lorimer halted to glare at them with his remaining good eye. He hissed furiously, but the spurts of poison were less than before. His black leathery hide and the stubs of his tentacles oozed dark blood.

Ivarr remembered his battle with Fafnir, and pushed the lingorm relentlessly toward the river in spite of its tail-lashings and spitting and hissing.

"This is the end, Lorimer," Ivarr panted, as the Alfar came up beside him, their swords ready. "I swore I'd kill you for Birna, and now you will die."

The lingorm dived at him feebly, hissing and snapping its teeth, too weakened to dodge the ringing blow Ivarr dealt it. The creature staggered, wavering dangerously close to the edge of the river cliff.

"He's dying!" exclaimed Finnvard triumphantly, taking a bold whack at the monster's tail and scuttling back again.

"Dying but not yet dead," gasped the voice of Lorimer. "Strike your death wound, Scipling. I am finished fighting you."

The lashing coils were quivering, and the vicious battered head sank to the ground. Ivarr did not hesitate; he darted forward and sank Glimr to the hilts in the lingorm's pale underside once and then again. The creature suddenly convulsed with a terrible shriek, lashing around in a fury. One of the remaining tentacles fastened around Ivarr's arm as he struggled to withdraw the sword and Lorimer bellowed, "When the great ones die, they never die alone!" With his dying strength Lorimer rolled toward the edge of the river cliff, dragging Ivarr after him in a path of gore.

The Alfar uttered a screech of horror and threw themselves on the monster's flailing tentacles and coils in a vain attempt to prevent him from going over the cliff with Ivarr. The creature's death struggles tossed Eilifir and Skapti aside, but Finnvard and Egills and Flosi hung on as if they intended to perish also.

Ivarr instantly saw what was happening. It was the work of a moment to snatch Birna's knife and cut through the leathery tentacle. He leaped back to safety, shouting to the tenacious elves to let the lingorm fall. They tumbled away, and the lingorm slipped over the edge limply, rolling gradually, lifelessly beginning its plummeting descent to the hungry river below. The carcass snagged a moment before dropping when the sword caught in the rocks, tearing away the black hide until a shower of gold began clattering down the face of the cliff. Then, with a final lurch, the lingorm was gone. The Alfar rushed to the edge of the cliff to watch the huge black creature splash into the river in a scattering of bright gold, winking in the newly risen sun. The river seized its prize gladly, nudging it gently around the rocks, then snatching it and swirling it away.

"Gone again," Ivarr said wearily. "The sword that slew two dragons."

Svartarr's Doom and lawgiving was held that night on a hilltop overlooking the river. The festive atmosphere had reached a new pitch when the rest of the dwarves were given the electrifying news of the death of Lorimer at the hands of the Scipling hero. Perhaps the most satisfying event was the return of Ottar by Andvari, who held fast to the lad's hand and scowled around suspiciously at the fires and merry-making until he presented his young charge to Svartarr himself and none other. He would have then preferred to scuttle back to his beloved river, but Svartarr detained him and ceremoniously awarded him with a magnificent gold chain and medal to wear around his neck and a complete set of fine clothing. Andvari tried not to look too terribly pleased, but he was downright awed when Svartarr advanced him to the rank of brown dwarf with all its benefits and privileges.

"And I'm not through yet," continued Svartarr, as Andvari tried to slink away again. "I now wish to offer you a permanent commission and residence in the halls of Svartheim in the capacity of Chief Warder of the Treasury in commendation for your years of guarding the Drangarstrom treasure so faithfully, and for saving my precious son Ottar."

Andvari shook his head, then shook his entire self vigorously. "I thank you for the offer, yes indeed, I'm sure you have a fine treasury with plenty of gold and jewels, yes, it's a fine offer, but you see I know every piece of my own treasure as if it were a dear friend, and your treasure would be like a roomful of strangers to me. I must get back to the waterfall and watch for all those pieces to start washing down again so I can catch them, the poor things. I wouldn't know how to behave in a fine castle, with so many people running around, no, no, I wouldn't like that at all. Just leave old Andvari to his cave, and thank you kindly." His creaky voice finally failed him as he looked around at the sea of friendly dwarf faces, and his feet moved in a continual edgy dance, as if longing to scuttle away any instant to his cave.

Ottar darted from his father's side and caught him. He inserted his slim brown hand into Andvari's gnarled fist and looked up into the old pinched face. "You'll come and see me again sometime, won't you? It was such great fun swimming in the river and riding down the rapid. Promise we'll do it again sometime?"

Andvari's lips twitched in an unfamiliar smile. He winked slyly and glanced around, whispering, "Of course we shall,

347

but you mustn't tell anybody. Farewell, Imp!"

"But wait!" Skapti cried, but Andvari had vanished. "Drat! I wanted to hear how he found Ottar. The old clam, he won't say a word he doesn't have to."

In a clear voice, Ottar said, "Then I'll tell you how it happened. I was roaming around in the marshes of the lake region where the whole trouble began. Lorimer was prowling around, up to no good, and I resolved to spy upon him in my fylgja form. Against orders, I fear. I regret to say I slipped away from my teachers—" He glanced contritely at his father. "I set about spying on Lorimer. I never imagined he would know me in my disguise, but he did, and I was captured. He carried me a long way, through terrible cold and winds of power until we reached the great river where he said I would die. He dropped me in the water, and I would have drowned, but I came against a big rock in the middle and there I sat all alone for two days. I was terribly hungry, and a big fish kept swimming around to look at me. I wished I could catch him and eat him, but I'm glad I didn't, because it was Andvari. He finally took me to his cave and we became friends. We lived there for a very long time, and then the gold was taken, which led me back to my father. I know I was disobedient, Father, and I've caused you a lot of trouble, and I am very sorry."

Svartarr coughed and nodded, keeping his hand on Ottar's shoulder, as if to assure himself his son was indeed safe and sound.

"I feel like a nithling for robbing the poor old fellow," Flosi said, "and I hope he finds all his gold again. But mostly I'm grateful that I didn't really kill Ottar in that otterskin. You can't imagine how glad I am."

Svartarr withdrew a package from his cloak and opened it to reveal the pelt of an otter. "I'm going to keep this always," he said. "This is the otterskin that nearly cost me my life and my kingdom. I'm going to keep it to remind me to be less hasty and less of a beast when my temper is aroused. I was ready to cause a war with my old friend and ally Elbegast. I hope you fellows will convey my apologies to him when you return to Snowfell.''

After much congratulating and celebrating, they left Svartarr's Doom and travelled northward. Svartarr had given them all new clothes and seven stocky little ponies. Ivarr silently bid Glimr farewell as they paused for their last look at the Drangarstrom, telling himself it would someday appear in Andvari's treasure hoard, where it certainly seemed more at home than it ever would in Fishless.

He thought about Fishless continually until they were almost to Snowfell. Thoughts of Birna's empty hut gave him a sudden strange pang. It seemed a lifetime away although he had been gone barely a year. He knew he had to go back.

The elves clamoured in protest, cajoling him to stay. Regin remained aloof, scowling thoughtfully.

"Regin, tell him he's wasting himself in Fishless!" exclaimed Finnvard in dismay. "How can he even think of going back to fishing and farming? Ivarr, I've seen your future and it's hopelessly prosperous and happy and you're going to become an important chieftain someday if you go back, so you'd better stay here with us, where things are far more chancy. We'll try to find you one more dragon, if you like.''

"I've got something to do at Hvitafell," Ivarr said. "Birna is still running my life, I fear. I'd like to continue her work, if I can. Her death left a gap, somehow, and I'd like to practice her healing powers for the injured and ill of the Alfar. Her house is a gateway between the two realms which must be kept open. Regin, I could use your help.''

Regin shook his head. "I'm far too green to teach you much. What you need is a clever teacher who has a great deal of knowledge, and I know exactly who you need." He pulled a black leather pouch from his satchel and gave it to Ivarr.

Ivarr opened it incredulously and looked within. With a shout of horror, he nearly dropped the bag. "It's Grus! Regin, is this a joke?''

Grus chuckled anxiously. "Lorimer jettisoned poor old

Grus, or he wouldn't have ended up as he did. I'm a wicked old thing, I assure you, but Regin has thrown the fear into me until I'm trembling in every limb, so to speak. I won't lead you wrong. I know all about healing and herbs. I've quite allowed my magic to go to my head, you see.''

Ivarr shut the bag and put it into his saddle pouch. ''I suppose I ought to say thank you, Regin. Grus will keep me reminded of things I might prefer to forget. But, well—it looks as if I've decided. How soon can I be sent back to Hvitafell?''

Regin studied his map. ''There's a gateway not far from here—perhaps five miles.''

Finnvard gasped. ''So soon? I'd hoped at least to show you I can make the best butter tarts in Snowfell. You can't imagine how I long to be promoted back to inactive duty. I've proven abundantly to myself I can fight when I need to, but I much prefer a challenge no bigger than a kitchen. We're not all intended to forge swords and kill dragons.'' He looked at Flosi, who was going to apprentice himself to a smith as soon as he reached Snowfell.

Five miles passed swiftly, in spite of their dawdling, and at last Ivarr was ready to be sent back to Hvitafell. He looked at the long faces of the Alfar from the centre of the ring of stones. ''You'll be all right, all of you. Skapti, I know Elbegast will realize at last what a fine leader you are and assign you to one of his finest regiments. Egills, I expect you to ask for something sensible to do—''

''I rather like the idea of a little house and a large garden,'' Egills said with a sigh, ''and a large audience to tell my favourite lies to. That's not too much to expect, is it?''

''And Eilifir—'' Ivarr looked at the silent Alfar and shook his head. ''I could never figure you out, except that you must have more great adventures before you.''

Eilifir solemnly shook his hand. ''Come back and find me sometime, and I'll take you on adventures that will make Fafnir look tame. There are places no one has explored, Ivarr, and since I shall be the first to discover them, you might as well come with me.'' He smiled then, still as

350

mysterious and puzzling as always.

"I'm last, as usual," Flosi spoke up, stepping up to shake hands with Ivarr. "I hope you can manage without me there to annoy you, Ivarr. I don't see how you can leave just as I begin to like you, but don't expect you've rid yourself of me. I shall visit you often, and if you're not careful, I may set up a forge someday in the Scipling realm, as one of the Dainns did. Goodbye, Ivarr."

Ivarr turned to bid Regin farewell, wishing he could apologize for his suspicions of the old wizard, but found he couldn't speak at all.

"Well then," said Regin gruffly, clasping his hands around Ivarr's with a strong grasp. "I've got you to thank for delivering me from the bondage of Lorimer. I hope we shall both use that gateway on Hvitafell very often. If ever you need me, just send for me with this." He put a small packet wrapped and sealed in wax in Ivarr's palm. "Goodbye. Bless you, Ivarr."

He raised his hand in farewell, and instantly the hills and scarps of Snowfell began fading into the mist. Ivarr felt dizzy and unsteady, as if the world reeled beneath his feet. Glancing down, he saw something orange streaking toward him, and a soft weight hit him full in the chest. He collapsed to the ground, which was just as well; he was very dizzy.

In a moment a querulous voice startled him from his stupor. "Well, you're home now. Let's get on with your herbs and smelly potions. It is rather pleasant to be back so close to my dear old barrow, I must admit."

Blinking, Ivarr sat up, immediately recognizing the voice of Grus and the green fells and mossy crags of Hvitafell. Sheep were grazing on the fell below him and he could see a fishing barge sculling across the firth. He stood up, recognizing Birna's cloak on his shoulders, which felt good in the early spring chill. He strode quickly toward the fold in the hills where her little turf house had stood; to his great relief, it was still there. Inside, it was dusty and undisturbed.

"Here we are, Grus, safe at home again," he said, installing Grus in a place of honour on a top shelf where he

351

could supervise and complain about the dusting and cleaning.

Ivarr lit the fire and began heating water for tea. His lonely temptation to summon Regin abated, although he still missed Flosi's banter and Finnvard's cheerful retorts.

Grus suddenly interrupted Ivarr's rather mournful thoughts. "There's something at the door, Ivarr. You'd better be careful. This is a dangerous trade you've chosen for yourself, keeping a gateway to the Alfar realm."

"Tush. You don't frighten me, Grus." Ivarr nonetheless opened the door a cautious crack to peer out. Something gave the door a gentle but decisive push, and in stalked an enormous orange cat, announcing himself with an affable "Mmmroww!" and rubbing against Ivarr's shins, purring loudly.

"Finnvard?" Ivarr knelt down, incredulous.

The cat responded with another yowl, and after a minute inspection of the tiny house he settled himself on the hearth-rug and shut his eyes, as if he never intended to go wandering again.

THE END